"The Engineers were th_____, __l Brognola stated. "We even tried tracking electronic communications to them, but their defensive software is too good. We're operating blindly."

"And it's not like it would be easy to find. If the Israelis haven't found and exploited that facility after four decades, it's hidden well," the President mused.

Brognola pinched his brow. "So you can see why we're still behind the eight ball here. We know who we're looking for, and we know their intentions. But as it is, we're still in reactionary mode, instead of a preemptive posture."

"It's something," the President offered.

"They only have to get far enough ahead for a second to launch an attack that could kill millions, though."

The President's mouth thinned to a hard line. "It's your operation, Hal. You've pulled this country out of the fire so many times, it's not like you're betraying national secrets to the North Koreans."

"No, but we are working with a few," Brognola admitted.

The President winced.

DON PENDLETON'S

STONY

AMERICA'S ULTRA-COVERT INTELLIGENCE AGENCY

MAN®

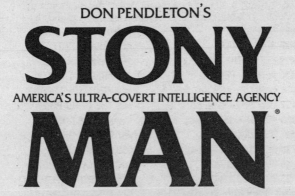

DEADLY
PAYLOAD

A GOLD EAGLE BOOK FROM
WORLDWIDE®

TORONTO • NEW YORK • LONDON
AMSTERDAM • PARIS • SYDNEY • HAMBURG
STOCKHOLM • ATHENS • TOKYO • MILAN
MADRID • WARSAW • BUDAPEST • AUCKLAND

First edition February 2008

ISBN-13: 978-0-373-61977-1
ISBN-10:   0-373-61977-4

DEADLY PAYLOAD

Special thanks and acknowledgment to
Douglas P. Wojtowicz for his contribution to this work.

DEADLY
PAYLOAD

PROLOGUE

Jason Kovak ran his fingertips across the smooth shell of the unmanned aircraft, a smile coming unbidden to his lips. It was a simple machine, with a standard propeller engine mounted under a housing that protected it from detection by thermal imagers. Even so, it ran much more coolly than a rocket thruster. The powerful computer in its bulbous nose would steer according to data flowing from its forward-looking radar, avoiding collision with terrain. That was only on autopilot, while utilizing an artificial intelligence program. Inside the sloped head there was also a tight beam transceiver, capable of picking up signals from a thousand miles away to be directed by remote control. Riding beneath wing mounts on two hard points were six high-powered missiles, their noses fitted with television cameras for precision fire.

"How many do we have?" the Israeli asked.

"Enough for what you wish," Cortez answered. His handsome, tanned features and black, silken suit reminded Kovak of an unmasked Zorro.

Kovak nodded. "We'll need quite a few. With some optional payloads. You're sure you can get enough?"

"Generosity, promises whispered," the Argentinian said, stroking his neatly trimmed pencil mustache. "I have my means."

Kovak nodded. "I won't dig too deeply, then."

"This is a big step for your side," Cortez said.

"My side?" Kovak asked. "I don't have a side anymore. Not after we've been betrayed."

"And so you're turning to us," the Argentinian concluded. "You can't get much more anti-Israel than our consortium."

"Israel and the Arab nations are partners now," Kovak said. "Bedfellows, seeking out peace accords when for millennia they've assailed the land promised to our people. They forget the Holocaust. It was a blip in history, done by a German madman long dead."

"So you're going to destroy your country?" Cortez asked. "Not that we mind. After all, Mossad's been hunting the Consortium's family and membership for decades."

Kovak chuckled. "There's a little sting, I'll admit. But the Mossad is a joke, knuckling to political correctness and cowardice. The Consortium isn't on an anti-Jew kick now, because it has other problems. Both of us have other things to worry about. Betrayals, weakness and weakened, corrupted leadership that needs a slap in the face to wake up. We have the same goal. We are one, building a better future."

Cortez nodded and held out his hand to the Israeli. "A world without our different headaches."

"Engineering the new tomorrow," Kovak said, referring to the name of the alliance. "If anyone wishes to stop us, they'll run face-first into a united front."

THE FIRST STRIKE of the united front known only to a few as the Engineers of the New Tomorrow came at dawn at a terrorist camp just five miles north of Damascus, Syria, in the mountains that formed a natural border with Lebanon. The camp was used by Syria to train and arm members of the Popular Front for the Righteous Liberation of Lebanon, a splintered offshoot of the Palestinian forces in the Lebanese countryside.

The strike was preceded only instants before by the soft hum of propeller-driven unmanned aerial vehicles, which drew the attention of the sleepy camp guard. The guards were used to being buzzed and observed by the Americans with their Predator drones, but every so often the Pentagon wanted to look as if it was taking a more offensive stance, and dropped a couple Maverick missiles into their backyard. Nothing that would obliterate the widely dispersed camp. Still, the groggy guard called out a warning, but by the time the words left his mouth, it was too late.

The first three rounds were white phosphorous, which burst thirty yards above the ground. They had been perfectly spaced and timed, clawing trails of burning waxy smoke spreading wide and arcing down into the unprepared camp. Half-dressed men, hearing the cries of alarm from the sentries, had burst from their tents and run right into the searing rain. As the WP struck their flesh, whether or not it was exposed or protected by clothing, it melted through, destroying skin and muscle until it burrowed down to the bone.

The lucky ones passed out immediately, while dozens of others ran screaming in horror at a pain that could only be torn out on the point of a knife. Lebanese insurgents and Syrian advisers twisted and writhed, grinding into the muddy ground, trying to drown the burning fragments of white phosphorous, but once exposed to air, the deadly element was unquenchable. Flesh around the fragments cooked and peeled away from bone in a slow, murderous torture.

The second wave of missiles from the UAV drones came unheard, the screams of the wounded and dying filling the air until the shrill rattle of 77 mm artillery rockets was right on them. These landed amid the semipermanent prefabricated buildings where supplies were stored. Thermobaric warheads struck with earth-shattering force, ripping Quonset huts to pieces and destroying anything and anyone still inside. Assault rifles and rocket launchers meant to slay the enemies of Syria in Lebanon were turned to pulped and mangled piles of wreckage.

A lone round sizzled into the communications hut and scoured it from existence with a blast equal to six sticks of dynamite. A radioman inside was cut off in midrequest, begging for help and support from the Syrian military when he and the hut were blasted into oblivion. The largest piece remaining of the Syrian communications officer was the size of a pencil eraser.

As smoke roiled into the sky, the circling drones whirled into position to launch phase three. Like hightech vultures, the quartet of drones pumped out a sheet of staggered rockets. It would have seemed overkill had it been conventional explosives or white phosphorous, but instead, cakey yellow clouds erupted from each artillery rocket strike. The ugly ocher fog spread across the camp. The cries of the wounded suddenly fell silent as the cloud washed over them.

One rocket round had landed, unexploded, its fuse apparently having malfunctioned. While the manufacture was undeniably American, the writing on the side was Arabic. The unmanned drones themselves were identical to the machines given to Egypt by the United States government as part of a multibillion-dollar lend-lease agreement.

Syria, stung with betrayal over the loss of dozens of its troops to an Egyptian sneak attack, threw out accusations, crying out in hatred against politicians in Cairo and Washington, D.C., vowing revenge.

Shock waves rippled across the globe.

PHASE TWO OCCURRED within thirty minutes of the attack in Syria, but it occurred in Panama. Memories of the invasion that had deposed Manuel Noriega decades earlier had never really left the public's mind. The full might of the United States armed forces had crushed down and taken out Noriega's government and forces. The American liberal elite had accused the Reagan administration of using overkill against the Panamanians, to the point where AC-130 gunships were said to have slaughtered citizens and soldiers alike as they raked neighborhoods with dozens of machine guns and cannon in synchronized fire.

Those wounds were yet fresh and raw, despite the long years since 1989. The United States consulate still had its share of protesters out front, anger sharp and focused over lost loved ones. They were peaceful, and they carried candles for a midnight vigil commemorating the anniversary of the invasion. Mournful hymns in Spanish hung in the air as the protesters said goodbye to loved ones once more and called upon God for justice in an unjust world.

The Marines at the front gate had grown used to this, and relaxed only a little. Policy had been to keep their rifles cold at all times, but the warrior elite knew better. Cold weapons in Beirut had cost 249 brothers their lives, and even though the Panamanians were armed with nothing more dangerous than candles, there were enough of them that the guards had their M-16 A 4s hot and ready.

Somewhere behind them, a weapon opened up, and the armed Marines whirled at the sound. It took only a few moments for them to recognize the roar and chatter of an M-240 medium machine gun—standard Marine and Army issue, as well as being hugely popular throughout Europe. It could burn off 7.62 mm rounds at 850 rounds per minute, and was deadly out to a thousand yards. The Marines crouched, believing themselves to be under attack, but the haunting hymns had been turned to screeches, a horrifying wail, as if someone had dragged a needle off one track and let it go on a recording of hell itself.

The Marine guards whirled and saw unarmed civilians twist and thrash as 7.62 mm NATO rounds chopped brutally into them. Bodies collapsed and screams of panic filled the air. By the time the Marines realized what was going on, the unmanned drones swung over their heads, brass raining from their belly-mounted machine guns. The two, sleek UAV craft climbed to swing around for another strafing run. The embassy protectors took shots at the airborne marauders. However, the killer drones had climbed out of the effective range of their M-16s.

The aerial predators whirled and sliced down again, streams of high-powered lead erupting from their gun pods and ripping into the helpless crowd.

Marine Sergeant Zachary Admunsen pulled out his equalizer—an AT-4 antitank rocket. Hitting an aerial craft would be difficult, but Admunsen wouldn't let civilians die without an effort. He triggered the rocket, giving one of the two drones some lead time. The warhead connected with the high-tech aircraft and blew it in two. The tail end whirled like a dervish and chopped off the right wing of the second Predator. It speared forward and crashed, relatively harmlessly, into the roof of the U.S. consulate, bursting apart into splinters. The semidisposable drones hadn't been intended to survive heavy ground resistance, but being unmanned, their loss was only a small monetary setback, not the life of a skilled pilot.

Still, Admunsen was stunned to see that he'd taken out both attackers with a single shot.

By then, though, it was too late. The damage had been done and the throng of protesters had been dispersed. Corpses littered the ground, forty-seven dead and another dozen wounded. Most had been victims of gunfire, but others had been trampled in the mad flight to get out of the machine gun's thunderous scythe of lead and fire.

Once more, accusations flew.

CHAPTER ONE

"So why are we investigating the destruction of a terrorist camp in Syria again?" T.J. Hawkins whispered to Calvin James as the Zodiac boat hummed toward the Lebanese coast. "If you ask me—"

"Well, I didn't," James retorted.

"Well, if you did, whoever took them out did us a favor," Hawkins answered.

"Really, mate?" David McCarter asked as he scanned the shore with his field glasses. "A chemical weapons attack on an unfriendly country, using American materials. That's a favor to the U.S.? I'd hate to see what you'd call a slap in the face."

"The PFRLL were some of the sickest bastards in the Lebanese equation, though," Hawkins stated. "They never cared about civilian casualties when they made their attacks. It'd have been our job, sooner or later, to take them out."

"Sooner or later, sure," Rafael Encizo answered as he worked the rudder's till, keeping them on course despite a crosscurrent. "But then, we also need to figure out who has a small automated air force. The drones responsible for the attack could end up in the hands of someone who might turn them against a city."

"Well then, that'd be a whole new mess o' pig shit," Hawkins admitted.

Encizo nodded, returning his attention to guiding the inflatable raft. The muscular little Cuban's steady steering was born of years spent by the sea, either diving or working boats. Between him and Calvin James, Phoenix Force had the training to handle almost anything on the water. The inflatable raft would be collapsed on the shore and buried before they went inland. If necessary, the raft could be dug up and used to exfiltrate from the country, but McCarter had other avenues out of Lebanon, just in case the investigation took them on a new path.

"Welcoming party," Gary Manning announced as he spied the beach through the scope of his Heckler & Koch PSG-1 rifle.

Hawkins's hand tightened on the grip of his G-36, but his trigger finger rested on the receiver.

"Keep your booger hook off the bang switch," he remembered his drill instructor bellowing in basic training. It was second nature for the Southerner, by now. Even as a Ranger, he practiced as a professional, not until he got it right once, but until he never got it wrong. That mentality was pushed even further as a veteran member of Phoenix Force, one of the most elite combat units in the world. The five handpicked Stony Man warriors had been chosen for their experience and ability. All of them were highly trained commandos.

"They spot us yet?" McCarter asked Manning.

"No. They seem to be waiting for someone else," Manning said. "Their attention is more to the north."

McCarter drew his finger across his throat and the Stony Man commandos fell silent. Only the muffled Mercury engine made any sound, and even then, it was a soft hum that was easily swallowed by the lap of waves. Phoenix Force lowered its profile, lying in the bottom of the raft, only Encizo and Manning breaching the tops of the inflated Kevlar pontoons to steer and to observe the mysterious group on the shore.

McCarter pointed to James and patted the grip of his knife. He nodded to Encizo. The stocky Cuban flicked a thumbs-up to the fox-faced Briton and adjusted their course a little farther to the south.

So much for the plan of burying the raft, Hawkins mused. With unknown forces on the shore, they would have to scuttle the inflatable raft, slashing through the rigid nylon pontoons. The weight of the motor would drag it down, and Phoenix Force would swim a hundred yards to shore.

Hawkins fed Encizo's rifle into a water-tight bag, since he was steering. He did the same for Manning's PSG-1, while the powerfully built Canadian switched to McCarter's field glasses to maintain surveillance of the unknown enemy.

"There," Encizo stated softly. He turned off the engine and James slashed the inflated tubes to starboard while McCarter took out the port side. The raft collapsed almost instantly, Mediterranean seawater rushing in and engulfing Hawkins. Within a few kicks, Phoenix Force had swum free of the sinking raft, and Hawkins handed Encizo and Manning their waterproof packs.

So far, their plans had been preempted, but then, an average day of work for Phoenix Force rarely went as they hoped. However, the team had been formed to take care of things when nothing had gone right. Adapt and overcome was their forte.

HERMANN "GADGETS" SCHWARZ was no stranger to Central America, and he was no stranger to the morass of its constant threats and violence. Going over the files that described the evidence of the Panama assault, he tried to gain the measure of who they were up against this time out. In the past, the warriors of Stony Man Farm had battled all manner of threats in the canal nation, from renegade secret policemen who killed for their fascist beliefs to Chinese espionage agents trying to gain control of the canal to drug dealers who had flourished under the former dictator. Often, multiple parties entwined, and even forces theoretically on the same side, like Communist rebels and the Red Chinese government, were at odds against each other. Then again, whenever Able Team went south of the border, it was never simple and easy.

"Never a lack of targets on these operations," Carl Lyons said. "Shoot in any direction and you'll hit a bad guy."

"Just the way you like it," Schwarz replied sardonically, putting the file away. "Simple and bloody."

Lyons grunted. "If I wanted to fuss over geopolitics, I'd have joined Phoenix Force."

Rosario Blancanales, fondly known as Pol, looked back at the pair from the balcony and sighed. "As if a caveman like you could run with that bunch."

"I am a pretty good detective, you know," Lyons responded. He looked at the list of murdered civilians, his heavy brow furrowed. "It could have been an assassination attempt."

"But making it look like the U.S. did it?" Schwarz asked.

"Well, the Venezuelan government has no love for our leadership in Washington," Lyons replied.

"Leadership in Wonderland?" Schwarz asked.

"Well, you know what I mean," Lyons returned. "But no one on the list of the dead fits in with people who'd have pissed off the head Communists in Caracas."

"Just women and children," Schwarz said. "Killed to smear America's name across the headlines in innocent blood."

Lyons shrugged. "The papers are already full of the U.S. being bloodthirsty brutes for Iraq. Like we needed any more vilification?"

Blancanales cocked an eyebrow.

"Sorry," Lyons said. "That last caveman comment got me breaking out my five-dollar words."

Blancanales grinned, but the smile didn't last long. "But why UAVs?"

"It has to be linked to the mess Phoenix is investigating over in Lebanon," Schwarz said. "And don't forget, we've had our own encounters with rogue drones in the past."

"The Farm never did figure out who supplied that Egyptian general with so many Predators," Blancanales answered. "This might be more of the same."

Lyons frowned, "Then we can find out who's behind it and shut it all down."

"Before they start a global war," Schwarz mentioned. He looked at the files on the attack. "We just need to figure out where the drones launched from. Maybe then we could learn who made them and work our way up the food chain."

He pored over detailed photographs of the wrecked unmanned drones that had hit the crowd at the consulate.

Nothing identifiable had survived the crash of the second, and the AT-4 rocket had blasted everything to garbage.

"Nothing on the technology front?" Blancanales asked.

"Bulk, cheap Chinese electronics, rewired to handle the demands of duplicating Predator UAV technology. Some brilliant improvisation, but no evidence of who put it together," Schwarz said. He shook his head. "Untraceable."

"Nothing is untraceable," Lyons retorted. "We'll find a handle. And when we do, we'll twist until we get some answers."

There was a knock at the door and all three Able warriors' hands fell to the grips of their holstered handguns. Lyons answered the door and admitted their contact, Susana Arquillo. She was a CIA field agent assigned to Panama. Her skin was darkened and bronzed by the near equatorial sun. Her hair had been long and dark in her file photograph, but in person, it was trimmed short and pulled back into a tight bun. A few strands of white feathered through it to make it seem lighter. Arquillo's full, lush lips parted in a smile.

"Carl Ryder?" she asked.

"That's me," Lyons said.

"And you can confirm who I am?" Arquillo asked.

"Gadgets, run her prints," Lyons told Schwarz. "If you're not who you're supposed to be…"

Arquillo's eyes dropped to the rubber Pachmayer grips poking out of Lyons's waistband. "I won't be walking out of here. But what if I'm packing explosives?"

Lyons looked her over, hard blue eyes scanning the way her jeans hugged her curvaceous hips. Her blouse hung, unbuttoned and tied together at the bottom, a dark red tank top constraining her full breasts. His hand patted around her waist and found her compact 9 mm Glock on one side and a tiny .38 Special tucked away on the other. "I don't think you could be hiding too much under there."

Arquillo was relatively tall, five foot nine, and athletically built. She cocked an eyebrow as she pressed her fingertips to the flat scan plate Schwarz held out for her. "Ever hear of a charger?"

"You don't strike me as the kind of woman who'd want to go out with an eighth of a stick of C-4 detonating in her ass," Lyons said.

"Besides," Blancanales added, holding up a portable "sniffer." "This thing would have smelled explosive residue on you."

"Thorough," Arquillo noted.

"She's clean," Schwarz declared.

CHAPTER TWO

Gary Manning observed the unknown group on the beach, ignoring the salt drying and congealing with sand in his soaked BDUs. There would be time to change into fresh clothing later, and it was a minor discomfort. The group's activity was clearer now from their position on the beach. It was a work crew, unloading containers from transport trucks onto a beached barge. His lips drew into a tight line.

"Unmarked containers," he said. "But the shape is unmistakable."

"UAV transport crating," David McCarter answered as he lowered his binoculars. "We lucked out here."

"Except, if we were lucky, we would have a Zodiac raft to shadow the barge to its destination," Manning said.

"I'll contact the Farm," McCarter suggested. "It'll be a breach of radio discipline, but they can keep an eye on the craft while we continue our inland push."

"We're still going into Lebanon?" Hawkins asked.

"These things were delivered somewhere. And we still have to touch base with Unit 777 and the Mossad. They've been noticing some unusual activity in Lebanon."

"UFO sightings," Calvin James muttered. "If they weren't one of the crack units in the region, I'd have thought they'd gone nuts."

"Unidentified aircraft aren't always spawned by little green men, *hermano*," Rafael Encizo chided his partner. "And some of those UFOs might have dropped chemical weapons into Syria. I'd still like to keep a tail on them."

McCarter lowered the satellite radio. "Barb has a Keyhole watching the barge. The Farm isn't going to lose track of it."

James nodded. "Which means we can concentrate on keeping up with the trucks."

"Not necessarily," Manning interjected. McCarter and James regarded their partner quizzically as the brawny Canadian observed the convoy through his sniper scope. "The trucks aren't moving."

McCarter ran a mental tally of the enemy vehicles. There were three tractor-trailer combinations and half a dozen pickup trucks. The pickups had six men a piece, and who knew how many crewed the eighteen-wheelers, but the Phoenix Force commander figured between forty and fifty men for this operation. The rules of engagement for this mission had nominally been to avoid enemy contact, and any unavoidable conflict had to be undertaken with a maximum of stealth. Five against fifty was not going to be a silent struggle, no matter if all of their weapons had been suppressed. The element of surprise only went so far.

"Even more bad news," Encizo noted as he lowered his scope-equipped MP-5. "That barge didn't go more than five hundred yards out into the water."

McCarter glanced back, then watched the trailers. He swept them with his binoculars, eschewing optics for his machine pistol. He lowered them. "They set up a transmission antenna."

James looked out toward the barge. "We only saw them unload one of the trailers onto the barge, with workers who had come out of the back of a second."

"The third is a control center," Hawkins said. He took a deep breath and lifted his binoculars to watch the barge along with James and Encizo. "It's parked?"

"Looks like they're setting up to launch the UAVs," James noted.

"Get on the horn to the Farm," McCarter said. "We've got a major emergency. Rafe, Cal. Time to hit the water."

Encizo grimaced. "Both of us?"

"I appreciate the offer, but that barge has to be put down before they can launch," McCarter ordered.

Hawkins looked up from his satellite phone. "Got the Farm."

"Barb?" McCarter asked.

"What is it, David?" Barbara Price asked.

"Have the Israeli air force go on alert. We've stumbled on another bit of provocation," he told her. "That barge is a floating launch pad."

"Should we get someone scrambled out to you?" Price asked.

"Syria is on full alert as it is. Any friendly aircraft who'd hit this place would only provoke them and their allies in Lebanon," the Briton explained.

"What kind of enemy forces are you looking at?" Price continued.

"Thirty to forty ground troops. Lord know how many in the trucks, but a group went out on the barge," McCarter explained.

Price covered the mouthpiece on her end for a moment, then spoke to McCarter again. "An air strike might make Damascus squirrelly, but we have a way around that."

"What've you got?" McCarter inquired.

"An artillery unit in northern Israel. They lob some explosives across the border into Lebanon every so often," Price mentioned.

McCarter frowned. "We're danger close, and I'd like to take one of the trailers intact. If we can get hold of the hardware and servers used to operate their drones, we could slip you chaps into the back door for some deep-down digging."

"Ten to one's tough odds, David," Price said.

"Worse than that," McCarter admitted. "I sent Cal and Rafe to the barge to sink it."

"We drop one shell in the vicinity. It'll cut the odds, and less likely to blow everything to hell."

The Briton handed the phone to Hawkins and contacted James and Encizo on his Los Angeles SWAT Headset— LASH. "How soon to the barge?"

"Another two minutes," Encizo said.

McCarter took the phone back from Hawkins. "How far is the artillery site from here?"

Price gave the coordinates.

"A minute and a half flight," McCarter figured.

"That's what we figured. Coordinates?" Price asked.

McCarter handed the phone to Manning, who had been observing the operation. The Canadian read off coordinates he figured through his map skills. Manning's mathematical skills and navigational abilities were second to none, and if anyone had a chance to spot for an artillery shell fired from dozens of miles away without benefits of laser targeting, it was him. Manning gave the Briton the phone.

"Your artillery is on its way," Price promised. "It'll be there by the time the others make their move on the barge."

"What can we expect?" McCarter asked.

"We have a reserve unit dropping some payback on a Palestinian group. You'll get a 155 mm Copperhead from a Doher," Price said.

"Cover your heads, lads. It's going to get loud," McCarter promised.

Manning slung his sniper rifle and drew his Glock 34. He'd eschewed a machine pistol for the precision rifle, but compromised by carrying two of the chosen sidearm for this mission. The second Glock was set up for close-quarters combat, equipped with a blunt four-inch suppressor, a 20-round extended magazine and, on a rail under the barrel, a mounted gun light. The suppressor provided a semblance of stealth without sacrificing stopping power for the hollow-point rounds within, and the light, even if it wasn't activated, served as a means of steadying the already mild recoil of the G-34 in rapid fire. The Glock was also one of the most accurate and easy-to-shoot handguns on the planet, second only to McCarter's own beloved Browning Hi-Power.

McCarter relegated his MP-5 to a backup role, drawing his Browning in anticipation of a fast, nasty mop-up. And it would be quick and nasty. While an artillery shell would take out a good number of the enemy force, no barrage would ever completely obliterate opposition. But it would soften them up. Hawkins stuck with his MP-5, not trusting his skill with a handgun to be as high as Phoenix veterans Manning and McCarter.

The Briton looked out over the water.

The two minutes that James and Encizo had estimated were almost up.

KNIFING THROUGH THE WATER like they were born to it, Rafael Encizo and Calvin James closed on the barge. The Phoenix Force pair drew their fighting knives in anticipation of first contact with the crew of the barge, but their observations showed that the men on board were busy preparing unmanned aerial vehicles for launch. Just before they reached the hull, they noted canisters labeled with the universal symbol for biohazard.

Encizo and James shared a nervous, knowing glance as they realized the implications of their failure. Whoever these men were, they were planning to launch an attack, utilizing a similar lethal contamination that devastated the Syrian camp. Four UAVs sat on the deck of the barge, laden with four canisters each on underwing mounts normally meant for Maverick antitank missiles. The size of the containers promised a potential of death for thousands if they struck in a metropolitan center.

Both Phoenix force commandos realized that Israel had many port cities that would provide tempting targets for the airborne death-bringers.

On the shore, a thunderclap split the air, which served as the starting gun for their assault.

Encizo gripped the rail of the barge with one hand and hauled himself onto its deck, staying low. In his off hand, the Cold Steel Tanto Combat knife was held in an icepick grip, the chisel-pointed, razor-sharp blade shielded against his forearm so it wouldn't reflect the work lights on the deck, even though he had the concealment of a crate. James surfaced and crawled onto the barge fifteen feet away, also behind a transport container. The barge itself was twenty yards long, but much narrower by a factor of four to one, five yards wide. It was a garbage scow that had been pressed into service as an aircraft carrier to launch the drones. Since the UAVs were designed for short takeoff and landing, even with underwing payloads, the length would be enough for the launching task.

The engines on the first one strummed to life and Encizo realized that if it started moving, tragedy would fall on an Israeli city. The stocky Cuban sheathed his combat blade and shouldered his machine pistol, quickly detaching the suppressor on the MP-5, knowing that he'd need every ounce of power to damage even the relatively flimsy and disposable aircraft.

He focused on the engine cowling, situated two feet above and away from the biohazard canisters mounted underwing, and opened fire as soon as he had a clear sight picture. The German-made machine pistol chattered out its popping death song. Men on deck dived for cover at the sound of Encizo's attack, shocked at his sudden appearance. The engine cowling perforated in a dozen places as full-metal-jacketed bullets smashed through the pistons running its propeller.

The Predator knockoff lurched forward a few feet, smoke pouring from the damaged engine, but it rolled to a halt as the propeller caught and froze on broken pistons.

James moved from behind cover as soon as Encizo opened fire and concentrated on two of the enemy who were reaching for their weapons. All the men on the barge were armed with at least handguns, and the two who were reacting had AKM folding-stock assault rifles. James ripped a burst of suppressed fire into one of them, stitching him through the face and shoulders. The other man had gotten to his knees and fired a quick salvo from the hip that missed the black Phoenix Force pro by inches. James tucked down deeper and sliced the rifleman from crotch to throat with a half dozen Parabellum slugs. The enemy gunner flopped over the side of the barge, disappearing into the Mediterranean.

Encizo scurried behind the cover of his crates, keeping one step ahead of the handgun fire that chased him. The Cuban took a few potshots, but was hampered by the fact that four drones were parked on the deck laden with poison-packed containers. He didn't want to risk dumping contagion into the Mediterranean to have it wash ashore in a populated area.

Saving one city would have been a waste if other civilians were sacrificed because of sloppy work. He still fired a few shots, high and wide, to keep their attention on him and give James, who had a better angle on the defenders, a chance to take them out.

James didn't envy Encizo's position as human target, and he ripped off more bursts from his machine pistol, tagging every enemy target he could find. Unfortunately the enemy had realized that as long as they cowered behind the biohazard containers, they were relatively safe.

James disabused them of that concept by dropping prone and targeting legs and feet with his machine pistol. Bullets smashed violently through tarsal bones and knee-caps with equally devastating and crippling results. The conspirators crashed helplessly to the deck, falling away from the lethal cylinders of contagion that they sought to use as shields. Flat on their backs and bellies, they were easy targets for James and Encizo to finish off.

The Cuban crouched behind a crate and swept fallen survivors with submachine-gun fire. It was a cruel and callous effort, gunning down the injured, but these men still held handguns that they could use in a last-ditch effort to breach one of the bioweapon containers as a final act of revenge.

"All clear?" James asked, moving swiftly around the bodies of the dead and the inert drones.

"No movement," Encizo answered.

"We can't leave these things," James stated, looking toward the shore.

"No," Encizo agreed, "but we can take them with us."

James looked at the deckhouse. "I've got it."

"Maybe we won't be too late to help out," Encizo concluded as the barge turned toward the shore.

It WAS NO DIFFICULT TRICK to misdirect a laser guided 155 mm artillery shell utilizing a broadcast pulse from a satellite slaved to Stony Man Farm's control. The M-712 Copperhead was one of the first and most successful of laser-guided, cannon-launched munitions, with a range of ten miles, and carrying nearly fifteen pounds of Composition B as its warhead. With a velocity of detonation at 8050 meters per second, 1100 meters per second faster than TNT, the Copperhead shell possessed awesome destructive ability. Aaron "The Bear" Kurtzman distracted the single Copperhead round from a flight of twenty aimed across the northern border between Israel and Lebanon against a Syrian-backed militia. Well within the ten-mile range of the laser-guided shell, the M-712 altered its guide path and split off from the main flight.

Kurtzman continued to track their hijacked shell in flight, painting Manning's target via a satellite-mounted laser. The computer genius took into account atmospheric refraction, but he held his breath as the warhead, loaded with the equivalent of fifteen pounds of TNT, was dropped, as McCarter had noted, "danger close" to the men of Phoenix Force. One variation in humidity or air temperature and there was a strong possibility that there wouldn't be enough left of McCarter, Manning and Hawkins to scoop up inside a matchbox.

The satellite registered the detonation of the Copperhead, and Kurtzman looked at his screen for the IFF codes on Phoenix Force's LASH communicators.

They were still in operation, unmoved by the concussive eruption of the deadly warhead. However, even as the dust cloud rose and thickened over the battle scene, obscuring the reconnaissance satellite's visual coverage of the battle scene, McCarter's, Manning's and Hawkins's signals burst into motion toward the convoy of conspirators.

"Good luck," Kurtzman whispered.

WHEN 138 POUNDS OF LASER-GUIDED missile landed, even if only fifteen pounds of it was made of high explosives, it made an impression.

The impact and detonation kicked up a wind that blew harshly over the heads of McCarter and his partners. The convoy itself was rocked as riflemen standing guard in the open and their pickups were lifted and hurled by a concussion wave that traveled at 26,000 feet per second. The tractor-trailer rigs shook mightily, but their enormous bulk had protected them from being flung around like children's toys. A column of dust and smoke rose from the impact crater, and bodies were strewed about. A pickup that had been two yards from the Copperhead's landing point was compressed as if it were an empty beer can, and rolled toward the beach. Other trucks were simply flipped to varying degrees.

While some of the drivers inside might have survived,

McCarter felt confident that those inside the crushed pickup kicked toward the Mediterranean like a gigantic metal beach ball were instantly dead. Rushing from behind cover with his sound-suppressed Browning in fist, McCarter was first into action. Manning and Hawkins were only heartbeats behind him, their own weapons at the ready.

The Phoenix Force commander charged toward the remnants of the convoy. A stunned rifleman jerked to his hands and knees, wagging his head to shake out the cobwebs. McCarter, not needing to have an armed soldier at his back, cleared those cobwebs away with a fast double-tap of Parabellum rounds, coring the gunner's skull. Hawkins and Manning sighted other potential enemies, ripping suppressed fire into them before they could return to their senses and form a defense of their Predator ground-control operation. It was fast and brutal butcher's work, but considering that the odds against them could still be twenty against three, there was no doubts slowing the three professional warriors.

The closer to the blast crater they got, the less movement they encountered, though McCarter paused for a half step at the sight of one survivor. A soldier guarding the convoy gasped, holding the almost skeletal remains of his right arm out to the Briton. The Arab's face was a sticky red mess and his jaw worked up and down, unintelligible sounds waiting through shredded lips. McCarter hammered three shots into the ghastly figure, ending the man's suffering as he continued in his hard charge toward the trailer that Manning had identified as the main control center.

Here, the guards had managed to recover much more quickly, even if they did sway uneasily on their feet, senses reeling from the hammer blow dropped by an angry god into their laps. McCarter dropped to one knee and pivoted like a human turret, his Browning sweeping enemy heads, trigger breaking like a glass rod every time his front sight crossed a body. At six shots a second, he wasn't going to approximate the rate of fire of a submachine gun, but each round went exactly where McCarter needed it to go, faces exploding as 9 mm bullets smashed into them with blinding speed.

With eight shots dead on target in a shade over a second, McCarter rose from his kneeling position and continued his rush. In the heartbeat between kneeling and accelerating to a full run, he automatically replenished the partially emptied Browning with a new 13-round magazine.

Manning and Hawkins raked the flanking survivors among the guard force with their own weapons, giving McCarter the freedom to continue toward the operations control trailer. He was three feet from the top of the steps at the back of it when the door slammed open, a dazed, bloodied technician staggering into view. The Briton lashed out with his left hand, grabbing a fistful of the man's shirt and shoving him back into the control center, the Browning in his right chugging two shots through the technician's heart. The flap holster on the man's hip might only have been for show, but he was armed and was going to send a weapon-laden flight of drones to attack an Israeli city. Cored through the heart, the technician was now a lifeless shield of flesh and bone as the Briton heaved him through the doorway.

Someone inside had some presence of mind and cut loose with a Makarov pistol, but the low-powered 9 mm bullets couldn't penetrate the dead man McCarter held in front of him. Most of the lights inside the trailer had been knocked out, only one bulb illuminating the far end, though liquid crystal display screens threw a soft but dim blue glow over the interior. Shaken technicians struggled to get out of the way of the Phoenix Force commander's stampede through their quarters. The Briton tapped off three shots at the gunman who'd drilled his own dead comrade. One shot was a miss, but the second and third shots were as straight as a line of rivets, cutting two gory holes in the shooter's throat. Head nearly severed, the armed technician flopped across his computer table, keyboard and liquid crystal monitor crashing to the floor of the trailer.

A drone operator lunged at McCarter from behind, his arms spread wide to grab the wily fox-faced Briton. Instead of catching him in a bear hug, the technician caught the point of McCarter's elbow in his solar plexus with bone-breaking force. Suddenly unable to breathe, the man collapsed to his knees, giving McCarter a moment of freedom to shove his corpse shield into a second feisty drone operator who tried to swing his chair as a club. Both men's bodies collapsed to the floor, McCarter pinning the chair-wielding technician down forever with two rounds from his Browning.

The choking operator reached out, trying to grab McCarter again, and this time the Stony Man commando whirled and snapped his heel into the conspirator's nose, crushing it flat and driving the bone into his brain. Four down, he thought, looking around the shadowy trailer, scanning for more opponents. He'd almost completed a full circle of his search when two Makarov bullets stung his armored load-bearing vest. The enemy gunman had some training, and that saved the former SAS commando, since most people concentrate on the center of mass when shooting. McCarter's center was protected by Kevlar and polymer mesh chain link calibrated to stop a .44 Magnum or AK-47 bullet. Lightning reflexes spurred the Phoenix Force leader to return fire, zipping five shots into the gunman from crotch to sternum.

Opened up like a gutted calf, the last drone operator fell to his knees, folding over his spilling entrails and dying.

"Report in," McCarter called over his com-link.

The others reported "all clear."

"T.J., bring the sat phone in here and hook these control computers up to the Farm," the Briton ordered.

He looked around the trailer, at the five bodies. The death toll for this mission was sure to climb. And given that even the technicians were willing to fight to the death, this conflict was going to be brutal.

McCarter took a deep breath and reloaded his partially spent Browning.

"So what else is bloody new?" he asked tiredly, holstering his pistol.

CHAPTER THREE

The Mercedes SUV bounced raggedly over the muddy trail through the Darien. A mountainous rain forest that formed an almost impenetrable border between Panama and Colombia, the Darien was a formidable force. Even though northern Colombia received constant radar scanning from various drug-enforcement agencies, the inland jungles and rugged mountains of the land bridge formed between the two nations provided innumerable hiding places for people not wishing to be found. Uninhabited, hot and rainy the area also could befuddle an army of people searching for fugitives. While building a base within these territories would be extremely difficult, a curtain of inhospitable jungle and choppy, hill-broken terrain provided a hard-to-penetrate barrier.

"But that barrier is useless against flying machines like an unmanned aerial vehicle," Schwarz said.

The SUV's front right tire dipped into another pothole that hurled the members of Able Team and Susana Arquillo around like rag dolls. Carl Lyons held on tightly, fighting to maintain control of the 4WD vehicle as the terrain threatened to hammer them insensate with the passenger compartment of the SUV.

Lyons glanced over at Arquillo. She clutched the sides of her seat to absorb most of the frantic thrashing, but even so, her pert, sleek little bosom jostled with each rut slam.

"Are you aiming for these potholes, Mr. Ryder?" Arquillo snapped. "Because if you are, just pull over and I'll do five minutes of jumping jacks for you and then you can drive sanely."

Lyons's attention had already returned to the road.

"You've driven in this mess before," he growled. "You know these roads suck."

"Besides, you're not Ironman's type," Blancanales said. "You can count to ten without using your fingers."

Lyons grunted in annoyance, weaving between two huge puddles. They were already soaked to the skin, as the humidity in the jungle was a stifling blanket, even without raining. They'd also hit one inescapable puddle that was three feet deep and stretched along ten feet of road. The interior of the vehicle was soaked with brown, brackish water as there was no way that they would drive the SUV with its doors attached. The roof, however, had a canvas canopy that prevented them from being brained by low-hanging branches. The fabric covering, however, breathed enough to keep the three men and their female companion from suffocating in the vehicle.

"How're we doing on the navigation?" Lyons asked as they neared the coordinates where Arquillo's informants had sighted UFOs.

Schwarz looked at his heavy-duty PDA. A GPS map on its screen was laid over a real-time photographic image of the countryside, satellite imagery transmitted from Stony

Man Farm to give Able Team every bit of information they needed on the go. The PDA itself was made with solid-state electronics and encased in a tough metallic shell. The screen was made from quarter-inch thick Lexan over a liquid crystal display. The keypad was a touch-sensitive pad under a fireproof Nomex screen with numbers and letters installed. The clear Lexan screen didn't interfere with the "touch screen" controls, which could be operated with any pointed object, from a dagger point to a pencil or stick scrounged from the environment. Schwarz knew that a stylus was easy to lose, having been a tech geek who'd lost several dozen expensive and inexpensive models for far less durable pocket data assistants.

"Another five minutes on... Hit the brakes!" Schwarz snapped. The Mercedes SUV screeched to a halt, its front end plowing into another pond-size puddle that sprawled across the road. Schwarz wiped muddy water off his screen and squinted. He tapped the screen with a pencil, increasing magnification. "We've got company."

Lyons pushed the SUV into a lower gear and powered out of the puddle, crushing through thick foliage at the roadside. He kept going, weaving between tree trunks until the canopy of the forest gave them concealment.

Able Team and Arquillo left the vehicle, grabbing their combat packs and weapons as they did so. All four of them carried SIG 551 assault rifles. Chosen for a durable, mud-and grit-proof AK-47-style action, but with the ability to utilize American 5.56 mm ammunition and M-16 magazines, the SIGs had fourteen-inch barrels, light and compact enough for jungle or close quarters fighting, but still with enough power and reach for long-range engagements. Lyons's version had a cut-down Remington 870 shotgun

"Masterkey" modification attached under his barrel. A small 5-shot 12-gauge allowed the Able Team leader some versatility in breaking the back of an enemy ambush with buckshot, or punching holes through stubborn locks as a breeching weapon. Normally, the Masterkey system was limited to rifles that could mount the M-203 grenade launcher, and the SIG rifles were designed to carry Heckler & Koch grenade launchers, a completely different form of bracket. However, since Blancanales didn't want to give up the M-203 grenade launcher he favored, and demanded for his SIG 551, Stony Man's master gunsmith John "Cowboy" Kissinger redesigned the M-203 mounting sleeve for the short-barreled SIG's forearm. The shotgun and the grenade launcher modifications to the assault carbines gave the team a force multiplier and the ability to destroy enemy vehicles or defensive positions with several ounces of high-explosive power. All four carried heavyweight 77-grain match-grade hollowpoint ammunition to make up for the 5.56 mm round's loss of velocity out of the 14-inch barrel of the SIGs.

Spare magazines were tucked into the pockets of their Safari vests, which concealed their handguns. The lightweight outer shell and multiple pockets also disguised the vests' inner lining, a blend of lightweight chain mail and mesh-woven Kevlar capable of stopping a hunting rifle round cold. Coverage was incomplete, because the sleeveless designs were meant for hot weather, and nothing protected their heads, but the garments, dubbed by codesigners Schwarz and Kissinger as Hot LZ vests, provided enough of an edge to split the difference between attacking in full commando gear and blending in as civilians. Since the Panamanian public was leery of American troops, Able

Team decided that low-profile "soft" civilian clothing was its best option.

Schwarz checked the screen on his PDA, live footage pouring in to inform him of the presence of two darts in the air. He pegged them as the Predator knockoffs. Only the sensitivity of the National Reconnaissance Office satellite feeding Stony Man its real time imagery made the patrolling drones visible against the jungle beneath. He pocketed the PDA and looked in the back of the SUV, making certain he left nothing behind.

"Shame, too. I liked this bucket," Schwarz grumbled as he trotted to join the others away from the SUV.

"The road's compromised somehow," Lyons said. "But it sure didn't look like any electronics could have survived in this environment."

"No sensors," Blancanales replied, "but there's a possibility we might have been picked up by low-level radar. A tight beam wouldn't show up on any detectors, not if it were scanning down into the hills instead of providing umbrella-style coverage."

"More like a spotlight," Lyons said. "It wouldn't even be seen from space?"

"No. Not in a tight beam sweep," Schwarz explained. "It was just blind luck that the drones I spotted on my map…"

They heard the thrum of motors fill the air. Softer and more subtle than conventional aircraft due to enclosed ducts, the Predators were designed to have a stealthy profile in their role as observation aircraft. Six shadows rocketed over a gap in the canopy overhead, speeding to the north.

"Six?" Schwarz wondered outloud, confused.

"How many did you see?" Lyons asked.

"Two…and they were a lot higher up," the electronics genius answered.

Arquillo looked toward the Mercedes SUV, nestled in the shadows of the tall trees bracketing it. "Well, if they've passed already, it should be safe to get back in…"

The CIA agent's musing was answered as a finger of smoke stabbed down through the treetops as quick as lightning. An explosion struck the SUV dead-center, splitting it into two burning halves that flopped away from each other like dying fish on dry land. The concussive blast rolled over Arquillo and pushed her to the ground.

Lyons grabbed her and hauled her to her feet. It took a few moments for her explosion-rattled senses to register that they were running, slicing through the rain forest as streams of machine-gun fire ripped down in their wake, lead, splintered branches and dislodged leaves falling in an unnatural storm behind them.

She shrugged loose from Lyons and kept up with Able Team's frantic pace through the jungle, staying one step ahead of the sweeping scythes of automatic fire that lashed at their heels.

ROBERTO DACOSTA DIDN'T BELIEVE in much. Though the majority of South America practiced Catholicism, or occasionally some other form of Christianity, DaCosta considered himself a fairly reasonable man, enlightened above the need for some invisible friend in the sky. Let the fools who worked under him throw their lot in with an imaginary father figure with magical powers, he thought. DaCosta made his own fortune and didn't need any psychic crutches. Right now, overseeing the loading of an oil tanker with millions of gallons of petroleum, earmarked for the

United States, the oil man realized what real power was. The Venezuelan had command over billions of dollars worth of product, and had the ability to deny substantial portions of another country the fuel they needed to warm their homes or to get to work in the morning.

DaCosta didn't believe in much, but he believed in his godhood. At his whim, he could strangle the wheels of progress to a halt and cast nations into chaos. A smile crept across his sun-bronzed face, a corner of his mouth turning up. He wouldn't really, but the thought shot him through with a jolt of adrenaline as powerful as any cocaine. In his role as supervisor at the Maracaibo petrochemical complex, he was paid handsomely, and had his share of mistresses for when he grew bored with his wife, or when the slowly aging slut was busy with some cabana boy or another. He'd even had occasion to enjoy a trip to Thailand, blowing a large bonus on some forbidden fruit.

He didn't need to sweat under the sun, among the white buttons of oil storage containers spread out in rows along the Gulf of Venezuela, or get his hands greasy in operating pipes. Hundreds toiled under DaCosta's leadership. Still, his bronzed flesh glinted in the noonday sun as he stood on a catwalk overlooking the oil transferral. His secretary could handle the paperwork, and any important phone calls would be routed through the cell phone hanging on his belt. DaCosta preferred to be outside, watching, paying attention to the domain that he ruled with unequaled power. He'd been, secretly, part of the two-month oil strike that had hit at the end of 2002, cajoled by an offer of several million dollars to hurt the government. That was when he realized his true godhood.

His cell warbled on his belt.

"What is it?" he asked, annoyed at the interruption of his dreams of grandeur.

"Sir, the coastal patrol spotted something a few minutes ago, passing Los Monjes," his secretary told him.

DaCosta was about to dismiss it, but knew that Los Monjes islands were a point of contention between Venezuela and Colombia. "Smugglers? So? Colombia sends smugglers all the time around the Gulf."

"Well, with the trouble in Panama with unmanned attack aircraft…" his secretary began.

"The coastal patrol can handle a few enemy airplanes, right?" DaCosta asked.

"They lost track of the unidentified aircraft."

DaCosta felt a moment of weakness. From his position atop the catwalk, he could see north, along the bottleneck between Lago de Maracaibo and the Gulf of Venezuela for miles and miles. Needlepoints of white, five or six of them, were visible in the faint distance across the glassy waters of the now placid gulf.

The Venezuelan oil man swallowed hard as they wove around the stern of an oil tanker, moving with synchronized precision like a school of deadly fish.

Suddenly he realized that his godly power was a stack of cards that could be knocked down, and he watched the personification of the ill wind that was going to collapse it.

NORMALLY, THE PREDATOR UAV drone was a low-powered, propeller-driven unmanned drone. It had been developed from early cruise missiles, the space normally reserved for a warhead payload replaced with advanced optics, transmitters and cameras. Unfortunately the cruise missiles, with their supersonic engines, were grossly inefficient at gathering intelligence, passing too quickly through an enemy territory. It was good for a first-glance of forces in a region, but commanders knew the benefits of real-time transmissions. Something slower, with longer staying power, was necessary. As such, the winglets were increased in width and area to allow more surface to catch air and glide, and the jet engine was replaced with a more fuel-efficient prop-driven motor. Now, crossing the sky at under two hundred miles an hour, the Predator was an ideal eye in the sky, able to hang around and orbit throughout an entire battle, or maintain a long-term watch on enemy movements across distances. The slow-moving Predators could also be equipped with weaponry that made them ideal assassination platforms, as proved in Afghanistan against al Qaeda forces.

The Engineers of the New Tomorrow, however, had brilliant designers on their side. Not only were the UAVs modified for multiple weapon platforms, such as machine guns, artillery rockets or even biochemical weapon payloads, but the ENT had developed a lightweight rocket engine that fit into the housing of the prop unit on their modified Predators. The additional wingspan helped stabilize the drones at near sonic speeds, and all that high-tech electronics were replaced.

In the case of the Maracaibo assault, the payload was a medium-size thermobaric warhead. While larger thermobarics were a step below a nuclear warhead, the modified Predators, reverse engineered back to being cruise missiles, were still devastating weapons. Originally, these particular warheads were meant for clearing underground installations such as those encountered in Afghanistan. Producing a cloud of airborne fuel, which was ignited to the same temperature as the surface of the sun, the fuel-air explosion had enormous power, capable of incinerating even the most persistent biological or chemical weapon.

Used against the armored white tanks dotting the shoreline, it was like a sledgehammer brought down on a row of candy buttons. The Predators spread out evenly, their blast radius a mere 500 meters, but more than enough to cover a large portion of the petrochemical complex. All six detonated simultaneously.

Roberto DaCosta, standing on his catwalk, was spared the raw fury of being caught in the cloud of vaporized fuel igniting across three kilometers of shoreline. The flash, however, was blindingly hot and his exposed skin was scourged with first-degree burns. A concussion wave of superheated air thrown off by the explosion slammed him against the railing of the catwalk hard enough to leave a hairline fracture along his pelvis and lower back, as well as deep tissue bruising. The combined pain made him collapse, his arms flailing for the support of the rail.

Instants later the wind returned, but in the opposite direction, pulling with the force of a tornado as the atmosphere fought to fill the momentary vacuum caused by six thermobaric warheads detonating in unison.

DaCosta howled in fear and terror, clinging to the railing for dear life. Below, he could see the complex's workers being thrown around like rag dolls by concussion and implosion waves.

The winds finally stopped, but the heat grew worse. DaCosta looked back and realized that 1500 square kilometers of oil storage field was a blazing inferno, millions of gallons of petroleum fueling a fire that convinced him that hell truly did exist. The sky turned deep black as thick, choking smoke spread out, a smothering blanket that spread across the city of Maracaibo.

THE DRONES WERE RELENTLESS in their pursuit of Able Team and Arquillo. While their brethren were en route to unleash relentless hell and fury on a defenseless city, moving at high subsonic velocities, the patrol Predators hung at a relatively lazy ninety miles an hour, long wings picking up the wind to provide lift beyond what their forward velocity supplied. Even so, their initial strafing runs had proved fruitless, simply because the only means that they had for picking up the fleeing humans was thermal imaging. In the hot and humid atmosphere of the rain forest, however, it was impossible to get a clean lock on the Stony Man warriors and their CIA ally. The SUV had proved to be an easy target, simply because its mass of metal and hot engine proved a much easier target for even tropic-hazed sensors.

Unfortunately the metal in their weaponry and equipment provided the tight-beam radar spotlight with a small means of tracking them. It was a tiny, low-profile signature, but still enough to give the operators of the drones something to lock on to.

Blancanales, his senses tuned by years of experience in jungles across the globe, found a cave and ushered the others into it. It was small, and a tight fit, but once inside, they were shielded not only from streams of light machine-gun fire, but also the probing radar beams that hunted them through the rain forest

Arquillo was crouched, hands on her khaki-clad knees, reddish hair damp and soaked, covering her face as she gulped down air to replenish herself from the frantic run.

Lyons rested a hand on her shoulder and she glanced up at him. He offered her a canteen of water.

"Damn near got us killed suggesting we go back to the SUV," she panted before taking a swig of tepid water. She swallowed, knowing that she needed the moisture.

"We're alive," Lyons told her. "No harm, no foul."

Arquillo straightened and leaned her head against the cave wall. She dragged a curtain of sweat-dampened hair from in front of her eyes and looked over Able Team. "I still let my guard down too soon."

"Well, it's not like we can drive you back to a day-care center for CIA agents, can we?" Blancanales asked, winking. "Someone blew up our ride."

Schwarz breathed slowly and deeply, willing his body's autonomic reactions to subside so that he could concentrate on his PDA. Inside the cave, under a sheet of heavy rock in the side of a hill, he'd lost satellite contact. He switched the device over to transmission scanning and moved closer to the mouth of the cave.

"Isn't he going to give our position away? One good shot with a rocket like before, and this cave becomes a tomb," Arquillo said.

"Nah. I'm on passive scan, this unit has radar-absorbent paint over its metal, and I left my rifle with Pol," Schwarz mentioned as he studied the screen.

"Checking to see if the spotlight is near us," Arquillo concluded as she watched.

The electronics expert nodded. "See, they can sweep the hillside with relative impunity because it's a tight beam. No radiation spills over to be noticed, even by sensors checking the area, unless they're right in the arc of the beam."

"Which the PDA is," Lyons said. "You don't pick them up, they can't pick us up."

Blancanales looked at Schwarz. "They're still sweeping the area?"

"Yeah. And even if the spotlight is off us, those drones still have thermal sensors. It won't be efficient, but after wasting so much ammo, they might just see what they could do with more rockets."

The ground shook violently and Arquillo ducked. Dust rained from the roof of the cave, making her cough.

"See what I mean?" Schwarz asked, crouched near the mouth of the cave.

"We could just shoot them down," Lyons growled.

Blancanales shrugged. "So then they'd send forces on foot after us."

"I'd rather go one on one with enemy soldiers than cower from rocket strikes," Lyons countered.

"Got a point there," Arquillo agreed. The rumbling thunder of artillery rockets slamming into the hillside around them was unnerving and left her feeling impotent and helpless. At least in a gunfight, she knew she had an even chance to survive and win.

Schwarz looked at the roof of the cave. "Don't worry. The tunnel's holding up. We're under enough rock that it'll take a direct hit to bring it down."

A loud thunderclap split the air in the cave, and Arquillo and the Stony Man warriors curled up in reaction to the nearby explosion.

"Say something else to tempt fate, smart-ass," Lyons grumbled.

Schwarz held a finger up to his lips, then pointed to the roof of the cave. The rolling thunder of the air strikes had stopped, the drones' rocket pods spent and empty. Schwarz grinned. "I was counting their shots. That was it."

"Good," Lyons answered. "With any luck, they'll send out a patrol. It'll be a relief to have a human opponent."

CHAPTER FOUR

It didn't take long for Phoenix Force to grab the hard drives out of the controllers' computers. They just ripped open the casings and sliced the IDE cables. The hard drives were durable and fit into Manning's backpack.

While Manning and McCarter were tearing apart CPUs, James, Encizo and Hawkins were repairing the tires of one of the pickups. The Toyota pickup was a bit old and weathered, but an inspection showed that the vehicle was in good running condition. All it took was a tire change, and it would be back in action. The pickup would be less conspicuous than the covered trailers, as well as having the benefit of maneuverability.

Hawkins scrounged the other vehicles and found spare gasoline canisters.

"All set?" Manning asked James as he topped off the pickup's tank.

"Yeah," James replied. "Time to go?"

Manning looked at his watch. "We've got a minute."

"Okay," James said, screwing the cap on the jerri can.

"No, we've got a minute to reach minimum safe distance," Manning explained.

"Aw heck. We were supposed to be coming in quietly," James muttered.

McCarter slid behind the wheel and started the engine. Hawkins and Manning squeezed into the front with the Briton, while Encizo and James clambered into the truck bed. Encizo's and James's darker coloring would be less conspicuous in the Lebanese countryside than the other members of the team, who looked distinctly European.

Manning's estimate of a minute to reach minimum safe distance was spot-on. Utilizing distract mechanisms already in the trailers, as well as some "Eight-balls"—one-eighth of a stick of C-4 plastic explosives—Manning had wired the drone operations centers well. The trailers ripped violently apart, but there was little flash. Electronics and corpses were ground to bits by the detonations.

While Manning had done his demolitions work, McCarter took fingerprints from the dead, utilizing a fingerprint scanner. Now, as he drove, Hawkins plugged the scanner into the sat-phone-linked laptop and uploaded information to Stony Man Farm.

"Barb, see if these are current Syrian operatives," McCarter had text-messaged along with the data file.

Hawkins looked up from the laptop. "Bear says that it'll take a few hours for them to check the records for certain."

"To narrow it down, tell them the unit we saw on the sentrics. They might have been veterans of the same group," McCarter suggested.

Hawkins typed that message back to the Farm's Computer Room. It took only a few moments to get a reply.

"Bear says thanks. He'll see what he can get on the sentries," Hawkins said.

"How's our schedule, Gary?" McCarter asked.

"At this rate, we should be five minutes early to our meet with the Egyptians," Manning answered.

"Of course, that doesn't take into account running into local factions."

"Just a little more drama for the evening in that case," McCarter said. "We won't stay and fight."

Manning was about to say something when McCarter sailed the pickup three feet into the air after plowing through a rut in the road. The truck plopped down and shook Phoenix Force around.

"Not that we'll be running into anyone with antiaircraft weapons."

McCarter grinned. It was a long-standing joke between the two that the British pilot drove as if he expected vehicles could fly. Manning had grown used to his driving, but he still held on to his seat with white-knuckled strength. From the bed, Encizo and James grumbled and complained through the cab's rear window.

"Hey, David, we don't have seat belts back here!" James growled.

McCarter kept up the breakneck pace. Drivers weren't known for cautious pace in the Lebanese countryside, and the Briton was following suit. "When in Rome" was a savvy strategy for blending in. It wasn't as if there were highway patrolmen on these dirt roads. No headlights were visible on the horizon in any direction. Manning scanned out the windows for operating lights on any aircraft, but the sky was merely sprinkled with immobile stars.

"Anything back there?" McCarter asked.

"Just two rattled people," Encizo complained. "No lights on the horizon."

"Give a shout if you see something," McCarter said.

"Who the hell's gonna catch up to us?" James asked.

"You know our luck," Manning quipped.

Hawkins shook his head. "Probably a rocket-assisted APC."

"Don't tempt fate," Manning cautioned.

Something sparked in the distance, a star of light on the ground. It wasn't a single headlight, and moments later, the snap-crack of bullets lashing past the truck filled the air. Machine-gun rounds hurtled by so quickly, Phoenix Force could hear the breaking of the sound barrier.

McCarter killed the headlights and swerved hard, breaking off their previous course. The Toyota pickup jerked and jostled as it rolled over rough ground and clumps of vegetation. Encizo and James were silent in the back, holding on for dear life so they wouldn't be ejected when the truck hit the next bump.

The star of gunfire turned into a sidelong flare, tracer rounds scratching streaks of red in the black night. Whoever the gunner was, he was searching for Phoenix Force's pickup. The teardrop-shaped muzzle-flash fattened and turned into a circle, bullets raking the ground around the pickup. McCarter hit the brakes and drove toward the machine gun. The arc of fire swung past and sliced into the night. Bullets had drilled into the pickup's bodywork, and the windshield sported three new white spiderwebs where bullets ricocheted off.

The weapon was a light machine gun, the rifle rounds at the extreme limit of their normal range, lacking the power to smash the safety glass.

"Everyone okay?" McCarter asked, skidding the pickup to a halt.

"Yeah," James said, crawling out of the bed.

Manning and Hawkins piled out of the cab, the Canadian went prone behind a bush and locked his sniper rifle's scope on the distant gunner.

"What is it?" Hawkins asked, sliding beside him.

"An armored personnel carrier," Manning grumbled. "Not the one you ordered, though. Just the good old-fashioned roll-along. No rocket boosters."

Hawkins grimaced. "Some days you eat the bear, some days the bear eats you."

"Too much Information there, T.J.," James joked. "Whatever happened to 'don't ask, don't tell'?"

Hawkins winced, remembering Aaron Kurtzman's nickname.

McCarter threw the American members of Phoenix Force a harsh glare, then leaned to Manning.

"Is it alone?"

The big Canadian swept the terrain around the APC. "It's an old Soviet-style APC, so it could either be Syrian or Syrian allied. The ground is uneven around it, and I can't see anything else. Range out is 750 meters, give or take."

"I said we wouldn't stand and fight, but driving in the dark without headlights is starkers, even by my standards," McCarter said. He consulted his map, illuminating it with his refilter flashlight. The low frequency of light put out by the ruby-colored lens wouldn't travel far to betray their position, especially at that range. He did a quick bit of reckoning. "We can leave the pickup and continue on foot."

"Double time," Hawkins said, looking over McCarter's shoulder.

"Get on the link to the Farm and tell Aaron that we ran into some interference," McCarter ordered.

"Shit, " Hawkins muttered. "David…"

McCarter looked at the laptop screen and clucked his tongue. "The paratroopers were dishonorably discharged. Syrians were dealing drugs to their fellow soldiers. They were assigned to operations here in Lebanon. And we've dealt with enough heroin coming out of the Bekaa Valley to know who they could have hooked up with."

"Drug dealers attacking Israel?" James asked.

"Muslim drug dealers," Encizo corrected. "The Jihad has used narcotics money to supply terrorist groups with almost bottomless funding."

"The kind of funding that can afford ten heavily armed UAV drones and two eighteen-wheelers loaded with computer software," Manning added.

"There's no solid confirmation that those paratroopers went into the Lebanese heroin trade, yet," McCarter said. "We'll have to check on that once we make our rendezvous."

"The APC is moving," Manning announced.

"Headed our way?" James asked.

"A straight beeline," Manning said. "Give me a few moments. Move on ahead, I'll catch up."

Phoenix Force took off while Manning took another stick of C-4 from his pack and divided it up, setting it on the fuel-filled jerri cans and replacing the gas cap to the tank. He wired them to one central detonator. There was a chance that the APC would hose down the truck with its machine gun at a distance, but either way, the explosion would erase any evidence of Phoenix Force presence in Lebanon.

If militia men did inspect the truck, there was a better

likelihood that they would disturb the cans in the back and set off one of Manning's tripwires, removing another squad of gun-toting militiamen from the Lebanese conflict. Shouldering his sniper rifle, Manning took off after his friends. His long legs fell into a loping pace that ate up distance effortlessly. He slowed to accommodate the others once he caught up with them.

Five minutes after leaving the truck, a fireball flashed, lighting the night behind them. The outline of the APC and two military-style jeeps appeared, backlit by the flowering blossom of their pickup. One of the jeeps flipped and bounced off the APC.

"Seventy gallons of petrol will do that," McCarter quipped.

Manning knelt and surveyed the blast site with his rifle.

"They tracking us?" Encizo inquired.

"They're dealing with wounded, " Manning informed them. "We'll have plenty of time to get out of sight by sunup."

"Ground cover will obscure us after another two hundred yards, and it's two hours until sunrise anyhow," James mentioned.

"That's no reason to sit around discussing the weather," McCarter said. "Let's roll."

"ALL MANEUVERS GO according to plan," Javier Cortez said. "At least until contact with the enemy. We've got activity in our Middle Eastern and Central American arenas."

"Someone's noticed us," Kovak said. "I see that Tel Aviv is still quiet."

"The fight was diverted." Ling Jon spoke up. "An outside group of hackers broke into the network and commandeered the drones. We shut down on first notification, initiated defensive—"

"Their system will have taken a beating from your defenses," Kovak noted. "What about the other scheduled attacks?"

Ling smiled. "The fuse is lit in the China Sea, and Kashmir is about to rock."

Kovak took a deep breath and glanced at Cortez. "You're looking to start every war you can imagine."

"So many juicy-looking powder kegs," Cortez answered with a grin. "We're making a whole new world, Jason."

"There's going to be enough of a planet left after China gets set off?" Kovak asked.

"I'm fully aware of what plans Beijing has, and the West's projected response," Ling explained.

"Beijing will take the attack as an excuse to make a move on Taiwan. The British and Australian navies will move to protect Taiwan, and of course the United States will throw in. One or two more Chinese ships sunk—"

"And China will take a potshot at the Western navies," Kovak concluded. "World War Three."

"Just like the chest-beating in South America," Cortez said. "Colombia and Venezuela responded exactly as we wanted."

Kovak looked at the world map. The Engineers' software was monitoring international tensions. Earlier that day, the Republic of Georgia suffered an attack from Azerbaijan The Azerbaijani government claimed innocence, but the city of Gardabani was hammered by HVAR artillery rockets and antitank missiles launched by unmanned drones. Muslim separatists took the opportunity to start riots across the city, killing police officers and soldiers.

The Russian-controlled Commonwealth of Independent States, already on the edge because of infighting between ethnic groups in the region, was on full alert. The Russian president offered to send a few divisions of troops into Georgia to help enforce the peace, but the leadership in Tsiblisi remembered that Russian troops had swallowed the independent government in 1921. Leery eyes remained locked on Moscow, wondering if this was a ploy by hardliners who wanted to rebuild the old Soviet empire. And now Beijing was being poked, the sleeping dragon baited with the jewel that was Taiwan. It was no secret that the People's Republic of China lusted after the independent island nation, and had all forms of contingency plans to take the little country. Taiwan was ready to fight, but it knew that if its Western allies faltered, it would lose the battle and China would be reunited.

With tensions in South America, the Middle East and the Commonwealth of Independent States, Britain and America would be stretched thin, making the road to Taiwan wide and ready. The projected spark of violence between India and Pakistan over Kashmir would leave the globe with a hair trigger.

"This should confuse matters," Cortez said. "Our previous two hot spots were major oil conflicts."

"Lebanon?" Kovak asked.

"Syria and Israel border on major oil-producing nations who are members of OPEC. The start of an all-out war between those two would affect Egypt and Saudi Arabia, not to mention the potential of other OPEC states that dislike Israel to step in and join the party," Cortez said.

"Those countries tried that. Israel beat them down. And we have nukes now, remember?" Kovak reminded the man.

Cortez smirked. "That's part of what we're counting on. We're lighting the match on as many fuses as we can."

Kovak nodded, looking at the map. "And when the bombs go off, the topography of the world alters. Radically."

"The Old World, the New World, the Third World, everything breaks down into anarchy," Cortez explained. "Barbarism and chaos run rampant. Riots infect the streets, governments crumble and, eventually, everyone will look to who has enough power to bring them peace and stability."

Kovak's eyes narrowed. "The tank attacks on Israel, a while back. Utilizing Marshall Plan hardware…"

"A test run. Now, we can see how the world responds to our operations, and we can anticipate them," Cortez said.

"This has been a long time coming," Kovak noted.

"We needed to build up supplies. The drones for bringing hostilities to the edge and pushing them over," Cortez continued. "But we have other facilities. Storage areas, set up around the globe, stocked with the kind of firepower we'd need to emerge from the ashes of civilization as the new tomorrow's government."

"And forcing nuclear, biological and chemical attacks across the globe thins down the herd you want to run," Kovak concluded. "After all, you might have a fairly strong organization, but even you can't rein in six billion humans."

"No," Cortez admitted. He smiled. "I don't blame you for feeling overwhelmed."

"It's not every day someone sets the wheels of Armageddon in motion," Kovak stated.

Cortez chuckled. "Yes. The backup plan."

Kovak looked at Israel, specifically the Northern District. To many Christians around the world, this was to be the location for the battle of Armageddon, specifically in the Jezreel Valley, not far from the Golan Heights. Several historical battles of Meggido had been fought across the history of humankind.

Jammed in the armpit between Lebanon and Syria, and containing the contested Golan Heights, the Northern District was a lightning rod for tension and violence. Between angry and hostile enemies, this region had seen countless acts of terrorism and posturing, from rocket artillery attacks from Lebanon to massed troops on the border with Syria. On the Israeli side of the equation, angry settlers engaged in brutal vigilante violence against native Arabs, murdering and intimidating countless people.

Kovak had engaged in copious amounts of such intimidating violence until the cowardly government gave in to "peaceful concessions" and gave the land back to the Arabs. Settlers were wrestled and hijacked from their homes. Kovak then realized that the Promised Land had fallen to the forces of evil. He wasn't the only one, and together, they had formed an unofficial wing of the Mossad called Abraham's Dagger. Made up of current and former Mossad agents, they took the actions that the government was too weak to commit. Now, hunted by their former comrades, Kovak and his allies were out in the cold.

Their future involved either jail or a shallow, unmarked grave.

Kovak's loyalty to Israel burned away like gasoline under a blowtorch.

It was time to start over.

That meant forming an alliance with South American Nazis and anti-communist Chinese rebels, among dozens of other splintered cells, disillusioned and rejected. Alone, none of them could have made much of a difference, just a few minutes of carnage-bloodied footage on the evening news.

Together, they were the Engineers of the New Tomorrow.

The world would bathe in blood, and be washed clean by the tide of war.

Kovak looked at Cortez and nodded grimly. The future would involve strange bedmates, but in the end, it wouldn't matter. The past was up for execution, and after the chaos, he could see the Dagger and the Nazis as allies. Old hatreds had no place when there was a world to rebuild.

They would be too busy trying to fight off mutual enemies.

THERE WERE TWO GROUPS meeting in the cave when Phoenix Force arrived at their rendezvous. But that was to be expected. Though Israel and Egypt were locked in a "cold peace," each side watching the other in response to enemy actions, they were at peace, not war. There was a healthy measure of distrust, but there was also a camaraderie between the two nations when it came to fighting terrorism. The same ultraradical Islamic groups that swore to destroy Israel also sought to overthrow the government in Cairo because it was not vehemently Muslim enough, nor willing to crush the tiny nation of Jews to its northeast. Peace talks and diplomacy was a wide-open avenue between the two, and such openness was an anathema to terrorists who wanted nothing less than extermination of a foreign presence in the Arab world.

In the minds of the Mossad and Egypt's General Intelligence Directorate, the ancient history that tied Cairo and Jerusalem together was just that—ancient history. A new era called for new responses and allegiances. While the GID had been formed to respond to the Mossad's attempts to undermine Egypt's fighting ability against Israel, the threat of terrorists often threw them together as allies.

"Is this a private party, or can anyone join in?" David McCarter said in greeting at the mouth of the cave. The muzzles of automatic weapons swung in his direction, but the black-and-white checkered keffiyeh dangling in his left hand was the indicator he was an ally. While the keffiyeh was traditional head garb of violent terrorists, holding it like a limp flag in his left hand showed disdain for the cloth in Arab cultural mores. The left was the unclean hand, and primarily holding such a sacred item in a left hand while the right was free was an insult to the PLO and the Fatah movements.

The muzzles pointed to the dirt.

"Bring your people in, King," the Egyptian leader said. "You can call me Mahmoud."

McCarter nodded to the Egyptian.

"I'm Reiser," the Israeli offered.

McCarter made a hand gesture to the rest of Phoenix Force. Encizo and James remained just outside the cave entrance, along with pairs of Egyptians and Israelis who served as perimeter guards, and to keep the others inside polite.

There was tension, but the real concern was an outsider stumbling onto this situation. Considering that most outsiders in the Lebanese countryside were armed members of one of several militia groups, the noise and violence would be considerable, drawing unwanted attention if the alliance didn't take them down swiftly and silently.

"Have you heard about the latest situations?" Mahmoud asked.

"Pakistan and India?" McCarter inquired.

"Border crossing with troops and air support from these damned drones," Reiser explained.

"Troops," McCarter noted with some surprise. "Any positive identification?"

"Most likely insurgents who found Iraq too hot to handle," Mahmoud stated. "Not much was left for identification. They grabbed their wounded when the Indian fire base they assaulted hit back hard. Drones packed with napalm crashed into the Indian compound, killed the troops and destroyed most of the remains of the fallen assault force."

"India would love for Pakistan to have made an offensive move," McCarter commented. "Kashmir has been a sore point between those two for years. It would be the perfect excuse to close it down once and for all."

"Trouble is, both sides have nuclear missiles," Reiser reminded him. "With a billion noncombatants in the subcontinent, that solution might be all too final."

"There's trouble between Georgia and Azerbaijan," Mahmoud noted. "Venezuela was also attacked. Maracaibo is in flames, literally."

"This is much bigger than we thought," McCarter said. He filled in the Egyptians and the Israelis about the aborted drone attack on Israel.

"Ex-Syrian paratroopers turned mercenary," Reiser mused. "Deniable, but that wouldn't matter much to our government if it had succeeded. Every insult must be answered in kind, which would involve firing a nuclear warhead into a Syrian city."

"Even if they were not guilty of this particular offense," McCarter added. "Because the world has seen that Syria is anything but innocent of malice toward the Israelis."

"Just like Colombia and Venezuela are hardly the sweetest of friends, or Pakistan and India, or Georgia and Azerbaijan," Mahmoud rattled off. "Someone's taking advantage of deep-seated hostility to start a war or five."

"Who and why?" Manning asked.

"Someone with ambition." One of the Israelis spoke up. "Couldn't help with the other option."

"Doesn't narrow the field down much, does it?" T.J. Hawkins quipped.

"That's why we're here," Mahmoud said. "If we figure this out, perhaps we can head off the main insanity."

"Which means China might be next," another Egyptian said. "It doesn't seem like there's a situation that might lead to a nuclear exchange than something involving Taiwan. The Taiwanese don't have the bond, but the U.S. and Britain do, and they'd need to have that kind of power to take on Communist China."

"We'll keep our eyes peeled in that direction," McCarter replied. "Good thinking."

The Briton's brow furrowed as he remembered a report from Able Team's Hermann Schwarz, about cheap knock off electronics from China. He hoped the cyberteam at the Farm would figure out that possible connection in the near future. Otherwise, he'd bring it up at their next scheduled teleconference.

That was, if this odd alliance survived long enough to report in.

CHAPTER FIVE

Barbara Price stared at the screen, not believing what she saw—a submarine from the People's Republic of China floating, belly-up, like a slaughtered whale, flame and smoke bleeding into the sky.

"For too long, we have dealt with the hostile ring that the Communists have wrapped around our tiny island nation. Now the so-called mightiest military in the world will see what power unrestrained truly is!" the announcement said.

The video and voice were coming through a live feed, broadcast over multiple frequencies. It was a slap in the face to Beijing, their navy now one ship smaller, split apart. Considering the number of drones that had been utilized in attacks recently, it was no surprise that they were getting broadcast quality video sent around the world.

"How's the trace on the signal?" Price asked Aaron "The Bear" Kurtzman.

"Uplinks are bouncing all over the place," Kurtzman said. "We've got some trails leading back to Taiwan, but more are scattered all across the Pacific. We've even got relay pulses coming from San Francisco and…"

"What?" Price asked.

"Panama," Kurtzman stated.

"China could take the path of least resistance and use the relays going through Taiwan as evidence for a retaliatory strike," Price mentioned.

"Which means we have to work fast," Kurtzman explained.

Price frowned. "Surely with all these attacks going on, utilizing similar MOs, the world would see that it's being yanked on a chain."

"Rational leaders would realize that," Kurtzman said. "But you've got these people working on the raw nerves of leaders who have grudges. I mean, how many times have our teams put down agents provocateurs in dozens of other conflicts?"

"Too many to count," Price answered. She pinched her brow between her eyes and sighed. "You'd think they'd learn by now."

"The bad guys go with what works," Kurtzman said. "And we keep stopping them cold, so the world's leaders don't get a chance to learn any better."

"Check on that transmission from Panama. Home in on it," Price ordered. "I've got to make sure that we can keep our government from misbehaving."

"My eyes are wide open," Kurtzman said, returning to his keyboard.

Price left the Computer Room and headed to her office. She picked up her phone and began conferring with her contacts in the CIA and NSA, making certain that the word got out about the uncertain origins of the Chinese submarine video. Both agencies confirmed Kurtzman's findings, though it took some cajoling to get their admissions. Intelligence agencies were notoriously tight-lipped about their information, even among their own departments. Price's contacts, however, were people she knew when she worked for NSA, and they shared a mutual respect. While the Department of Homeland Defense had been devised to eliminate jurisdictional disputes and information smoke stacking, the reality was that petty rivalries often strangled the flow of intelligence between those who needed to know.

Price's hot line rang and she picked up. It was Hal Brognola.

"What's happening, Hal?" she asked.

"The president is working on building a case for Beijing not to take action against Taiwan. Information from the CIA, NSA and the U.S. Navy has given him enough counterindication to work on, but it's not going to be too easy," Brognola said. There was a short pause. "Good work."

"Sometimes intelligence and logic can prevail," Price replied. The past few hours of wheeling and dealing over the phone had left her with a throbbing headache, but relief flooded her after hearing Brognola's news. "What about the other fires on?"

"FARC has stepped up action, making it difficult for Colombia and Venezuela to step down. Both sides are on full alert, and it's hard to tell the difference between terrorist activity and legitimate military action," Brognola explained. "The National Reconnaissance Office's notes are that northern and central America are pretty heavily masked. Electronic surveillance is difficult, and orbital cameras are being obscured by all the smoke from Maracaibo."

"I got the same from Aaron," Price answered. "We're doing our best, though, and Able is on the ground."

"If anyone can shake answers loose, it's Carl," Brognola admitted. "Keep in touch with him."

"I suppose we don't have to worry about any more international incidents with all this going on," she said with a sigh. Price checked her screen and received McCarter's report on the meet in Lebanon. She saw the postscript, and as usual, the men of Phoenix Force demonstrated knowledge and political awareness. The report came in just minutes before the video on the Chinese submarine, and McCarter had voiced concerns about the conspiracy they were in conflict with attempting to spur tensions over Taiwan.

"David can be scary sometimes," Price murmured.

"Don't tell me that. I've driven with him," Brognola quipped.

"I mean, he and the others were concerned about China being the next hot spot the drones hit," Price corrected him.

Brognola clucked his tongue. "Oh, that. Last time I checked, the average IQ of the members of Phoenix was around genius level."

"Dummies don't last long in field operations," Price replied. "I'll see if there's anything new on the Chinese front, and see if there's any breakthrough in Panama."

"I'll brief the President on what you're sending me," Brognola replied. "He's headed to New York to speak with the United Nations."

"Talk about tap dancing on thin ice," Price remarked. "After the world accused the U.S. of overreacting to Iraq, the President calling for cool heads…"

"There's no other choice, Barb. Either we get the world to put its sabers down and look for the real cause, or World War Three hits," Brognola told her. "It's world-saving time again. And we can't screw up."

"I know, Hal," Price answered. "We're on it."

"Never doubted that," Brognola replied. He hung up.

CARL LYONS CROUCHED, the SIG 551 Masterkey cradled across his knees as he peered through the foliage at a pickup wending its way across a dirt road. The back was covered with a tarp, and two dirt bikes with submachine-gun-armed riders rolled parallel to it. Two more dirt bikes snarled into view, coming from the direction that Able Team had marched from.

"They'll know we got out of the SUV," Susana Arquillo whispered to the Able Team leader.

Lyons nodded toward the riders. "They have radios, so they'll have reported the lack of corpses back at the drop-off."

Arquillo looked up. The thick tree canopy overhead blocked the sky, but with some forms of imaging, they might as well have been hiding under clear plastic wrap. Her lips were drawn tight.

"Nothing in the air." Schwarz consoled her. "We're okay for now."

"They won't have to send aerial scouts for us," Blanca-nales countered. "They know they're our targets. If we're not charred skeletons in a burned-out vehicle, then we're on our way to check them out."

"We'll be answered by some serious security, in that case," Arquillo said.

"Good," Lyons answered.

"That's good?" Arquillo quizzed.

"The more protection we run into, the more important the base, and the more answers we'll get after we crack it open," Lyons explained.

"That's Ironman," Schwarz quipped. "He's a Pollyanna, looking for a silver lining in every cloud."

"More like a Silvertip hollowpoint in every .45," Lyons corrected him. "We'll stick with the road, but keep to the forest. Pol?"

"I'll take point," Blancanales answered, accepting the role. The eldest Able Team member was at home in tropical jungles and could lead the group through the densest of rain forests with nimble ease. Schwarz was a jungle warfare expert, as well, but he was busy monitoring a frequency meter to determine enemy activity and watching for drones being directed toward them. With Schwarz glued to his PDA monitor, it was up to Blancanales to watch for more terrestrial challenges.

The Stony Man warriors and their comrade continued parallel to the road the motorbikes and pickup took for a few minutes when Schwarz gave the hand signal for them to stop cold.

Arquillo and Lyons crouched deeply. The leaves of the canopy were thick overhead, but to some forms of detection, they might as well have been standing on barren tundra.

"Tree trunks, break up our pattern," Schwarz whispered, crawling into the crooked fingers of a tree's roots for cover. The others did the same, sweeping leaves and mud over themselves. The ambient temperature of the forest floor would allow the leaves and mud to mask their humanoid heat patterns, however, all the metallic gear they carried would provide enough to lock on with focused radar sweeps. Even the pound of metal in Arquillo's polymer-framed Glock would register.

Schwarz inwardly hoped that because of the low-cost Chinese electronics in the unmanned drones, that they wouldn't have the technical capacity to operate a focused beam radar sweep. He doubted it, though. The drones were supposed to be untraceable, but the enemy would undoubtedly want prime-quality gear for the UAVs protecting their home base. He braced his SIG and aimed toward where the PDA's sensors picked up the drones' approach, ready to empty a magazine of 5.56 mm NATO rounds into the Predator.

The thrum of engines sounded overhead as the UAVs took up an orbit. There were two of them, Schwarz's monitor picked them out as they described a lazy circular arc overhead, setting Able Team and their ally perfectly in the middle. The electronics genius scowled.

"Found us," Schwarz said. He still stayed close to the tree trunk, but the mulch of the forest floor was no longer needed. "But these aren't armed."

"The last time they hosed us down from the air, they got bupkis," Lyons growled. "This time, they want confirmed kills. That means…"

The buzzing snarl of dirt bikes rose to a crescendo in the distance, but then stopped. Blancanales gestured toward where he placed the enemy's last position. His SIG, equipped with an M-203 grenade launcher, swept the forest.

Lyons squirmed out of most of his gear and laid the SIG Masterkey beside it. The only metal he had left on his person was his combat knife and his Kissinger-tuned 1911 pocket revolver and spare ammunition. It was still a significant amount, but the Able Team leader had been briefed well by Schwarz about the radar capability of the Predator drones. His sheathed magazines, pocketed revolver and battle knife, under radar-absorbent ballistic nylon, would provide a negligible signal for the drone to pick up. He threaded a suppressor onto the barrel of the .45 auto and nodded for the others to do the same.

The implication was clear.

His teammates dumped their gear except for their handguns and knives.

Arquillo was about to do the same, but Lyons shook his head.

"You're our anchor," he told her in a low whisper. "I know you're okay with fighting, but this isn't going to be self-defense. This is going to be slaughter."

Arquillo frowned as she gripped her .45. "I can handle myself."

Lyons shook his head. "If things go tits up, I need someone with a real weapon, not a handgun, giving us cover fire."

The CIA agent's eyes narrowed. "Because I'm a woman?"

"Because you're not a member of our team, and you haven't done what we have," Lyons said. He stalked off into the forest, his modified-for-silence .45 a dark, grim bit of high-tech in his fist.

Tso Ku killed the engine on his Kawasaki and slid off its seat. The heat was stifling, but it was a familiar cloak. While the rain forest here smelled different, strange plants and animals compared to the jungles of Thailand where he served as chief of security for heroin plantations, it was familiar territory. The rules were the same as back in Thailand, even if their aerial cover was far more sophisticated. Somewhere above the treetops, rotating around their target site, the Raptors, Predators updated and renamed by the Engineers of the New Tomorrow, kept high-tech eyes on their prey.

He clutched his Heckler & Koch G-36 K, a fine, sturdy piece of hardware that was as well suited to the jungle as his old AK-47. While his shirt stuck to him with damp sweat and sticky humidity, his vest didn't add an unwanted burden of extra heat while providing a layer of protection against even full-powered rifle slugs. ENT had gone to great lengths to give Tso all he needed to be successful in this new environment.

Tso pulled his out GPS monitor. The Raptors had picked up his team on its radar, the steel in their weapons and gear giving them away to invisible high-frequency beams. There was some scattering of the signal, tiny blips away from their main targets, four people who had wandered into the jungle.

No, they hadn't wandered. They'd survived one of ENT"s distracting traps and a strafing run. The Mercedes SUV left burning at the cliff was mute testimony that the strangers weren't wayward tourists. It was a quality, expensive piece of equipment, and charred gear in the back indicated that the four of them were well-armed and looking for trouble.

Tso sneered as he silently answered that the fools had found trouble.

Using hand signals, Tso had his men spread out. They were a mix of Filipino, Thai, Mexican and Colombian, all experienced in jungle operations, and ENT had trained them together to form a cohesive team to the point where they could communicate entire thoughts with gestures and glances. FARC had made the mistake of trying to enter their territory, and the ragtag terrorists, forty strong, had fallen to the well-honed ENT security force under Tso, despite two-to-one odds. Tso hadn't lost a single member of his team.

Tso had seven men with him, leaving the others to protect the base. If anything happened to this group, Aceveda would lock down the facility. The Thai commander didn't think that this group could handle two-to-one odds, but they had managed to survive a Raptor attack involving machine guns and an antitank missile. Firepower wasn't everything, and Tso was under no illusion that even his team's level of training made them invincible.

There was a soft cough off to his right and Tso hit the ground hard. A Filipino ENT sentry also fell, but not out of survival reflex. The ENT gunman's face had been obliterated by a suppressed pair of bullets, smashing his cheekbone and ejecting his brains out the other side of his skull. One glassy eye stared at Tso, unblinking in its accusation.

There was no room for silent communication now. Not with hostile marauders in their midst.

"Ambush!" Tso bellowed, slithering into the foliage as slugs dug up mud near him. He triggered his G-36 K, slicing a wide arc in the forest before reaching the cover of a tree trunk. Other assault rifles chattered, and Tso could see their muzzle-flashes in the dimness of the canopy's shadow. "Check fire! Check fire!"

The ENT commander slung his rifle. The weapon would give his position away. The rifles they selected for this operation were chosen for their compactness, but that same short barrel also produced a flare that would point right at him. Even with the muzzle brake taming the explosive gases to a mere spark, it was still bright enough to give away his position. Tso pulled his pistol and looked for movement in the trees. His team was smart enough to set their assault rifles aside, going to handguns in the darkness. A pistol wasn't a preferred weapon, but with stealthy ambushers, their longarms would prove to be a hindrance, giving aid to the enemy.

Thumbing back the hammer on his pistol, Tso took to the shadows, hunting the demons of the forest.

CARL LYONS DELIBERATELY MISSED the apparent leader of the enemy strike force, throwing away ammunition in the course of forcing Tso to reach cover. He rammed a fresh magazine into the butt of his .45 and snicked on the safety. He wanted the Asian alive, or at least in good enough condition to survive a couple of questions. From his position in the middle of a patch of shadowy, moss-encrusted roots, he was invisible, the 1911's suppressor rendering his low-flash ammunition invisible to view from Tso. The direction of the bullet impacts in the ground might have drawn the commander's attention, but his assault rifle spit wide of the mark.

"Loudmouth's mine," Lyons whispered over his LASH radio.

"Roger," Schwarz answered. "Remaining three fair game."

Lyons slid a phosphate-coated Ka-Bar fighting knife from its sheath. A dull black, even to its razor-thin, flesh-slicing edge, it was a shard of night hidden among the shadows. Tso and his crew would obviously be alert for the sound of a suppressed handgun. Even though the muzzle-flash was swallowed by the steel tube, and the roar of the bullet was reduced to a cough, there was still enough sound for a nearby opponent to lock on to a target. Wiping out half of the investigating force had been easy with the initial shots, and even from cover, Able Team had been relatively secure against return fire.

The ex-cop saw Blancanales glide from behind a tree and wrap a muscle-knotted arm around the throat of a Hispanic gunman. The Colombian's eyes went wide as the former Black Beret's forearm closed over his throat, cutting off his air. Blancanales didn't give the ENT sentry a chance to strangle to death, even though his grasp had been tight enough to crush the man's windpipe. Another black-bladed combat knife punched through the bone and cartilage of the Colombian's breastbone, spearing through the thick trunk of the aorta beneath it. The point had missed the guard's heart by an inch, but with a wicked twist and a hard rip, the knife had rendered the blood pump useless by severing the major artery. Blood pressure dropped like a rock and the Puerto Rican's victim didn't even have the strength for one final thrash, his arms and legs dropping limply like wet noodles to the forest floor. Dark, cold eyes stared lifelessly at Lyons as he circled behind a second of Tso's commandos.

Lyons lurched from the shadows, his hand wrapping around the Asian's face, palm clamping over the gunman's mouth while he slammed his Ka-Bar into his reedy, brown neck. The thick Bowie-style blade carved through arteries and windpipe in one savage intrusion. Lyons cranked on his knife handle as if it were a cantankerous stick shift, pulling the knife forward.

The wiry little Asian tried to scream, his arms flailing into the big ex-cop's face, and the guard's windpipe resisted the Ka-Bar, hanging on with rubbery tenacity. Unable to pull the knife forward, Lyons twisted the blade around and shoved back. His adversary's eyes rolled crazily as the phosphate-coated edge crunched and ricocheted between vertebrae, parting cartilage. Nearly decapitated, the ENT soldier's corpse fell instantly still. Lyons wiped the blood off his blade and looked for the team's commander.

The Thai security commander's handgun revealed him, bullets cracking loudly. Lyons whirled and spotted Schwarz, diving for cover, pulling the body of his last ENT victim along with him as a shield. Tso howled in rage and reloaded his handgun.

Lyons let his knife fall and lifted his silenced .45. He aimed low, striking the ENT guard in the rear.

Contrary to comedy, anything more than a load of bird shot in the gluteous maximus was guaranteed to cause major injury. One of Lyons's 230-grain hollowpoints rounds, stopped cold, deforming as Tso's pelvic girdle absorbed its forward momentum. Unable to deal with 350 pounds of force, the hip bone shattered. The second round tore through fatty tissue and muscle to burst Tso's bladder, ripping out a half-inch chunk of groin muscle. Either wound would have made it impossible for the Thai to stand upright. Together at once, they dropped the ENT commander to the forest floor in blinding agony.

Blancanales rushed to the wounded man, kicking the gun out of his hand before checking his wounds.

"He'll live?" Lyons asked.

"Missed the femoral artery, but he's bleeding badly," Blancanales said. He pulled a small tube from his medical pack and poured a black silt into Tso's groin wound. It was gunpowder, and the Able Team medic ignited it with an electric lighter.

The Thai gunman thrashed in agony as his bloody wound was cauterized shut, damaged blood vessels sealed off as they cooked instantly.

Lyons leaned onto Tso's throat, his hands clamped on either side of his neck.

"Speak English?" Lyons asked.

"Go to hell," Tso answered.

"Good enough for me," Lyons replied. "We're going to have a little talk."

Tso coughed violently. "Or what? You'll torture me? Didn't you hear that torture was illegal?"

"How long do you think it'll take for you to die in this jungle?" Lyons asked.

Tso's eyes narrowed.

"You're a cripple. There's no way you can walk out. And even if you could crawl one hundred miles to the nearest city, I'm pretty sure you'll succumb to a few dozen infections. You'll never go anywhere on your two feet regardless," Lyons stated.

"You cauterized my gunshots," Tso said, his voice a nervous warble.

Lyons rolled his eyes and pulled his Ka-Bar. The blade sliced into Tso's upper arm, opening the skin. "How many cuts do you think we'll need, Pol?"

"Just that one," Blancanales replied. "Any more, and we'd run the risk of jaguars finding and finishing him off too soon."

Tso's features paled instantly.

"You know," Schwarz said, "the cats aren't the real threat. I'd be more concerned about ants or maggots."

"Actually, the maggots would be helpful," Lyons told Schwarz. "Maggots only eat necrotic flesh and leave healthy, uninfected tissue alone."

Schwarz nodded. "There's that. But you're talking about garden-variety maggots. There are flesh-eating larvae in these jungles that burrow down and even gnaw into living bone."

Tso grimaced. "You wouldn't do that…"

Lyons frowned. "You just said, we Americans can't torture you. And you've done nothing for us to give you a quick, clean death."

The Thai looked at the hard-faced members of Able Team.

"Nice try," Tso said. "I'd find a way to make it quick for—"

The sound of his shoulder dislocating and separating exploded across Tso's consciousness like an atomic blast. A red curtain of blood replaced his vision, his ears resonating with the rumbling echoes of his cracking bones and popping cartilage. He returned to reality, the taste of his sour bile in his mouth, the stench of vomit next to his head. He didn't remember throwing up, but it had to have been while his consciousness disconnected. His arm was a limp, useless mass of twisted muscle and bone.

There was no one to be seen around him.

"Hey…" he croaked. His throat was raw from yelling, or maybe the acid in his bile searing unprotected esophagus.

There was no answer and he twisted, looking around.

"Hey! Hey! I'll talk!" Tso shouted.

The forest was empty, except for the corpses of some of his men. He tried to roll and crawl, but with only one arm and a shattered pelvis, he was helpless, motionless. All he could do was clutch at leaves and roots, unable to pull his lifeless limbs along. He saw the handle of his pistol poking out of some leaves and reached for it. Fingers sank into mud and he pulled. It seemed to take an eternity to shift only an inch, and two of his nails had been pried out by the roots due to his efforts. Bloody tips stung as they sank into the dirt for more leverage and haul himself closer to the pistol.

He was drenched with sweat, and his cut was burning from the effort. Tso looked at the puckered brown skin, seething with infection. With another tug, he felt the rubber grips of his pistol and he pulled it closer. It felt lighter, and he looked at the magazine well.

Empty.

Maybe there was a round in the chamber. He thumbed

back the hammer and pressed the muzzle to his temple. The trigger tripped and the hammer fell with a loud clack.

Tears cut through the sweat and grime on his cheeks.

They'd left him with an empty gun, to taunt him with the faint hope of a swift end.

"There are twelve more men at the base," Tso called as loud as he could, feeling something pop in his throat. "Twelve men, with machine guns, and motion detectors as well as UAV drones!"

Tso took another deep breath and repeated his cry.

He shouted his report five more times, for a total of seven, when he heard the crunch of wet leaves under boots. His throat tightened as he looked up to see Carl Lyons standing over him. He held a 9 mm pistol by the barrel handle presented for the Thai.

Tso reached up, swallowing. His fingers wrapped around the grip. He turned it over, and there was no magazine in place.

"You've got one shot," Lyons told him. "Use it wisely. We won't give you another."

Tso nodded. "My people will tear you apart."

The ENT commander tilted the barrel of the pistol between his lips and pulled the trigger, getting the hell out of Panama.

CHAPTER SIX

The covert conference had reached its conclusion long before, giving McCarter time to report in to the Farm. The Mossad and Unit 777 operators were calling in, as well. All three teams were resting, burning away the morning hours so that they would travel in the heat of the day. It was harder going for all three groups, but fewer people would be out, and Phoenix Force and its allies would be less obvious.

McCarter's neck hairs rose and he looked toward Gary Manning who had tensed up at the cavern's entrance.

"Drone," Manning whispered, his HK sniper rifle gripped firmly.

That awoke the entire group. Squinting, the Phoenix Force commander could barely make out the tiny speck against the sky. Though they were painted white, the Predator drone was difficult to see, the colorless hull blanking out against the halo of sun-blazed sky or clear blue. Manning's face was set in a grimace of disgust.

"What's wrong?" McCarter asked.

"It's been following an orbital path around the cave for at least two minutes," Manning replied. "And it had been following that course when I first saw it. I should have noticed it earlier."

"You're only human," the Briton said.

Manning quirked an eyebrow. "I'm supposed to be better."

"How did you even notice it?" Mahmoud asked. "It's keeping the corona of the sun at its back."

"Sharp eyes," Manning answered. He shook his head. "It's high enough that it can't be heard, and staying near the sun keeps it secure against thermal imaging. I'd caught odd movement in my peripheral vision, so I used an old eclipse-gazing trick."

Manning pointed to his cap. Small, circular vent holes near the crown to allow the seventy-five percent of body heat expelled through the head and shoulders to escape unhindered, was part of most headgear. He took the cap off and held it over a map that he'd put face down. He kept his fingers over all but one of the pinholes, and a disk of light showed on the map in his broad shadow. A dart-shaped object crossed the disk of light.

"Son of a bitch," Reiser growled. "How did they know…"

Rafael Encizo spoke up, "One of your men is missing."

"Kohn?" another Israeli asked. "He was supposed to be watching the mouth of the cave from the wash running past."

"He's long gone," Calvin James interjected. "I don't see any sign of him anywhere."

Mahmoud looked at Reiser, his lips pulled tight. Dark eyes studied the Mossad commander for a moment. "Your suspicions were correct."

Reiser sighed. "Let's move…"

"We'd be right in the open," Manning countered. "And our allies tell us that those drones can be armed with anything. One of our teams encountered machine-gun fire from the drones."

Mahmoud looked up toward the sun, but the harsh glare made it impossible to see anything. He turned away. "They've also attacked with rockets, and this cavern would make a handy tomb with one warhead."

"Who did you suspect Kohn of working for?" McCarter asked Reiser.

"There's an organization made up of former and current intelligence officers and private citizens," Reiser began.

"Abraham's Dagger?" McCarter prompted.

"You've encountered them before?" Reiser asked. "I lost a good friend investigating those bastards."

"Not personally," McCarter replied. "But I do know of two operations they've been involved with. A Palestinian refugee camp, and the attempted assassination of several UN relief workers."

"Abraham's Dagger lives up to all the bad press the Israeli government gets," Mahmoud stated. "They've caused Egypt enough headaches."

"We try to do damage control," Reiser said. "Trouble is, they have the unspoken approval of too many hard-liners in charge. The Dagger did enough to seem legitimate and supportable, but then they go and kill children of terrorists or people who could link them to atrocities."

"That explains hitting a terrorist camp in Syria, but a flight of drones was sent toward Israel with bellies full of chemical weapons," Hawkins reminded them.

"The Dagger has felt betrayed by the proper government," Reiser told him. "A major terrorist attack, killing thousands, would give them all the support they'd need to make whatever first strikes they wanted. Naturally, they'd get all of their supporters out of the target area so that the Dagger's agenda could be hawked in the aftermath."

"Scary bastards," Hawkins rumbled.

A Mossad commando scurried across the wash and crouched near the mouth of the cave. "We've got an unknown force coming toward us."

Manning shouldered his MSG-90 and scanned the horizon with its high-powered scope. "Armored personnel carriers and jeeps."

"An advance party, commandos on foot, are working their way closer," the Israeli told them.

"Kohn's buddies," Reiser said with a sneer. "I'm going to kill that little fanatic…"

"Save it," Mahmoud told the Mossad commander, putting a calming hand on his shoulder. "We should get out of the cave."

McCarter looked at Manning. "Got a good withdrawal route?"

"Two. The other would take us right down the throats of the advancing force," Manning stated. "But all have cover against that Predator up top."

McCarter looked at the horizon. "We'll take that route."

"You're going to hold them off?" Reiser asked. "No. We'll all withdraw."

"Actually, we weren't intending on holding them off," James said, knowing his commander. "We'll knock a few answers out of those chumps."

"He's right," McCarter said. "We might have a chance to interrogate an enemy prisoner or three."

"He never takes the easy route," Manning added. "You two withdraw and go on to your phase of this operation. We'll contact you if we learn anything."

Mahmoud nodded. "Allah be with you, my friends."

McCarter's eyes narrowed, a mirthless grin tightening his lips. "God's going to sit this one out. We've got the devil's work to do, mate."

CAPTAIN ZING HO, a North Korean officer, heard the American woman's voice on the phone and took a deep breath, his stomach flip-flopping. It had been a while since a mysterious warrior had given him a new lease on life, saving him from a massacre in an illegal chemical weapons lab. The tall man in black protected him, and later, a group of computer hackers smoothed over all the wrinkles left by association with Major Huan. Now, as a military attaché in the North Korean consulate in Beijing, he had been contacted by the tall warrior's allies, given access to a fistful of information.

"We need to make certain that cool heads prevail here," the woman said to him. "The documents in your e-mail will help with that."

"North Korea, being the voice of reason?" Ho asked.

"It's a long shot. Just present it to the ambassador," Barbara Price informed him. "You know that Ambassador Chong is a good man. So do we. He could do a lot to defuse the situation."

Ho nodded. "Nobody wants China to go to war with the British and American fleets over Taiwan. Too much chance of things going nuclear. And we're right in the backyard in case a few megatons fall short."

He paused for a moment. "But, won't your contacting me show up on the Chinese government's radar?"

"You know that deal with the search engine and the Chinese government?" Price asked.

"You're kidding me," Ho said.

"Nope. Putting the blocks on those searches also gives us a lot of wiggle room for covert communication. The same scrambling encryptions are protecting every e-mail and Internet broadband phone communication that we are putting through," Price answered.

Ho took a deep breath, feeling safer now. "You arranged that?"

"More of taking advantage of a blind spot," Price told him.

Ho looked at his printer. Sheets piled up in the output tray. Even at eight pages a minute, it seemed to take forever. "Tell your man…thanks again."

"He doesn't do it for the gratitude," Price explained. "But when I see him again, I'll let him know."

"Provided the world doesn't turn into a smoking crater," Ho muttered.

"The documentation you have will go a long way toward cooling that off," Price returned.

With the overview finished and a CD-ROM burned containing actual records, Ho was ready.

"Thanks," Ho said.

"If this works, thank you," Price countered.

Captain Ho popped the CD from his drive, took the overview document and headed for Ambassador Chong's office.

"WITH THE NORTH KOREANS confirming the information we've sent our contacts in the Chinese intelligence community, we might actually pull this off," Price said hopefully.

"Taiwan is a tempting prize," Kurtzman stated. "The hard-liners who want all of China unified will be hard to dissuade."

"We just have to keep playing the back alleys," Price answered. "Keep hitting the Red Chinese with reason until they back down from their urge to hit the Nationalist Chinese for retaliation."

"Reason has rarely been an effective tool against invasion," Kurtzman replied. "If an administration is gung ho and ready for battle, almost nothing slows it down. For every war that we pulled the plug on, another took place somewhere else."

"So just because we have misses, we're supposed to give up?" Price asked. "We didn't shut down because we couldn't prevent the Towers from falling. And we didn't give up because the President ignored our recommendations of force application in Iraq. We just keep plugging to save the world, whether it wants it or not."

"I'm not saying to throw in the towel," Kurtzman said. "I'm just not counting on this to be resolved by common sense, which isn't as common as you'd think."

"We've made a difference before. It's what we do. Batting a thousand isn't possible, but humanity's still here."

Kurtzman nodded. "You're right, Barb."

"How is everything on the files we pulled out of Phoenix's haul?" Price asked.

"Hunt's going through it. He's thorough, and there's a lot of herrings and worms crawling around in there," the computer wizard explained. "It's not going quickly, but he's pulling clues out of the drive."

"I just thought he was slow," Price said with a wink and a grin.

"We've got Akira for the twitchy work," Kurtzman said. "But if you want someone who can filter every single ounce of usable info out of an infected hard drive, nobody is better than Hunt. I'm glad we've got Carmen to be this band's virtual bass player, keeping the rhythm." Akira Tokaido, Huntington Weathers and Carmen Delahunt were the members of Kurtzman's crack cyberteam.

"I got word in from Striker!" Tokaido announced.

Price froze and looked over at the young hacker. "He's reporting in already?" Mack Bolan had been deployed to the Republic of Georgia.

"With all these major wars popping up, I'm not going to waste any time," Bolan said over the speakers. "Georgia is hot, but I'm picking up signs of our troublemakers already."

"Any clue as to who they really are?" Price asked.

"No. They're working through ex-KGB agents," Bolan answered. "But the usual suspects are putting up a pattern. Disillusioned and abandoned true believers, passed over by a world that's evolving into something new."

"What do you get when someone binds together large numbers of rejected fanatics?" Price asked.

"A world on the verge of war," Bolan concluded. "We know who the savages are recruiting for their crusade. With the way they're pushing things, it's easy to see that they're going for a complete annihilation of the status quo. They're promising a return to the old ways, or at least cleaning the slate so they can reclaim their old glory."

Price grimaced. "So, potentially they have thousands of operatives out there."

"Thousands of pawns, but I haven't gotten any names out of the people I've interrogated," Bolan stated. "Just rumors and leads."

"You know I don't have to tell you to keep on it, or to be careful," Price said.

"Take care." The Executioner signed off.

Price took a calming breath. The future looked dark, but glancing around her, she knew that there was a light at the end of the tunnel. The full power of Stony Man Farm, from Mack Bolan down to the cyber team, wasn't alone in staving off Armageddon. Even if Price hadn't given American and foreign intelligence groups nudges closer to the truth, there were people out there striving for peace and sanity.

Whoever was out there was playing a game of manipulation, and Stony Man engaged in games of countermanipulation. Price filled a mug with Kurtzman's swill and took a sip. The coffee, harsh and rancid, kicked her awake. With the action teams, it would appear to an uninformed observer that the Farm was a brute-force solution to complex geopolitical problems, but Price knew the truth. With gathered intelligence and subtle information sharing, the Stony Man crew stopped as many terrorist plots with information as with a flurry of bullets. Now, with the mysterious enemy working on multiple fronts, it was as if Price were facing a twisted mirror image. So far, they hadn't encountered highly skilled strike teams, but the enemy had high tech weaponry that had nearly been the end of Able Team.

"Any word from Carl?" Price asked Delahunt.

"They had me give them some orbital imagery of a location in the Darien," the redheaded computer expert answered. She wiped her brow and looked at her screen. "Unfortunately, all we have are a couple of entrances in a hillside. Someone installed an underground installation, though."

Price looked at the imagery that Delahunt had pulled up. "Not too many options for them to get in there."

"No," Delahunt replied, "but Carl will find a way."

"Keep on it," Price told her. "See if you can find any back doors."

"I'm looking for air vents. We'll see if there's anything like that on the thermals I'm downloading," Delahunt replied. "But if the enemy is sharp enough to get generic knockoff electronics from China, then they might have designed the vent system too small for infiltration."

Delahunt returned her attention to the screen, her brow furrowed in concentration.

Price returned to Kurtzman.

"Ambassador Chong already contacted the Chinese government with his findings," he told Price. "You were right about Chong."

"Of course," Price said, distracted. "How about Phoenix? What's their situation?"

"The Bekaa Valley's hot. I just spotted a large force closing in on their rendezvous," Kurtzman explained. "Satellite also picked up this."

Price looked and saw the Predator drone over the impending battle scene. She pursed her lips. "It looks just like ours."

"A perfect knockoff externally," Kurtzman said. "If we could capture one or two intact, we'd have a better handle on how good a copy it is."

"Doesn't seem likely unless we capture one on the ground," Price replied. "But, Able Team has found an underground installation."

"Gadgets knows Predator UAVs inside and out. All he needs is a few minutes with one to figure out how legitimate they are," Kurtzman explained. "He might even be able to pin down exactly which models they were copied from."

"Maybe," Price said. "They just have to get into that base first. Can we get any support for Phoenix?"

"Not without setting off Syria," Kurtzman answered. "Israeli or U.S. aircraft in the region would convince the Syrians that we're coming after them, even if we're just dropping ordnance in Lebanon."

Price grimaced. "Good luck, David. Good luck to all of us. We need it."

"CARM CAME THROUGH FOR US," Schwarz said, looking up from his PDA. "She found a small emergency exit."

"Going in through the out door." Lyons grunted.

"Oh…so many wrong things to say," Blancanales groaned. He winked at Arquillo.

"Let's scope out the back door," Lyons said. "If we make too much racket cutting through, we'll end up bringing down too much heat on our heads."

"And if they have anything useful, it'd give them time to destroy the evidence," Schwarz stated.

"Quiet and careful," Lyons added. "At least until it's too late for them."

"But it better be quick," Arquillo said. "They know we took out their advance team."

Blancanales nodded. "Quiet and careful doesn't mean slow, lady."

"Not for us," Schwarz added.

Lyons memorized the map on Schwarz's PDA screen. "Let's roll. Time's wasting and we owe these idiots a few magazines."

CHARLES KOHN SHIFTED HIS FEET nervously as he stood before the ENT commander's jeep. "You should just obliterate the lot of them."

Ariel Fuqua smirked at the Mossad turncoat's discomfort.

"What's so funny?" Kohn asked.

"You're afraid that you'll be found out?" Fuqua asked.

"I just don't want any of them escaping and hunting me down," Kohn snapped. "If they get away, even if the world ends, I know Reiser, and he'll hunt me down."

"Do not worry," Fuqua said. "They'll die. We just will see how much they know."

"They have an idea of what's going on," Kohn reminded him. "If they don't have the name of the Engineers of the New Tomorrow, then they might shake it loose sooner or later."

One of Fuqua's lieutenants spoke up. "The drone reports movement at the cave mouth."

"Making a break for it," Kohn muttered. "If they get away…"

"They won't," Fuqua said.

He raised a microphone to his lips. "Mortar crews, open fire."

A line of pops ripped the air behind a row of personnel carriers and Kohn winced. Arcing shells disappeared into the blazing sky. From the sound of them, they were 81 mm mortars, which meant that they could drop devastating amounts of high explosives. He held his breath and waited the final seconds of the artillery shells' aerial transit.

In the distance, explosions blossomed on the hillside where the covert teams had met for their conference. A second later the rumbling of blasts hit his ears. Clouds of pulverized stone and smoke filled the air.

"Drones can't see through the smoke," Fuqua's UAV liaison announced.

"Our ground forces will confirm," Fuqua stated.

He turned to Kohn. "Once the mortars hit, that was their cue to move in."

Fuqua lifted his microphone back to his lips. "Gunners, prepare to give ground forces support."

The 30 mm cannon mounted atop the BTR-80As swiveled in their turrets, aiming at the cave that Kohn had abandoned. He hoped that it would be enough, but he knew that others had tried to kill Reiser. The veteran Mossad commander was as difficult to kill as an infestation of cockroaches. The Promised Land needed to be scoured pure, and half-assed bleeding hearts like Reiser, chumming up with Egyptians, were poison to that cleanliness.

"No contact yet," the radio relayed. Kohn looked from the speaker to Fuqua.

"They got away?" the Dagger man asked. "Or did the mortars…"

Fuqua's driver suddenly jerked, his forehead detonating.

Charles Kohn pulled his Uzi and hit the dirt.

The enemies of ENT had escaped their trap and were striking back.

CHAPTER SEVEN

Carl Lyons hadn't been chosen to be the leader of Able Team because of his brute strength and ability with a gun alone. As an experienced police officer and an undercover federal agent, the brawny blond ex-cop was quick at thinking on his feet, and thinking outside the box. So when he looked at the back door that Carmen Delahunt found on satellite imagery on Schwarz's PDA, something stirred his instincts. Examining it thoroughly with his own eyes, his doubts had been confirmed.

"It's a trap," Lyons announced.

"Totally," Schwarz agreed. "But it's the only way in. The more conventional entrance is too well covered."

"If they pop a bomb, they don't even have to waste a bullet on us," Blancanales mentioned. "There, at least they'll have to work to mow us down."

"And we'll have to work our asses off to keep them from being shot off," Lyons replied. "No, this isn't going to cut it."

"So, what?" Arquillo asked. "We turn around and go back?"

Lyons shook his head, frowning deeply. "The secondary entrance on the other side of the hill…"

"That's the launch hangar for their Predator drones," Schwarz said. "The doors are controlled from within and too heavily armored to breach."

"But they're remote control," Lyons replied. "Probably even cued to the UAVs' IFF."

The electronics genius smiled and quickly sent Delahunt a text message.

He turned to Lyons. "She's going to give us time to get back to the hangar, and then have the ComSat broadcast a wide-spectrum signal to act like a garage door opener for us."

"Let's do it, then," the Able Team commander said. "Up for another fast hump?"

Arquillo shook her head. "Not on the first date. But I am ready to haul ass to the other side of this mountain."

Lyons rolled his eyes.

"Hey, don't blame me for the fact that all this military lingo has a ton of double entendres," Arquillo countered.

Having made the trek in a half hour the first time, taking care to avoid potential pitfalls, Able Team and Arquillo were able to traverse their back path in a third of the time. Once there, they returned to the original roost where they had observed the mountainside. Below, the foliage was cut low in a wide arc around the main entrance. The face of the hill was scoured down to the rock, which was thick and heavy enough to hold off even the heaviest conventional artillery. Tree limbs jutted here and there, but nothing drooped low enough to provide the team with concealment. Halfway up the mountain, under a lip of foliage-topped stone, was another entrance, secured from satellite and aerial view as the outcropping poked out fifteen feet over the tall doors. There was a small access path, three feet wide, too rough to have been carved, but flat enough to walk.

"How long will it take?" Lyons asked Schwarz.

"Give it a minute to run through the whole spectrum," the electronics engineer replied. "And given the hydraulics about fifteen seconds for the door to rise high enough for us to get through."

"In the meantime, we have to worry about potential sniper positions," Blancanales stated.

"Got them marked off from our last time here?" Lyons quizzed.

The eldest member of the team pointed twice. Lyons memorized the positions and nodded. The two potential sources of gunfire were in Vs of boulders.

"Our enemy gunners are behind enough cover to be immune to anything but precision grenade fire," Schwarz noted.

Blancanales patted the loaded breech of his SIG's grenade launcher. "The first one to open up will get some high-ex forty. But if both positions are hot . ."

Lyons ejected the shells from his Masterkey attachment and inserted three shells in its tubular magazine. "I've got that covered. The minigrenades Cowboy whipped up for me don't have the same punch as your M-203, but I can send them out faster."

"Just make certain you clear the chamber and change the loads to regular buckshot when we get inside. I don't want the backwash of even a 12-gauge grenade knocking all of us on our asses if you cap off indoors," Blancanales admonished.

"I know," Lyons said. "Any shooting will be done with the rifle part."

The door jerked and started to rise. Up above, the Com-Sat had finally hit the remote-control frequency for the hydraulic door and it started to move.

Blancanales took the point, grenade-launcher-equipped SIG at the ready. Lyons was hot on his heels, and Schwarz and Arquillo weren't far behind.

Blancanales's instincts were dead-on as a muzzle-flash erupted from the closest defensive gunnery position he'd scouted. The Puerto Rican commando had his grenade launcher ready for the attack, however, and he triggered a blast at the notch between boulders. A cone of smoke and concussive waves erupted from the V-cut in the boulders and that gun immediately stopped. Lyons had felt the peppering of two bullets against his protective body armor, but he didn't allow himself to slow down and he concentrated on the path. One misstep and he'd tumble fifty yards down the smooth rock face, landing where his broken body would be hosed with other machine-gun fire.

Arquillo's heel skidded off the narrow stretch, but Schwarz lunged out and braced her against a fall with the frame of his assault rifle. The CIA agent slid against the rock face, her eyes wide with shock, but she kept on putting one boot in front of the other, beating a path to the hangar door.

Lyons watched the second potential defensive position, but nothing flashed. They only had ten more yards until they were inside the hangar. Even if they made it in, there were a dozen enemy guards inside. He didn't think Blancanales's grenade had done more than disable the machine gun, and not its operator. There was also the thought that they might encounter enemy technicians pressed into emergency service as fighters against intrusion. Amateurs thrown into the mix were an unknown variable. Professional soldiers had one set range of reactions, but rookie gunmen were too erratic and wild to anticipate.

Blancanales dived and slid under the hangar door. The wiry former Black Beret somersaulted into a crouch and scanned the hangar, his rifle's muzzle following his eyes. The lack of gun play told Lyons that they had the hangar to themselves, at least for a moment as he stooped below the rising door and charged in more deeply.

Like formations of dull-white, winged sharks, the Predator knockoffs, twelve in all, rested quietly, six on the left, six on the right. There was room for another eight in the hangar, but Lyons could account for the missing group— six that had self-destructed in Maracaibo, and two shot down by U.S. Marines in Panama. Off to one side was an arsenal, fenced off by chain links, for assorted machine gun and rocket pods. A cargo elevator was at the very back, the top landing of a staircase visible to its left.

"Probably have worse payloads stored deeper in the base," Schwarz noted as he and Arquillo entered. He looked around for the manual door close and hit the control just as the second scouted defensive position opened up. Arquillo ducked away from the door, wincing as splinters of bullets peppered her right leg where they self-destructed on the lip of the floor.

"You okay?" Lyons asked as he looked at how she skipped to one side.

"A few stings," the CIA agent answered.

"Pol, take a look. I'll watch the stairwell," the Able Team leader said. He looked at Schwarz, but the electronics expert was already doing his job, examining the drones, gathering intelligence about the faux Predators. Once Blan-

canales finished looking at Arquillo's injuries, they would
be able to concentrate on the defense of the hangar until
the next stage of their infiltration.

GARY MANNING'S FIRST SHOT against the commander's
driver was the signal for Phoenix Force to explode into action. It was easy to tell the commander, because Manning
recognized Kohn. When the driver's face exploded under
the hammer force impact of 170 grains of jacketed open-
tip lead, the Abraham's Dagger member dived to the
ground in a near panic. The enemy commander sprayed a
blast of autofire as he took cover behind the frame of his
vehicle, but not knowing where the Canadian sniper hid,
Fuqua's ammunition was wasted ripping apart empty air.
Manning switched his point of aim toward the communications officer and stroked the trigger on his silenced HK,
punching another 7.62 mm round through the hollow of his
throat. On the way out of the hapless communication man's
rib cage, Manning's slug also wrecked the radio strapped
to his back. Corpse and shattered circuitry sprawled in the
sand, littering electronics and pouring blood in a slowly
widening puddle.

An armored personnel carrier's gunner swiveled his cannon turret to look for the sudden attackers, and he thumbed
down the spade trigger of the big gun, ripping out 30 mm
shells in a wide arc. As his commanding officer bellowed
for the gunner to check his fire, Calvin James stopped the
trigger-happy soldier's fusillade cold with a hand grenade.
The concussive force of the MK-3 A-2's eight ounces of
TNT didn't penetrate the truncated cone of the turret, but
the ferocious forces released upon detonation twisted the
cannon's barrel irreparably. The gunner hadn't stopped fir-

ing when the grenade was thrown, assured of his invulnerability inside of the armored carrier, but the breech of his cannon exploded violently as the shells had nowhere to go. The weapon's action came apart, chunks of steel sheering through flesh and bone, leaving the hapless gunner a lifeless stump. James broke from cover and raced closer to the APC, using it for cover between himself and his next position. He knew full well that he'd given away his position, even if the suppressor masked most of the sound and muzzle-flash from his gun. It was broad daylight, and angry voices called out as he was spotted.

That was the former SEAL's intention. As he ran a serpentine pattern through the scrub toward a gully, weaving out of the aim of the soldiers left behind at the armored vehicles, James provided a misdirection. He skidded head-first into the wash as waves of automatic fire rippled into the stony lip of the rut.

Encizo had been only a few yards away from where James had started this conflict, and as gunmen spun in reaction, triggering their weapons, he lined up on a squad. Shooting an enemy in the back reeked of distasteful cowardice, but outnumbered and outgunned, the Cuban was practical enough to strive for every ounce of advantage he could get on a superior force. Three soldiers dropped with hot Parabellum rounds burning in their backs before the rest of the squad realized that they were outflanked. Encizo's MP-5 sawed the head off a fourth gunman as he spun in reaction to Phoenix Force, and Manning's lethal, silenced sniper rifle blew a deadly hole through the neck of the last enemy guard.

Four soldiers chased after James, counting on the support fire of their allies to give them cover. They hadn't

counted on T.J. Hawkins perched behind a boulder ten
yards from the rut that the black Phoenix force commando
had dived into. They didn't spot the ex-Ranger as he pivoted from behind the boulder and ripped off swift, short
bursts from his suppressed machine pistol. Two gunmen
collapsed like sacks of potatoes, their bodies flopping and
tripping the two survivors. One of the Arabs recovered
from his stumble, milking a salvo of AK-47 fire toward
Hawkins, but his only reward was a flight of hot 9 mm
slugs burning across his waist, courtesy of Calvin James.

"Forget about me, motherfuckers?" James shouted. The
taunt once again anchored the attention of the armored
carriers' defenders who raked the air the Phoenix Force
medic once occupied with a storm of autofire.

David McCarter hated wagging one of his men out in
the wind like a piece of bait, no matter how well he could
fight back and survive incoming fire. However, after long
years of combat in both Britain's elite Special Air Service
and countless missions with Phoenix Force, he knew one
simple, cleansing method of dispelling dread. He used it
as fuel to rip through enemy forces, a jolt that spurred
adrenaline in his lean, long limbs. Exploding from cover
and descending upon the APCs from their blind spot, Mc-
Carter closed with the rear door of one of the carriers. The
Briton recognized the design immediately, a BTR-80A,
top-of-the-line military equipment for the mid-90s. If its
squad of eight soldiers had embarked, along with those of
seven other carriers, only the artillery crew remained, one
poised at the 30 mm 2A42 autocannon and its coaxial
PKTM 7.62 mm machine gun under a truncated cone of
bulletproof steel. McCarter lobbed another MK-3 A-2 concussion grenade through the rear hatch of the APC and

slammed the door shut. Though it didn't possess a fragmenting shell, the extra ounce and a half of TNT in its fibrous body made up for the lack of deadly shrapnel, especially in the confines of an armored vehicle.

Screams rose to a crescendo as the enemy realized their deadly fate, but they were drowned out by an earthshaking roar. Overpressure crushed the internal organs of the BTR's crew instantly. McCarter threw open the rear hatch and scurried inside. He pulled the mangled corpse of the gunner out of his spot and took command of the 2A42 cannon. The rest of his team needed heavy backup now that the blaze of gunfire was attracting the attention of the commando force sent to root out their cave. Taking aim, McCarter speared a lance of cannon fire past two BTRs toward a platoon of soldiers rushing back to their staging area. Each 30 mm shell detonated with limb-ripping force and the Briton's initial burst ground the gunmen into hamburger.

The two BTRs started to move, engines firing up, turrets swiveling to take out McCarter, but the one on the right rocked violently as Hawkins bounced another high-explosive grenade under its cab. The gunner spun his turret, milking out bursts from his PKTM machine gun at the boulder shielding the Phoenix Force warrior.

McCarter took the reprieve to concentrate on the BTR to the left, raking it with a double blast of cannon shells. The HE rounds tore through the thick protective armor as if it were tissue paper, and shook the enemy vehicle. Its turret stopped moving as McCarter had targeted the gunner's compartment. He returned his attention to the charging Arabs returning to the convoy. He held down the trigger on his own PKTM and ripped off a long, raging stream of 7.62 mm fire. With the power and velocity to reach a thousand yards, the bullets didn't slow down when they struck the ENT commandos only fifty yards away. Sliced down like stalks of wheat in a thresher, the soldiers' charge was broken.

Rafael Encizo saw Charles Kohn racing away from the scene of his betrayal, and took off in a ground-eating run. Though smaller, with shorter legs than the reedy Kohn, the Cuban was in much better physical condition, and he pumped his legs harder to catch up with the fleeing Israeli. Encizo was tempted to pull his Cold Steel Tanto knife from its sheath and gut the traitor, but cool professionalism took over. Phoenix Force needed answers, and the swarthy Cuban slammed into Kohn with a flying shoulder-block. Kohn collapsed to the ground under Encizo's weight, and struggled to squirm free. Encizo grabbed Kohn's wrists and twisted them violently to the small of his back, then pushed them both up between his shoulder blades. Caught in a double chicken wing, the Israeli had no response except to whimper and kick ineffectually. Encizo looped the traitor's wrists together with a cable tie, then gripped his MP-5, looking for the man's co-conspirators.

T.J. HAWKINS DIDN'T ENJOY being the focus of so much attention from the BTR's gunner, but he knew that aside from lobbing a grenade blindly over the top of his boulder, there wasn't much that he could do. With Encizo going after the Mossad turncoat, and James off to the side, that would not only be sloppy work, but dangerous to his partners. He threw James a quick glance, and the ex-SEAL popped up from his cover, raking the front of the BTR with his MP-5. It was a waste of ammunition, but it caught the attention of the gunner, and the heavy rain of 7.62 mm lead swept away from Hawkins's boulder to chop at the lip of stone protecting James. The Southerner swung from around his cover and scurried closer to the armored personnel carrier. The firing ports were open in the back, and he snagged one with his free hand, stuffing the muzzle of his machine pistol into the hole.

He burned off the entire magazine, pivoting it around in the firing port. The BTR picked up speed in a wild panic as 9 mm full-metal-jacket rounds bounced off steel intended to deflect .50-caliber slugs. The BTR's heavy machine gun fell silent and Hawkins felt something grab the muzzle of his MP-5. He let go, as he'd exhausted the weapon's payload anyhow, and swung to another firing port. He could see the gunner and he shoved the muzzle of his G-34 through the gap, tapping off two shots. The pistol's rounds burrowed deep into the crewman's chest, hollowpoint slugs deforming and shredding flesh and bone in their wake. While the machine pistol was loaded with hardball, in case they needed to shoot enemies wearing body armor, the pistols they carried were filled with jacketed hollowpoint rounds for maximum stopping power. The crewman slumped and Hawkins's MP-5 dropped free from the firing port. Defanged, the armored personnel carrier rolled wildly to escape the battle scene and Hawkins took a moment to stuff an M-67 fragmentation grenade through the port he'd jammed his machine pistol into. Falling away, he was out of danger as the shrapnel bomb detonated, jets of flame and smoke venting from the firing ports. The BTR rolled, unguided, until it crashed into a rut, drivers killed by a lethal sheet of razor wire fragments and explosive pressure.

McCarter paused in raking the ENT soldiers long

enough to swivel the turret and rake the fifth enemy BTR, knowing there were still two more hostile, armored vehicles in the area. He swept the 30 mm cannon from stem to stern, slicing the vehicle open down the middle. The Briton didn't have time to celebrate as his BTR rocked under an impact. Thrown from the gunner's seat, McCarter couldn't see what was going on, but he could make an educated guess. His teammates had disabled the weapons turrets on the other two APCs, and one of the drivers had taken it upon himself to use good old-fashioned brute force to take down the Phoenix Force commander. A second jarring impact rocked the BTR-80A, and McCarter found himself inside a rolling tin can, the concussion-crushed corpse of an enemy gunner flopping on top of him.

"Gary!" McCarter bellowed into his LASH.

"No need to shout, David," Manning replied with cool, smooth logic.

Calvin James saw the BTR-80A slam into the armored personnel carrier that McCarter had commandeered and looked at the column of gunmen the Briton had raked with its turret. Soldiers staggered, shell-shocked from the incessant pounding from 30 mm cannon shells and whipping lines of 7.62 mm machine-gun rounds. McCarter had decimated the force.

Actually that was a misnomer. Decimation meant killing one in ten. McCarter had cut the enemy's fighting force down to one-third of its former numbers with merciless barrages of HE shells and flesh-shredding bullets. However, twenty gunmen were still more than enough to cut down Phoenix Force with bloody efficiency, especially with Encizo occupied with the Mossad turncoat and McCarter being slammed by a rampaging mechanical rhinoceros.

James cut across the battlefield now that they'd cleared out most of the opposition. His goal was a jeep littered with the corpses of its driver and gunner. The vehicle had a pintle-mounted RPK machine gun, a belt-fed variant that was hooked to a feed canister. A surviving member of the convoy was racing toward the vehicle, as well, and he spotted James. Whoever gained control of the light machine gun would have control of the battlefield.

James fired his MP-5 from the hip, missing the enemy rifleman with his first burst. Fortunately the near miss was enough to throw off the Arab's own aim, a salvo of 7.62 mm slugs slicing the air over James's head. The Chicago-born Phoenix Force Pro shouldered the machine pistol and shot again. Using the sights, he cored the enemy gunner through the upper chest, a quartet of slugs chopping through ribs and upper thoracic cavity, severing air passages and major blood vessels. The gunman collapsed to the ground, dying fingers yanking the trigger, but merely pumping lead into the sand at his feet.

James leaped atop the jeep and racked the bolt on the RPK machine gun. The enemy strike force, twenty-strong, closed with the battle scene. There was no time for anything fancy, so the Phoenix Force medic mashed down the trigger and ripped off steel cored bullets at 800 rounds per minute. The light machine gun ripped out its death load, sounding like a balloon sputtering air through a flopping valve. High-velocity slugs raked whipsaw across the enemy strike force.

The soldiers attempted to fire back or to dive for cover, but under sustained bursts of the RPK, there was very little that they could do. They either stood their ground to fire accurately and were mowed down by high-powered bullets at thousands of feet per second, or they sprayed wildly and jumped behind the protection of outcroppings. Either way, James followed every opponent he could, glad for the steel mount on the back of the jeep to control the RPK's recoil. Brass flew in a golden arch of tumbling empties while the muzzle darted around, focusing on this target and that for a fraction of a second, long enough for the fragile human at the other end to absorb up to thirteen .30-caliber bullets before moving on.

Encizo mopped up, using his MP-5 to take out gunmen who were outside of James's reach.

A third crash rammed into the tumbling BTR, and McCarter landed under the pillowy body of an Arab gunman. A moment of panic struck the Briton, but he managed to hurl the corpse off him. The third impact turned into an extended push, shoving instead of rolling McCarter's carrier along.

"I took out the driver," Manning said, "but you'd better get out of there."

"Don't have to bloody tell me twice," McCarter snapped, lunging for the rear hatch.

"Now you know how we felt in the back of that pickup," James cut in.

"I love you, too," McCarter replied. "I take it from the banter, we've cleared out the opposing forces."

"I've got Kohn under wraps, and you broke the backs of the commandos when they tried to take back their vehicles," Encizo mentioned.

"I cleaned up your leftovers with an RPK mounted on one of the jeeps," James added.

"So where's T.J.?" McCarter asked.

A breathless reply came back. "Chasing down the enemy commander."

CHAPTER EIGHT

Susana Arquillo wanted to tell Rosario Blancanales that her leg was all right, but the Able Team medic wasn't going to have any of it. She had a two-inch gash in her calf through her khaki pants that the Able Team commando washed out with a squirt of saline, then pressed gauze into and covered with duct tape. The silvery adhesive stuck to her flesh with a vengeance, preventing any infection from crawling around the edges, and even if it did, the medication in Blancanales's sterile gauze would combat it.

"You don't mess around with open wounds in the rain forest," Blancanales explained to her.

"Thanks," Arquillo replied. "Now, can we get back to work?"

"Be my guest," Blancanales said.

The CIA agent limped over to Lyons and crouched beside him, her SIG 551 carbine resting across her knees. "Any movement?"

"None so far," Lyons answered. "How's the leg?"

"A flesh wound," Arquillo replied.

"You can move?" Lyons pressed. "I saw you limp."

"It smarts, but I'm not slowed down."

"Okay. Follow me," Lyons ordered.

He turned to Blancanales. "If we get in too deep, haul ass out of here."

"Yeah, right," Blancanales replied.

Arquillo knew this team wouldn't abandon one of its own, even without reading the tone of the Puerto Rican's voice.

Lyons finished stuffing his explosive 12-gauge rounds into their loops on his vest. The miniature shotgun grenades had blue plastic housings, as opposed to the red or yellow polymer casings for his buckshot or rifled slugs. He thumbed a red-shelled buckshot round into the breech of the Remington 870 Masterkey under the barrel on his SIG assault carbine, and closed the breech. "Come on."

Lyons lead Arquillo down the metal stairwell, the rifle-shotgun combination held so that the big ex-cop had access to the 12-gauge. Arquillo felt a surge of comfort at that. Anyone who popped into view would be swept away by a thunderous storm of buckshot in the confined quarters of the hillside complex. She didn't relax, however. Despite the firepower and her protective body armor, she was still just a human being, mortal and relatively fragile, despite the toughness that had carried her this far into the inhospitable jungle to a secret cave complex.

Back in the hangar, while Blancanales had been cleaning out her wound, she watched as Hermann Schwarz had disassembled one of the drones completely, taking multiple photos with a digital camera. The Able Team electronics genius had been thorough and meticulous in examining every inch of the Predator drone, and though he hadn't said anything about his discoveries, the look on his face was one of concern.

It was apparent that Able Team's resident military technology expert had found the answers he was looking for about the origins of the unmanned aerial vehicle. Lyons had brought her up to speed about the rest of the crisis points flaring around the globe, though he was tight-lipped about how his organization was responding to all of these menaces. With trouble brewing in Russia, the Middle East, Kashmir and China as well as here in Central and South America, Arquillo was fully aware that the fate of the world rested in a precarious balance.

Lyons stopped and he held his hand to Arquillo's stomach to hold her up. She pressed against the wall and tucked the stock of her SIG against her shoulder, ready to shoot at the first sign of trouble. The Able Team leader leaned close to her ear and whispered softly.

"Movement at the end of the hall. I make two to four hostiles."

Arquillo didn't poke her head out to confirm the ex-cop's observations. Instead she quirked an inquiring eyebrow.

Lyons slid an MK-3 A-2 concussion grenade from his harness. On open ground, outside, the powerful little weapon only had a two meter radius of lethality. However, inside an enclosed space, such as the hallway bristling with defenders, Arquillo knew that the concussion grenade's deadliness was increased exponentially. She opened her mouth and when Lyons threw the grenade, she let loose a yell to equalize the pressure inside and outside of her ears.

The Able Team leader's toss planted the minibomb in the midst of the defenders at their positions, timed perfectly so that when it landed, it detonated. Eight ounces of TNT produced an enormous amount of pressure at ground zero, the ENT guard closest to the miniblaster dying as blood vessels ruptured under a massive concussion. A second defender might have survived with only minor disorientation, except that the fuse rocketed along on the force of the explosion it triggered, one ounce of steel mechanism sheering through his forehead and turning his head into an excavated canyon of jagged bone.

One of the ENT guards staggered into the open, his surviving partner curled up on the ground in a fetal position. The ENT rifleman brought up his HK to avenge his dead and crippled friends, but Lyons swung into the hallway, the 870 Masterkey bellowing with 12-gauge thunder. Eight double-aught buck pellets perforated the Colombian defender's rib cage, burrowing .36-inch paths of destruction through vital organs, arteries and muscle tissue. The gunman jerked backward and flopped into a lifeless heap on the floor.

Lyons pumped the Masterkey and moved into the hall. The last surviving defender, rolled up in a ball, coughed up black syrupy goo from his lips, his eyes, nose and ears trailing rivers of blood where the MK-3 A-2 induced massive internal damage on the hapless gunman. Lyons reached into his pocket and pulled out his snub-nosed Colt Python and ended the ENT sentry's suffering with a .357 Magnum slug to the back of his head.

"That commander said twelve," Arquillo reminded him.

Lyons thumbed a shell into the tube magazine of the shotgun. "Twelve guards and who knows how many more."

"So it's not eight to go," Arquillo noted. She took a deep breath. "Didn't give me much to do."

"There's no guarantee that these gunmen were all made up of the professional security staff," Lyons warned. "So don't count your chickens."

He scanned back and forth at the T-intersection the dead

men defended, then pressed his throat mike. "Gadgets, got news for me?"

"Hangar destruct mechanisms are disabled," Schwarz replied. "And Pol's transmitting back to the Farm."

Lyons grimaced. "How long do you need?"

"Another minute," Schwarz told him. "I took a lot of pictures."

"So what's the bad news?" Lyons asked.

"Better than perfect copies of the Predator UAV drones sent to Egypt on the lend-lease program," Schwarz explained. "These designs have been improved and streamlined, even using knockoff electronics. The hangar bay also had miniature jet turbines in modular housings."

"Just the thing to upgrade observation drones to cruise missiles?" Lyons asked.

"On the nose, Ironman," Schwarz congratulated him. "Whoever built these could have made a fortune in the aerospace community if he were straight up."

"Well, he doesn't sound like he's interested in just making money," Arquillo interjected. "Not trying to jump start the end of the world."

"Why be rich when you can be God?" Lyons asked rhetorically as a means of explanation.

"Hell," Arquillo murmured.

"Done," Blancanales announced. "We're on our way down."

Lyons continued looking for signs of enemy response. "Hustle. These guys might not wait too long to start destroying anything we can use to shut them down."

T.J. HAWKINS RACED ALONG the Lebanese countryside in hot pursuit of Ariel Fuqua. Still rattled from riding an armored personnel carrier like a rodeo cowboy, it took a few moments for him to get to top speed, and Fuqua was running full-tilt at a pace that would have made an Olympic sprinter proud. Hawkins was tempted to pull his G-34 and put a couple shots into the enemy's legs, but Phoenix Force would need a prisoner to interrogate.

There was too much of a possibility that Hawkins might clip Fuqua's femoral artery and the ENT commander would bleed to death before answers could be mined out of him.

"Just gotta bring you down the old-fashioned way," Hawkins growled.

The enemy leader spun and pulled his gun, firing a burst that nearly caught the ex-Ranger in the chest. Instead, Hawkins dropped prone, sliding on his chest and skidding through the dirt as bullets chopped the air over his head. Fuqua continued to track Hawkins with his rifle, bullets chasing him.

It was a calculated gamble. Fuqua would either kill the Phoenix Force commando and escape, or force Hawkins to kill Fuqua in self-defense. Either way, the secrets of ENT would be maintained for a few moments more. Fuqua hadn't counted on Hawkins, however. Though he was the youngest and newest member of one of the world's most elite counterterrorism teams, Hawkins was still smart, skilled and qualified enough to be among their ranks.

Discipline kept the Southerner from triggering his MP-5, and honed reflexes kept him out of the path of Fuqua's fusillade. Hawkins wasn't going to be dissuaded by Fuqua's assault rifle, and he left his weapons where they hung on his lean, powerful frame. Cutting through ruts of sunbaked sand, hardened to the consistency of rock, he dodged and evaded bullets as they snapped through the air at supersonic speeds. It helped that the ENT commander wasn't firing from the shoulder, using his sights and pivoting like a turret. Hawkins ran a zigzag pattern, tumbling under Fuqua's stream of fire and coming up on the other side, charging closer to him.

Fuqua adjusted his aim, but the momentum of his rifle had swung him way behind the curve. By the time he brought around the muzzle of his rifle, Hawkins was within fifteen feet of the conspirator, running up a rock as a ramp. The Phoenix Force warrior's path took him seven feet into the air, and the terrorist's rifle chattered its last rounds into the stony shelf that Hawkins ran on. Fuqua snarled and reached for his pistol, but as his hand touched the flap holster, Hawkins leaped the rest of the way, crashing down on the gunman with bone-jarring force.

The two men collapsed into a heap, Fuqua absorbing the majority of the punishment. Hawkins pushed hard under the man's jaw, clutching his throat and pushing his head back into the ground. Fuqua's lean, dignified face distorted into a mask of rage, but he only had one hand free, the other arm pinned under Hawkins's knee.

"Get off me," Fuqua growled.

"Right. I'll really do that," the ex-Ranger said, squeezing the conspirator's throat more tightly. Fuqua thrashed violently, twisting to break his adversary's grasp, all the while clawing at the American's face with his free hand. That left the Phoenix Force commando's hands full, one pinning the prisoner to the ground and the other fending off attacks, all while Fuqua squirmed more and more to get out from under him. Hawkins let go of Fuqua's throat and grabbed his shoulder with the recently freed hand, the other gripping the terrorist's wrist. Tucking and rolling, Hawkins dragged Fuqua around, hitting a shoulder roll and utilizing his full weight to leverage the ENT commander into the air and then face-first into the ground. There was an ugly, disgusting crunch as Fuqua's shoulder dislocated, and Hawkins snapped his boot into the small of the conspirator's back.

That took a little of the fight out of the man's sails, but Fuqua still squirmed, trying to slither out of Hawkins's grasp. Twisting the dislocated limb, Hawkins brought the commander to heel on a leash of blinding pain. Fuqua forgot all about the pistol in its flap holster, but then the Phoenix Force pro didn't blame him. With the popped shoulder and his face jammed into burning hot, hard-packed sand, Fuqua's senses were overloaded. Just the same, Hawkins plucked the pistol from its resting place and jammed the muzzle into the base of his spine, never relenting his grip on Fuqua's much-abused limb.

"Behave. We don't need your legs to question you," Hawkins grated.

Fuqua could only sputter an unintelligible response. An engine rumbled in the distance and Hawkins tensed but returned his attention to the prisoner when he saw James standing atop the approaching jeep at the controls of an RPK machine gun.

"Look what I found," Hawkins said, keeping his attention on Fuqua. "Can I keep him?"

McCarter got out of the jeep and sighed, looking at the ENT commander. "I don't know. Rafe has his own souvenir, and you guys promised Barb that you wouldn't load up on gifts for yourselves."

Fuqua tried to turn his head to see the other prisoner,

but Hawkins dug the muzzle of his own pistol into his high cheekbone. "Did I tell you to behave?"

A second jeep rolled up, driven by Gary Manning. In the back, Rafael Encizo guarded Charles Kohn. The Mossad turncoat was bound, and his eyes and mouth were covered by duct tape. McCarter helped Hawkins secure Fuqua the same way, leaving him blind and unable to communicate. For an extra measure of security, Fuqua was put in the jeep driven by McCarter.

Calvin James's medical skills would be put to the test, and both Kohn and Fuqua would give up their secrets to scopolamine.

HERMANN SCHWARZ AND Rosario Blancanales had told Carl Lyons and Susana Arquillo that they were on their way down, but they didn't say which way they were coming. The enemy, if they were listening, would simply assume that all the invaders would form one cohesive strike team cutting through the insides of the complex. Even if they weren't listening, the machine gunner who had opened fire on the hangar would have reported that all the intruders were inside. Blancanales and Schwarz scoped out the remaining machine gun nest, Schwarz using a periscope attachment to his digital camera. Utilizing levels of resolution far above commercial devices, Schwarz was able to see through the V neck of rock, spotting the muzzle of an enemy machine gun. Magnification increased, and he was able to see over the rear sights of the emplaced weapon. No gunner hunched over the controls.

Pivoting the periscope, Schwarz scanned the other positions they'd spotted on their first approach to the facility built into the mountainside.

"Clear," Schwarz whispered.

Blancanales nodded and hurled a coil of rope out of the hangar. The Puerto Rican had strapped the warhead portion of a 70 mm high-velocity artillery rocket to his pack. Rappelling with his full pack was no problem, and even the additional mass of a nine-pound M-151 high-explosive style warhead didn't provide him with difficulty. He scurried down the side of the mountain, Schwarz providing an over watch using his teammate's grenade launcher in case a machine gunner showed up.

When Blancanales reached the ground without attracting enemy fire, Schwarz grabbed the rope and followed after. He carried a second of the antipersonnel warheads on his back. While Schwarz had a significant quantity of C-4 explosives, the two artillery rocket warheads would provide the extra oomph to rip open the entrance of the hidden base.

Landing next to his friend, Schwarz saw that Blancanales had already packed the first warhead under a sheet of rock. Unfortunately, the M-151 70 mm rocket warhead was designed for fragmentation over a large area. The flat plate of rock would help focus the explosion. Schwarz had to make due with two smaller boulders, but he still managed to pack the M-151 tightly against the opposite side of the doorway. The Able Team duo took cover behind a shelf of stone and Schwarz thumbed the firing stud on his radio detonator. Smoke and broken stone filled the air, but augmented by half a kilogram of C-4 plastic explosives, the artillery rockets tore open the entrance of the hillside complex easily.

Blancanales swung around the boulder and triggered the M-203 grenade launcher mounted under his SIG 551.

The 40 mm round in the breech was a buckshot round, turning the wide-mouthed launcher into a massive shotgun. A flight of .36-caliber pellets whirled and whizzed through the shattered entrance, cutting through the smoke to elicit screams of dying agony on the other side of the cloud. Blancanales brought his firing hand back to the grip of the carbine and he charged forward, Schwarz hot on his heels.

There was no satisfaction in the sight of shattered bodies and dismembered limbs as they cut through the entrance. It was a cold, deadly task they were up to, as it always was. Cold-blooded response was needed to deal with cold-blooded murderers.

"How many?" Blancanales asked, looking over the carnage.

"Three and change," Schwarz replied. It was a grisly evaluation, but the two men had to figure out how many enemies were down.

"We have no guarantee about how many there really are with our count and Carl's upstairs."

"Nope," Schwarz answered. He sighed. "Just be prepared for anything."

"Nothing new on this front, then," the Puerto Rican said.

The Able Team advanced carefully, one moving forward at a time in a leapfrog, each covering the other with his carbine. The interior of the base was oddly familiar to the pair as they went through the hallways.

"It's a continuity of government installation," Blancanales finally said.

"Yeah. A U.S. design," Schwarz agreed. "Probably to maintain control of the canal area in the event of a nuclear war. A forward base, set away from major population centers, but still within range of the Canal."

"Even if it took a hit from a few nukes, it would still take only a little effort to be put back to use as a shipping short-cut," Blancanales mentioned. "Railways, highways and airports could be obliterated, but boats would still work."

"To think, that used to be a moot point for a while," Schwarz murmured.

"We'll take care of it, pal," Blancanales consoled. "We just have to figure out where they'd put the major electronic control center."

"This looks like a standard spiral-staircase style COG facility. Everything would be on the inner coil at the middle," Schwarz replied. "Putting the main nerve center at the deepest part of the mountain would protect it from a ground-zero detonation."

"No wonder they set up shop here," Blancanales said. "These COG centers are modular enough to bring in new equipment as well as store older supplies."

Schwarz shook his head. "They're utilizing U.S. military equipment and long-forgotten Continuity of Government facilities. Stuff that's slipped through the cracks."

"You think you have an idea on how to track down things further?" Blancanales asked.

"We've had a few conflicts with renegade U.S. factions making use of COG facilities before," Schwarz noted. "And even if we didn't, the Bear would have the ability to locate all the old records of these bases."

"We just have to live long enough to tell the Farm about this," Blancanales admonished. "Hold up."

Schwarz knelt next to his teammate at the corner of an intersection. A muzzle of an enemy rifle poked out of a doorway before disappearing behind the doorjamb. Schwarz took out his digital camera and hooked on the fiber-optic periscope lens, peering around the corner. Image magnification revealed hidden forms in other doorways.

"So much for the estimation of only twelve guards on hand," Schwarz whispered. "These guys have no muzzle discipline."

"Technicians," Blancanales replied. He quietly slipped a concussion grenade into the M-203's breech. "Someone has to take care of the UAV drones."

"Figure a couple experienced soldiers with each group," Schwarz added. He took a moment to convey this information to Lyons and Arquillo over his LASH communicator, as well as the layout of the base as a Continuity of Government headquarters. "They probably sent the bulk of the skilled troopers toward the hangar, since that was our primary assault vector."

"But the commander still had the presence of mind to leave someone guarding the back door," Lyons replied. "Okay. We've got things covered."

Schwarz nodded to Blancanales, who triggered the concussion grenade. The corridor became an envelope of fire and ear-shattering roars.

The Able Team moved in to mop up.

THE KNOT OF RESISTANCE that Carl Lyons saw prompted him to reload his Remington 870 Masterkey with the 12-gauge minigrenades. Hanging back, he heard the thunderbolt of Blancanales's grenade from several levels below. When the less-disciplined technicians jerked in reaction to the distant blast, the Able Team leader poked the Masterkey down the corridor and emptied the four microbombs as fast as he could work the shotgun's slide.

Susana Arquillo popped around the other corner and fired

bursts from her SIG carbine toward the defending forces, chopping high-velocity bullets into those not torn apart by the quartet of grenade detonations. Lyons quickly joined her, shifting back to his 551's trigger and raking a stunned enemy guard with a torso-ripping line of 5.56 mm slugs.

Lyons was about to take a step forward when his instincts told him that the skirmish had gone too quickly and easily. He was in midturn when an air vent exploded open, two black-clad commandos dropping through the ceiling. One crashed into the big ex-cop moments after he shoved Arquillo out of the way. The other tumbled into a somersault, missing the CIA agent who was his intended target.

With the steely muscles that gave veracity to his nickname of Ironman, Lyons shrugged violently to his feet before the ENT commando who'd dropped on his back could solidify a stranglehold around his throat. The enemy gunman, roughly 200 pounds, flew off his shoulders like a rocket and slammed into the corridor's wall. With reflexes like a coiled spring, Lyons spun and powered a Shokotan knuckle strike into the attacker's sternum, ribs cracking. Blood burbled from the defender's lips as he slid to the floor, staggered.

Susana Arquillo was a tough and scrappy fighter, but outweighed by fifty pounds, it was all she could do to keep her enemy's knife out of her throat. Lyons could see the muscles knotted in her lean, brown arms as the commando tried to spear her on his blade's tip. The Able Team leader quickly put a halt to the murder attempt by driving a snap kick into the guy's kidney.

Blinding pain folded the black-clad killer at the waist, depositing him at Arquillo's feet. The CIA agent tugged her vest aside and drew her customized .45, tapping out three shots in rapid fire. Lyons didn't even have to look as he heard the commando's dying grunt. Instead, the ex-cop turned and kicked the gun out of the corpse's hand.

"Thanks," Lyons said.

"You saved my ass, I figured I'd return the favor," Arquillo answered. She took the momentary pause to reload the .45, and then she picked up her SIG 551 where it had fallen.

Lyons winked. "That's what partners are for."

He scooped up his fallen weapon, jarred from his hands when he'd been tackled, and continued on into the COG facility.

CHAPTER NINE

"Ariel Fuqua," Barbara Price announced as the lean, handsome face of a blue-eyed, brown-haired man appeared on the screen for Hal Brognola. "He's the first link in the conspiracy that we've managed to get in custody."

Brognola gnawed on his unlit cigar for a moment, looking over the printouts from the cyberteam. "Israeli."

"Member of the Mossad, but he's been believed dead for the past fourteen months," Price told him.

"Hmm. He managed to rise from the dead to lead a strike force inside Lebanon," Brognola stated. "So how did they learn even that much about him?"

"Charles Kohn, another member of Abraham's Dagger, spilled the beans under scopolamine," Price explained.

Brognola held up a report. "So Bear's come up with this much. What else is there?"

"The organization involved is called the Engineers of the New Tomorrow," Price stated. "We don't have too much on them. Kohn and Fugua both said that the Dagger has been recruited into their central elite. But they're not sure who else is a part of the organization."

"We have a name, though," Brognola replied. "We have at least that much to go on."

"But the whole thing still is a jigsaw puzzle, and the only bits we have put together are the four corners. No borders, nothing in the middle," Price complained. "Sure, we'll be able to put more pieces together, but this is taking time, and did you hear about Kashmir?"

"A Pakistani armored division across the border got hit by artillery," Brognola stated. "Hard to tell if it was Indian military equipment or if it was our troublemakers."

"I had Bear look into it. We've got the cybercrew spread pretty thin, trying to put out the Chinese fires and giving our field units support, so the data from the attack on the Pakistani forces is inconclusive as of yet," Price told him. "However, we've managed to tap some resources in China."

"You're not going to say who, though," Brognola answered.

"Only if you need to know," Price responded. "They're hard at work tracking down leads. It's pretty thin, but with our contacts inside North Korea's embassy, we might manage to find a good lead."

"What's the word on Able Team?" Brognola asked.

"Off the grid," Price explained. "But it hasn't been long since their last contact with Carmen."

"That's in the Darien?" Brognola pressed.

"Yes," Price said. "Carmen's been digging into how that base could have gotten there, but there's no records in regard to recent construction activity."

"Might be older," Brognola stated. "An already-existing facility."

Price tilted her head. "There's nothing in the Panamanian government records. And we checked Colombia."

"The U.S., Barb," Brognola corrected.

The Stony Man mission controller squinted her eyes. "Continuity of Government?"

"Precisely," Brognola commended her. "It's a long shot, but get Carm on it."

"Striker did mention that there was a dangling thread from that operation to start a war between Israel and Egypt a while back," Price said. "General Idel had been in contact with someone who disconnected just as he went for the knockout."

She took a deep breath and squeezed her brow. "The picture's becoming a little clearer now, but what we're pushing against isn't too pretty."

"It rarely is," Brognola agreed. "We can only hope that if they're going for this kind of all-out global catastrophe, all of their cards are on the table."

"It might be likely. This is a full-court press on their behalf," Price stated. "I'll check our files for foreign-based COG units."

Brognola nodded, fitting the files into his briefcase. "The President is really feeling the heat, Barb. The war hawks want us to come down on Colombia and Venezuela, and they're not too happy about China's saber rattling."

"But then we've got the grass-eaters accusing him of fomenting this tension on his own," Price said. "You know how those conspiracy theorists are. How the attacks on the Towers and the Pentagon were faked."

Brognola shook his head in disbelief. "Those people are just projecting their own lack of conscience onto whichever leaders they don't happen to agree with at the time, Barb. It's a lunatic fringe."

"One that draws considerable attention," Price interjected.

"We're not spin doctors, Barb," Brognola replied. "All

we can do is save the world from the people shooting at it. The loudmouths and the idiots will have to be dealt with by someone else."

"Good luck with the President, Hal," Price said.

Brognola gave her a slight wave from the door and then left for the White House.

ARIEL FUQUA REMAINED silent as he was tucked into the corner. The plastic cable-tie around his wrists was tight, digging into his skin, but he'd already endured one round of drugs and was nearly sure he revealed little in formation. He could hear the mysterious men talking about the ethics of administering another dose so soon.

Blindfolded and gagged, he wasn't able to taunt them, but the information between his ears was perfectly safe. They might have destroyed his multinational strike team, but so far, they were losing the war when it came to information gathering.

A rough hand pulled the tape off Fuqua's eyes, and the Israeli blinked, getting used to light once more.

"Rise and shine, Ariel," Calvin James said. He had a needle in his hand.

The tape came off his mouth.

"Ah…Dr. Farrow," Fuqua replied, masking the discomfort of his raw lips. "Back for another go?"

James tapped the needle, a bubble floating to the front.

"You won't get any answers out of me, regardless," Fuqua stated.

"Who said we need answers from you anymore?" David McCarter asked.

Fuqua looked around and saw Charles Kohn, eyes wide, jaw slack, chest unmoving, bound by his side.

"See, we can't afford to have you talk to your buddies in the ENT," James said. "So, I figure a double dose of scopolamine should be enough to keep you quiet."

"Sorry," McCarter apologized, though the smile on his face put a lie to the word. "But we don't have room in our vehicle to take you home with us. Besides, we've got business."

"So why not use a bullet?" Fuqua asked.

"We're saving them for people who count," McCarter informed him. "Besides, leaving a bloody mess would only ensure that you're found sooner."

Fuqua chuckled. "I'm not afraid of dying."

The needle poked into his neck and James squeezed the bulb.

In a panic, the ENT commander jerked, blood squirting from the puncture caused by the needle. Fuqua tried to kick them both away and started to scream, but McCarter clamped a hand over his mouth.

"Hold him still," James gritted. He refilled the syringe, disgust covering his face. "Bad enough I have to give out a lethal injection because you're too pussy to torture—"

"Shut the hell up, Farrow," McCarter replied. "They put a goddamned idiot under my command, always giving me shit for my decisions. He should—"

The Phoenix Force leader was jerked violently away from Fuqua, and the ENT commander couldn't believe his eyes as he saw "Farrow" draw his fist back, drenched in blood.

"You fucking…" McCarter snapped. He launched himself before he could finish what he intended to say, leaping at James. The two men rolled, exchanging savage blows.

Fuqua wasn't going to look a gift horse in the mouth. His dislocated shoulder hurt like hell as he stretched his wrists under his butt, yet he didn't give up. He only hoped that the two men would continue fighting each other too violently to pay attention to him. Fuqua got both hands under his feet and he got up, bound wrists in front of him now. He spotted the window and threw himself through it. It was dark outside, which would be to his advantage. Even if the five mystery commandos could see him in the shadows, they would be torn between another lengthy, time-consuming hunt or bugging out to their next mission objective.

Long, loping strides put distance between himself and his adversaries. He felt lucky that the men had left him his boots, otherwise crossing this terrain at full speed would have been impossible. As it was, he tripped, crashing to the ground on his injured shoulder. Searing pain crossed his clenched eyes in a sun-yellow sheet of agony, but he supported his weight on his good hand, his feet pushing against the ground to launch himself forward.

Fuqua wasn't quite certain where he was, but a sprinkle of lights, like amber stars, glimmered in the distance. Once he hit the town, he could contact his ENT allies, to warn them about the discovery of their operation. He could only hope that the Engineers were merciful enough not to execute him outright.

DAVID MCCARTER WIPED the red-tinted syrup off his jaw as soon as their prisoner leaped out the window. He licked his lips, then smirked. "Pancake syrup?"

"It was in the MREs we brought," Calvin James said. "Mixed it with ketchup."

The Briton chuckled. "Might not be a hit with kippers and biscuits, but you might have something for the barbecue."

James licked his knuckle off, then grinned. "Add a little jalapeño…"

"Hey!" Hawkins grumbled. "You two finished comparing recipes like old ladies?"

"How's the tracking signal?" McCarter asked.

"It's still strong," Hawkins said. "But if he puts two and two together, he's going to ditch his boots."

"He won't," James answered.

Hawkins rolled his eyes. "Posthypnotic suggestion. I thought you were smarter than that voodoo shit."

James and McCarter shared a knowing glance. Phoenix Force, before the addition of Hawkins, had encountered their fair share of Caribbean criminals and terrorists who utilized varying degrees of "voodoo" sorcery, even drug-created zombies.

"Cal's practiced at hypnosis," Encizo said, "and using a diluted dosage of scopolamine, Fuqua was put in a highly receptive state."

"Remember, it's a posthypnotic suggestion," James said. "I told him that we would be too distracted by our fight that he could get away. He'd have tried to escape anyhow. This just made him more receptive."

"And he won't think to look for a tracking beacon installed in the heel of his boot," Manning added. "David and Cal's role playing only cemented his opinion of us as unprofessional enough to think of that."

Hawkins glanced at the window Fuqua had thrown himself through. "Well, he did buy it. But what's to say he just won't find a rabbit hole and disappear? Common sense might override your suggestion to find his bosses."

"What would you do if you escaped from the enemy?" McCarter asked.

"Check to see if I had a tail, or any tracking tags," Hawkins began.

"Then what?" McCarter pressed.

"Find a way back to you guys," Hawkins admitted.

"It's just basic instinct. Find your team and your buddies," James said. "That's how we can be certain of the hypnotic suggestion. Simple psychology, assisted by some pharmacology."

"I'll believe it when he leads us right to his pals," Hawkins grumbled. "And if it does, I'll bite the head off a chicken and dance around in my underwear."

The others winced at the mental image.

AARON KURTZMAN SNEEZED as he was working on tapping the telephone communications in the tiny Lebanese town that Phoenix Force had let Ariel Fuqua escape to.

"They must be talking about me," he muttered, wiping his nose with a tissue and tossing it in the wastebasket. On a side monitor, Kurtzman was tracking Fuqua's movement thanks to a small electronic tracking tag inserted in the ENT commander's boot. He was inside the town. Kurtzman looked at his primary monitor, his digital ears peeled for signs of Fuqua contacting the rest of the ENT.

It would have been a long shot of a plan if it hadn't been for Stony Man Farm's unmatched electronic intelligence-gathering capabilities. Kurtzman was monitoring the tracking beacon from a British satellite, while a Middle Eastern telecommunication's company was baring all its secrets over an Internet leak constructed by Akira Tokaido.

Connection tracking software poised like a swarm of hungry piranha, waiting for the first drop of blood in the water. As soon as a telephone connection was made,

Kurtzman's programs would pounce on the trail, following the data stream as fast as lightning. Even if the connection broke, wisps of electronic data would still linger for enough time to complete the lock down and track back.

The Farm was operating without a warrant, but since they weren't going for a conviction in a court of law, that didn't matter. The niceties of the law were fine for standard operations, but against an international menace sparking off an extinction-level global war, the rule book was out the window. It was the same gray area that Stony Man always operated in. The cybernetics team and the warriors in the field bent and twisted regulations that hindered other organizations, but in operating above the law, they were able to strike against those who obeyed no law.

Kurtzman's software flashed to life, programmed data packets blazing through the phone lines half a world away at the speed of light, chasing down the telephone call that Fuqua made to his contacts.

"Show time," the computer wizard said over the sat phone link to Phoenix Force. "He's calling for help."

"ANY PARTICULAR BREED OF CHICKEN you'd like to bite the head off?" David McCarter asked Hawkins.

Hawkins sighed. "Cal, you were right."

"Bear's got our next location," Encizo announced. "And Hal's going to arrange for Fuqua to be picked up."

"Good job." McCarter looked over the Cuban's shoulder at the screen. "Israel."

"He's narrowing it down, but it's taking some time," Encizo said.

Manning frowned as he consulted a map. "I guess our

penetration of Syria's called off, then. Something's troubling me with all of this."

"Syria and Egypt throwing down would be a bad war, especially if Syria went through Israel to get at them," James observed. "Tel Aviv would back up Cairo if it came to that. But that would slow down Syria, make them less likely to start the war."

"But if it could be made to look as if Israel started the conflict, and took some serious damage, their enemies would move right in," Manning explained.

"Israel is either goaded into making a first strike, or it's made to appear that they hit first," Hawkins said. "Right?"

"And when that happens, who'd have the kind of firepower and willingness to nail Israel hard?" McCarter asked.

"Iran would, but their nuclear program is still in the plodding stages," Encizo said. "Unless…"

"We've already seen them use thermobarics in Maracaibo," McCarter noted. "Who's to say they don't have the ability to lend a few nuclear warheads to Tehran."

"Nobody in the Arab world would blame Iran for nuking Israel in response to a first strike," James said.

"Guys, incoming message." Hawkins spoke up. "It's Able Team. They've got something for us."

CARL LYONS FINISHED HAULING the corpses of the ENT base staff into a storage room, then closed it off. It was sweaty, dirty work, but it was better than stumbling over dead bodies in the control center.

Hermann Schwarz had broken through the base's mainframe security with the assistance of two of the technicians who had lost their nerve. With their untrained partners killed, the techs figured that they'd have a better chance with the intruders.

Originally, there had been half a dozen technicians, but when they'd opened fire on the last of the professional soldiers, the revenge and response had been swift and merciless. Blancanales had attempted to keep a third alive, but his injuries were too much. However, the life-saving effort had not been lost on the survivors.

"How's it going?" Lyons asked Arquillo as he returned to the control room. Schwarz and the technicians worked feverishly at the mainframe.

"The self-destruct mechanism for the entire base is disarmed," Arquillo answered. "Right now, they're switching to backup Internet access and contacting your people."

"Good news," Lyons said. He had helped to separate the bodies of the reluctant soldiers from the professional true believers. It was hard, but he shut out the guilt creeping in at the thought of burning down the inexperienced fighters. They were part of an operation that had claimed the lives of hundreds of noncombatants and threatened millions more. The survivors working for them had switched sides only because they didn't want to be needlessly sacrificed.

Reluctant soldiers, yes, but they also assembled, programmed and controlled machines that delivered chemical weapons and deadly explosive payloads to crowded cities. If anything, the technicians had proved far more murderous than their rifle-toting comrades. Just because they didn't pull the trigger didn't mean that their hands were bloodless.

Blancanales was outside, transmitting over their sat phone back to the Farm, so they didn't need the base's computer for communication, but if there was going to be any way for Kurtzman and his crew of hackers to break into the enemy's network, accessing the mainframe would give them an advantage.

That meant reconnecting the mainframe to the outside world without setting off built-in security protocols that would fry the system.

Schwarz looked up from his work and nodded to Lyons. The ex-cop walked over to his friend.

"They're helping out, and we're making progress, but they're still a little squirrelly. They don't want to be punished for helping out," Schwarz told him. "And the looks you're giving them aren't making them feel any better."

Lyons looked at the turncoats. "Tell them I don't trust them. If they want me to not look like I'm going to eat them for dinner, they better damn well make me happy."

Schwarz chuckled. "I'll be a little more specific. I don't think you want them bending over for you."

"Just tell them to do their jobs before I decide I need more target practice."

"Gotcha," Schwarz answered, returning to the mainframe's access terminal.

Arquillo regarded Lyons for a moment.

"What's wrong?" he asked.

"Just wondering if you'd stick around for a while when this is over," Arquillo said.

"Much as I'd like to, we don't get a lot of downtime," Lyons answered. "And, chances are we're not going to be staying here much longer on this leg of the crisis."

"Oh," Arquillo replied, disappointment coloring the monosyllabic response.

Lyons glared at the technicians, burning off the unbidden guilt at gunning down their partners, indignant that he felt sorry for wiping out the mechanics who assembled remote-controlled murder machines. "Trust me, Susana..."

Arquillo nodded. "Yeah. I always think it's pretty stupid to get involved with coworkers. It always looks so phony in movies when that happens. All that tension and violence, and somehow the hero and the girl still sneak off to some corner and get hot and sweaty. I never understood why they did it."

Lyons raised an eyebrow as Arquillo stepped away. He suppressed a smile. For a CIA agent, her hints were as subtle as a baseball bat in the face. If they had some time once everything was hooked up and secure, the prisoners locked away tightly, he'd continue that line of conversation with her. Lyons had been guilty of that "unrealistic" interaction before.

Whenever he was close to death, he wanted reminders of life. A lot of the time he made do with Blancanales's and Schwarz's joking. But when he had access to someone he was attracted to, the temptation for more was overwhelming.

He remembered, though, what that had bought some of the women he'd been with. Flor and Julie were the first two who'd sprung to mind, lovers who'd been drawn into the dangerous world of Able Team. Flor had died in the line of duty, and Julie had been assassinated for reasons unrelated to Lyons's duties. In either case, and in other scattered instances, Lyons felt it was because it was his doing. He was a lightning rod of violence. Bad karma, as Gadgets Schwarz called it.

Women who could otherwise take care of themselves, crack shots and tough as nails, still ended up dead. Lyons didn't believe in curses.

Arquillo looked at him from across the room.

Lyons did believe in luck, coming in waves. And you had to ride that luck to the very end, and if it ran out, you still pushed it, making more of it. Life was too short to worry about what could happen somewhere down the line.

"We're hooked up," Schwarz interrupted.

"Good," Lyons growled, still staring at the two prisoners. "Lock them away. When we get transportation out of here, they'll be on their way to a jail. But for lesser charges than they really deserve."

The technicians understood Lyons's implication. Relief and nervousness fought for control of their faces.

"All right. Let's fill in the Farm about the Continuity of Government base," Lyons said.

CHAPTER TEN

"The network is too well shielded from external influence," Aaron Kurtzman explained to Barbara Price. "Even with a direct hookup to their facility in the Darien, there's enough black ice protecting their connections that we can't dent it. Whoever set this up really knew what they were doing."

"So, we can't locate the individual Continuity of Government facilities?" Price asked.

"Communications between different redoubts are impossible to track. Even contacts outside of the network, like with Fuqua, are blunting our tracking programs," Kurtzman stated. "We only have one real bonus on our side."

"Hunt," Price said.

"He's hard at work tracking down references, no matter how oblique, to COG facilities set up around the planet," Kurtzman said. "On top of that, he's going over what we can access of the network with a fine toothed comb."

"What about Akira? He's usually good at thinking outside the box when it comes to hacking a network," Price suggested.

"He is, but right now our team's spread pretty thin," the Bear explained. "Also, the black ice isn't the only defense this network has."

"Logic bombs. We rustle the wrong data node, it blows and sends out worms," Price concluded.

"Right," Kurtzman said. "Hunt's taking it slow and careful, but some of these are on time release. Areas we considered clean and safe suddenly pop a booby trap. Akira's on it, putting out the fires, but cleaning up after a viral attack is a mess."

"So how is Hunt going to be our ace in the hole on the network?" Price asked.

"We're getting a map of the Continuity of Government facilities outside of their system," Kurtzman said. "They can stop us on the outside, cybernetically, but we can still give our teams locations to bring down the hammer in person."

"Able Team took out one facility, so far. We just find the others, and hope they're part of the Engineers' network," Price said.

"Like here. We set up a trace on Ariel Fuqua's communications. We lost the trail inside of Israel. The Engineers' setup scrambled our tracking programs so that we can't narrow it down to anything smaller than the northern district," Kurtzman said.

"And Hunt's found information about a forward facility in Israel," Price mused. "Probably put there in the sixties, when we had military advisers in country."

"In the Meggido Valley," Kurtzman announced, showing her a photograph of the region.

"The plains of Armageddon," Price said, looking at the satellite photo. "Disturbingly appropriate."

"McCarter and the gang were brainstorming, and they

wanted us to make certain that there was something in Iran," Kurtzman added. "Hunt's checking, and we might have something installed there, from when the shah was our buddy."

"It's easy to start a nuclear war when you can fire from both sides of the conflict," Price pronounced grimly.

"Now that we know what to look for, we can steer Jack and Striker," Kurtzman said. "It's still going to be a tough prospect, taking out these bases."

"They're designed to survive the end of the world," Price replied, understanding the situation. "This also explains where they plan to hole up while the world tears itself apart."

"And come out of hiding with the kind of equipment necessary to take control of everything left over," Kurtzman concluded.

"No doubt the Engineers erased as much as they could of the COG base records," Price said. "Hunt's going to have his work cut out for him."

"The Meggido base seems our strongest lead," Kurtzman explained. "We'll arrange for Phoenix Force's pickup and take them in-country."

"Without letting Tel Aviv know, just in case Abraham's Dagger has ears to the ground," Price mentioned.

"David said to be as loud and blatant as necessary. He wants the ENT on alert and responding to them in-country," Kurtzman corrected her. "This way, we'll know if we're on the right track."

"I hate how they use themselves as bait," Price grumbled.

Kurtzman grinned. "Ever hear of the alligator snapping turtle?"

"From T.J.," Price replied. "Why?"

"The alligator snapping turtle is one of the biggest, most heavily armored turtles ever, and yet it feeds by leaving its mouth open, and exposing a tiny, delicate-looking worm-like part of its tongue to fish. The fish comes in expecting a snack…" Kurtzman began.

"And it becomes the snack when this big, nasty, heavily armored turtle snaps its jaws shut," Price concluded.

"David setting his team up to be hit by an enemy ambush is exactly like that little worm on the turtle's tongue. It looks like an easy target, but the truth is, those little fish are swimming right into the jaws of the biggest, toughest predator in the swamp," Kurtzman explained. "Besides, it's not an ambush when you know you're walking into it."

"Too hairy for me," Price said.

"Me, too," Kurtzman replied. "But that's why we're not on Phoenix Force."

Price looked at the aerial photograph of the Meggido Valley. "Amen, Bear. Amen."

JACK GRIMALDI PULLED his twin Glock 17s pistols from his double shoulder holster and opened fire, the two polymer-framed handguns barking in unison. He hadn't been anticipating any difficulty in hooking up with two members of the Farm's blacksuit program who had been on the ground, investigating in Pakistan. The two young men were of Arabic descent, and they assured Grimaldi that everything was all right with their reconnaissance of a potential nest of troublemakers in the Kashmir conflict.

However, if it was one thing that Grimaldi had learned, it was that trouble hit when you least expected trouble. Too often when he'd been in the field with Mack Bolan or ferried Able Team and Phoenix Force to their missions, things went bad.

As it was, the blacksuit he knew as Amad clutched a blood-soaked shoulder while Isdan fired on a strike team of assassins who had them pinned down. Isdan's 9 mm Star 1911 knockoff locked empty and the young blacksuit ducked back, fishing for more magazines.

That was when Grimaldi decided to make his presence known, cutting loose on the hit men They appeared to be Pakistanis wearing battered old military jackets and packing submachine guns. The ace pilot took out one with the twin streams of Parabellum rounds ripping out of his Glocks, sawing two lines of bullets up the gunman's chest.

The remaining trio of hit men reacted swiftly and violently, if not altogether accurately to Grimaldi's intrusion in their ambush. Machine pistols ripped wild arcs of lead into the air, tearing apart the wall that Grimaldi had been standing near, bricks exploding under their assault. The ace pilot, however, had dropped to the ground, focusing on a second Pakistani gunman with his left-hand Glock.

The two follow-up shots to the assassin might have been unnecessary, but Grimaldi didn't trust anything less than a .44 Magnum to positively punch through a human skull for a dead-center hit. The pilot twisted out of the way of a chopping salvo of pistol-caliber slugs that pounded into the cobblestones he'd been lying on. One bullet struck a cobblestone at an angle and ricocheted across his shoulder.

Isdan reloaded his Star and rejoined the conflict, hammering two shots into the chest of the shooter who tried to spray Grimaldi's intestines on the ground. The Pakistani killer folded under the twin impacts and dropped to his knees.

Amad leaned around the corner and triggered a stubby,

heavy revolver at the fourth of the would-be killers, .45-caliber bullets smashing gory holes through the shooter before he could target Isdan. Amad tucked the barrel into his belt and thumbed the latch. The revolver seemingly broke in two, empty brass chucked out of the cylinder. With his one, bloodied hand, he fed stubby bullets into the old Webley .455-caliber revolver, closing the action.

"You guys okay?" Grimaldi asked.

"I'll live," Amad said. His normally tanned face had grown a shade paler, and the grit in his voice was enough for the Stony Man pilot to realize that he wasn't as hale and hearty as he pretended to be.

"Jack, we've got more enemy contacts closing off the street." The voice of another blacksuit cut through his earpiece "We'll engage…"

"Belay that. Avoid contact until my signal," Grimaldi ordered. "You guys are not disposable."

He reloaded the Glocks and tucked them back in their holsters. He gathered up two machine pistols and spare magazines from the dead Pakistani hit men, then handed one to Isdan. "I think they're Pakistanis, but you might know better."

Isdan looked at the corpses as he accepted a machine pistol. It was a Type 56 7.65 mm machine pistol, made in China. "If they are, they're ethnic Arabs."

Grimaldi loaded a magazine into his depleted weapon. "Any clue as to where they came from?"

"Not without hearing them speak," Isdan admitted. "And, unfortunately, they weren't interested in small talk."

Grimaldi pulled a Browning Hi-Power from the belt of one of the killers and handed it to Amad. "So you don't have to practice one-handed revolver reloading."

Amad smiled weakly and struggled to his feet. He tucked the 9 mm pistol into his pocket. "Thanks."

"Don't mention it. We've got a few hurdles to jump before we can get your arm taken care of," Grimaldi explained.

"Then let's get crackin'," Amad growled. "I'm feeling a little light-headed."

The blacksuit's reply was an understatement, and Grimaldi contacted the blacksuit he'd brought along. "Wallace, how many bad guys do you count?"

"Six of them. Five are on feet, but one's manning a Land Rover," Wallace answered.

"Don't compromise your vehicle," Grimaldi ordered, "but take out that driver."

"Loud or soft?" Wallace inquired.

Grimaldi smirked, liking the blacksuit's spunk. "Make sure they hear it back on the Farm."

"Oo-rah." Wallace signed off.

The enemy gunmen were visible for a moment, but Grimaldi held his fire, not wanting to waste ammunition on uncertain hits. Besides, he was waiting for Wallace to shake up the attack.

A 40 mm grenade turned the Land Rover into a vibrant blossom of fire and spitting metal instants later. One of the hit men jerked upright, clutching an arm wound, and Isdan tapped off a shot burst into his face. Shrapnel from the exploding Rover had drawn the hit team's attention, and Grimaldi charged their position. Isdan and Amad stayed where they were, sniping with their weapons when the gunmen realized that they had been outflanked.

Grimaldi's Type 56 chattered out a snarling tune as it riddled the rib cage of one of their hunters and he reversed the machine pistol, crashing the tube-steel stock hard across the jaw of a second killer. The Pakistani killer tumbled backward into an insensate heap. Isdan and Amad took out the last of the would-be murderers, .455 Webley and 7.65 mm ComBloc slugs ripping him apart.

"Wallace!" Grimaldi called. "Wounded and a prisoner."

The pilot jerked the stunned assassin to his feet, disarming him.

Wallace pulled up in a Toyota pickup, and together, Isdan and Grimaldi dumped their prisoner into the bed as Amad crawled into the shotgun seat.

"Bro!" Wallace called to Isdan.

"Shit, brother," Isdan replied. "You're Wallace?"

"Let's move," Grimaldi stated. "Before you two are conducting your reunion in a Pakistani military prison."

The pickup took off toward the Stony Man pilot's base of operations.

They were one step closer to getting answers in the Kashmir conflict, and Grimaldi had gotten all of his people out alive.

It was a pretty good day so far.

"THAT'S THE ONE WEAK LINK in your idea," Mack Bolan said over the satellite phone. "While the CIA might have had some means of setting up safehouses in the Soviet Union during the cold war, they didn't have the facility to make a Continuity of Government base, even in Georgia."

"What about Turkey?" Price querried.

Bolan looked at his prisoner. The man stirred, and the Executioner snicked the safety off on his massive Desert Eagle, resting the muzzle against the Georgian's nose. "Good morning, sleepyhead."

The prisoner swallowed audibly and began to sputter in Georgian.

"In Russian, please," Bolan growled. "Unless you'd like me to set you free right now."

The conspirator's eyes locked on Mack Bolan's finger on the trigger of the Desert Eagle. He realized that his release would come in the form of a bullet through the brain. "I am sorry…"

"We'll see," Bolan said. He set down the sat phone, switching it to speaker function so that the Farm could record the results of the interrogation. "I spoke with Oleg, and he said that you were stockpiling weapons and equipment."

"I'll kill Oleg, that blabbermouth," the prisoner snarled.

"Too late for that," Bolan answered coldly. "But if you want, I'll arrange a meeting between you two, Smirov."

Smirov remained silent.

"Who wants all those goods?" Bolan pressed.

"I'm not allowed to say," Smirov stated, his voice tense with fear.

"Die now for sure, or be on the run and have a chance of surviving to old age," Bolan told him. "It's all your choice."

Smirov's eyes narrowed in spite. "There is no choice. You simply do not stop these people."

Bolan shook his head. "I don't believe anyone is unbeatable."

Smirov's lips tightened. "They're former KGB."

"Nothing new to me," the Executioner returned.

"Nobody escapes the Komitet," Smirov snapped.

Bolan fished in his pocket and dropped a medal on the floor between them. Smirov looked at it as if he'd taken a live, angry cobra out of his pocket. "I did. Tell me where to find them, and they'll never bother you again."

"It's…it's you…" Smirov whispered, fear and awe washing his defiance away.

"Talk, Smirov. My time's getting short," Bolan told him. "And if my time's short, yours is shorter."

The Georgian spilled his guts.

THE PRESIDENT USHERED his advisers out of the office and locked the door behind them. He regarded Hal Brognola for a moment. "You look like hell."

"Things just got much more complicated," Brognola explained. "You know of the Continuity of Government program, correct?"

The President nodded. "Top-secret facilities were set up around the nation during the fifties in the event of a global nuclear war. When the cities and the national power structures were destroyed, there was a hiding space held in reserve for world leaders and a select portion of the population to fall back to."

The man grimaced for a moment. "Though, I'm not particularly thrilled with the concept of how the survivors were to be chosen if what I read is correct."

Brognola shrugged. "Someone decided to utilize several of those facilities before their expiration date came up, apparently."

"But these people—the Engineers of the New Tomorrow, that's what they're called, right? These people are operating around the globe."

"Unfortunately the COG program was never limited to American shores," Brognola told him. "Forward bases were placed in areas that would be considered vital during the cold war. And apparently, the Engineers are not limiting themselves to the American program."

"Possible Soviet locations?" the President asked. "It seems reasonable. They want to redo the whole world, and since they're starting conflicts in what used to be the Russians' backyard, they might have access to some of their facilities. The damnedest thing is that after the wall came down, the KGB must have wiped the records on half of those hidden bases off official records, if they'd even waited that long."

"Stony Man has closed down a couple of them in conflicts with the Russian *mafiya*, but there's no way that those were all of them. Striker just reported in from the Georgian Republic that he's located a possible ENT nest," Brognola stated.

The President frowned. "And there's no guarantee that they're not operating in facilities on American soil either."

"Considering that the ENT erased the tracks on what appears to be dozens of bases from the FEMA mainframe, as well as other databases, it's highly likely," Brognola replied.

"And even if we knew where they were, it'd be a one-takedown-at-a-time operation. Those places were designed to survive a nuclear conflict. Not that we'd drop a five-megaton bomb that close to Colombia and Venezuela when they're ready to slaughter each other," the President replied.

"Fortunately, the Engineers' headquarters in the Darien has been neutralized. We're sending in a mop-up and recovery team to Panama to pick up Able Team," Brognola told him.

"That's good news. But I can just tell that there's worse ahead," the President said.

Brognola nodded. "Right, sir. We're tracking a facility down in Israel. The Meggido Valley."

"We had an operation in Israel?" the President asked.

"In the sixties. The United States sent military advisers and forces to help train the Israeli military. Part of it was to spy on their forces at the time, part of it was to bolster the strength of an ally in the region, and apparently, to set up a forward covert operations facility," Brognola explained.

The President looked at the file that Brognola had shown him. "No location on this base?"

"The Engineers were thorough. We even tried tracking electronic communications to them, but their defensive software is too good. We're operating blindly," Brognola said.

"And it's not like it would be easy to find. If the Israelis haven't found and exploited that facility after four decades, it's hidden well," the President mused.

Brognola pinched his brow. "So you can see why we're still behind the eight ball here. We know who we're looking for, and we know their intentions. But as it is, we're still in a reactionary position, instead of a preemptive posture."

"It's something," the President offered.

"They only have to get far enough ahead for a second to launch an attack that could kill millions, though," Brognola stated.

The President sighed. "I've got the CIA and the NSA working overtime on this. Maybe I could send in some special operations team to help out."

"The other agencies are getting all the targeting data we can acquire as we get it," Brognola said. "No one is being cut out of the loop. In fact, we're working through assets all across the globe."

"You're feeding potential enemies intel?" the President asked.

Brognola stiffened. "People we can trust, even if they're not Americans."

The President's mouth thinned to a hard, lipless line. "It's your operation, Hal. You've pulled this country out of the fire so many times, it's not like you're betraying national secrets to the North Koreans."

"No, but we are working with a few," Brognola admitted.

The President winced. "That's why Ambassador Chong is playing the peacemaker."

There was a knock at the door.

"Sir," an aide said, stepping in, "we have information on an incident in China."

"What happened?" the President asked.

"There was a terrorist attack on the North Korean embassy in Beijing. Other than that, details are sketchy."

Brognola excused himself. He had to get back to Stony Man Farm.

CAPTAIN HO HAD MANY THINGS to attribute to the big man in black who'd rescued him from a conspiracy. One of them was the knowledge that he'd better be armed at all times. As such, he kept a 9 mm NP-228, a NORINCO knock-off of the excellent SIG-Sauer P-228 pistol, on his person at all times. Though he had a Makarov in a flap holster on his dress belt, it was strictly ceremonial. Regulations dictated that it be kept empty, even in its sheath. The NP-228, however, was nearly as small as the Makarov, but held twice as many shots of more powerful 9 mm Parabellum ammunition. Ho made sure that every bullet in the gun, as well as in the two spare magazines worn in a covert shoulder holster, hidden under his loose dress shirt, had their round noses clipped flat by his pocket knife, scored with an X on the new, blunt plateau. It was a poor man's version of a hollowpoint, but even if the Xs didn't inspire expansion, the clipped tips still contacted dramatically more flesh than a regular hardball round. Ho's slender torso and wide, muscular shoulders combined to hide the powerful handgun well.

It also helped that the North Korean military didn't believe in tailored clothing, even for ranking military attachés.

Ho was on edge, and in violation of regulations, he'd even had a round chambered in the barrel of his holstered Makarov, a full 8-round magazine of 9 mm Mak ammo in the butt. Barbara Price had contacted him that the enemy, the Engineers of the New Tomorrow, had been striking back at the investigative efforts.

"I hope you have a means of protection," Price warned.

"I do," Ho answered. One of his care packages from his American benefactors had contained a Kramer T-shirt style ballistic vest. He was wearing it, even though he knew that it wouldn't provide much protection from a full-powered assault rifle. It'd give him a shred of a chance, however, and protected him from handgun bullets, even fired from SMGs.

"Are you okay, Ho?" Ambassador Chong asked in the back seat of his official limousine.

Ho turned his gaze from the window and looked over the elderly statesman. "We've been putting the lie to whoever is trying to spark a war between China and Taiwan, sir. You've been at the forefront of this effort, and that might make you a tempting target."

Chong smiled warmly. "I never expected to die of old age, son. But do not worry about me. I've lived a good, long life."

"Not long enough. The PRC still wants to take a bite out

of Nationalist China," Ho said. "Let's finish this, and then you can retire as much as you want."

"Indeed," Chong replied. "I do not want my grandchildren to grow up in a radioactive wasteland."

Ho nodded and turned his attention to the window. They were nearly back to the embassy after a meeting with PRC liaisons. Chong didn't seem disturbed that they were doing the work of a covert American agency, but then, the elder statesman was a man who worked for peace. In this case, the Americans were allies, protecting the whole globe. It would have been easy for these mystery men to smear North Korea for past infractions, but instead, only the truly guilty had been dealt with—permanently—and those like Ho, caught in the cross fire, were given a clean slate. The final cause was peace, and the justice that enforced such a peace.

Something flashed in the captain's peripheral vision and he lunged for Chong, wrapping his long, lean arms around the ambassador, cushioning him as the limousine jerked violently. In the aftermath, Ho would realize that his body recognized the hurtling enemy automobile on instinct, and lightning reflexes had enabled him to leap to Chong's protection. But in the moment, all the North Korean captain knew was that he'd wrapped himself around the ambassador moments before both of them crashed into the roof of the overturning vehicle. The right side doors were crumpled inward by the impact. Despite the fact that the limousine was armored against even heavy-caliber machine-gun fire, the raw horsepower of even a compact automobile outdid the ballistic forces generated by a bullet that weighed only an ounce.

Chong blinked dazedly as Ho crawled toward the leftside doors. The limo was upside down, and outside he heard the chatter of automatic weapons. The attaché paused long enough to rip open his uniform shirt, pulling the NP-228 pistol from its holster. He pulled the Makarov from its flap holster and stuffed the small pistol into Chong's hands.

The statesman flicked off the safety in a smooth, natural movement, and did a press check to see if there was a round in the chamber. For a man of peace, he certainly knew his instruments of battle. "A couple of handguns aren't going to be enough against submachine guns, Captain."

"The purpose of a pistol is to keep you alive long enough to reach a heavier weapon."

The undamaged door shook as an assassin tried to pull it open. The lock had given the two Koreans a moment of respite, and Ho cocked his NP-228, then flipped the lock controls. The door flew open as the gunman on the other side lost his balance. A second assassin was caught out in the open, and the captain fired twice, burning two dumdum bullets into the killer's belly. The Asian collapsed into the doorway, and Ho ripped the machine pistol from his lifeless hands.

The surprised hit man recovered his balance and wits, swinging the muzzle of his weapon toward Ho, but the captain opened fire with his NP-228, rather than bring the fallen assassin's weapon to bear. Five mangle-tipped bullets butchered through enemy flesh and bone, the X-cuts causing the slugs to split and deform as they struck heavy bone. The hit man gave a horrific final death howl as the mutilated bullets exploded inside him, churning internal organs.

Ho decocked his pistol and stuffed it into his waistband, inspecting the weapon he'd gotten from the enemy. It looked like an MP-5 at first, but the North Korean saw writing in Spanish on the frame. He grabbed spare maga-

zines from the dead hit man's corpse, pocketing them. Behind him, Chong kept his Makarov at low ready, muzzle
aimed at the rear window in case a reflexive flinch made
him pull the trigger. The statesman's muzzle discipline
would prevent an accidental shot in Ho's back.

The two surviving North Korean bodyguards opened
fire on the assassins, but the killers were prepared for the
ambassador's defenders. The only thing they hadn't
counted on was a slightly paranoid young military attaché.

A grenade bounced toward the limo's door, and Ho
opened fire on it, the Chilean machine pistol's rounds striking the miniature bomb and kicking it away from the overturned vehicle. Ho hauled up the corpse of one of the
assassins as a shield, just in case, a moment before the grenade detonated. Shrapnel and shock waves buffeted the
body in Ho's grasp, but no lethal fragments got into the
body of the limo.

Heavier weapons opened up, cracking loudly. Ho recognize them as the AK-47s used by his Korean comrades.
Killers flopped and crashed in the street, perforated by
rifle fire. More grenades exploded outside the armored
limo, but Ho lunged out and slammed the door shut. The
overturned vehicle shook under the blasts, heavy plating
deflecting shrapnel and the worst of the concussion from
the explosions.

Ho looked back at Chong. The ambassador began to
rack the slide on his pistol, ejecting five shots. One for
every pistol round that had been fired by the North Korean
captain.

"Better hide that NORINCO in your belt, son," Chong
informed him. "Wouldn't want the man who saved my life
to get in trouble."

The statesman pocketed the ejected ammunition and winked.

Ho sighed, still gripping the enemy's machine pistol.

They'd live to fight another day.

CHAPTER ELEVEN

Hal Brognola got off the helicopter and ran to the SUV where Barbara Price was waiting for him. "What's the news?"

"Ambassador Chong is okay," Price said. "A military attaché was on hand and heroically protected Chong."

"Striker's buddy from North Korea?" Brognola asked.

Price smiled. "He brings out the best in everyone. The North Korean government's on edge now. They're accusing Beijing of not looking after the safety of their representatives. Several RPNK soldiers were killed in the assault, and that's not going over well with Pyongyang."

"Two steps forward, three steps back," Brognola grumbled, climbing into the SUV. He pulled out a cigar and clamped it between his teeth. "What's the word from the field?"

"Jack Grimaldi hooked up with some blacksuits we had on the ground in Pakistan, but not before their cover was compromised," Price stated. "The enemy is on to us."

"How much?" Brognola asked.

"At first, we thought that it was just a fluke that Phoenix Force encountered an Engineers' strike force. However,

Akira has picked up a few phantoms in our network," Price explained.

"Phantoms?" Brognola asked.

"Very discrete information scoops. Basically, it looks like the ENT is keeping ahead of the situation by means of some very powerful computer taps," Price said. "And a couple of phantoms have been found in our mainframe after we'd broken into their own system."

"Shit," Brognola swore. "How badly have we been compromised?"

"We've got Carmen engaging in damage control, but it started when Hunt went into the system Able Team captured in Panama," Price stated. "Luckily, our Internet communications are extremely sanitary, and voice exchanges have not shown any form of tapping. Extra layers of scrubbing are going on on all data going in and out of the system, but I think that's how they homed in on Ambassador Chong."

"He'll be all right, though?" Brognola inquired.

"Yeah. The North Korean Diplomatic Security Agency dispatched a backup special operations team to Beijing for extra muscle," Price said. She looked at the Farm's main building. "Bear ran background checks on all of their members. They're clean and can be trusted to protect Chong."

"Never hurts to be too cautious," Brognola admitted. The SUV pulled up in front of the farmhouse and the head Fed got out. "What else?"

"Well, Jack has a prisoner. A Green Beret team in Pakistan is helping out his group, and they're interrogating the guy," Price stated. "The Green Berets are under the impression that Jack and his crew are with the CIA."

"Wonder who gave them that idea?" Brognola mused.

Price grinned. "Able Team's still waiting for Task Force 160 to move in and pick them up. And Phoenix Force is heading for Israel."

"What's the delay on TF 160?" Brognola asked.

"We're not the only people operating in the area. Between inserting SF teams to keep an eye on the rowdy Colombians and Venezuelans, and extracting stranded CIA assets," Price said.

"Right. And Jack's busy halfway across the world," Brognola noted. "So used to having him as everybody's taxi service."

"They're fine. Gadgets is still hacking the mainframe, looking for threads back to where these guys have their main headquarters. Trouble is, the Engineers were thorough about compartmentalizing their operation. They figured we might hit one or two of their cells before they started the real fireworks," Price surmised.

"What about our crew here at the Farm?" Brognola asked.

"The COG base's black ice is too thick. We can't hack it, even with our system. That's okay, Gadgets is nearly as good as Aaron when it comes to breaking open systems," Price said.

"Striker?" Brognola asked.

"He's checking out that stockpile of supplies in Georgia," Price said. "He's gone to radio silence, but said if we don't hear from him, we're to get on the horn to his friends in RI to send in a Spetznaz team to clean up."

Brognola shook his head. "How about the China conflict, aside from the ambassador?"

"Nobody's aware of our allies in the region. Or if they are, our people haven't had a hard contact yet," Price told him. "Mei Anna is good, though, so she shouldn't have picked up any tails."

"And if she gets into trouble? Who can bail her out?" Brognola asked.

Price frowned. "Mack, Able and Phoenix are busy elsewhere. She'd be out of luck."

"You always put such a cheery spin on things, Barb," Brognola grumbled as he entered the farmhouse.

CARL LYONS CHECKED the door to the office where they'd placed the prisoners. He'd made certain to wreck the outlets and jacks in the walls before putting the technicians away.

"But…but we helped you." One of them spoke up. "Why are you locking us in this trashed armpit?"

"You'd like to have Internet access or a phone, or some kind of entertainment?" Lyons growled.

"We don't need to be treated like mad dogs."

Lyons regarded the man with a cold gaze that forced his target to break out into a cold sweat. "You also helped to incinerate hundreds of people in Maracaibo."

The other technician took that as a hint to enter the office quietly, no courage left in him to look at the brawny blond ex-cop. "Come on, Dave…"

"No, Kelsey," Dave protested. "We never killed anyone ourselves."

"Who assembled the drones?" Lyons asked, stepping closer. "Who fitted them with jet engines to turn them back into cruise missiles? Who loaded their warheads?"

Dave swallowed hard, but his indignation wouldn't allow him to back down.

"Dave, let the wookie win," the other pleaded.

"No!" Dave snapped at his friend. "We did what we could to help you."

Lyons shook his head, then tapped Dave under the chin

with the muzzle of his Colt Python. The slender technician's eyes widened and he backed away, looking at six inches of heavy under-lugged black barrel aimed at the hollow of his throat. "Behave. Or I will rip your arms out of your sockets and beat you to death with them. As far as I'm concerned, you're as much a cold-blooded murderer as the guys paid to pack the assault rifles. You might have a sweet deal where you won't be executed for slaughtering everyone killed by those missiles you cobbled together, but I am willing to say 'fuck that deal' and send you to the devil with any more provocation."

Dave tried to suppress his shudder of fear and revulsion. It didn't work. "We'll make ourselves comfortable, somehow."

Lyons locked the door securely.

"You don't have to play tough guy and bully around the little girly men, Conan," Susana Arquillo said.

"That one thinks he's absolved of all his sins just because he decided he didn't want to be sprayed all across the ceiling by my rifle," Lyons countered. "And he'll cut a sweet deal to escape any prosecution and retribution for what he was truly responsible for."

Arquillo brushed aside a careless lock that had fallen on Lyons's forehead. "Carl, you look like you're ready to explode. Come on…"

Lyons's eyes narrowed. "Susana, this isn't pent-up sexual tension."

"No, but I think keeping you focused on something other than twisting those punks' heads off will be good for both of us," Arquillo answered. "Or did I pick up the wrong vibes off of you?"

"And what about the prisoners?" Lyons asked.

"Pol's around the corner, waiting for us to clear out. He'll keep an eye on things. He got off the sat phone with your people, and said that TF 160's forty-five minutes away," Arquillo said. "Or do you want me to take a page from your big book of cavemen, beat you on the head with a club, and drag you back to my cave?"

Lyons caught Blancanales peering around the corner. A wink from his elder partner let him know that the situation was stable.

Lyons took a deep breath and flushed the anger out of his mind. He leaned in close to give Arquillo a passionate kiss. "Your cave, huh?"

Arquillo winked. "Yeah. Let's get a move on. I don't want you to have to run after the helicopter with your pants around your knees."

DAVID MCCARTER PERCHED in the doorway, smoking a Player's cigarette, wishing he had a Coke with him. Instead, he settled down, keeping an eye on the street. The others should have been here by now, and he noticed a wide-shouldered woman in a full burka and hood walking toward him. The woman had a basket in her hands, which were oddly concealed under the fabric of her sleeves. It took him a moment to realize that the figure was stooped, but it was something that would have escaped a casual observer. His mouth curled into a smile as he dropped the cigarette, smashing it out with his toe.

"Women aren't supposed to be seen talking to strange men, especially us Europeans, Mahmoud," McCarter chided.

"How'd you guess it was me?" the Egyptian leader said, holding up an onion for McCarter to investigate. He gave it a shake as if for emphasis.

"Reiser wouldn't have needed to stoop," McCarter answered with a grin. He pointed at another of Mahmoud's onions. "We have Fuqua back under control."

"His allies aren't going to pick him up?" Mahmoud asked.

"They're smarter than we thought. We do have some leads," McCarter admitted.

"But you're not going to share them, are you?" the Egyptian asked.

"Not yet. We have to move fast, and asking nicely will only slow us down," the Briton answered.

"Try not to make a mess in my backyard," Mahmoud admonished.

If that was an attempt to get a little more information out of the Phoenix Force commander, it didn't work, but McCarter didn't blame him for trying. "The only thing we're interested is preventing war."

"With our help, you'd get things done much more quickly," Mahmoud stated.

"The enemy might also know if we're coming," McCarter replied. "I'm sorry, but like I said, this has to be fast, silent and deep. But if things do get hairy, you'll get a call to go exactly where the mop-up's needed."

"That bad, eh?" Mahmoud asked.

The Briton nodded. "Sorry."

"God speed, then, Mr. King," Mahmoud said.

"I just hope that's fast enough," McCarter said, taking an onion and dropping a coin and a folded note in Mahmoud's basket. The note contained the location where both Kohn and Fuqua were packed away. "Good luck getting out of here."

Mahmoud winked. "I've got my ways, too."

McCarter separated from the Egyptian commander. He had a rendezvous with the rest of Phoenix Force.

JACK GRIMALDI SWUNG the MD600N helicopter low over the Pakistani border toward an installation that Hunt Wethers discovered missing during a comparison of data backups in the Farm's records. During the Soviet invasion of Afghanistan, U.S. forces had been welcomed into Pakistan to help train their army in the event that the Russians wanted to expand eastward. With the end of the cold war and Soviet expansionism, the Pakistani people and the freedom fighters they'd sent into Afghanistan to help their beloved neighbors forgot about the succor they received from the United States, only seeing a hateful enemy seeking their moral destruction.

But Jack Grimaldi, after the efforts of the Special Forces A-Team that interrogated their prisoner, with fact corroboration from Stony Man Farm, had his intel. Charlie Mott piloted a second of the McDonnell-Douglas MD600N helicopters. The aircraft were ideal for stealthy operations due to their six-bladed design. The newer 600Ns were longer than the old MD500s, capable of carrying seven passengers, albeit in cramped quarters. That made it easier to carry the thirteen-man Green Beret team and also bring along Isdan. While the Green Beret team had been chosen for its skills in local dialects, Grimaldi wanted to have an extra pilot on hand, as well as having a translator.

He knew that there were members on the team who would be able to pilot the McDonnell-Douglas helicopters as well. Though he wasn't usually a field operative, Grimaldi had been in the thick of battle countless times, alongside Mack Bolan, Able Team and Phoenix Force. And one thing he'd learned from the other warriors of Stony Man Farm, was that if you lead men in combat, you lead from the front.

The MD600Ns buzzed low to the ground and landed

atop a plateau overlooking a canyon. Grimaldi looked to Isdan who took the controls, keeping the bird hot. Two members of the A-Team stayed back with the helicopters, equipped with M-60 machine guns to defend their ride out, or to provide aerial fire support in case the ground team was overwhelmed. It wasn't a squadron of gunships and artillery support like Grimaldi would have preferred, but it was something. "Isdan, I know that the Farm's watching our backs here, but keep your ears open."

"Belt and suspenders, Jack," Isdan replied. He patted an MP-5 in a scabbard next to his leg. "Ears open, and my hand never too far from a weapon. If I hear anything on the local frequencies, I'll let you know."

Grimaldi nodded. He checked his rifle, an AKMS. The 7.62 mm round was as common as grass in Pakistan, and even out of the stubby AKM barrel, the bullet had superior punch and penetration to an M-4. Brutish and reliable, the AKMS wouldn't be out of place, and was a vital part of the Green Berets' foreign operational armament. Loaded down with 30-round magazines and grenades in his vest, Grimaldi was ready for front-line combat. He unfolded the AKMS's wire stock and shouldered the rifle as soon as his boots hit the ground.

"Captain." Grimaldi greeted the Special Forces team leader.

"Mr. Grayson," Captain Ralph Busiek answered. His skin had been tanned dark behind his thick curly brown beard. The Green Berets operated under relaxed hygiene in the field, finding that thick dark beards helped to disguise their identities as Americans in the Middle East. Grimaldi's own Italian features and weathered good looks helped, but he couldn't help feeling out of place, relatively clean-shaven. Even so, the past several days had allowed the pilot to grow stubble enough to darken his jaw, but nothing like the Special Forces operators. "Ready to accompany us into the facility?"

Grimaldi took a deep breath. Busiek was hiding his reluctance to bring a stranger along with his team into combat. Unit integrity was an important aspect to the success of special operations teams, and even a stranger with a high level of skill didn't possess the same kind of cohesion and continuity of the original squad had. But Grimaldi wasn't going to order men into a situation that he wasn't a part of. What risks they faced, he'd face, as well. "Lead the way, sir."

Busiek nodded, but the pilot could still feel the doubt and distrust in the air.

"Captain…"

"Call me Ralph," Busiek replied.

"Ralph, I know that the Green Berets believe strongly in continuity. I'm not here to contradict you. I'm just here to make sure that people entrusted to my leadership aren't sacrificed," Grimaldi stated. "I'm a team player."

Busiek sized up the Stony Man ace. "Fine. But if we get killed, don't expect us to cover your ass."

Grimaldi chuckled.

The Special Forces team embarked toward the facility entrance.

JASON KOVAK PACED NERVOUSLY. "We should have sent someone for Fuqua."

"He was bait," Cortez answered. "And we're lucky that they can't penetrate our electronic defenses. Our computer techs repulsed dozens of probes. Good probes at that."

Kovak's eyes narrowed. "But he's been compromised.

Who knows what kind of information they've gotten out of him."

"They've gotten enough," Cortez replied. "We're dealing with a behind-the-scenes operations force. We've already lost the Canal control juncture, and Pakistan is reporting an incursion in their facility."

Kovak frowned. "Sounds familiar. Especially the descriptions that Kohn sent in before we lost contact with our strike force. Five men who are deadly effective. Nobody is sure who they work for, but they've been linked to everyone from the CIA to Interpol."

"I recognize the makeup of the reported investigation team that met up with a CIA agent in Panama City, as well," Cortez said. "They've clashed with earlier incarnations of my organization. A trio, lead by a muscular blond man. And this three-man operation is rarely cozy with the CIA leadership."

Kovak recognized the description. "It's been years since they've been active in Europe and the Middle East on a large scale. An A-Team?"

"Perhaps. The whisper stream has a few names for them," Cortez responded. "And if it weren't for the fact that many of my cohorts had been slaughtered by those three, I'd give the stories about them the same veracity as a chupacabra sighting."

"We've come all this way, and urban legends are popping out of the woodwork to stop us," Kovak muttered.

"Now you know why we brought you here, out of the way," Cortez said.

Kovak sighed. The Continuity of Government facility they were in was huge and well stocked. It was the main headquarters for the Engineers' main operation, where they intended to mastermind a global collapse, and fortify themselves before emerging from the rubble of civilization to begin anew. Stockpiles of food, equipment and weapons were housed in deep, underground caverns under a sheath of bedrock that could blunt a fifty-megaton detonation right on top of them. Shielded from radiation, with water recycling and even a small nuclear power plant, the facility was bleeding edge state of the art, even three decades after its inception. Satellite uplinks gave the headquarters access to the whole globe, monitoring every part of the planet. Computers with constantly updated and upgraded hardware, software and security connected with the Internet, were shielded from prying enemy eyes through cybernetic stealth programs.

"I don't like being in the enemy's backyard," Kovak told Cortez. "Especially since this mystery enemy has started locating our covert facilities."

"This place is off their main maps," Cortez stated.

Kovak looked out the window of the underground office. It overlooked weapons stockpiles with equipment spanning from World War II standards to the most modern high-tech armor and guns. One corner, a closed-off concrete bunker with biohazard signs, was prominent as technicians transported sealed lead canisters from the blockhouse to a freight elevator. "And when we launch our spark?"

"The Predators are meant to be ultralow profile," Cortez stated. "Besides, we'll hit the ELINT data collectors for the U.S. with a wave of static just before we fire off our cruise Predators."

Kovak nodded. "An electronic intelligence blackout would help."

"Not having doubts about the Meggido Valley phase, are you?" Cortez asked.

"When the Lord flooded the world to cleanse it of human corruption and villainy, He promised that when He next sought to judge humanity, it would be cleansed with fire, not water," Kovak said. "This will be that judgment. I will not weep for the pretenders who infest God's promised land."

Cortez nodded. "Good."

There was a buzz at the intercom of the office. It was Ling, the Asian head of computer operations for the Engineers. "We've got identification of an enemy operative in the Georgian Republic."

"Do you have a name?" Cortez asked.

"Matt Cooper," Ling stated.

Cortez looked at Kovak. "That name ring a bell?"

The Israeli shook his head.

"His description is interesting," Ling added. "Check your monitor."

The remote liquid crystal display flashed to life and a grainy photograph of Matt Cooper appeared on the screen.

"This is footage taken from a security camera at Smirov's black market warehouse," Ling announced. "Does that look familiar?"

Kovak squinted. The man on the screen was tall, broad-shouldered and leanly powerful under a skintight dark uniform. The tape loop showed him gunning down two Georgian smugglers with a large, heavy handgun, and moving with the speed and grace of a panther. Ice water poured into the Israeli's bowels.

"When he clashed with Abraham's Dagger he was called Colonel Brandon Stone," Kovak stated.

"Neither registers in any records," Ling announced. "He must have access to a cybernetic backup crew that deletes mentions of him."

"The same crew who tried to hack into our network?" Cortez asked.

"Given their tenacity and skill, it's highly possible," Ling answered.

Kovak looked at the video loop. "How are you doing on blunting their penetration of the system?"

"It's hard, constant work. These people don't give up," Ling admitted. "Our only saving grace is that they are divided between hitting us and defusing the disinformation and confusion we've sown so far."

"They're setting back the hostilities," Kovak grumbled.

Cortez clapped Kovak on the shoulder. "There is no way that any amount of computer hacking can dispel the hatred and hostility of an Israeli first strike with nuclear weapons."

The Israeli grinned, imagining Syrian, Saudi and Egyptian cities disappearing in flares of atomic fire. The sweetest thoughts ran across his mind's eye when he envisioned Moscow rocked and reduced to a radioactive crater. Israel's cries for innocence would vaporize instantly in heat that rivaled the corona of the sun, and the United States would also be burned, charred to a crisp for supplying the tiny Jewish state with nuclear power, even if it was involuntary. The retaliation against the two nations would be instantaneous. Britain would suffer similarly. Other nations, pushed to the brink by waves of violence spurred by ENT, would open fire on their opponents, rather than be caught flat-footed by megatons of exploding devastation.

"Really, how is a handful of people going to stop us?"

Cortez pressed. "We are gods who have soaked a rickety house in gasoline, and now, the match merely has to be dropped."

"So why not do it now?" Kovak asked.

"Timing," Cortez answered. He gestured toward the screen. "Just because the mosquitoes are biting doesn't mean we must flush into the open where the tigers can pounce. A base here or there is one thing. Exposing ourselves to concentrated defenses from the world's air forces would be suicide."

Kovak nodded. "If our enemy knew how to shut us down completely, they'd be directing more overt powers against us. You're right. Hasty reactions would disarm everything."

Cortez nodded. "Be patient and stay the course, Kovak."

The Israeli looked out the window to the blockhouse, watching sealed nuclear warheads transferred to the launch bay. The future was bright, even if the glow came from clouds of radioactive fire.

CHAPTER TWELVE

Crouched inside the ductwork intersection of the underground facility, Bolan slid an eight-round magazine of .44 Magnum hollowpoints into the grip of his Desert Eagle.

"Mr. Cooper!" a voice boomed over loudspeakers. "Mr. Cooper, there's no need to make this difficult on yourself! We're working to build a whole new world, scoured clean of corruption and rot."

Bolan thumbed the Eagle's safety back to safe and holstered it before squirming into a vent and slithering with snakelike agility through the metal corridor. Were they hinting at an alliance? If so, their suggestion was falling on deaf ears. The Executioner battled against corruption, but in his world, there was no room for the culling tactics of the ENT. The loss of any noncombatant lives in his battles was an abomination to Bolan.

The narrow vent split off, and Bolan slithered to the right, stopping at a grating that overlooked a part of the supply warehouse. He'd been here minutes earlier, and the corpses of dead Russians and Arabs littered the floor. Defending security forces had moved on from the scene, and

Bolan punched the grating out of his way, hooking the lip of the vent, and dropped headfirst out of the hole. Still holding on, he allowed his feet to swing over his head and then he let go, landing on the floor in a crouch. The Desert Eagle was out and in his right fist, safety snicked off and ready to greet all comers. It would have to do until he substituted his lost rifle with a replacement.

Unfortunately the ENT security teams were professionals. They stripped the dead of rifles and handguns, and had even policed Bolan's fallen Bizon PP-19 submachine gun. Judging from the volume of enemy fire, and the helical magazines in the dead men's pouches, they were armed with Bizons, too. The Executioner didn't blame them. The compact design combined the rugged and utterly reliable Kalashnikov action design with a 64-round 9 mm magazine in a compact, folding-stocked weapon.

Even grenades had been stripped from the dead, denying Bolan an opportunity to raise hell. There were weapons inside various crates, but getting them open would be too loud and take too much time, drawing the attention of the guards.

"Cooper, you know that the world needs to start over. There are too many useless creatures populating its surface. Humanity is collapsing under its own weight, descending into insanity and madness. Just take a look at the incompetent leadership of your nation over the past two decades, regardless of political party," the announcer continued, trying to woo Bolan out of hiding.

The Executioner put his Desert Eagle away and drew his knife, stalking like a phantom in the shadowy maze of crates. His silenced Beretta hung under his left armpit, but even the chug of a suppressed bullet would attract too much attention if he couldn't grab an enemy rifle quickly. The conspirators were highly trained, and one misstep would be the end of him.

The enemy gunmen moved in pairs or trios, watching each other's backs, their muzzle discipline exquisite, never aiming at or crossing their partners. The ENT soldiers moved with the practiced grace of professionals, which meant that Bolan would have to work to earn every kill he could get. The Executioner edged closer to his foes, palming the Beretta. He targeted a duo, but waited to see that they weren't being covered and observed by another unit of guards. The maze made ambushes easy, but it worked as well for his enemy as it did for him. The two-man squads could simply have been bait for Bolan to betray his hand.

The Executioner timed his attack, then lunged. The Beretta 93-R in his left hand coughed out a 3-round burst, high-velocity 9 mm bullets chopping into his enemy's face and rupturing his skull into a mist of bone splinters and blood. Bolan speared with the knife in his left hand, striking his second opponent just above the hip, eleven inches of Bowie steel slicing the Arab guard's kidney in two. Bolan released the coffin-shaped handle and plucked his enemy's Bizon submachine gun from limp and lifeless fingers, then dropped into a shoulder roll as an enemy gunman caught sight of him, crying out an alarm in Russian. Bizon and Beretta swiveled toward the alarmist, and twin bursts of full-auto fire chopped into the Russian, bowling him off his feet. The guard's two partners, both Arabs, spun around the corner, aiming high, intending to hit a standing opponent, but the crouched Executioner sawed them off at the waist with the whipping hose of 9 mm rounds from his Bizon.

"Cooper! This is your last chance! Join the future or be culled with the rest of the useless…" the announcement speaker blared before Bolan silenced it with a burst from the Beretta. The intercom squelched and exploded in a warbling moan as electronics detonated.

The Executioner put the 93-R into its holster and grabbed ammunition from the dead men, feeding the hungry submachine gun. With a vest stuffed with 64-round helical magazines, and sixty-five shots in his weapon, Mack Bolan greeted the next-wave of ENT defenders.

If they wanted to unleash a cleansing flame upon the Earth, they'd have to face the Executioner's own cleansing fire.

JACK GRIMALDI PROVIDED covering fire for Captain Busiek as he crossed the hallway, his AKMS ripping out swarms of 7.62 mm steel-cored slugs at the defenders. The enemy inside the facility was a mix of Asians, from the sound of their shouted communications Cantonese speakers, and locals from al Qaeda cells. The AKMS ran dry and Grimaldi ducked back behind cover, ejecting his magazine and feeding it a fresh one.

"Just who in the hell are these guys?" Busiek asked.

"They call themselves the Engineers of the New Tomorrow," Grimaldi replied. "And they look like they're a lot more global than we imagined."

A Green Beret triggered an RPG-7 rocket toward the heavily defended intersection and ducked back. The warhead detonated with earth-shattering force, shredding Chinese and Arab alike in a single blast. Grimaldi had doubted the efficiency of bringing the RPG-7s into the underground facility, but the Green Berets had shown him exactly how effective they could be. Utilizing antipersonnel shells that mixed notched razor wire and high-concussion explosives, they were able to clear out enemy forces, even in the confined quarters of the corridors. The fact that the Soviet-designed rocket-propelled grenades ejected their shells without producing the choking backwash of an American-style LAW rocket made them ideal for the close-quarters combat.

Grimaldi and Busiek advanced cautiously. The level of opposition that they'd encountered was incredible, and the Green Beret team had burned off one-third of their ammunition already. Two of the Special Forces commandos were wounded, but nimble first aid had prevented serious threat to their lives. Busiek ordered them to secure a fallback point in the complex so that if the A-Team had been repelled, they wouldn't be cut off from the surface.

Busiek paused and checked the corpse of one of the Chinese killed by the RPG blast, then frowned. "No identifying tattoos."

The Green Beret captain pulled out a digital camera and took shots of the man's face, then dipped the corpse's fingertips in its own bloody wound, then pushed them on a clean spot of tile floor to get fingerprints to photograph.

"Not the cleanest way to get prints, but it beats severing fingers," Busiek noted.

"No arguments with that," Grimaldi replied. He checked around the corner and ducked back as rifle fire chopped at the corner. "Found the next tier of defense."

Busiek pocketed his digital camera and pulled a grenade from his harness. "I'm glad you're not concerned with preserving the facility."

"Hey, these things were designed to survive a nuclear

war. A few explosions inside shouldn't make things too difficult to navigate," Grimaldi stated.

"Got a point there," Busiek said, whipping his fragger around the corner. It skipped down the hall, spoon popping free as it tumbled toward the entrenched enemy. It exploded a few feet short of the defenders, eliciting screams of pain, but return fire flared violently, sheets of automatic fire splashing on floor, walls and ceiling like leaden rain. "Holy shit…"

Grimaldi winced as sections of the wall disintegrated under enemy gunfire. "They brought out the heavy artillery, too."

"No kidding," Busiek stated. "From the sound of it, they've got a 12.7 mm machine gun and a lighter belt fed."

Green Berets behind them opened fire, hammering out suppressive streams of fire.

"They're trying to flank us!" Truman, one of Busiek's sergeants called.

"Between a rock and a hard place," Grimaldi growled.

"More like an avalanche," Truman answered. "Grenade!"

The Green Beret swung his AKMS like a golf club around the corner, catching the enemy projectile in midskip and launching it back toward the ENT defenders. It got only a few yards before it detonated, the shock wave knocking Truman to the ground. Grimaldi scrambled to the man's side.

"I'm okay," Truman answered, sitting up. He was dazed, and a piece of shrapnel opened up his forehead, caking his face in blood. Two more Green Berets continued to launch suppressive fire against the flanking forces while Grimaldi tore a strip of Truman's do-rag into a bandage to keep the blood from pouring into his eyes.

"They're not afraid of pumping grenades at us, either," Grimaldi commented.

Busiek fired around the corner and ducked back behind the shattered wall as more heavy machine-gun fire closed in on him. "They're trying to cover their people this way, too. We can't stay put."

Grimaldi grimaced. The two Green Berets' fire was holding the enemy back from throwing more grenades, but their suppression couldn't last forever. And under the hammering cover fire of the heavy machine guns of the defenders, more ENT guards would be able to capture Grimaldi's team in a pincer. The pilot plucked his last two hand grenades from his harness. Truman took two more, and the two warriors thumbed out their cotter pins.

"Three, two…" Grimaldi said. He tossed his pair first, throwing high while the floored Truman rolled his mini-bombs low.

The corridor, packed with enemy flankers, erupted into a cloud of smoke, dismembered limbs and clumps of flesh spraying as the combined power of four grenades cut loose in unison.

"On me! Truman, you and these two back up the captain," Grimaldi ordered. He charged down the shattered hallway, AKMS spitting as more flankers tried to block the invaders' advance.

Screams and autofire rattled in the air, the underground hallway disintegrating into an abattoir for the Engineers' defense forces. Grimaldi and his backup spotted the defenders' machine-gun nest. The heavy weapons sprayed out brass as they chopped away at Busiek's defensive position. An RPG-wielding Green Beret leveled his rocket launcher and fired at the ENT soldiers while Grimaldi and two others cut loose with their rifles. The heavy warhead exploded, ripping apart the machine-gun nest, mangling the heavy weapons and turning their gunners to a pulpy mass.

Those spared the initial blast were cut down mercilessly by Grimaldi and his allies. He reached the next junction and looked down the hall to see Busiek limp into the open.

"You okay?" the ace asked.

Busiek winced as he tightened a bandage around his thigh. "Took a flesh wound. We're getting chewed up pretty good."

"Never said this would be easy," Grimaldi answered. "That's why I didn't want you going in without me."

Busiek nodded. "Thanks for the backup."

"I should be saying the same to you," Grimaldi replied. The Green Berets were stripping undamaged weapons and magazines off the dead to replenish their dwindling supply. "Come on, we've got a long road ahead."

LING JON LOOKED at the security footage coming in from the two facilities under siege. In Pakistan, a special operations team had hit with shattering force, while the Soviet counterpart facility in the Georgian Republic had been invaded by one man. He frowned in response to how badly the defenders were faring, even though he realized that each of the facilities used as spark points were staffed with expendable forces.

It was a cold-blooded strategy, but the destruction of modern civilization wasn't undertaken by those without a sense of ruthlessness. Those in the forward bases, charged with unleashing the hounds of Armageddon, were sacrificial lambs. If their underground bases survived the global conflagration, then excellent. If they didn't, then they gave their lives in the glorious cause of cleansing the world.

Ling didn't doubt that Cortez picked the soldiers for these facilities for their disposability, or their willingness to sacrifice their existences for what they perceived as a noble cause.

"How are we doing?" Cortez asked, interrupting the chief technician's thoughts.

"Not well. If this keeps up, we'll lose the Pakistan-India conflict," Ling stated. "However, tensions are high enough in the former Soviet republics that reprisals can start a war, especially with our Meggido launches."

Cortez's mouth set in a hard, cruel line.

"You don't want to lose Georgia?" Ling asked.

"It will be inconvenient. Especially since the facility we have there is a vital stock point," Cortez stated. "That's why we had so many forces guarding it."

Ling nodded. "But we know where it is. And that man is alone. I doubt he'll have someone to clean out the facility in his wake. At least before we unleash the war."

"Doubts are one thing. But you forget the firepower we have stocked in the base," Cortez stated. "He could deny the facility to our surviving forces with the firepower we have on hand."

Ling frowned, watching the warrior at work on the view screen.

"He's a one-man army. Though he's been put on the run at least three times during his assault, he's always fallen back and destroyed his attackers and continued on," Ling noted. "If anything, he's progressed further and faster than the entire Special Forces platoon in Pakistan."

"Sanitize the base," Cortez ordered.

Ling glanced to him. "But the remaining forces…"

"They're dead anyhow," Cortez replied. "Release nerve

gas through the whole facility. I don't want him squirming his way out of that hellhole."

Ling sighed and hacked into the Georgian facility's command center.

THE EXECUTIONER WRESTLED with the Russian giant, his forearms clamped around the titan's throat in a death grip. Normally, Bolan was strong enough to break a man's neck from this position, but the Russian's neck muscles were simply too powerful.

With the strength of a grizzly, the giant flipped Bolan off his shoulders with a single shrug and kicked him in the face. Only razor-sharp reflexes kept the blow from tearing Bolan's skull from his shoulders, and even then, he was left dazed by the impact. On automatic pilot, he clambered back and away from the massive killer.

Unfortunately, in two strides, the huge Russian was right on top of Bolan and wrapping a huge paw around his throat. The Executioner caught sight of his Desert Eagle out of the corner of his eye and stretched for it, but the mighty hulk lifted Bolan with one hand and hurled him twenty feet down the tiled corridor, away from the massive pistol. The Russian stooped and picked up the Desert Eagle, making the foot-long hand cannon appear like a pocket pistol in his huge paw.

"Such a cute little gun," the Russian said. "It almost fits me like a glove."

Bolan got to his hands and knees, blood drooling from a busted lip. The Russian leveled the Desert Eagle, but the Executioner didn't flinch as the gun jerked in the giant's paw. He'd left the .44 Magnum weapon on safe, locked and cocked. It would take a moment for his powerful opponent to figure out how to desterilize the pistol and put a bullet into Bolan. In that time, the Executioner reached into his sheath and drew his coffin-handled Bowie knife, charging like a rhinoceros

Bolan, at six-three and two hundred pounds, was normally considered a big, powerful man, but the Russian was a full foot taller and one hundred pounds heavier. The giant's bulk was lean, however, and he reacted with nimble agility, sidestepping Bolan's main attack. The Executioner had kept his knife hidden during his charge, though, lashing out at the last moment and raking its razor-sharp length across the Russian's belly. Skin and muscle parted, and the huge killer clutched his wounded gut. He pulled the trigger on the Desert Eagle again, but Bolan's thumb safety kept him alive a moment more.

Spinning on a dime, the Executioner dropped to one knee and in a fencer's lunge, speared the seven-inch blade through the Russian's groin. When the hilt stopped on contact with skin, Bolan gave the Bowie a cruel twist and wrenched the carving edge sideways.

The Desert Eagle slipped from pain-numbed fingers as the giant's blood pressure suddenly dropped, gushing out of his carved groin through severed femoral arteries. Bolan withdrew the knife and crashed his forearm into the side of the Russian's head, spinning the big killer around. The Bowie flipped into an ice-pick grip and Bolan sank the point into the juncture of the mortally wounded defender's neck and shoulder. The blade sliced apart muscle, broke bone and tore apart blood vessels in one wicked death stroke. Using the knife as a handle, Bolan flipped the big man's corpse aside.

He bent and retrieved his Desert Eagle. The Beretta and

the Bizon were several yards up the hall, torn from the Executioner's hands in the giant's initial assault. He had to admit that the Russian had taken him completely by surprise with a stealth that belied his seven-foot, three-hundred pound bulk, but Bolan had recovered from the initial attack and used his brains rather than try to outfight the titan at his own game.

Bolan still felt dizzy when alarm Klaxon blared wildly. Puffs of cold, compressed air burst from fire-control nozzles in the ceiling, but then, only a deadly hiss followed, no streams of flame retardant leaving the ceiling.

The soldier reached into his combat vest rapidly, instincts informing him of the invisible threat pouring out of the deadly nozzles. His hands tingled and were going numb almost immediately; tearing open the pouch containing his atropine syringe felt like a Herculean task. The hiss of escaping nerve gas and the howling Klaxon whirled in the Executioner's consciousness as he wrestled his syringe free. The pouch was kept close to his centerline, so that all he had to do was bat off the cap on the atropine with his unresponsive left hand and spear the needle into his chest.

He collapsed to his knees, struggling with the cap, his fine motor control disappearing under the nerve gas assault. In the distance, screams of the dying mixed with the alarm's shrieks. Flashing red lights colored his dimming vision to the color of hell when he finally wrenched the tip of the atropine syringe. Bolan pushed the needle deep into his chest and squeezed with all of his might, feeling the shock of the drug fighting off the paralyzing effects of the lethal gas. The Executioner trembled and collapsed, his strength disappearing in a final flash as chemicals fought it out in his bloodstream, but he never lost consciousness.

It felt like an eternity before he could move, but the chronometer on his wrist told him it had only been a mere five minutes. Pulling the syringe from his chest, he discarded it.

The Engineers had gone to extreme measures to eliminate the Executioner, but failed. He staggered to his feet and limped toward the control room.

He had to inform Stony Man Farm of the desperate measures the ENT were willing to go to, to ensure their victory.

JACK GRIMALDI WIPED his brow as he looked through the control room. It reminded him of Stony Man's Computer Room, thousands of miles away, while Busiek and his battered Green Berets worked feverishly to connect their satellite communications to the computer network.

A patrol of two Special Forces sergeants returned to the control room, looking haggard. "No remaining pockets of resistance, Captain."

"Good job," Busiek said.

Grimaldi took a deep breath, then regarded the screens on the wall. An electronics intelligence sergeant had temporarily disconnected the facility from contact with the rest of the COG network. It was a precaution when an initial examination had shown multiple methods of base sterilization, from explosives to nerve gas. The Green Berets quickly shut down links to the outside world to prevent a self-destruct signal to penetrate the base.

"We're hooked up to the antenna," the electronic specialist said.

"Time to call home," Busiek told Grimaldi.

"Thanks. You guys are faster than Ma Bell," Grimaldi quipped. He picked up the phone and dialed the Farm. The phone's internal encryption circuits scrambled the call to discourage tracing and snooping. He'd have to be fast, however, because a previous cyberspace encounter between the Farm and the Engineers had unleashed bugs into Stony Man's nerve center.

"Jack?" Barbara Price asked on the other end of the several thousand mile link.

"We've got the Pakistan base, Barb," Grimaldi told her. "No losses, but we have wounded."

"Good work," Price said. "Striker just got in contact with us before you connected to us. He said that the Engineers might try to destroy the base by remote control."

"Luckily, the Green Berets with me recognized multiple self-destruct mechanisms built into the base," Grimaldi replied. "They've got us locked off from outside interference."

"Which means we can't plumb their systems, either," Price replied.

"Unless you have a tech support team in the region to keep the base's computers safe from ENT attack," Grimaldi replied.

"Not right now," Price told him. "The most we can give is a force to secure the base, and transport out for the more seriously wounded."

"How soon will they be here?" Grimaldi asked.

"Give it a half hour," Price said.

"We can hold out that long."

Price paused for a moment. "What's the status on the drones?"

"They were in the process of finalization for launch," Grimaldi answered. "Their propellers were replaced with ramjets, and they hadn't set up their payloads yet. We've been looking, but there are no warheads in the facility."

"And with loss of contact," Price began, "the Engineers know they'll have to use another launchpad for their missiles."

"Where?" Grimaldi asked.

"That's the big question," Price admitted. "I just hope the other teams can find out where."

CHAPTER THIRTEEN

T.J. Hawkins lowered his binoculars as he looked at the Israeli border. Barbed wire and protective emplacements were everywhere.

"Tell me again how we're going to get past all that security?" Hawkins asked.

"The old-fashioned way," David McCarter replied.

"I was afraid you'd say that," Hawkins said. "You know, if we got help from the Mossad, we'd be able to keep our gear."

"That would only slow us down and compromise the operation," Gary Manning countered. He'd just finished digging a six-foot hole for their battle gear and Calvin James tossed him a load-bearing vest. Rafael Encizo had stripped ammunition out of magazines and was burying it elsewhere. Separating the weapons from their magazines and their ammunition made it difficult for anyone who stumbled onto one of their salvage piles to have access to useful equipment. Bullets buried naked and unpackaged in soil would be too exposed to the elements to be reliable. Magazines were disassembled, their springs and followers stripped out and tossed in with the bullets, leaving the mag tubes as useless aluminum canisters.

James and Manning had disassembled the rifles and submachine guns, smashing the bolts with rocks to further render them useless. Phoenix Force regretted damaging perfectly good weapons, but they didn't want terrorists to stumble across a stash of high-tech firearms. The only guns that they had left were their personal backup pistols and their Glock 34s, with attendant gun lights on under mounted rails. Hawkins managed to find empty spaces in the vehicle's frame to put the handguns and spare ammunition. The usual hiding spots would be searched thoroughly by Israeli border guards, but Hawkins and McCarter knew all the potential spots on the vehicle where security would look. They improvised and managed to find places for ten combat pistols. Unfortunately, in the pickup, there was no room for their longer weapons, so their dismantling and sterilization was a necessity.

McCarter wasn't concerned by the momentary setback. It wasn't the first time that Phoenix Force had penetrated a hostile border without the benefit of packs loaded with equipment. The only things that Phoenix Force retained from their penetration into Lebanon, other than the intelligence they'd acquired, were common street clothes bought in a market and the pickup itself. He looked over the vehicle, making certain nothing remained that could identify the team, or make them appear as weapon-smuggling foreign agents, which was a good trick, because that was exactly what they were.

"Okay, Cal, Rafe, take the truck," McCarter said. "T.J., head to the pedestrian checkpoint to the north. Gary and I will take it to the south. If the Engineers have people inside Israeli border security, or are monitoring it, they'll be looking for all of us to cross at the same point."

"As it is, they might recognize the brown people crossing," Encizo mentioned.

"That's why Calvin's driving you. Your complexion makes you local enough to raise suspicions that you're a Palestinian, minus the semitic features," Manning stated. "But, sorry about this, Cal, having a black man drive you in will lower suspicions."

"Ain't too many brothers in the Lebanese 'hood," James quipped.

"The roughing up we've taken over the past day or so should give us credibility when we say that we're reporters who got in over our head and lost our equipment," Encizo added.

"Be careful, guys," James called, pulling away.

The men of Phoenix Force separated and made their way to the next leg of their mission when they saw the distant forms hanging in the sky. It was an optical illusion, however. The reality was that the forms were descending upon the border at over 150 miles an hour.

Unarmed, the Stony Man warriors could only watch as the Predators swooped down for their brutal air strike on the checkpoints.

HERMANN SCHWARZ STUDIED the screen of his combat PDA as the Task Force-160 Black Hawk carried them out of the Darien at high speed. The UH-60 Black Hawk was one of the fastest combat helicopters in military service, and loaded down with only Able Team and Susana Arquillo, the bird managed a few more miles an hour than if it had a full complement of troops. For all the velocity with which the chopper raced toward the JUNGLAS forward base in the Colombian countryside, Schwarz's brain spun faster, going over the data he'd managed to compress into the pocket computer.

"Something up?" Blancanales asked.

"I was looking at the log of transmissions out of the COG facility," Schwarz responded. "There are a few signals that are disturbing. I worked out a map of where the Darien base was transmitting to."

He turned the screen to show Blancanales.

"So they were communicating with someone to the north," Blancanales said. "Cuba?"

"It's a possibility, but I doubt it," Schwarz answered. "Aside from Gitmo, there aren't many cold-war era operations in Cuba that Castro wasn't all over like ugly."

"According to Barb, Striker tracked down one of the operations to a facility in the Georgian Republic," Blancanales said.

"Gadgets thinks that we might be looking at enemies hiding on U.S. soil." Carl Lyons spoke up. "A COG facility that slipped through the cracks, and probably has enough firepower to nuke the planet all by itself."

"And in all likelihood, it would be like cracking open NORAD mountain," Schwarz added.

"We've practiced for that eventuality," Blancanales stated.

"Yeah, but that's with Bear and the others preventing nuclear missile launch. All the Engineers have to do is open the garage door and let the nuke-tipped pigeons fly," Lyons countered. He looked at Arquillo.

"Hell, in the time I've known you three, I wouldn't doubt you'd be the ones who'd get the 9-1-1 if bad guys took over NORAD," Arquillo stated. "But that doesn't give me anything as to who you really are."

The helicopter veered suddenly and dropped altitude, skimming low over the treetops, and Lyons knew instantly why. "Oh fuck."

Blancanales and Schwarz looked out the window, seeing an armed Predator drone slicing across the starboard of the Black Hawk. Looking out the port windows, they saw its twin. The door gunners swung into action, strafing long bursts from their machine guns, the UAVs swerving to avoid taking fire.

Lyons slammed a magazine into his SIG and opened a window. "Take them down!"

Blancanales led one of the Predators as it pushed hard to keep up with the Black Hawk. It had almost swung into position where it could rake the helicopter when Pol held down the trigger on his assault rifle. The nose cowling ruptured under multiple hits, but the Predator was unphased, swooping away to get a better angle on its target. Unfortunately for the drone, in its spiraling escape, it had been flushed into the firing arc of one of the door gunners. The XM-134 buzzed violently, its six barrels tearing off slugs at 3000 rounds per minute, splitting the air with the sound of ripping canvas magnified a thousandfold. The unmanned vehicle burst apart under the heavy-caliber onslaught.

The armored shell of the Black Hawk sparked and sang under the second drone's assault. The chopper suddenly climbed, nose pointing straight up as the Predator continued on past below. As the helicopter rose, Able Team, Arquillo and the door gunners spotted more of the unmanned aircraft closing in on them.

"I'm calling for COIN fighters," the pilot shouted. "But hang on, we're going full evasive."

Lyons's left forearm bulged and rippled as he held on to a handhold, his right hand guiding the SIG 551 through the window and popping rounds into the aerial hunters. "Anything in the air besides these bastards?"

"Lucked out. We've got Broncos coming back from a fire-support mission," the pilot responded. "They're two minutes away."

Schwarz's feet slipped from under him as the Black Hawk banked violently to avoid a blast of enemy fire. "It's going to be a long two minutes."

"Just let's make sure these fuckers don't hassle us for two minutes!" Arquillo snapped. She emptied a magazine at a drone, clipping its wing. The Predator slowed, falling behind the faster, more maneuverable helicopter, but against multiple aerial opponents, cutting the bird off at the pass, the pilots were doing everything they could to keep the UAVs from hitting them. Escape would require being an easy target for too long. An unguided rocket passed close under the belly of the Black Hawk, its smoking trail testimony to how closely Able Team and the crew had avoided death.

The minigun on the starboard side ripped out another metal-chewing burst, but the Predator juked out of the path of the stream, suffering only minor damage. In the meantime, its under-wing-mounted M240s clawed violently at the Black Hawk. The door gunner returned fire, hosing the enemy drone with his minigun when an artillery rocket cut loose. The gunner swung the multibarreled weapon toward the puff of smoke, and the sheet of XM-134 fire detonated the rocket yards short of the Black Hawk's shell. Unfortunately, the force of the explosion was powerful enough to launch shrapnel through his window. The gunner grunted as a shard of metal punched through his shoulder and dropped him to the floor of the helicopter.

"Pol!" Lyons shouted.

"I've got him," Blancanales answered, moving to the wounded man's aid. Lyons slung his SIG 551 and grabbed the controls of the XM-134. He lacked the heavy protective armor of the door gunner, but the minigun was far more likely to take out an enemy Predator drone than his small-caliber assault rifle.

Lyons swiveled the flesh-shredder and triggered it, the six-barreled monster roaring with unmatched fury as it split the UAV down the center. A line of tracers mixed in with the conventional ammunition produced an almost liquid stream of blazing red fire that poured into the enemy craft. The armored helicopter jerked under another assault, but the pilot was good enough to minimize the machine gun damage. However, the airman was more concerned with keeping out of the path of unguided rockets that ripped from launch canisters. The other door gunner knocked a third of the sharklike sky drones out of the sky before the Black Hawk shook. The starboard side of the helicopter was engulfed in smoke, the pilot barely saving everyone by tilting the ship enough to turn a direct hit into a glancing graze from an artillery rocket. The missile tumbled crazily past the Black Hawk before it speared into the ground at an angle that set off its impact fuse.

As it was, the cabin was thick and hazy with rocket exhaust, the remaining door gunner clawing at scorched features as superhot gases burned his skin. Even though the door gunner wore protective vests and helmets, over the top of the miniguns, they were still close to the windows, and superheated exhaust gases generated only inches from the skin of the helicopter proved devastating. Able Team and Arquillo had jerked far enough from the windows, protecting their faces, but by the time the burning cloud reached them, it was only uncomfortable warmth, not burning smoke. As it was, the cabin was thick with choking smoke. Despite the fumes, Schwarz took over the other XM-134 and continued to pump out harrying bursts against their attackers.

Another explosion rocked the Black Hawk, and the co-pilot let out a cry of pain.

"Pete took shrapnel from a near hit through his leg," Jenkins, the pilot, called back. "I'm keeping us in the air, but we're not going to last long."

Lyons didn't acknowledge the grim news. He targeted another Predator and hosed it. The UAV corkscrewed to get out of the way, but it took a couple of bullets in its engine cowling, slowing. "Look for an opening and go for it!"

With only two pursuers operating at full speed and agility, the pilot had more of a chance to leave the drones behind.

The Black Hawk spun off and hit the full throttle, pushing closer to 200 miles per hour, outstripping the Predators for a moment. On the straightaway, the helicopter had a better speed than the two unmanned vehicles, at least according to the raw specifications. Unfortunately, the more sedate pace of the drones suddenly picked up. As one, the twin crafts pivoted and raced faster.

"Improved engines," Schwarz growled. He tried to get a better firing arc on the enemy craft, but the two missiles were dead on their tail. Forward-pointing weapon pods opened up, ripping across the Black Hawk, keeping the Able Team electronics genius from leaning out and engaging them with his rifle. Bullets sparked and ricocheted against the helicopter's armored hull.

Lyons cursed as a stream of enemy bullets smashed the barrel mechanisms of his minigun, rendering the XM-134 useless. "Go low and continue evasive! They're faster than they should be!"

Jenkins wove and pushed the bird lower to the ground. The Predators swooped past, having easily 50 mph on the helicopter. They parted paths, but came in on the side where they'd targeted Lyons's minigun. The Able Team leader and Arquillo shoved their SIG 551s out the windows and opened fire, but the Predators swooped in close, moving too fast to be easily targeted by the assault rifles. The 5.56 mm NATO rounds they put out didn't have the same authority as the heavier guns of the Black Hawk or the M-240 wing mounts on the Predators. So even if they hit, the bullets would only cause minor cosmetic damage.

An artillery rocket lashed close to the TF-160 helicopter, and the pilot banked hard to pull it out of the shock wave. At the low altitude, they were within range to be buffeted by the explosive missiles and Schwarz grunted as Lyons stumbled into him.

"Those Broncos better get here fast," Lyons growled. "You okay?"

"You ain't heavy, you're my brother," Schwarz replied, shoving him off. "They're taking advantage of the blind spots we've got open."

"We're down to one minigun," Blancanales said. The door gunner with the scalded face had grabbed an MP-5 from the weapons locker, but the short-range 9 mm machine pistol was equally as helpless against the enemy drones. It was all up to Jenkins. So far, he'd kept the Black Hawk

ahead of the heavier weaponry of the Predators. A 70 mm
artillery rocket would destroy the aircraft with a direct
hit. The shell of the transport helicopter was invulnerable
to 7.62 mm machine gun fire, and the rotors could take
direct hits from 23 mm explosive shells.

But Jenkins's luck couldn't last forever. An artillery
rocket swooped through the rotor diameter. While the warhead's impact fuse missed the wide dish of spinning blades,
the titanium and fiberglass blade of one rotor smashed
through the center of the missile. Impact with the rocket
bent and deformed the rotor blade, and the Black Hawk
lurched violently.

"Hang on!" the pilot roared as the chopper spun crazily
in the air. He struggled to maintain control of the bird. It
still had all four rotors, but one blade was damaged, ruin-
ing the aerodynamics of the spinning lift-surface. Robbed
of agility, the helicopter was suddenly vulnerable. The
Predators swung out slowly, with lazy confidence.

Miles away, the enemy operators had to have taken a
moment to gloat over their impending victory.

Lyons could feel his stomach sink and he jammed his
SIG carbine through the window, emptying his last magazine at it, vowing not to accept death quietly.

One of the Predators broke apart under a hail of high-
powered machine-gun bullets, crumpled remains raining
to the forest canopy below. The other Predator jerked and
opened fire, spraying bullets and artillery rockets at the two
OV-10 Broncos that came onto the scene at nearly 300
mph. Wing pod-mounted miniguns on the forward observation craft ripped out streaming columns of tracer-illumi-
nated flame, sawing the remaining craft into confetti with
a combined assault.

"Black Hawk, are you in need of assistance?" one of the Bronco pilots called.

"We can limp back to base," Jenkins stated. "but we'll need an escort."

"We've got our eyes open for you, pal," the other Bronco pilot called. "Anyone hit on board?"

Lyons looked over the others and gave Jenkins a thumbs-up.

"Two with shrapnel injuries, and one with minor burns on his face," the TF-160 pilot announced.

"Medics will be there to take care of them," the Bronco pilot promised.

"Thanks," Jenkins said.

He turned to Able Team. "When we touch down, there'll be a military Lear-class jet to take you north. Those drones might be fast…"

"Considering they were reverse-engineered into cruise missiles, it could get really bad," Lyons replied. "But I doubt our enemies will try again."

"Good luck," Jenkins offered.

Lyons nodded. "Thanks. We'll need it."

IT WAS EITHER THE UNLUCKIEST day of Corporal Keith Bohr's life to be on guard detail at the Israeli-Lebanese border when the mysterious assault drones came out of the sky, spitting machine-gun bullets and artillery rockets, or fortune smiled upon him in the form of the men of Phoenix Force.

It had been a standard, quiet afternoon on the border, checking refugees for smuggled weapons or drugs coming out of Lebanon. His M-16 hung on its sling across his stomach. It would be an hour before children, schooled across the border, would be coming back, and the traffic had thinned out when he heard the strumming drone of propeller-driven engines. Bohr looked up to see the darts swoop out of the sky. Curiosity gripped him at their sudden appearance when a pickup truck blazed up to the border gate at full speed, hitting the brakes and skidding out in a cloud of dust.

"Down!" a man with a British accent commanded, leaping out of the bed of the truck.

Lean and fox-faced, David McCarter grabbed Bohr and his partner Yuri and threw them to the ground instants before slashing fingers of automatic fire clawed the earth where they'd stood an instant before. McCarter had his Browning Hi-Power out, but he knew that there was no way he could hit an object that high up and far away, skimming through the air at 150 mph.

The gatehouse disappeared in a flash of thunder as eight pounds of explosives on a 70 mm dart smashed into it. The shock wave rippled across McCarter's back, and out of the corner of his eye he could see Gary Manning brace himself against the concussion. With the strength of an ox, he rode out the thunderclap and continued forward.

"Who…What?" Bohr was lost and confused. He was a border guard and while he might have been prepared for an assault by enemy mortar positions, snipers or other grounded troops, the sleek aerial drones were akin to an alien invasion.

"Keep your head down," McCarter told him. Manning reached the wreckage of the gatehouse and cut to a machine gun mounted on a jeep. Since the Predator operators hadn't seen anyone at the vehicle, they only wrecked it with bursts of M-240 fire, saving artillery rockets for bigger targets. Holes had been blown in the fence, and what few pedestrians who had been waiting to cross between the countries had scattered at the first rip of machine-gun fire. At all of the border checkpoints for a five-mile stretch, Predators swooped down with brutal vengeance.

McCarter opened fire with his Browning, ripped from its hiding space in the pickup. When Phoenix Force recognized the drones and their intent, they knew that the advantages of smuggling pistols into Israel were outstripped by the need for firepower to assist the Israeli defenders suddenly under assault. Betraying their armament was a small price to pay if it could help them protect lives.

Manning leaped into the back of the jeep and swung the mounted MAG-58, the European version of the M-240, to face the attacking Predator. The big Canadian was taking a big risk as he swept a storm of 7.62 mm NATO rounds across the Predator. Jerking from newly gained damage, the drone somersaulted in the air to dive on the lone machine gunner in the jeep.

McCarter looked to see Bohr roll over and shoulder his rifle, adding to Manning's defense against the diving drone. The Canadian dropped behind the bulk of the jeep and tucked in tightly as an artillery rocket speared into the earth five yards in front of the vehicle. Thousands of pounds of steel shielded the brawny Phoenix Force sniper from mortal harm, though the concussive overpressure rocked his senses to near uselessness. The Predator zoomed over the heads of the other Stony Man warriors and the border guards, not twenty feet above them and charging at lightning speed. McCarter cut loose with his pistol, the others firing after the speeding missile. The drone, already weakened by Manning's machine-gun assault, shuddered as more bullets slammed into it at point-blank range. Mc-

Carter didn't know whose shots did the trick, but the UAV tilted out of control and dug into a crater bisecting the border fence. Fiberglass split and splintered into thousands of pieces on impact.

McCarter raced to Manning's side. "You okay?"

"I screamed to equalize the pressure in my head," Manning answered.

The Briton looked at the mounted machine gun, but the artillery rocket warhead had bent it into a lump of modern industrial art.

"Clear the area!" Calvin James ordered at the top of his lungs.

Bohr got to his feet, then reached out for Yuri who eyed the five strangers.

"What the hell is going on?" Bohr asked.

"World War Three," Rafael Encizo told him. "And on the other side of this border is the answer."

Yuri looked at the Cuban, distrustful. "How are we supposed to justify letting armed foreigners across the border?"

"Because we're friends of Israel, and we're trying to prevent an Apocalypse." T.J. Hawkins spoke up.

Bohr looked at the American for a moment. "Yuri, how many hillbillies do you know who are Palestinian terrorists?"

Yuri looked at Hawkins. "And his gang did help protect us."

"We can talk all day, but the other drone operators noticed we took out one of their own," Encizo mentioned. "Clear the target area."

"Let them through," Bohr said. "If we get into trouble because of these guys, I'll take all the heat."

"Thanks," James said.

"It's your ass," Yuri warned.

"At least I still have an ass to put on the line, thanks to them," Bohr returned.

Bohr and Yuri joined the men of Phoenix Force as they raced to the Israeli side of the border, losing themselves in the streets of the border settlement before the Predators could seek them out.

CHAPTER FOURTEEN

"These people lead charmed lives," Cortez said grimly. "They survived Predator assaults, a mechanized division and in one case, even nerve gas."

"We did use chemical agents in Syria, and almost did the same in Israel," Ling replied.

"They'd have to be foolish not to have atropine injectors on hand in case of chemical attack," Kovak agreed.

Cortez smashed his fist into the table. "That doesn't matter! What matters is that we still have enemies hounding at our heels!"

"If they knew who they could trust," Kovak interrupted. "Then they would have made their way into Israel under official escort. And there's been nothing in channels about that."

"But our scorching of the border checkpoints ended up only giving them an opportunity to slip past," Cortez growled. "They even shot down one of our Predators, then ran like hell. By the time we caught a glimpse of them in that shantytown at the border, Israeli jets mopped up the rest."

"You knew the dangers of operating in Israel. We're nothing if not efficient," Kovak said.

Asid Rabbani, a Palestinian at the conference table, grimaced. "Your people have gotten sloppy of late, Jew."

Cortez's glare froze the Palestinian in a heartbeat. "I will truck no petty differences in this facility, Asid. Our peoples have failed, collapsed under their own rot."

Rabbani swallowed. "I'm sorry, Kovak."

"I understand your frustration," Kovak returned. "We'll make things better, after the cull."

"Unless," another man, an African named Abbas Gidorran, interjected. "Unless they can track us down, even here."

"This is one of the most secure places on the planet," Ling explained. "It would take an asteroid the size of Alaska landing right on top of this mountain range to damage us."

"Nothing manmade is impregnable," René Dujon, a Frenchman, replied.

"So, one little display of competence among our enemy, and you're looking to surrender?" Kovak asked. He turned to Cortez. "And you spoke so highly of how we were going to cleanse the world. We're in full force here. There is an army, literally, down here. And we have enough firepower to break California off into the Pacific Ocean without even trying. Why are you so uptight?"

Cortez glared at Kovak for a moment, then looked at the table where he'd cracked the veneer. "I do not suffer incompetence well."

"Our failures have not been through incompetence," Ling pitched in. "Our failures have been because of a synergy of skill, audacity and pure toughness on the part of our foes."

"We also have a clue as to what to expect," Lee Shinjoh, a Japanese man, added. "If not exact capabilities, then we have rough numbers of enemy forces we're facing. And we can gauge just what exact level of opposition they can bring against us by examining their previous encounters with us."

Cortez nodded. "Then we prepare for their coming. They're too smart and too skilled to leave us at large and unhindered."

"We do have a saving grace," Dujon said. "Our operations are spread across the globe, and they cannot concentrate their abilities in any one area. While the former Soviet republics have been calmed, and the Pakistani crisis downgraded, there is still China and the South American conflicts, and the Middle East is no closer to peace than it was twenty years ago."

"Things are not as bad as they seem," Lee Takarov, their Russian recruit, added. "At least for our plan. And even if Pakistan isn't the origin of a nuclear first strike, they will take advantage when our Chinese contingent unload on New Delhi, right, Ling?"

"Absolutely," Ling replied.

"We continue," Cortez answered. "I just want to know which of you has the willingness to see this through."

Everyone at the conference table agreed.

"Kharpal, send a message to your Taliban friends in Pakistan. I want increased violence to keep the government on its toes and to draw off attention from the Americans supporting them," Cortez ordered. "Ling, you know the drill for China."

The Chinese man smiled, tight-lipped like a satisfied toad.

Cortez had stirred up the nest, looking to see if his pawns would be shaken. While some hostilities floated to the surface, the conspirators maintained their cool. Their will was strong enough to carry them through the threat of the American teams harassing them.

Now all he needed was to pull the trigger on worldwide suicide. When humanity's teeming herds were thinned, control would be in his grasp.

But he needed one last piece of the puzzle to ensure total victory. It was a simple tool he'd had one of Ling's hackers compose for him, a time-delayed data packet. The hacker performed her task with subtlety and eloquence. The woman was expendable, so Cortez gave her a drugged drink. Intoxicated by spiked alcohol, she was easily given a lethal overdose of Ecstasy.

Cortez knew about the covert agency that sponsored field operatives, or at least knew enough to realize that it could be his cat's paw.

As he built up his multinational conglomerate of terrorists, rebels and anarchists, he knew that such men would be hard to keep on a short leash. He trusted a few of them, but others he knew would try to split off into their own post-apocalyptic feudal kingdoms. He'd searched long and hard for the kind of opposition that could clean out his organization of potential deadwood, leaving him with a lean, hungry conquering army.

Cortez was familiar with the three commandos dogging him. He'd been a part of an organization that had been decimated by the American juggernauts. The commandos had been instrumental in clearing out the upper echelons of the organization allowing Cortez to rise within the ranks. The five-man team remained a mystery to him. As did the lone man.

But the exact details of their identities didn't matter. All that was important was that Cortez could manipulate them into action against the Engineers, to provide a tempering furnace to forge the organization into a stronger tool and to pare away whatever deadweight existed.

Then, when civilization crumbled, there would be one gleaming spire of strength rising from the rubble to begin a new golden age, starting with his rule.

All it would take was the data packet, and the tireless skills of the cybernetics team to discover and decipher it. It would require a keen eye and a sharp mind to locate the information within, but anything that wasn't a challenge would be immediately suspect as bait for a trap. And that just wouldn't do.

SUSANA ARQUILLO JERKED awake. The wrinkles of Carl Lyons's shirt had left lines on her cheek where she'd fallen asleep on his shoulder, comforted by his nearness. Though she'd told herself that this was only a quick fling, something to work off tension, both stress and sexual, she'd grown comfortable with the man. When she'd learned that she was to accompany them back to the U.S., she was secretly happy. Practicality told her it was because her cover might have been compromised by working together with the trio of American commandos, and would have been recognized by the Engineers of the New Tomorrow. Staying with this team protected her from reprisals by whichever pawns the ENT could throw at her.

Lyons smiled at her as her brown eyes sleepily blinked, looking around the cabin. "Feeling better?"

"Yeah," Arquillo answered.

"It's almost time to land. Better put on your seat belt," Lyons told her.

She gave him a kiss on the cheek. "Thank you."

Arquillo buckled in and the plane landed at Holloman Air Force base. She kept an eye on the windows until the wheels touched the ground, concern hanging with her after their near death in the Black Hawk when Predator drones attacked the helicopter. The C-21A Lear jet, however, was a reliable and fast-moving ship, enabling the transport of personnel across long ranges. The hop from Colombia to New Mexico hadn't even begun to tax the 931-gallon fuel tanks of the sleek aircraft, and riding on 3,500 lbs of thrust from each of its turbofan engine pods, it skimmed along at 530 miles an hour, eighty percent of the speed of sound. Enemy drones would have a difficult time tracking the jet. Now, under the protective canopy of Holloman's defenses—ground based missile launchers and high-tech fighters—she felt a little safer.

"Forgot to tell everyone to put their trays in the upright position," the pilot confessed as he looked back from the cockpit.

"Somehow we survived," Blancanales joked in return. "Don't worry. We won't file any complaints with the airline."

"We won't? But what about those cake frequent-flier miles?" Schwarz quipped.

"Knock it off, Gadgets," Lyons grumbled, getting up. "Don't mind our buddy. When they dropped him on his head as a kid, he bounced like a superball, so we can't even claim brain damage for him."

"Seriously," Schwarz said, "thanks for a smooth flight."

Able Team and Arquillo disembarked and were greeted by driver and a jeep.

"Pickup for Steele, Lopez, Garcia and Brooks," the driver said.

"That's us," Lyons answered.

"I've got orders to take you to our communication center," the driver replied. "You're due for a conference."

The comm center was empty, but that didn't prevent Schwarz from running a top-to-bottom sweep for bugs left to spy on them, finding two actively transmitting, and hardwired bugs that, while they didn't transmit radio frequencies, did have their own unique electrical currents. He stripped them out, and finally proclaimed it safe to talk with the Farm.

"You sure it's safe for me to be here?" Arquillo asked.

"You've earned our trust," Lyons said. "And we won't be talking about anything that would give away our group."

Barbara Price appeared on the video monitor and directed her words to Arquillo. "We've made arrangements with Langley for you to be attached to our team. You won't be doing any further front-line operations, but you can serve in a support role."

"Ah, miss?" Arquillo asked.

"I'm not going to have you get in front of a bullet," Price told her. "But I don't want you to feel useless while we have you in our version of protective custody."

"It is my decision to risk my life, however."

Price nodded. "And it's my decision to keep you from getting in too far over your head. We're looking for the Alpha site where the Engineers are working from. Once the team finds it, the level of opposition will be almost insurmountable."

"Automated security systems with robotic turrets, nerve gas, and that's not counting an army," Lyons added.

Arquillo pursed her lips. She caught a momentary glimmer of softness in Lyons's eyes.

"Pol, Gadgets and I are old hands at cracking nuts like these," Lyons added. "And we've seen too many allies torn apart when we've come against heavily entrenched opposing forces."

The pain that flashed for a moment on his face spoke volumes. This had been the first hint of weakness in the man, but it was also a legitimate concern. Arquillo had been a DEA agent before she was in the CIA, so she had some self-defense training, but when it came to a full-force hard contact, she knew that she'd never be in the league of DEA's SWAT or the Special Forces soldiers who would back up field agents. She didn't have the level of training and experience to take on a whole enemy base. She'd carried fewer supplies and equipment in her vest than the others simply because she didn't have the same body mass as the three men. Trying to move in full combat kit, as she'd glimpsed in the lockers just off the communication center, would be like trying to do ballet with concrete blocks encasing her feet and hands. Even against the dozen ENT guards and their unskilled technician backup, she'd come close to buying it in battle several times. Against the main ENT headquarters, she'd simply be outclassed. It wasn't sexism on Lyons's or the mission controller's part. It was just cold, logical practicality.

"All right," Arquillo answered.

"Good. Otherwise I'd have to punch you out and handcuff you to the rafters to keep you safe," Lyons said, getting mean and lean again.

Arquillo grinned.

"How's the progress on finding the Alpha site?" Lyons asked.

"Slow. Hunt's running through records for all the old Continuity of Government installations, but there's a lot of garbage data," Price said.

Lyons nodded. "If anyone can find that needle in the haystack, Hunt was born to do it."

"I know," Price returned. "And we've got transportation on standby to get you there."

"What about the other fronts?" Lyons asked.

Price sighed. "I've sent Striker and Jack to hook up with a Chinese contact. David and the boys are in the dragon's mouth."

Lyons nodded. "So a few problems have been resolved?"

Price shook her head. "Not completely. You know how the eastern former Russian states are. Pakistan's still hopping mad, but we've got our diplomats massaging egos over Kashmir."

"All things considered, I'd rather be in a firefight than have to stroke off a cranky politician," Arquillo murmured. She paused and saw Gadgets grinning at her.

"Don't worry, Susana," Schwarz consoled her. "Easy targets like that, I'm too classy to razz you on."

Arquillo sighed. "Which means he's saving it to bust your chops, Carl."

Schwarz winced, and Blancanales chuckled. "She got you there, Gadgets."

"Get some sleep and some food. It could be a long wait," Price interjected into the team banter. "And when we find 'em, you'll need to move fast."

"Right," Lyons said. "Able Team over and out."

Price's face disappeared from the monitor.

PHOENIX FORCE SET UP SHOP in a hovel in an Arab neighborhood. The conditions were cramped.

"Compared to this dump, the Zodiac felt like a ninety-foot yacht," McCarter grumbled.

"I don't know," Encizo replied. "This would count as a penthouse suite with bedrooms for twenty back in Cuba."

"Definitely feels like my old crib back in the projects," James countered.

"You'd think the leader of the team wouldn't join in on the stand-up comedy," Hawkins complained.

"Now, T.J., just because you left your sense of humor in your other BDU pants," Manning interrupted. "Let them de-stress."

"How do you slough off stress?" Hawkins asked.

"Unless David's driving or flying, I don't experience stress," Manning admitted.

Hawkins grinned. "Well, we at least have the base of operations set up now. Who's going out for the guns?"

"David and I," Manning told him. "Our Arabic's the best of the group."

McCarter nodded in agreement. "You stay back here. Yours is passable, but if we get nicked, it falls back to you three."

"Works for me," Hawkins answered. "I know we'll be stuck with AKs anyhow."

"Is that a bad thing?" McCarter asked. "I used to swear by them when this team first hobbled together."

"Yeah, but you like your guns like your broads...old," Hawkins countered.

"I prefer the term proved and reliable," McCarter countered. "A college cheerleader doesn't know how to throw a pot noodle on the stove and put a damp rag on your head when you're under the weather."

Hawkins grinned, then got back in contact with the Farm to apprise Price of the situation.

CHAPTER FIFTEEN

Huntington Wethers looked at the screen, his face an impassive mask. `

"Something's wrong?" Carmen Delahunt asked.

"I found an old record of Continuity of Government facilities, dated from the late 1960s," Wethers stated. "From what I've located in the database, it is as complete a listing of facilities as I've encountered. Other records had been located and compromised by hackers, presumably working for the Engineers to cover their tracks."

"So, it's good news," Delahunt declared, looking at the screen. "Or is it?"

Wethers nodded grimly. "Considering the timing, I am skeptical of the sudden discovery of this content."

"You've been scanning data for hours, Hunt," Delahunt told him. "I just started my shift. Let me sniff around to see if it's bullshit or not. You might have just lucked out and found the Golden Egg."

"If I did, I'm suspicious at the placement of the nest, and wish to count my fingers after touching said egg," Wethers replied.

Delahunt trusted her partner's instincts. If he felt it was foul information, a potential trap for Stony Man's cybernetics crew, then she'd have to be careful. Embedded viruses and logic bombs had been sown throughout the computer systems that the Farm had connected with, programs that were the equivalent of poison pills for any hacker's system, left behind to render deeper investigation useless. Over the past few days, Delahunt had had to shut down two of their servers because of corrupted data. Total isolation, cleaning and rebooting had been required.

Wethers rose from his seat and exited Computer Room, heading for the staff lounge.

In the meantime, Delahunt was combing through the data file. She picked up the phone and got Barbara Price's voice mail. Price was busy, burning up the lines coordinating various intelligence agencies. So far, in the wake of Bolan's and Grimaldi's activities in the former Soviet Union and Pakistan, the CIA and NSA were able to come up with evidence for various hostile governments to realize that their enemies were not pounding at the gates to incite war.

Delahunt didn't envy the President. Pakistan and Azerbaijan were throwing fits as Muslim extremists were spurred to violent uprising. The timing was too convenient for it to be anything other than the Engineers at work. When their main bases had been compromised, the ENT fell back to civil unrest, obviously relying on them to keep tensions percolating in the background until they picked the proper moment to unleash their final assault. Considering the stockpile of supplies Bolan had discovered, it didn't take much for Delahunt to imagine that nothing less than a nuclear holocaust was the ultimate goal of the Engineers.

Secured away in covert bunkers, the ENT would bide its time as nuclear weapons flew and nations exhausted their armies in petty conflicts. Since the Continuity of Government facilities were specifically designed to provide a staging area for the United States government to rise from the ashes to reunify a disaster-blasted nation, the Engineers had been clever in their placement. Going through the Internet to delete all reference to their particular facilities had given them an invisible anonymity, to the point where they could have been hiding as close as Mount Weather, the most publicly "known" of all COG facilities. Mount Weather was even more heavily defended than NORAD's mountain, and contained massive computer mainframes and stockpiles that would preserve the branches of government from nearby Washington, D.C. Mount Weather was an active facility, a matter of public record, with a full staff and also tasked with updating the Federal Emergency Management Agency's records, everything from files on American citizens to contingency plans for man-made, natural and even cosmic level disasters. Mount Weather was the fallback for everything from nuclear world war to a 200-mile-wide asteroid crashing into Kansas.

Delahunt looked at the records that Wethers had discovered, and frowned. If Mount Weather was an indication of the kind of underground superfortress that the Engineers had managed to secure for themselves, then the field warriors of Stony Man Farm would be pressed to limits they'd rarely breached before. She wished that she could get Phoenix Force, Able Team and the Executioner together on one raid, but they were needed across the globe. Unfortunately, the planet-wide scale of the threat forced a dilution of Stony Man's forces. Backup from more conventional forces was out of the question. Two of the facilities were in other countries, and it had taken Barbara Price every ounce of pull she had to keep one Green Beret team under the enemy's radar in Pakistan. Besides, the People's Republic of China would be reluctant to work with U.S. forces, and Israel was a proud nation that had balked at interference before, prompting unsanctioned missions by Phoenix Force on previous occasions.

With the taps the Engineers had on the U.S. intelligence community, getting help at home for Able Team was also out of the question, if the Alpha site was even in the United States.

Delahunt looked over the source code for the data packet, going over it line by line, looking for what had set off Wethers's instincts. It was innocuous, except for one programming shortcut that she nearly missed. She took a closer look at it. Though the line was supposedly several decades old, Delahunt knew that the trick she was looking at in the source code was only a new development since the early nineties. It might have been a rewritten segment to restore the integrity of the data packet, perhaps copied from an earlier file, but it was out of place, a minor sliver of error that had given Wethers his pause.

The phone rang. It was Price.

"Barb, we've got a development down here. A listing of COG facilities," Delahunt said.

"So what's the problem?" Price asked.

"Hunt doesn't trust the source material, and I found a discrepancy in the data packet making up the file," Delahunt answered. "It couldn't have been written more than fifteen years ago, but all other indicators of its origin date back to the sixties."

"So it could be manufactured information, slipped in for what?" Price asked.

Delahunt stared at the screen for a moment. "Bait for a trap is one possibility. But I think it's more. This packet was hard to locate, buried so deeply, it would take a lot of brain power to dig up."

"Our specific form of brain power," Price concluded. "Like we've been strung along?"

"In every hard contact between our forces and theirs, we've managed to come out on top, but only barely," Delahunt mused. "It's almost as if we're passing an audition."

"In other words, if we couldn't figure out the clues, then we wouldn't have been useful to them," Price agreed. "We've been encountering all forms of small fry, but nothing deep and major. Everything we've eliminated has been peripheral and expendable bases, despite the secrecy and fire power of each."

"Why would they want us to locate them, though?" Delahunt asked.

"Recruitment to their cause? Or maybe we're going to be a control mechanism for the remainder of the organization," Price said. "After all, just because we can drop Able or Phoenix down their throats is no guarantee that we can derail their plan."

"It's been touch and go for a while," Delahunt replied. "But how would they know about us?"

"We don't exist in a void, Carmen. Just because you and the others scrub our involvement from recorded history doesn't dissolve rumors," Price stated. "Sure, we can pass things off to other agencies to credit them, but a brilliant and careful observer would be able to gather enough clues to figure out we at least exist."

"So it's not a direct attempt on the Farm itself. It's just trying to draw us out of the woodwork to perform some cleanup before the bosses take over." Delahunt thought out loud.

"An attack would clear out potential enemies," Price said. "People who would dissent against the main party line later on."

"Already planning his purges before he gains power?" Delahunt asked.

"Or providing a boogeyman to keep the team solid," Price replied. "After all, a common, almost untouchable enemy is good for bringing people together."

Delahunt smirked. It wasn't often that Price got political, but she had zero patience for political tomfoolery, such as when public figures created straw-man enemies like "vast right-wing conspiracies" or claiming that opposition to rights infringing policies "aided enemy terrorists." When it came down to it, Price, having operated in a world where she saw the outcome of such bogus manipulations, realized that in general, both political parties were populated by blood-sucking leeches who sowed fear and doubt as a means to maintain their power. The only real difference between politicians and the terrorist scum they crushed were the numbers of innocent bystanders ground into mulch as a result of their atrocities.

"Find an outside confirmation source on those facility locations that were knocked off the official map," Price ordered. "And see if we can get some kind of advance recon from the National Reconnaissance Office. The information is most likely legitimate, but I want us to be able to sidestep any traps the enemy leave behind."

"I'll keep it on the QT. The Engineers might be using our assaults to be the starting gun for their dash to the goal."

"Good thinking," Price returned.

Delahunt set to work.

HITTING THE STREETS, it didn't take long for McCarter and Manning to find their pigeon. He was a young Arab boy in his late teens. He was tall and reedy, with bony elbows that poked out from his sports jersey, making him look like a doe-eyed scarecrow. With his shirt hanging almost as low as a skirt, and a nervous, jerky gait, he took a puff on a cigarette, holding in the smoke for just a little too long.

"Hashish," Manning said softly.

McCarter nodded. "Where there's drugs, there's guns."

"And dopers have the money to spend on better quality gear," Manning added.

"Shall we?" McCarter asked.

"He's all yours," the Canadian said.

McCarter walked briskly past the youth, bumping shoulders with him and nearly knocking him off balance.

"Hey!" the young Arab snapped. His hand tugged at his dresslike sports jersey and McCarter stopped, giving him a hard glare, but not hard enough to spook the kid into running. The plan was to get him on their side, not start a gunfight or a chase.

Manning slipped up behind the kid and wrapped his hands around sticklike biceps. With a simple shrug, the Arab teenager was lifted from his feet and pressed face first against the wall.

"No PLO, no PLO," the youth cried in Arabic.

McCarter leaned in close, then pressed the muzzle of his

Browning into the kid's belly, hissing in Arabic. "We don't care if you're Yassar Arafat Junior."

"Oh no," the kid murmured.

"Relax," Manning cooed in his ear. "We don't want trouble with you. We just want to know where you get your product."

Big brown eyes widened even further. "No I don't deal hashish I just smoke it to take care of—"

The sharp front sight of McCarter's pistol dug into his belly, making him quiet down.

"Where?" McCarter asked.

A tear crawled from the corner of the kid's eye. Manning plucked the youth's handgun, a Beretta, from under the tentlike jersey, and slipped it into his pocket. "Tell us what we want, and we'll go away."

The kid gave up an address. McCarter patted him on the cheek. "That wasn't so hard, was it? Now run home."

"Here," Manning said. "T.J. was right about you liking old guns."

McCarter looked at the piece. It was a nickel-plated Beretta 1934, one of the most successful pocket pistols in the world, only outmatched by the Walther PPK on name recognition. It was as reliable as a fork, and nearly as simple in construction. The Briton smiled and tucked it in his back pocket. "Thanks."

The hash house wasn't far away, and confined to an apartment on the second floor. Manning knocked on the door with all the authority he could muster, calling out in Arabic. On the other side of the door, it had to have sounded as though someone had taken a jackhammer to it. He stepped out of the way an instant before the response, a hail of autofire, ripped through the door.

"They're no angels," McCarter announced, and he swung around the doorjamb and triggered his Browning the moment the front sight crossed a rifle-wielding gunman. Two shots punched into the hash dealer's center of mass, piercing his heart and hurling him back to the floor. "Stop wasting our ammo!"

Another of the gunmen swiveled at the shouting Briton, triggering a burst that missed as McCarter ducked behind cover. Manning popped out and cut loose with his Glock, chopping down the rifleman.

The doorway was clear and the Phoenix Force pair moved in swiftly. McCarter picked up the rifles and wrapped them in a loose-woven rug. Manning scanned for more threats, G-34 tracking. "Naturally, they don't have spare ammunition on them."

McCarter shrugged. "They'll have more elsewhere."

"True," Manning replied. He saw movement and tossed the bundle toward it. There was a howl of shock and automatic fire burned into the wall.

The Briton swung around and aimed at the panicked gunman. "Throw it down now!" he commanded in Arabic.

The hash house survivor threw his rifle away as if it were burning his fingers. "Don't shoot!"

McCarter came into the open and held the hash dealer under the gun. Manning retrieved the discarded rifles quickly.

"Got spare ammo for these?" McCarter asked. "And any more weapons in the house?"

The drug dealer pointed, shakily, toward the kitchen cupboard. "Don't kill me."

Manning opened the door and gave a low whistle. "Where'd you get all the hardware?"

McCarter glanced back to see what Manning meant and saw a stack of collapsing stock Colt Commandos, as well as bandoleers of spare ammunition.

"The men you killed ambushed an IDF patrol," the hash man said. "They brought them back here to sell."

"How many do they have?" McCarter asked Manning in English.

"Six," Manning replied. "And judging by the mix and wrappings, he isn't lying."

McCarter leaned in close to the cowering dealer. "The authorities will be here soon enough, with all this noise going on. I suggest you give them all the information they want, otherwise they'll get right nasty with you."

The Arab nodded, terrified. "I wanted nothing to do with messing with the Israelis. I just deal hash."

Manning had found a large gym bag and he stuffed the collapsible assault rifles into it, taking all of the ammunition. They left one of the smaller M-16s behind, as evidence of the dead gunners' wrongdoing. McCarter used a cable tie to secure the hash dealer to the stove's frame, and the Phoenix Force pair exited the apartment.

"Lucky break," McCarter noted.

"Kept guns out of the hands of the bad guys, took down a hash dealer and brought some ambushers to justice," Manning stated. "All in all, a pretty good day."

"We've still got the end of the world to prevent," McCarter told him.

"Anyone ever tell you that you're a buzz kill?" the Canadian asked.

"Anyone ever tell you you've been hanging around Gadgets too much?" McCarter countered.

The pair was half way down the block when jeeps full

of Israeli paramilitary police showed up, Uzis and Colt Commandos bristling.

Knowing that the hash dealer was in safe hands, Manning and McCarter took their gear and headed back to their base of operations.

WHILE PHOENIX FORCE WAS LEFT scrounging for weapons, Carl Lyons and his team were overlooking the care package from the Farm — Nomex jumpsuits and armored load-bearing vests, fitted specifically for each of them, as well as new weapons and gear. There was a suit and armored vest for Susana Arquillo, just in case.

The Farm had been certain that a full-out assault inside the Alpha site would trigger the Engineers' end game. Lyons and the team had no reason to disagree, so stealth would be the order of the game in this infiltration. The choice for the operation was the UMP-45 submachine gun. An improvement on the original Heckler & Koch MP-5, but chambered for the powerful .45 ACP cartridge, the UMPs were ideal for close quarters conflict and with their suppressors, they were among the quietest submachine guns ever built, thanks to the naturally subsonic velocity of the cartridge. Backing them up were their Kissinger-tuned 1911s, also equipped with suppressors. Stealth was needed, and to maintain that stealth, Able Team would need to stop their adversaries in the quickest possible time. Few handgun rounds accomplished that task faster than the .45, and few suffered as little when put through a "silencer."

"Well, we won't be undergunned," Lyons said after running a quick field-strip on his UMP. "Just outnumbered."

"You know what I hate about you, Carl?" Schwarz asked.

"My eternally sunny optimism?" Lyons suggested.

"Well, now it's you stepping on my punch lines," Gadgets commented.

Lyons grinned. "We've got time for you to come up with some new jokes, smart-ass."

"I've not begun to crack wise," Schwarz countered. He checked his PDA, slipping in flash memory cards with programming installed. "Though right now, I want to make certain that we can crack their mainframe defense when we penetrate the Alpha site."

"Then we can shut down their launch programming before they know we're in there," Blancanales said, hope coloring his words.

"I've been working on the transmission power feeds on the combat PDA," Schwarz replied. "We find a hookup for it, we can use the PDA as a link to Stony Man's network."

"Which will free us up for combat operations," Lyons concluded.

"As long as we can protect or secrete the linkage away," Schwarz said.

"Not as simple as it sounds," Lyons growled. "So what else is new?"

Blancanales held up an atropine injector. "Apparently Striker ran afoul of some bad stuff when he hit the base in Georgia."

"I detected a 'sanitization' sequence for the facility we were in, too," Schwarz said. "The mercenaries and the technicians were too interested in surviving to consider it, but according to Striker, someone connected to the Georgian base's security network and activated the nerve gas."

"Pretty ruthless." Arquillo spoke up, her voice low and trembling. "Nerve gas?"

"You push the syringe into your chest and squeeze when you start to feel your motor control failing," Blancanales told her. He showed her the atropine dose.

"That looks like it hurts," Arquillo mentioned.

"Well, it is supposed to punch through the chest wall," Blancanales explained.

Lyons shrugged. "If it's a choice between a sore chest and a lethal case of paralysis, you're going to quibble?"

Arquillo shook her head. "No way. This is just… A few years ago, the worst chemicals I ran into were highly flammable stuff used to cook cocaine. And there's not a big market for weapons of mass destruction in Central America. It's mostly Communists, rifles and drugs."

"The times, they are a'changin'," Schwarz quipped.

Arquillo puffed out her cheeks in a sigh of disbelief. She stepped away from them and looked over the Nomex jumpsuit meant for her as it hung on a hanger in a locker. "Your people had my size?"

"Just in case," Blancanales informed her, "we needed an extra pair of hands."

"We're going to be outnumbered," Lyons said, "but, my theory is, nut up and do it."

"I'm glad that shoe company went with the other slogan," Arquillo replied.

Lyons grinned. "Right. Anyways, if you're scared, there's nothing wrong with that. Fear makes adrenaline. Adrenaline makes you stronger and faster."

"So you're really scaredy-cat man?" Arquillo prodded.

"Yeah. Unfortunately, marketing nixed that idea in the bud," Lyons answered. "Just like the shoe ad."

"Oh, well," the CIA agent replied. She smiled to the others. "Just say the word. I might not be a human bulldozer like your teammate here, but another pair of eyes and another trigger-finger definitely could help."

"It couldn't hurt," Schwarz said. "But we've got everything under control. I've got an idea."

"Is it something as cheap as that one guy we chased?" Lyons asked. "Had that awesome truck bomb set to take us out, and he hits a pothole. Boom."

"How anticlimactic," Arquillo interjected. "And the government called you in on this goon?"

"We sort of just stumbled into it," Lyons admitted. "He was rooting around our organization. He wanted to blow our cover, but frankly, for someone who was supposedly such a fearsome threat he just went all stupid."

"If a pothole could take him out, he was beyond stupid," Arquillo commented. "You have a pothole, Gadgets?"

"I said I had an idea. Not a lame ending," Schwarz countered. "We're going to have to work for this, but trust me, we'll have it down."

"I knew you'd figure something out," Lyons said. "Let's hear it."

Schwarz began to outline the knockout punch against the Engineers.

CHAPTER SIXTEEN

Mei Anna looked at the tall man stepping off the passenger jet and her suspicions had been confirmed. Frank Juniper was as much a journalist as she was a sumo wrestler. She maintained her cool in approaching "Juniper" though. She'd wait until he got to the hotel, not drawing the attention of PRC intelligence or the Engineers of the New Tomorrow. She'd had a few close calls in recent days, picking up enemy tails. She knew the local PRC agents who followed her, and she'd behaved for them, but the Engineers' thugs were a whole new story.

Only her cunning had kept her out of a gunfight so far. She'd prefer to keep the violence to a minimum, but when she saw the big American, she knew that avoiding conflict was out the window. Bolan didn't look like a man who resorted to brute force to solve every problem, but he had the look of a man who wasn't called in to handle jaywalkers and overdue library books. His gait and the hardness in his eyes betrayed an intimate familiarity with violence, though there was none in his demeanor. He moved with fluid grace and subtle efficiency, like a trained martial artist, gliding from foot to foot as he walked. He glanced at her and locked his cold blue eyes with hers for a moment.

Mei Anna was impressed. She'd been keeping a low, stealthy profile, and yet he picked her up in a heartbeat. He winked and continued on his way. The acknowledgment was nothing that would be caught by anyone not in eye contact with him, but enough to let her know that he knew she was there. Mei looked around the airport. She saw one tail, but nobody who had been interested in Juniper so far. That didn't mean that there wouldn't be trouble out front.

Mei was conscious of the weight of her pistol hidden under the silken drape of her jacket. It was only a .22-caliber Walther, but it was small enough to hide on her slender frame, and it fit her hand like a glove. The P-22 had ten shots, and a threaded barrel in case it needed to be silenced. With a round in the chamber and the hammer down, all it took was a pull of the trigger to get into action. Mei had fallen for the little Walther, which was more accurate and easier to shoot than any other pistol she'd ever carried. What the .22 lacked in power, the Walther's accuracy and reliability made up for, able to put bullets into eye sockets at ten yards with a flash of the sights.

She had a second one secreted in her purse, plus extra magazines for the twin .22s. If real conflict were to start, she wasn't going to stick around and duke it out armed with the tiny little Walthers, but the P-22s would give her the opportunity to gain something larger and more powerful, or to run like hell.

Mei stepped out of the airport and into the bustle of people. Bolan was visible in the crowd, towering above the others, so keeping track of him wouldn't be difficult. Unfortunately, Mei had to keep her senses alert for those who blended easily into the population of Asians mulling about. Not all of them were ethnic Chinese. Japanese, Korean and Thai businessmen mixed in with the crowds, each with their own set of features as blatantly recognizable to Mei's Chinese eyes as the difference between an Englishman and an Italian would be to an American.

A wave of paranoia threatened to wash Mei away, but she kept her focus, skimming and weaving through the throng of people. She didn't focus long on any one person, a quick glance and evaluation, and on to the next. A pair of cold, hard, black ice eyes popped up in her peripheral vision, and she turned to see their owner walking with determination toward Bolan. Mei paused. For a moment she wondered if it was anger on the man's face, but she recognized only malice, not fury.

She fell into step behind the hard-eyed stalker, alert for any others in party with the man. He wasn't with SAD, the Communist Chinese intelligence agency. She knew them, and this man was Korean, which would be akin to a Klansman hiring a black man to be his spy and assassin. The racial enmity between Cantonese and Mandarin Chinese was tense enough, and in Asia, bigotry against other nations was virulent and hostile, especially on an institutional level. SAD wouldn't send a Korean into action on their own soil. Mei was glad that Ambassador Chong had established a rapport with the People's Republic's State Department at a level that transcended old bigotries. It wasn't perfect, and there was still distrust, but the North Korean statesman had defused much of Beijing's enmity toward Taiwan.

A lean, suntanned Thai came into Mei's line of sight, staying away from her target, but the two men acknowledged each other. The Thai's scowl was also one of cold determination. Mei kept her own features cool and placid, letting people move intermittently between herself and the tall, reedy Thai man. She avoided direct eye contact with him, not wanting to alert the Engineers' second stalker. Mei wondered how many more were in the crowd.

The hunters paused as Bolan clambered into a taxi that drove off.

"Well, he's out of the fire," Mei said softly to herself.

She turned to find herself a cab when she bumped into something the size and mass of a brick wall. Mei staggered back, trying to recover her balance when the slab of humanity she'd bounced off of reached out and took her by the wrist.

"Naughty little girl," he murmured. Mei was shocked to see a sumo wrestler in the crowd. She hadn't noticed him, or even sensed when he'd snuck up on her, but with the speed he snared her wrist, it was obvious that his bulk was carried lightly, with quickness and agility.

Mei reached for the Walther in her jacket when the man's other paw clamped it to her side, digging the polymer grip hard into her hip. Trapped, she struggled to twist free, but it was like trying to wrench herself out of hardened concrete. There was no sign of stress or strain on the Japanese man's face as he pinned her hands together. All that showed was a tight-lipped, turned-up smile of bemusement as she fought to break free.

"If you make a scene, I will twist your head off and peel it like an orange, little rag doll," the man warned in a soft, soothing coo.

More men surrounded Mei and she realized that her cover was blown by the Engineers. All this time trying to elude them, they finally caught her out in the open. It was a risk, making an early contact with McCarter's ally, but she wouldn't give these men any information. She sneered, but relaxed. Both Walthers and her spare ammunition were plucked from their hiding places, stuffed into pockets.

The Engineers had to have had eight men staking out the airport. Maybe even more, perhaps shadowing Bolan to his destination. The group obscured her from view as they headed, en masse, toward a bus. The sumo pushed her ahead of him, and Mei stumbled on the steps from the casual shove he gave her. Mei was convinced that somewhere in the giant's family tree, Godzilla had to have had a branch, because he felt strong enough to use Toyota pickups as free weights.

Mei glared at him, but looked for a seat. The Korean she'd first spotted took her by the arm and forced her onto a seat, then scrunched against her, her own Walther pressed into her ribs.

"You make a fuss, and nobody will hear a thing," the Korean growled. "We'll throw you in a ditch outside of town. That is…after we finish with you."

Mei nodded. She wasn't certain that taking a few bullets through the heart wouldn't be preferable to whatever tortures these men were willing to engage in. After all, they bandied around the threat of rape right off the bat.

Of course, just talking about it meant that she'd have an opportunity to escape. Professionals didn't engage in gang-rape, so she wouldn't be torn apart by them. Then, if these weren't professionals, just disillusioned psychotics with a modicum of skill, they'd give her an opportunity to squirm to freedom anyhow.

"If you think you can outsmart us," the Japanese giant said, looking at her, "you're wrong. I picked up some thugs to flesh out my team, and I won't be afraid to turn them loose on you. But if you try something tricky... You've got sharp eyes on you."

Mei frowned. Which were the professionals and which were the amateurs was uncertain. Anticipating what an amateur might do was almost impossible, and a professional usually had more than one contingency for an escape attempt. She was locked between a rock and a hard place.

Getting out of this mess would take a little outside help, but even if she couldn't get that, she'd figure some way to throw a wrench into the works. Unfortunately, it was starting to look like her best-case scenario to avoid torture was to die trying.

JIAHUA LOOKED OVER HER SHOULDER from the front seat of the taxicab and smiled mischievously. "Welcome to China, GI Joe."

"Nice to see you, too, Cello," Bolan replied. He opened a cardboard box set in the floorboards and was pleased to see that the Chinese operative had done well in picking up some items for him. Since he'd come in as a civilian, being armed would have been difficult. Bolan picked up one of the handguns in the box, keeping it low and out of sight, but he was able to examine it by feel.

"The new Beretta?" Bolan asked. The Px4 Storm was an evolution of an earlier handgun, the Cougar, replacing its aluminum frame with a reinforced polymer. Lighter, and more robust due to an enclosed slide, it was smaller than the U.S. Army's Beretta M-9, but with its adaptable grip frame, it could take the same magazines. He checked the control levers, and they went down, then sprung back up, indicating that it was converted to decock only, not a dedicated safety catch. Only by stripping all of the ammunition out of it would the pistol be rendered sterile. One pull of the trigger would be all that was needed to get it into action.

"I couldn't get you your usual gear, so I improvised. You don't mind, do you?" Jiahua asked.

"Nope," Bolan said. He looked at the magazines that came with the gun. One was a flush-fitting seventeen-rounder, but the other three were 20-shot sticks. Certainly it would be enough firepower. "No suppressor for it, but it's not much of a handicap."

Bolan racked the slide, decocked the hammer with the control lever and tucked the weapon into his waistband. The other gun was larger and heavier. For a moment, he thought it was a standard Colt .45, but when he turned it over, he saw the fat hole in the grip. "NP-30 high-capacity."

"I couldn't swing a .357 or a .44. Figured you might make up for the lack of punch with more .45s," Jiahua said. The taxi's progress was slow and laborious through the clotted traffic around the terminal, but that gave Jiahua time to scope out any stalkers on the road. Her eyes moved to the side mirror and she saw a throng of men push through the crowd and onto a bus. A flash of a familiar face chilled her blood. "Oh, shit."

"What's wrong?" Bolan asked as he loaded and tucked the big .45 away. He looked out of the corner of his eye and saw a hulking sumo wrestler climb onto the bus.

"We'd only made contact peripherally, but I recognize your other agent in the region," Jiahua told him. "She's been herded onto the bus."

Bolan frowned and settled down into his seat. "Anyone else watching us?"

"We've got a car stalled three lengths behind us. They

had an opportunity to pull around and get out of this mess, but they didn't take it," Jiahua explained.

The Executioner nodded. "I'm going to need a distraction so the tails don't blindside me."

"How much of one?" Jiahua asked.

"We'll need the taxi to get us out of here," Bolan explained. "And get out of the snarl."

Jiahua nodded. "I'll figure something out. When do you need the distraction?"

"Now," Bolan said.

The taxi screeched to a halt and one of the cars behind it slammed into the rear fender. Fortunately the old cab was built like a tank, while the cheap auto behind it suffered a crumpled hood. The Chinese woman got out and began cursing in Mandarin, as other cars swerved and a huge choke point formed in the road. Bolan slipped out of the cab, the frame of a Volkswagen van blocking the door he'd exited from the tail that Jiahua had indicated.

The Executioner scurried low and quick, weaving between cars. The bus that Mei Anna was on rolled onto the curb with every intent of driving on the sidewalk to get past the traffic jam. Bolan wasn't going to let a Stony Man ally be hauled away as long as he had breath in his lungs, so he circled around. He tore his knife out of its hiding place in the lining of his jacket and thumbed the release stud. Razor-sharp steel, actually a nonferrous alloy that wouldn't set off metal detectors, snapped out and the powerful retention spring held it in place as he jammed its wicked three and a half inches of blade into the bus's tire and slashed. Rubber parted and air sputtered out of the wounded inner tube.

Bolan jogged toward the back of the bus and sabotaged the rear tire as well. Another flick of the control stud on the switchblade, and the knife returned to resembling an innocuous black metal rectangle. He walked around the rear of the bus, the knife tucked into his palm. A couple of men came out of the doors to see what had happened to the tires. Staying in the blind spot at the rear corner of the bus, Bolan had the advantage, but if the Engineers had a savvy team working for them, they'd realize their sabotage in a heartbeat. The sight of Bolan walking past their windows would clue them in and endanger Mei.

Bolan didn't risk stooping below window level, in case the men looking over the damage turned to see him coming. He turned around the back, put his foot on the hood of an automobile behind it and reached up, hooking the roof of the bus. The driver of the car that he'd used as a booster honked and shouted angrily, but it was swallowed by the rest of the blaring horns and angry cries of drivers trying to find freedom. From up top, Bolan could see that the traffic jam caused by Jiahua had thinned the traffic on the other side of the taxi considerably.

For now, he concentrated on padding smoothly and softly on the roof of the bus, feet gliding rather than stepping firmly. He didn't have to skim on the roof of the bus too far — there was a hatch near the back big enough to get through. Bolan made certain that his shoulders would slip through the gap, then pulled another item from the lining of his jacket. It was a compact canister of OC gas. Again, its lack of ferrous materials made it invisible to metal detectors, but would have given him an advantage if he were caught, unarmed, at the airport. With a powerful stomp, he burst the hatch and threw the canister through the hole. The impact fuse, charged by hitting the safety switch on the container, jarred and detonated the container.

There were screams of pain and agony as the cloud suddenly expanded, and Bolan dropped through immediately after the muffled crump of the OC grenade's detonation, Beretta Storm in his fist. His lean frame slithered easily through the trapdoor, and he landed in the center of the aisle.

Choking, half-blinded gunmen staggered to their feet, the burning pain of capsicum extract inflaming the soft tissues of their sinuses and eyes, leaving them blind to the Executioner in their midst. Bolan got a quick visual of the bus's layout and where Mei Anna was seated, then moved toward her. He'd held his breath to spare his nasal membranes, but his eyes were already pouring tears down his cheeks. Where the men caught in the cloud were left blinded by their gushing eyes and ravaged sinus tissues, Bolan was used to the pain and able to focus. He blinked normally to wash the blur of tears away, not allowing the pain to slow him down.

Mei Anna was as afflicted by the tear gas as the gunmen holding her, but she at least had a focus to deal with. She was currently wrestling with an Asian man, twisting a small automatic pistol away from her. It cracked, and a .22-caliber slug punched into the window behind her head, spurring the Executioner to even faster action. He lashed out and grabbed a fistful of the Asian man's hair and yanked his head back. The gun in the Korean's hand strayed to point at the roof of the bus, another bullet triggering skyward.

Mei sensed that something was afoot when her wrestling partner jerked violently backward. Bolan chopped the butt of the Storm into the gunman's face, its plastic base plate having sufficient toughness to break the Korean's nose and split his forehead. The jolt of agony made the Asian buck, his neck popping before he went limp.

The Executioner didn't want to waste time to check if he was dead. "Mei, it's Juniper. Come with me."

He took her small hand in his, but she held back long enough to pry the Walther P-22 out of the Korean's numb fingers. She didn't want to go unarmed, and she'd gotten hold of the weapon without slowing them.

Bolan had taken three steps when a huge form lurched into the aisle.

"You're not going anywhere, little man," the sumo said. Though tears made his cheeks wet, the pain in his sensitive tissues hadn't appreciably slowed him.

Bolan brought up his Beretta, but the Japanese giant's hand flashed quickly, jarring the gun aside. The Executioner held his fire, not wanting his 9 mm bullet to go through the bus window and into the crowd. He let go of Mei Anna's hand and speared a knuckle punch into the sumo's solar plexus, but it felt as if he'd punched a section of sidewalk. The slab of abdominal muscles that wrapped his enemy's torso provided a cushion of protection against even Bolan's most powerful punches. The sumo drew a handgun from under his jacket, but Bolan grabbed the top of a seat to brace himself and launched a kick into the giant's jaw.

Neck muscles like rock kept the sumo's head from bouncing under the jarring impact, but his balance was lost as he staggered backward. Launching forward, using the seat as leverage, Bolan slammed into the unbalanced thug's chest with his shoulder. It moved him another step back, but a log of an arm crashed into the Executioner's shoulder blades, knocking the wind out of him.

"You're trying to knock me out?" the sumo asked with a chuckle.

"No," Bolan answered. He jammed the muzzle of the Beretta into his opponent's stomach and triggered the weapon into his entrails. The sumo's almond eyes widened in painful shock and he staggered back. "I was simply making sure you couldn't knock my gun away again."

The wounded ENT man clutched his shattered stomach, but still struggled to bring up his handgun. The Executioner leveled the Storm at the sumo's nose and pumped a 9 mm bullet deep into his brain.

Mei grabbed handful's of Bolan's jacket and rasped, "Go."

Bolan took that as his cue to continue toward the exit of the bus. Another gunman struggled to stop the soldier and his ally, but the Beretta barked again, coring out the thug's eye socket. Breathing through his mouth, he managed to hold off a wave of sinus agony for a moment more.

The gunfire inside had drawn the attention of the two who had exited to examine the slashed tires, and they were at the door. Bolan catapulted down the steps of the bus in a feet-first jump, catching the first of gunmen square in the chest, plowing him back to the street and over his partner. The three men collapsed into a heap, Bolan on top, and he stuffed the muzzle of the Beretta into the chest of the man he'd kicked. Three shots punched through the Asian's thoracic cavity and into the guy beneath him, killing them both. With the muzzle pressed to the man's chest, the sharp crack of the 9mm weapon was swallowed and muffled.

Mei Anna stumbled out of the bus, coughing and wheezing, blinking away her agony. Bolan tugged her down to her knees just before a spray of machine-pistol fire ripped at the side of the bus.

The tails obviously had decided to make their presence known, and they were armed to the teeth. Mei Anna, even though she had a gun in hand, was still blinded and stunned by the OC gas. When the rattle of automatic fire sounded, she pressed herself against a stalled car, using it for a shield. "Do we have a way out of this?"

"Taxi at the front of this snarl," Bolan answered. He used the hood of another car as cover and fired his Beretta at one of the SMG-armed gunmen. Two shots punched into the would-be killer's chest and threw him back onto his own vehicle's fender.

"The gunfight is going to draw unwanted attention," Mei said, trying to recover her faculties.

"We're almost out of here, come on," Bolan answered, taking her hand.

In a mad rush, the pair scurried toward the front of the traffic jam. Mei had the presence of mind to stoop behind the crouched Executioner, so the remaining gunman would have nothing to shoot at. Jiahua got back into her cab and revved the engine.

"Go, Cello!" Bolan ordered, pushing Mei into the back seat and diving in after her. The taxi roared to life and pulled away.

"Thanks for the rescue," Mei murmured. "I was so busy watching your back…"

"It's all right," Bolan told her. "You're alive."

Mei started to wipe her eyes with her sleeve, but Bolan stopped her.

"You'll only rub more OC into them, and that will hurt like hell," Bolan warned. "Cello, we need some place to rinse off this tear gas."

"You got it," Jiahua answered.

"You sure know how to make an entrance, Juniper," Mei muttered.

"This was just the opening round," Bolan told her. "And it'll only get harder."

CHAPTER SEVENTEEN

"How goes it?" Barbara Price asked, looking over Carmen Delahunt's shoulder as she tapped feverishly on her keyboard.

"The data packet seems genuine enough, especially going through Aaron's stored hard-disk information," Delahunt answered. "I've been picking it apart to see if there was anything inside of it which might be a logic bomb, but it's clean, and too small to hold infectious code."

"What about when Hunt discovered it?" Price asked. "He sifted through another database to find that data, which could have had tripwire alarms to inform the enemy of when we discovered it."

Delahunt nodded. "I looked into that, as well, but when Hunt came back after a quick nap, he told me that he made certain the node was isolated. No communications were sent out, and there was no active monitoring software in the area."

Price frowned as she looked at the screen. "I don't think they would have left this in place without some form of observation."

"That's what has us concerned," Wethers said, looking up from his screen. "Unfortunately, we're dealing with an ever-tightening timetable."

"Yeah. I heard about the violence at Beijing Capital International Airport," Price noted. "They almost anticipated Striker's infiltration of the country. Someone obviously has his photos."

"They were there," Delahunt said.

"They were there, but they didn't corner him," Price responded. "Unfortunately, he's not going to contact us for a while. Not with all the monitoring going on and Mack's history with SAD."

"Well, nothing on SAD's radar yet," Delahunt replied. "They're not looking for him."

"That's one small favor," Price responded. "Okay, I'm going to get Able Team in transit. We can't leave them sitting on their thumbs if we have a location for the Alpha site."

"You might tip off the enemy that we know where they are," Delahunt told her. "That is if they don't already know just by looking at this data packet."

"The old Heisenberg theory," Price said. "The act of observing data on the Web influences it."

"Not quite the Heisenberg uncertainty theory, Barb, but close enough in spirit," Delahunt replied. "Akira is skimming to see if anything had tracked out of our system to alert the Engineers. So far, we're secure on this end."

"Quantum physics never was my strong point," Price admitted. "I'm going to arrange transportation, but I know that Holloman is likely being watched closely, since that's where the Lear was scheduled to go after it left Colombia."

"Don't worry, Barb," Kurtzman cut in. "I'll shield off Air Force communications from the Engineers. We've studied their parasitic data tracking programs for long enough to give the USAF a form of immunization against prying eyes."

"Like inserting a dead virus into a person. You gave an inert code sample of the spy ware to the USAF system to digest and recognize," Price asked.

"Precisely. The Engineers might notice it and adapt, but hopefully we'll have a couple of hours' worth of a window to move Carl and the boys around the country," Kurtzman explained.

"Can you stretch it out? I'll need some lead time to get the guys in motion," Price said.

"I'll actively monitor and reinforce the USAF network then," Kurtzman said. "It'll take some work, but it's why you pay me the big money."

"We pay you?" Price quipped.

"Go play travel agent, Barb," Kurtzman grumbled.

Price grinned and made her arrangements.

WHEN SUSANA ARQUILLO WAS GIVEN the option of staying safe and sound among the security at Holloman AFB and joining Able Team en route to the Alpha site, she jumped at the chance to accompany them.

"We're heading to a place called Pollock Hill," Lyons said.

Schwarz smirked. "Probably named after the guy who wrote the article about Mount Weather."

Lyons quirked an eyebrow. "Some kind of conspiracy theory stuff?"

"Real thing. Not far from Stony Man there's a honking huge Continuity of Government facility designed to be the President's fallback point in the event of a planetary disaster," Schwarz said. "Of course, that's what it was back in the seventies. This guy, Richard Pollock, did a major article on the fallback site and its purposes, using congressional reports."

Lyons frowned. "And so, that forced the government to build another facility, since in writing that article, Pollock painted a big bull's-eye on top of the hideaway."

"That was sort of the idea," Schwarz answered. "But frankly, if you were going to hit Mount Weather, you'd have to use the kind of firepower that could crack the East Coast off the mainland and sink it into the Atlantic. We're talking major league firepower."

"So Pollock Hill, where is this place?" Arquillo asked.

"According to Carmen, it's in Utah," Lyons explained. "Green River."

"Green River?" Schwarz asked. "Hmm. Makes sense. For a while, there were rumors that it was the new Area 51."

"Rumors?" Arquillo inquired. "But those were disproved. The place is completely dead. The last time anything happened there was 1974. It's in 'caretaker status.' One of the foremost Area 51 conspiracy theorists went there and found no activity there."

Lyons tilted his head.

"Why do you think I paid attention to the UFO sightings in Panama?" Arquillo asked. "This kind of tinfoil hattery sometimes leads to real intelligence."

"Fair enough," Lyons said. He'd encountered threats from ninjas to the alleged "walking dead" as well as instances of shamanic magic. While they'd all resulted in some form of logical resolution, it still left Lyons's normal skepticism on hold while his curiosity got the better of him. "Actually, if the site looked dead when a supposed crackpot was walking all over it…"

"Denk is not a crackpot," Schwarz interjected. "He's a military observer who keeps an eye on aerospace designs tested at Groom Lake. But even so, that article was written in 1997."

"Descriptions and photographs of the Green River showed smashed antennes and power lines. Nothing usable remained," Arquillo countered.

"See, I knew it was a good idea to bring her along," Blancanales said.

Lyons cuffed his partner's shoulder playfully. "If anything, that makes the Utah Launch Center even more attractive. It's isolated, six miles from the nearest town, and large, 3600 acres."

"Plus, you're talking about an underground facility, Susana," Schwarz mentioned. "The bunker looked dead and all the surface buildings were boarded up, but Continuity of Government facilities have all forms of above-ground cover."

Arquillo thought about it. "Where does this information come from?"

"Our Cyberteam thinks that it was planted information," Lyons said.

"So it could just be a trap," Arquillo mused.

"Absolutely," Lyons returned.

Arquillo chewed her upper lip and nodded. "So even if it is a trap…"

"It doesn't mean anything more than new people to interrogate," Lyons concluded. "If life gives you lemons…"

"Make lemonade," Arquillo returned.

"No. Shoot the sucker giving you lemons and go buy a six-pack. I hate lemonade," Lyons answered.

Arquillo grinned. "Anyone ever tell you you're nuts?"

Lyons pretended to think about it for a moment. "Not in the past half hour. But let's get moving. The bad guys won't wait forever."

LING JON GRIMACED as he worked feverishly at his computer station. The rest of his crew were working hard at their stations, and the level of tension in the room was thick as fog when Cortez entered.

"What's wrong?" the Argentinian asked.

"We lost contact with Holloman Air Force base," Ling replied. "All of our taps just vaporized."

Cortez leaned over Ling's shoulder, staring at the screen. "It looks like not just Holloman."

"The whole of the United States Air Force computer and communication network has been shut down," Ling said. "We're trying to key through other sources, but our software keeps bouncing."

"They immunized against your worms," Cortez mused.

"Absolutely," Ling replied. "The damnedest thing is that we've got other agencies monitoring them, but suddenly, we've got to break encryption on their data coming out."

"What!" Cortez exclaimed. Alarm crossed his features.

"Someone just blinded us," Ling stated. "We're cut off from the rest of the world. Nothing's getting through to us."

"How long before we can clear this up?" Cortez asked.

"It'll only be a few hours," Ling said. "We've got our sensors operating on our facilities, and there's nothing coming in on us. In fact, Israel and China are crystal clear to us."

"They must be moving their people into position," Cortez muttered.

"Who?" Ling inquired.

"Blinding us to their movements, at least for now," Cortez explained. "Have a reception team waiting for them at Hill. Just in case they are on their way."

"Wouldn't that confirm any suspicions?" Ling asked. "And how the hell did they learn about the launch center's COG facility?"

Cortez looked askance to the Chinese hacker. "Perhaps old hard copy, or even stored data backups from before your cleanup."

Ling frowned. "It'd take a lot of effort to sift through paper files, and the old tape drives."

"They managed to throw down a scramble on the Web," Cortez reminded him.

"Yeah. And they also managed to keep off our radar, despite all of my hunting for them," Ling added. "Careful and thorough cuts both ways. A trace here or there must have gotten through, just like the knowledge we have on their action teams."

"We'll go to Orange Alert for now," Cortez explained. "If they do show up, they'll need some major firepower to cut through the facilities' protective shields."

"They got into the Darien headquarters," Ling said.

"But, the Darien headquarters had a mountaintop hangar facility for their Predator drones," Cortez said. "With radio IFF controls for the hangar entrance."

"While ours are hard-wired into the old missile launch silo," Ling replied.

"There's no way they could break through the silo doors without bringing tons of military equipment," Cortez said.

Ling didn't look entirely convinced, but Cortez didn't want the man cluing in to his plan for his intended cull of Engineers' leadership when their enemy made their attack.

"I'll put the Fire Raptors on fifteen-minute countdown," Ling told him.

Cortez smiled. When the enemy commandos made their move, it would ignite the end of the world. The Fire Raptors, Predator drones reverse-engineered back to its original cruise missile configuration with ramjet motors and nuclear warhead capability, would be almost unstoppable, moving at twice the speed of sound and each warhead carrying 15-kiloton charges. Granted, it was nothing in comparison to the megatonnage produced by a conventional ICBM, but 15 kilotons would smash a city the size of Denver or Phoenix into a wasteland, leaving thousands dead and ten times as many dying from radiation poisoning, starvation and exposure. With a flight of three hundred of the Fire Raptors set up, the Engineers had enough to lay waste to major population centers across the country.

A widespread nuclear assault would force the hand of the armed forces. Martial law would be implemented, but the survivors of the widespread nuclear assault would be far from helpless. Survivalists and rural populations would balk at a military takeover and fight back. Mayhem would engulf the United States. And when the Green River facility launched its attack, China and Meggido would get the signal to begin their attacks. A further seven hundred Fire Raptors were primed for the purposes of hitting major cities across Europe and Asia. It had taken a lot of work assembling so many, but Cortez had the time and the resources to build such a vast network. The U.S. government and the Red Chinese had also helped, keeping supplies of nuclear-tipped artillery shells in their Continuity of Government stockpiles. The Meggido base was a particular boon, its covert base being equipped with an arsenal of five hundred M-33 203 mm artillery shells. Capable of being launched from the 3AD M-110 Howitzer, the M-33 had a scalable yield from 1 to 20 kilotons, despite their late seventies lineage. In the event that the Soviet Union ever backed a Syrian play to invade Israel, the shells would have been used by covert American forces in the path of the invasion to render Israel's northern border an impassable zone of nuclear destruction. The nuclear warhead that destroyed Hiroshima only generated a yield of 15 kilotons, so the 20-kiloton shells would be enough to smash armored divisions into radioactive scrap metal.

The 203 mm warheads also could be broken down and fitted into the nose cones of the redesigned Predator UAV drones with minimal effort. The warheads were dialed up to their maximum yield for a linear plutonium implosion to release the maximum damage and radiation on detonation. Cities wouldn't be fused into bowls of glass, as if when an ICBM would hit, but the Fire Raptors would pop the illusory bubble of civilization in their nuclear blossoms.

"It's finally here," Ling said, interrupting Cortez's musings on the Engineers' lethal arsenal.

"What is?" Cortez asked. For a moment he wondered if the enemy had found their perimeter.

"The end of today, and the beginning of tomorrow," Ling reminded him. "What we've worked for…it's coming. We're almost ready to remake world."

Cortez nodded. "First we have to burn down the failure that is today. Stay ready for their incursion."

"Yes," Ling answered.

Cortez smiled. Ling was none the wiser. Then again, Cortez had been skillful in the drug overdose of the winsome young hacker he'd seduced. She died in relative peace, content in thinking she was being given a substantive reward.

THE THUMP OF A HIP-HOP background beat began to reverberate from Carmen Delahunt's monitor and Huntington Wethers walked over to it. "I didn't know you listened to this kind of garbage."

"I don't," Delahunt said. "It's a virus."

"It's a repeated verse, too," Akira Tokaido said. "It sounds familiar."

"I thought you were mostly into speed metal or punk or whatever?" Delahunt asked.

"Well, it popped up in the soundtrack of a video game I like," Tokaido admitted.

"He spends all his time looking at the screen for us, and when he gets some free time, what does he do?" Wethers asked. "He looks at more screens."

"If you fuck with me, it's a must that I fuck with you," Tokaido muttered.

"What?" Wethers asked, startled at his fellow hacker's vulgarity.

"The rap verse. That's the lyric," Tokaido stated. "Typical macho rapper posturing, threatening revenge for any wrongs against him."

"Whatever happened to the Sharks and the Jets?" Delahunt mused. "So, whoever programmed this data packet, they slipped it in? Why not do something more destructive to our computer system?"

Tokaido took a look at the code, scrutinizing it. "You missed this little bit."

"The subroutine, no. I noted that it was out of place,"

Delahunt stated. "They didn't use shortcuts like this when this packet was originally dated from."

"But the shortcut has a reference. It's a number generator that creates a binary version of a URL," Tokaido stated.

"I'm so used to base IP addresses, I wasn't thinking in binary," Delahunt murmured.

"We've all been overworked. I didn't think of that myself," Wethers admitted.

"That's why the Bear has all of us as a team. Four pairs of eyes are better at two when you're doing heavy code crunching," Tokaido admonished.

Wethers returned to his station and entered the number generation code into his keyboard. "Gah… Pop-up attack!"

Tokaido and Delahunt looked at Wethers's monitor as random Web sites appeared, flooding his screen. Wethers was ready to kill his station when Delahunt stopped him.

"There's the odd porn site, but a lot of these are just pure random sites," Delahunt noticed. Suddenly the music began on one of the pop-ups. Wethers stepped aside to let the quicker, more manic Tokaido onto his station. The young hacker's twitcher reflexes cut through the additional pop-ups, clearing them away with rapid-fire clicks of the mouse until the page putting out the rap song appeared at the front. Tokaido hit it as a favorite place before additional pop-ups appeared, then killed the Web browser cold in a few strokes.

"You got it?" Delahunt asked.

"Got it," Tokaido said. "Fastest fingers in the West."

Wethers smirked. "Fast is fine, but accuracy is final."

Tokaido restarted the browser and opened up the bookmarks menu, tracking down to the recently added page. The rap song appeared.

It was a free Web log, maintained by an attractive young Asian woman.

"Wow," Tokaido said. "Pretty nice."

"She's got a few media files in her folder after that tune," Delahunt noted. "What's the one marked Last Will?"

Tokaido opened it up and the pretty young girl appeared on the screen.

"If you're watching this, congratulations on being good enough to find this. It means that Cortez hasn't underestimated your abilities as hackers. It also means that the fucker killed me," the young woman stated. "And since he fucked with me, it's a must that I fuck with him."

Tokaido's brow furrowed. "Damn shame. He murdered this girl?"

"And hundreds more, Akira," Wethers stated.

"I'm putting a URL on this video file, which will take you to a holding site where I secreted construction plans, key codes and other information on the Utah launch center's Continuity of Government facility," the young woman continued on the screen. "No hidden codes in this one, but I'm certain you won't trust me. Just be quick about making sure it's clean. This guy Cortez is totally nucking futs, if you get my meaning. I've got everything I know about the Engineers in data packets on the site, behind secure encryptions. The code is also part of this video file."

The young woman frowned. "So, get this guy for me. Kill him dead. I didn't know what his and Ling's plans were when we started this. I thought it was some kind of grass-eating grassroots peacenik movement. Instead, Cortez wants the Apocalypse. Also, if you've found this, we're damn near the deadline for his global assault."

The video file ended, the built-in player freezing on a frame with the Web site and encryption key code.

"Well?" Tokaido asked. "Trust her? Or worry that this is another trap?"

"Akira, break it down for us. Be ruthless. The first sign of a booby trap, torch the site and hit us with a protective firewall," Delahunt said. "I'm waking up Bear. Hunt, get back to supporting the President's Chinese peace efforts."

"On it," Tokaido and Wethers said in unison, getting to work.

It was the first real sign of hope. Carmen Delahunt smiled as she went to Kurtzman's break room, realizing the truism of the old cliché.

Hell had no fury like a woman scorned. And in the case of this one hacker, the fury reached out from beyond the grave.

AMBASSADOR CHONG SIGHED as the Chinese premier shook his head.

"What's wrong now?" Chong asked.

"The party thinks that if we're going to sit by and do nothing in response to these attacks, we'll be seen as weak," the premier answered. "I'm trying to think of a way to placate them, but there's very little to go on."

"Doesn't the fact that we just received word of a nerve gas attack in a Taiwanese subway give them some pause?" Chong asked.

"I sympathize with the victims of terrorism, but one of our military vessels was destroyed," the premier replied. "A few dead and a couple hundred injured civilians are not going to satisfy the war hawks in my administration. They want decisive action."

"And decisive action is being taken," Chong said. "The SAD is receiving reports from my people about the third party involved in this conflict."

"Yes, the Engineers of the New Tomorrow. We've got sources inside of Pakistan reporting about the discovery of a base used for inciting a conflict over the Kashmir region," the premier replied. "A base that had originally been placed there by the United States. I have people who are telling me you've been in communication with the Americans."

"They don't want a war," Chong told him.

"No, of course not," the premier replied. "But most importantly, they want Taiwan to remain fragmented from Mainland China, instead of returning to us."

"You honestly don't believe that the U.S. is inciting violence between you and the Taiwanese, do you?" Chong pressed.

"I don't. But the voices of dissent are not so easily quieted in my party," the premier told him. "As it is, we had a recent terrorist incident at Beijing airport. My sources are of the opinion it was related to the arrival of an American operative. This man is known to us."

Chong shrugged. "And how many times has he appeared in China to bring terrorism to your shores?"

The premier pursed his lips. "He has been in conflict with the aims of the People's Republic."

"If he is who I think he is, he has been in conflict with operatives of my government, as well, but only in instances where we have acted aggressively toward the West or its allies," Chong admitted. "However, in a few instances, he has prevented my government from being taken over by even more aberrant parties and stopped illegal activities within our borders. I'm certain that the man has assisted the cause of justice in your nation, as well."

The premier nodded slowly, as if he were struggling to keep the truth from moving his head in an affirmative. The truth won out, even though the words were not voiced. "He has not brought harm to a citizen of the People's Republic who has not been involved in oppressive or illegal activities."

"He's here to help. Not hurt," Chong said.

"He and his allies have interfered with our efforts to reunify China before, though," the premier countered.

"China will always be here," Chong returned. "He is but one mortal man. In a hundred years, your nation will be unified, and he will be dust in the earth. Provided we do not engage in the kind of violence that shall turn us all to ashes."

The premier smiled. "Would that you were in charge of your nation. Your wisdom is great, despite your birthright."

Chong chuckled at the backhanded compliment. "We've got a lot of work to do. As does the American. Something tells me that this crisis will come to a head."

"Let us hope that when it is over, we will have time to bring more sense to our world," the premier replied.

"BARB'S STILL IFFY about this intel," T.J. Hawkins told David McCarter as he was working from contingency plans based on the layouts of the Pakistan and Darien sites. "But she gave it to us anyhow."

"What's her hesitation?" McCarter asked.

"The source might have been planted by an enemy operative to lead us into a trap," Hawkins explained.

"We deal with traps all the time," McCarter complained. "Hell, half the time my arse is the proverbial worm on the hook!"

"Well, they're still trying to determine why someone on their side would be anticipating our activities," Hawkins said.

"That's not difficult." Gary Manning spoke up. "We've been around enough that there are rumors about our existence."

"We've made enemies who remember us," McCarter said. "We've influenced the world subtly over the years."

"First time I've heard hosing down terrorists with a MAC-10 being called subtle, David," Manning quipped.

"As low profile as we try to be, we'll always leave footprints. On a couple of occasions, we've come across enemies who recognize us. Not that they could pick us out on the street and assassinate us. Bear and the others prevent that by cleaning the record of mentions of us. But in the field, we're as recognizable as Nessie poking her head out of the Loch. Our anonymity is as much a weapon as our freedom from the constraints of 'rules of engagement.'"

Hawkins nodded, then saw the screen on the sat-phone-linked laptop flash with an incoming message, which he checked.

"The information's source has checked out," Hawkins said. "Akira did some hacking into who created the packet. The info's good, but the reasons still seem kinky."

"How so?" McCarter asked.

"Seems the leader of the Engineers, some guy named Cortez, wanted us to come in and clean out the weak members of his herd," Hawkins explained. "So he got one of the Engineers' hackers to make a packet for our cyberteam to find. Then he killed her."

"And she left insurance behind that if she died, Cortez gets whacked, too," Manning mused.

"So he wanted us to knock the chaff off his new world order," McCarter said.

"He must have been relying on sheer numbers and fire-power to stop our teams cold," James figured.

"But our little hacker girl, she slipped us the answer sheets under the desk," Encizo added. "So now we have an advantage again."

"Not much of one. We still have to take down the Engineers, one enemy at a time," McCarter said. "Luckily, though, that happens to be our specialty."

CHAPTER EIGHTEEN

On arriving at Hill Air Force base, Able Team and Susana Arquillo were greeted by one of Hal Brognola's contacts who had shown up with a gunmetal-gray Chevy Suburban SUV. The big off-road vehicle screamed "unmarked police vehicle" with its paint job and dark-tinted glass.

Lyons rapped the fender and nodded. "Armor-plated, with solid rubber tires. Practically a tank."

"FBI SWAT office expects this back in one piece," the man stated.

"Come on. What can we do to a tank like this?" Lyons asked.

The man folded his arms. "If you're the super Feds I think you are, crush it like can."

Schwarz waved his hand before the man's face. "We are not the spooks you're thinking of."

"Right, Obi Wan. Oh, well. Mr. Brognola will know who to blame when a high-ticket SWAT vehicle ends up crushed into scrap metal."

Schwarz shrugged. "I tried."

The man grinned and got into a waiting car, driving off.

Lyons, Blancanales and Schwarz loaded their war bags into the SUV while Arquillo took the driver's seat. The armored vehicle would give the woman a measure of protection against all but artillery rockets, and the lady CIA agent would be able to pull Able Team out of the fire if the odds against them were too heavy.

"No built-in chain guns," Arquillo said, disappointment sounding.

"You were expecting those?" Lyons asked.

"Well, I've seen them around," Arquillo told him. She blushed. "And I'd seen a few movies with some really cool jeeps with guns."

Lyons shrugged. "I keep asking for one of those, too, but for some reason, they always turn a little pale at the thought of me with a minigun."

"No, really?" Arquillo asked in mock disbelief.

Lyons rolled his eyes. "The burdens I must bear."

"Poor you," Arquillo mockingly sympathized.

"Come on, we're loaded up," Lyons told her. "Roll out."

"Yes sir," Arquillo replied. Her hand went down to the folded-stocked Heckler & Koch UMP tucked beside her leg in the driver's seat well. Assured that it was still there, she gave Lyons a smile. "I have a bad feeling."

Lyons nodded, his humor vaporizing with her pronouncement. He looked back at Schwarz and Blancanales, who were getting their UMPs out, laying them in laps under towels, despite the tinted glass of the windows.

"You know if we get into a firefight…" Lyons began.

Arquillo nodded. "I won't stop and make us an easy target. I do have some offensive driving training from my time in the DEA."

"Good."

"I'll also duck any incoming bullets, if possible," Arquillo promised.

"Hopefully that'll be a good strategy," he replied.

Lyons gave her shoulder a gentle squeeze with one hand, gripping his UMP's handle with the other as the Suburban left Hill's gates.

THE GUN METAL GRAY Suburban SUV rolled along toward the town of Green River, an unassuming vehicle in off-road country, handling the less than fully upkept roads much more easily than the Mercedes handled the rain forest paths in the Darien. Carl Lyons had been distracted before by Arquillo's sensuality, but now his focus was entirely on threats. They had been ambushed too many times on this mission for him to lapse into complacency when the Engineers had been at their heels at every turn.

As they approached the outskirts of Green River, Arquillo slowed, looking at Lyons.

"Cut through the town and risk bystanders being hosed in the cross fire?" she inquired. "Or should we cut around the town and risk a more direct ambush?"

"You only die once," Lyons said. "It's how you die that matters. Let's cut around the town."

Arquillo nodded and turned to an off-road path. There was too much of a possibility that the ENT would make its move near the town, and given their goal of starting wars in which millions of civilians would be killed, there seemed to be nothing to ethically prevent an ambush that would destroy a small town and its residents. Maracaibo and the preempted attack on Israel were fresh reminders of that form of ruthlessness.

"I'm picking up a carrier wave," Schwarz called, jolting Lyons and sending his adrenaline into overdrive. "Off the road now!"

Arquillo swung the wheel rapidly when the windows were darkened by a thick and heavy cloud. Gravity shut off, seemingly for an eternity as the blast that threw up the cloud lifted the SUV like a toy, flipping it around. Indecipherable shouts struggled against the roar of remote-control road mines for attention in Lyons's mind as his hands grabbed for handholds. His seat belt tugged against his chest as his forward momentum pushed him against the nylon straps. Fingers closed around the seat and door handle, and he tried to turn his head. Out of the corner of his eye, he could see Arquillo howling, clutching the steering wheel in a white-knuckle death grip. The door on her side of the armored vehicle was missing, and a puff of dust obscured her partially.

She was screaming, which meant that she was in pain. Part of him, the one that cared for the feisty agent, ached in response to her agony, but the logical part of his mind countermanded his emotions. Dead people didn't feel pain.

The SUV slammed to a halt, and Lyons grunted as the seat belt snapped sharply across his torso. Even the thickness of his body armor couldn't prevent the feeling that he'd been whipped by steel cable, and his UMP hurtled violently into the windshield, cracking the bulletproof glass.

The roof of the armored vehicle held, despite the force of its mass and velocity against the immovable earth beneath it. The Suburban SUV continued to tumble and Lyons's shoulder slammed into the bullet-resistant passenger window. Only by tucking his chin against his chest on reflex did he spare himself a crippling head injury, and luckily thick sheets of heavy muscle protected his shoulder joint. The vehicle came to a halt on its remaining three wheels, lurching to one corner as the front left tire and axle were peened away from the rest of the SUV by the force of a land mine.

Lyons recovered his senses and pulled his combat knife, slashing the seat belt in two swift slices. He wasn't going to struggle with the release mechanism, and he reached over to cut Arquillo free from the driver's seat. She looked at him, brown eyes wide with pain and fear. Her left hand was a mangled stump, fingers torn away by a chunk of the dashboard propelled like a guillotine blade. Her face was splashed with blood as she came into his arms, loosened from the constraining seat belt. He tugged on her as he kicked open his door.

"Pol! Gadgets!" Lyons called.

"We're fine!" Blancanales answered. His forehead had been split open when his machine pistol had bounced against it in the tumbling vehicle. "I got your UMP…"

"Gadgets?" Lyons called.

"Right here," Schwarz answered, helping Lyons carry Arquillo. The blast had to have deadened Lyons's senses partially for him not to notice his friend. "Holy hell…"

Lyons blinked as he pulled Arquillo and Schwarz to the cover of the back of the SUV, using its massive bulk as a shield. While it was damaged, it would at least stop enemy bullets from a few angles. Blancanales knelt, watching their exposed angles, subgun at the ready. "What?"

"Pol! I'll take sentry. Get here *now*!" Schwarz called.

Lyons's vision cut back in and he could see Arquillo. Her right leg was splashed with blood, and her pretty face was reduced to two colors, red and pale. She clutched at his forearm with her right hand, her left dangling as a bloody stump. He looked for Arquillo's left leg, but it ended just below her knee, another victim of the land mine.

"Don't," Lyons growled. "Stay with us."

Blancanales, the team medic, wasted no time as he pulled a packet of gunpowder out and poured it onto the remains of Arquillo's left leg. With a touch of his lighter, the powder burned, cauterizing blood vessels and ruined flesh to stop massive hemorrhaging. "Susana, hang on."

Arquillo's lips moved, but nothing came out. Pain had subsided to shock, but that didn't diminish the strength in her fingers. She bit her lower lip and winced as Blancanales tied rubber tubing from his first-aid kit.

"Carl, focus!" Blancanales shouted. "Do you have a concussion?"

Lyons's senses were operating selectively, and it was likely the shock wave from the land mine blast had affected him. "I'm fine. Take care…"

The rattle of a burst of .45 ACP rounds from Schwarz's UMP interrupted Lyons's order. He reached for the machine pistol that Blancanales had laid down and looked at Arquillo. "Let go…please."

The wounded woman's fingers let go of his forearm for an instant, and he pulled free. Reassuringly, the hand clenched into a tight fist. Blancanales still had work to do to save her life, but she had strength left in her body.

"Keep fighting," Lyons grumbled as he shouldered his UMP-45. From the road, a jeep had come into view, bristling with gunmen. Schwarz's initial burst had brought them to a halt, but they simply took cover behind their vehicle. Accurate bursts from the electronics genius's weapon kept them from engaging the partially exposed members of Able Team.

Lyons gave a hand gesture to Schwarz that he was going to flank the enemy. Schwarz nodded and continued supplying suppressive fire to the enemy attackers while his teammate ran, crouched and nimble, in an arc around the mop-up squad. They had to have expected that Able Team would survive the road mine attack, given the previous track record. He was ten yards from the jeep when he felt a rifle round clip his Kevlar-protected ribs. Dropping to the ground, Lyons twisted and looked for the sniper.

It was a triple layer of assaults, and only the fact that Arquillo had turned their SUV at the last moment had given Able Team a position that was just out of the firing angle of the riflemen on the ridge. Unfortunately the killers were out of range for his .45-caliber machine pistol, so Lyons turned and opened up on the gunmen at the jeep, sweeping them from their exposed flank.

Two of the ENT gunmen jerked violently, perforated by heavy-caliber slugs that smashed bone and shoveled flesh aside like half-inch bulldozers. One of the surviving ambushers dived away from the others to avoid being cut down and lurched right into Schwarz's sights. Instants later he, too, was lying lifeless in a roadside ditch, torso smashed to a bloody pulp by a trio of 230-grain man-stoppers.

The last gunman swiveled and fired, trying to take out Lyons, but the Able Team leader laid prone, too small a target covered by a small rut. The ENT shooter's fire dug harmlessly into sand and dirt, while Lyons's return fire stitched the would-be killer from crotch to throat.

"Get behind cover!" Lyons shouted to Schwarz. "Snipers are on the ridge behind me!"

The Able Team commander got to his feet and darted toward the jeep. At first movement, an ENT sniper launched a bullet, but in the heartbeat between reaction and the bullet's landing, Lyons was out of the slug's path and it chewed uselessly into the ground. Lyons was intent on reaching the jeep and he paused long enough to grab one of the dead men's M-16s. He launched himself across the hood of the jeep in a somersault, collapsing behind the vehicle's fender as sniper fire chopped into the other side. One of the dead ENT soldiers had fallen across the shotgun seat, and Lyons reached back, grabbing the dead man's bandolier of M-16 ammo. With a sweep of his combat knife, the pouch belt came loose and he pulled it to cover. The corpse jerked on the strap, drawing sniper fire that puffed out spurts of blood from its chest, undoubtedly enemy shots intending to keep Lyons from spare ammunition.

He reloaded the M-16 and looked back. Schwarz and Blancanales had moved Arquillo around the frame of the shattered Suburban, giving themselves more cover from the riflemen on the ridge.

Lyons saw the snipers settling into new roosts on the ridge, and estimated their range. It was about four hundred yards from the jeep he'd taken cover behind, nearing the extreme range of the 5.56 mm rifle that he had. Not insurmountable, but he'd have to push his marksmanship skills to the limit. At that distance he'd have felt better equipped with a 7.62 mm rifle or a .30-06. Unfortunately the realities of combat prevented him from showing up to every battle with a golf bag loaded with assault rifles fitted for the task.

He didn't even have a scope for the M-16, which meant he'd have to do it the old-fashioned way. Lyons clicked the rear sight of his rifle to four hundred yards and fired a ranging shot, aiming for one of the gunmen on the ridge.

A miss as good as a mile, as he caught the spark of the

bullet against the boulder his target had hidden behind. Lyons adjusted, aiming higher and fired again, this time with the selector on full-auto. Recoil made the muzzle climb more, and he burned off half the magazine before the jeep took a dozen hits in rapid fire. When the smoke cleared, he spotted another sniper dragging a limp form behind cover. He'd either scored a lethal hit or he'd wounded his target enough to force his allies to come to the rescue.

Behind him something thudded loudly and Lyons looked back to see Schwarz lowering the smoking muzzle of the M-84 Carl Gustav recoilless rifle for Blancanales to reload.

They'd brought the shoulder-mounted weapon to give themselves a means of opening up heavy bulkheads easily, or to cause massive material destruction in a hangar full of drones. Not exactly the lightest of weapons, the M-84 launched 84 mm shells to ranges up to seven hundred yards, and was able to punch holes through twelve inches of armor plating with a direct hit. On the ridge, the FFV HE 441B round struck and produced a thunderclap that Lyons could hear four hundred yards away. The man dragging his injured or dead ally was standing one moment, and then was yanked over the top of the ridge as if he were a puppet on a string. Designed for antipersonnel purposes, the warhead was packed with eight hundred steel balls wrapped around a high-powered core charge. The impact fuse ruptured the shell and spread out a lethal sheet of death.

Lyons took aim again and looked for more targets when a rifle bullet smashed the fender next to him. He ducked back down as the sniper cut loose, trying to make up for the windage to tag Lyons's head. Heavy-caliber rounds punched into the metal of the vehicle's fender, and the ex-cop crawled in the sand, finding another vantage point to fire from. Doing so would ruin his calculations and he'd have to find the enemy's range again, but it was better to do more work than to end up with a .30 inch hole in his face and his brains torn out the back of his skull.

The Carl Gustav roared again, launching a second shell. The enemy sniper stopped shooting and Lyons looked for his hiding spot. The 84 mm shell struck, raising a cloud and producing a rapidly expanding ring cloud, a dome of death as eight hundred steel ball bearings rushed away from the detonation at lethal velocities. He spotted movement from the enemy sniper and with a fresh magazine, Lyons triggered the M-16, hosing the general area, holding high and to one side to take into account range and wind.

Lyons felt the shock wave of a bullet after it slammed into the dirt inches from his elbow and he jerked back to cover.

"He's too well entrenched," Schwarz said over Able Team's throat mike communicator. "I can't tag him with anything less than a direct hit."

The SUV's engine chugged, despite the bullets that had chewed its fender. Lyons looked back at Schwarz. "Catch the rifle. I've got a plan."

Lyons quickly wrapped the bandolier of spare magazines around the rifle stock. The burly ex-cop launched the M-16 like a spear and Schwarz jumped out to capture it, ducking back as the sniper tried to tag the suddenly moving electronics genius. Lyons threw himself behind the wheel, cranked the vehicle into gear and stomped on the gas, spinning it around, rear tails kicking up rooster tails of sand as he steered toward the sniper's roost. Holding down the gas and grinding the gears higher to pick up speed.

The rifleman on the ridge fired, trying to track the

speeding vehicle, and once or twice, Lyons heard the clang of a bullet on the frame of the SUV. He drove at a maddened pace, each bump jarring his spine as he taxed the four-wheeled drive's off-road capacity to its limits. However, if he babied the suspension, the jolting and jarring effect of the terrain would be lessened, giving the marksman trying to tag him a clear and easy shot. Still, Lyons wove and steered with masterful skill. If the Suburban SUV came to a halt by slamming bumper-first into a rut, if being hurled from the driver's seat didn't break his neck, then the sniper would put a bullet in him at the first instant.

A 7.62 mm slug smashed the dashboard, inches from the steering wheel, and Lyons gripped the wheel tighter, maintaining his weaving course across the desert toward the base of the hill. It seemed like forever to cross the hundreds of yards to the base of the ridge, but in truth, it was less than a minute, especially since he wasn't driving in a straight line. Behind him, Schwarz was firing his M-16, though the roar of the SUV drowned out the crackle of the 5.56 mm's muzzle-blast with distance.

Lyons braced himself as the front wheels bumped up hard, and the side of the hill swelled toward the top of the ridge. From here on out, it was going to be all acceleration, and he tore down, keeping a straight course for the sniper. He ducked his head low behind the steering wheel, the hood sparking as the enemy gunman fired incessantly. Normally, the gunman would have taken off, but at under five hundred yards, Schwarz was able to keep him pinned down to the protection of his sniper's nest.

However, at point-blank range, Lyons would be on an equal footing with the ENT assailant. The UMP-45 was still slung around his neck.

The engine crunched and rattled, breaking apart under the enemy rifleman's constant onslaught. Unable to hit Lyons, he settled for taking apart the SUV's engine, but the vehicle had too much momentum. Despite having to overcome gravity up the side of the hill, he still could get the SUV within ten yards of the sniper's roost.

Lyons slithered out of the driver's seat as the shot-up vehicle died. Behind the cover of the front fender, he snapped open the UMP's folding stock and shouldered the weapon. The rifleman took a shot at the blond ex-cop, but the scope got in the way at such short range. Popping around, Lyons put the front sight on the sniper and triggered a burst at him. A volley of 230-grain hollowpoint rounds leaped across ten yards with deadly accuracy, catching the shielded gunman in the head and throat. Pieces of skull and divots of neck muscle exploded off of the marksman, tossing his corpse back into the cover of the nest.

He'd been shielded from the shorter range M-16 by distance, and protected from 84 mm cannon fire by the placement of boulders around him, but his exposed head and neck were nothing more than a bull's-eye at fifteen paces for a submachine gun fired from the shoulder. Lyons looked around the ridge, seeing if there were any more gunmen still capable of combat. More importantly, he was looking for their transportation to the ridge. He found it, another SUV with a motorbike strapped across the tail.

"Just what I need," he said, rushing for it. There were keys in the ignition, obviously in case the snipers had encountered overwhelming firepower. Lyons started it up and swung toward the access road, which would lead back to the road.

He didn't spare the horses getting back to Arquillo and the others.

"You got wheels," Schwarz noted.

"Take the bike and transfer what supplies you can," Lyons said. "I'm taking Susana to get some medical attention, and I'll try to catch up to you as fast as I can."

Blancanales nodded. "Good plan. They'll think we'll be turned back by this."

"I don't give a damn what they think," Lyons snarled. "I want to put these murderous bastards out of business now. We can't afford to stop everything just because one of us is injured."

Schwarz glanced at Arquillo. Though pale and haggard from blood loss and concussion, she nodded at the logic.

"Everything's going to go boom," Arquillo slurred.

Lyons got out and with Blancanales's help, slid her into the back of the ENT's SUV. Schwarz did a quick check on the motorbike with his combat PDA, then pulled out a pocketknife, tearing a transmitter out of some wiring under a panel.

"GPS transmitter," Schwarz explained while Lyons and Blancanales made Arquillo secure and comfortable in the back of the SUV. "Here."

Lyons pocketed the transmitter. "Good thinking. If we keep the two GPS transmitters together, they'll assume we fell back."

"I thought you didn't…" Schwarz began.

A cold glare from Lyons stopped him cold.

"We'll have to leave the Carl Gustav here," Blancanales said. "It'll be bad enough fitting the two of us with full gear on this bike."

"Gadgets, locate the GPS on the SUV," Lyons suggested.

"I'm already on it. You'll bring the artillery," Schwarz replied.

Blancanales helped to load the recoilless rifle into the SUV while Lyons stroked Arquillo's hair. She had a bottle of Ringers solution in her arm, part of Blancanales's first-aid kit, not something he'd have been able to keep with him in a pack, but didn't have to worry about packing into an SUV. The saline solution helped keep her pressure from dropping too low, without diluting her blood.

"I was expecting bullets, not bombs," Arquillo muttered, a tear crawling down her cheek.

"Shh," Lyons whispered, thumbing the drop away. "I'll get you to help."

"What about Pol and Gadgets?" Arquillo asked. "They'll need you."

"You need medical attention. I'll get back to my buddies in time to finish this party."

Arquillo blinked, lips quivering. "It's all my fault."

"No. It's Cortez's fault," Lyons replied. "You saved us by pulling off-road."

Arquillo clenched her eyes shut. "Don't blame yourself."

Lyons kissed her forehead. "I'll make sure everything's okay. But first we have to make sure there's a future for everything."

She took her hand in his and squeezed tight. "I know."

"Got the GPS!" Schwarz exclaimed.

Lyons took the second transmitter and pocketed it, as well. He got behind the wheel. "Save some bloodshed for me."

"You got it," Blancanales said as Lyons tore off toward Green River.

CHAPTER NINETEEN

"It's your choice, David," Barbara Price's voice said over the sat phone. "Make your move, or wait to coordinate with Able Team."

"What is Carl saying?" McCarter asked.

"He told Pol and Gadgets to make their move. He'd be with them as soon as possible," Price explained. "And we have the satellite overhead to black out the Meggido region so that they can't tell the other facilities that they're under attack."

McCarter looked to his team. "Carl said not to hold up the facilities to his own people. We'll make our move, too."

"All right," Price replied. "Good luck and godspeed."

"We'll take every advantage we can get," McCarter replied.

He broke the connection, then checked his Colt Commando. Loaded with a 30-round curved magazine, it might not have been the most effective weapon, but in the close quarters of an underground installation, utilizing an improvised suppressor to protect his hearing, it was still going to be a devastating tool. The failure of a short-barreled version of the M-16 was due to using it at rifle combat ranges, not using it as the room broom he intended to utilize it for.

"Shit, David," Hawkins muttered. "Why can't we just take on corporate goons shaking down watermelon farmers?"

"You love being a big damn hero, and you know it, mate," McCarter replied.

Gary Manning glared at his partners as they talked, then returned to working on the electronic lock. While not the genius-level tinkerer that Hermann Schwarz was, the brawny, brainy Canadian still knew more than a few electronics tricks. He and Schwarz worked together, honing each other's demolitions and hacking skills, so while Manning wasn't at a level to develop his own computer hardware, he was able to deactivate an electronic lock.

The door was an unassuming one, hidden deep inside a cavern at the western edge of the Meggido Valley. Concealed in the dark, the cave itself shielded by boulders, it was an emergency exit designed for forces to escape in case the underground facility became overrun by a combined Soviet and Syrian invasion force, despite the nuclear firepower of its artillery shells. There were other hidden exits around, but the vengeful young hacker had specified this particular covert entrance for the Israeli infiltration.

It was a risk, but Phoenix Force never expected fighting international terror to be easy or safe. They would have to trust the hacker, and the cyberteam's evaluation of her offered intel. The electronic lock opened and Manning transitioned to his Glock, clicking on the under-barrel mounted light. He had a full-length M-16 with a scope atop his weapon in the event that he might have to shoot across a wide area or down a long hallway. The G-34, with its 17-round capacity and five-inch barrel, would be ideal for close-quarters battle, the under-mounted light reducing the Glock's already light recoil to the point where rapid-fire would snap off with deadly accuracy. Nothing greeted the burly Canadian, and he entered the darkened hall.

Calvin James and Rafael Encizo flanked him in the corridor, their M-4 carbines equipped with barrel lights, as well. With muzzles aimed at the floor in front of them, they wouldn't put Manning in danger of an errant gunshot, but the splash of light off their weapons bounced off the floor, spraying illumination down the corridor. McCarter and Hawkins took up the rear, their weapons left unlit to conserve battery life and to not betray the true numbers of Phoenix Force's size.

"Well, it's not a trap," Manning said, probing ahead of the others, scanning for booby traps or hidden defenders. He nodded to the others, but the team still avoided bunching up. However, their pace picked up from a crawl to a smoother, quicker walk, but not so fast that Manning wouldn't miss seeing a trip wire or concealed enemy defender.

"Great," Hawkins muttered. "We've got clear sailing to go up against an army of entrenched enemy commandos with two hundred nukes at their disposal. I feel so safe and secure."

The Stony Man commandos trod softly into the darkness, James and Encizo killing their gun lights to lower their enemy's ability to see them. One mistake, and they wouldn't live long enough to see the world die in nuclear flame.

JACK GRIMALDI ACCEPTED the stubby AK from Mack Bolan, much to the consternation of Mei Anna as she sat next to Cello Jiahua in the cab of the pickup. They had been directed deep into the Chinese countryside by the information that Aaron Kurtzman and the Stony Man cybercrew had given them. Years ago, the river they were overlooking used to be held back out of the canyon by an ancient dam built centuries before. Mei looked at the rushing river, swept away by the People's Republic's desire for progress over its ancient cultural identity, destroying a centuries-old landmark and towns that had built in the canyon's length.

And now, it appeared that the dam had been flooded to further bury a Chinese Continuity of Government facility, built during the early stages of the cold war, when the nation had realized that it could neither trust the Soviet Union nor the United States. It was one of many, but the old canyon complex had been dug deep into the walls of the canyon to provide a sense of security. Somewhere at the top of the canyon was a hidden launch bay, originally intended for helicopters once the technology had been developed. Now, it was apparent that the bay doors would open to unleash an airborne horde of nuclear-tipped devastation to spread across Southeast Asia and the Pacific, branding the mainland as a target for global revenge among the shell-shocked survivors of a wave of atomic fire.

Grimaldi and Bolan were clad in neoprene wet suits, with gear loaded into waterproof pouches on their load-bearing vests. The AKs were waterproof, and their handguns could survive a deep-sea dunking in their holsters. They were going to swim to the bottom of the river in scuba gear, and enter an old, long-abandoned entrance from the bottom of the canyon. Rising from the pool, the Executioner and the Stony Man pilot would begin the process of clearing out an army of ENT conspirators intent on scouring the globe clear of humanity.

"You'll be outnumbered down there," Mei told the Executioner as he checked his rebreather's mouthpiece.

Grimaldi nodded, looking up from his weight belt adjustments. "We'd still be outnumbered, even with you and Cello on our side."

"If we fail, you call down the thunder, and run like hell," Bolan told the Chinese agent. "That's the way it has to be."

"You pulled my ass out of the fire, Juniper," Mei began.

"Which I'd have done anyway," Bolan returned, fitting his dive mask over his eyes. "You've done a lot for this effort, but if you want to back me up, then stay out of the fire and be the voice of reason. If this screws up, we don't want Beijing thinking they were the target of a first strike."

"So, the only options to stop all of this are two guys with guns, or a nuclear bomb?" Jiahua asked.

"Extreme times call for extreme measures," Grimaldi informed the Chinese-American CIA agent. She took a deep breath at the thought while the ace pilot checked the draw of his dive knife from its sheath.

"We're not going on a suicide mission," Bolan explained. "Jack and I know what we're doing."

Grimaldi gave the fender of the pickup a pat. "Get moving. We'll call when we're done."

Mei and Jiahua looked back at the pair of Stony Man warriors as they pulled away in the truck. The two black-clad men dropped into the river and disappeared beneath its turgid surface.

CARL LYONS REACHED the town of Green River in under five minutes, pushing the SUV to its limits. On the smooth, fairly well-paved roads, and with Susana Arquillo cradled gently and carefully in the back, padded with cushions and rolled-up blankets, he was able to keep the injured agent from suffering too much for his feverish pace. The small hospital was ahead of him and he swerved through the parking lot, leaning on the horn to get civilians out of his path.

Tires squealed as he came to a halt in front of the emergency-room entrance, and he pulled a badge on a neck chain from a pocket in his load-bearing vest as he piled out of the vehicle. He grabbed Arquillo and took her through the automatic doors, cradling her body in powerful arms.

"Hang in there, Susana," Lyons whispered gently in her ear as he pushed through the ER. It wasn't busy, and the security man at the entrance balked at the sight of the Able Team commando, dressed for war with weapons hanging off his back, carrying the badly wounded CIA agent through the emergency room lobby.

The guard rose to his feet, hand falling to the pistol on his hip when Lyons glared at him.

"Find me a gurney to put her on, or you'll be shitting that gun," he growled.

The security guard froze in horror before logic kicked in. He pointed to an orderly, who was already wheeling over a stretcher for Arquillo.

Nurses came up and helped Lyons place her on the rolling gurney.

"She's suffered burns," one of the nurses noticed.

"Emergency cauterization," Lyons explained. "Otherwise, she would have bled to death."

"What blood type?" another nurse asked, studying the bottle of Ringers stuck in Arquillo's arm.

"Type O," Arquillo whispered weakly. "Get moving, Carl. I can tell…"

The wounded agent faded for a moment, her eyes glazing over, then she clenched them shut and opened, renewed in their dark focus. "I can tell them. Go."

Lyons gulped down a desperate breath, then gave her hand a squeeze.

"Sir, you can't go. There's paperwork to…" the first nurse said.

Lyons looked at her. "Do I look like I have time for paperwork? I'll be back and make out all the goddamn forms you want."

The nurse paused, paling at the vehemence of the big Stony Man commando's statement. The security guard was between Lyons and the exit, and the SUV loaded with the heavyweight firepower Blancanales and Schwarz would need to back them up.

"I just need some identification," the guard told Lyons, nodding to the badge hanging on his neck.

"My identification can be gleaned from the bootprints on your face if you don't move," Lyons snarled.

The guard glanced at the nurse, and realized that being in an ER wasn't going to be any consolation if he continued to obstruct the armored commando seething before him. "Drive carefully, sir."

Lyons grabbed the GPS transmitters and stuffed them into a waste can, then shoved past the security guard.

Arquillo was in good hands for now, but every minute he delayed, his partners were facing deadly odds to stave off the end of the world. Lyons sped out of the parking lot, pedal to the metal.

CORTEZ FROWNED as he looked at the screen that Ling Jon brought up for him.

"They retreated?" Cortez asked.

"Apparently, the forces you dispatched injured one or more members of the team before being completely wiped out," Ling stated. "The GPS trackers have them in Green River Municipal Hospital. The ER entrance."

Cortez grimaced.

"Shouldn't we make our move?" Ling asked. "Launch now before they call in backup?"

"You think that if they had access to backup, they'd only have sent four people in the first place?" Kovak interrupted. "They've encountered our other facilities, and they no doubt realize what kind of opposition they're up against. They'd have called in platoons of Special Forces operators."

"Like in Pakistan," Ling added.

"You studied the communications. They managed to distract us and convince USSOCOM that it was a raid on an al Qaeda base," Cortez stated. "But we're on to that tactic now, and we've been monitoring the Pentagon, as well as every other law-enforcement agency in the region."

Ling frowned. "They have overcome tough odds before."

"Only by surprise," Cortez said. "We're prepared for them, remember?"

Ling looked askance at the Argentinian commander of the ENT. He looked as if he wanted to say something, but thought the better of it, remaining silent. Cortez filed that away. Sooner or later, Ling would end up as dead as his lady hacker. Except instead of a deadly overdose of Ecstasy, Ling would simply receive a lethal overdose of copper-jacketed lead in his head.

Conversely, Kovak appeared to prove his worth as a minion. Cortez was glad to have recruited the Israeli. Despite the fact that the Middle Eastern situation was rapidly unraveling, Kovak showed strength and leadership in the face of enemy adversity. As well, the renegades he led were working hard to sow the seeds of discord in the region, adding their efforts to Asid Rabbani's men, working in concert.

Tensions were high, but not quite high enough, and Cortez needed a few more hours of jumpy, edgy nerves on the part of world governments and militaries. Colombia and Venezuela were skirmishing at their border, and China had fired a shot across the bow of a Taiwanese tanker. Terrorist attacks across the globe were poking and needling things to the right fever pitch.

A good inferno couldn't spread without enough spilled gasoline.

"Maintain the guard force on full alert," Cortez said. "But we launch on schedule."

Ling's face darkened. "Yes, sir."

Cortez nodded to Kovak, gesturing for the Israeli to join him. The two men entered the hall, and as soon as they knew that they were alone, Kovak spoke.

"You want this commando team to hit this facility."

"I've been leaving clues for the only people who could conceivably stop us. I've been steering them and jerking them around, setting my own pace," Cortez said.

"Keeping your enemies close," Kovak surmised. "So that when you do make your move, you'll have them already indisposed."

"And to make certain that everyone who remains at my side is strong enough to lead the Engineers into the new world," Cortez said. "To set the world on fire, we first must see if we have been forged in flames hot enough."

"And these mystery commandos are the heat," Kovak stated. "Plus, it would be pretty likely that if we did launch, they would survive the apocalypse and be thorns in our side when we tried to take over the surviving population."

Cortez looked at the pistol in Kovak's hip holster. The Israeli hadn't reached for it, but he was still wary. Kovak grinned.

"Don't worry about me," the Israeli stated. "We've got a world to rebuild. Having them in our way would only make things worse. You've brought them right into our laps, into situations that there is no possible way they could survive."

Cortez nodded.

Kovak smiled. "You can trust me."

"Good," Cortez replied.

The conspirators continued to the cafeteria for some coffee. They wanted to be wide awake for the rebirth of the Earth.

SUNNY YAO'S DEATH had bothered Ling Jon for a while. Although he was aware of her taste for drugs and alcohol, he also knew that even at her most stressed, she wouldn't engage in a suicidal overdose.

The alert chime for an incoming e-mail popped up on his screen and Ling opened it. It was a mail from Sunny, with a link inside.

Ling felt bile sour his throat and mouth as he looked at the link. The message was sent a day before Sunny had died, or at least set up on a time-delayed release. Hand hovering over the mouse like it was a fetid rodent corpse, he steeled himself to open the link. He checked over his shoulder, then hooked his ear buds to the speakers so no one else would be able to hear.

He was directed toward a blog page, one Sunny had set up before her death. It was barren, with a generic, empty profile, no pictures, no music, and one frozen video file. Ling clicked it and watched Sunny.

"Jon, Cortez had me set up the Engineers. By now, whoever he wanted to put on our tails has deciphered my other information. You need to get the hell out of the Green River facility now," Sunny said. Her eyes were heavy and glistening with tears. "Whatever way I died, it was Cortez's fault. He wants to make sure that the Engineers will not fall to pieces, so he's staging an assault on our main bases just before the end. I'm screwing Cortez hard, but you need to get out, now."

The video shut down and the Web page he was looking at dissolved, disappearing into an error notification on his browser.

Ling sat there, looking at the screen for a moment, feeling as if he'd swallowed an ingot of lead. The page, faded into a 404 Error notice, glared bright white on the monitor, the world around him turning dark and fading. At first he thought it was tunnel vision, but then even the monitor flickered, losing electricity.

Ling reached for his key chain flashlight and clicked it on as the computer center went dead. Emergency lighting snapped on, and Ling cut off his pocket light. He went through his drawer and found a nickel-plated Glock 17. Loaded, with a round in the chamber, he had eighteen shots. He pushed the pistol into his waistband and took off, keeping the key chain light in his hand.

He wondered if he should find Cortez and put a bullet in the man's head, or just run, trusting Sunny's plan to avenge herself to take place. His chest ached as he realized that the young beauty, who he'd had a crush on, despite being her supervisor, had given him a chance to live. A final act of affection, made bitter and hurtful when he realized that he'd never see her again. Tendrils of pain tingled down his arms, all the way through to his hands as he gripped the key chain torch tightly.

"Damn you, Cortez. Damn you," Ling gritted, cutting through the halls.

ROSARIO BLANCANALES PAUSED as the lighting in the base cut out. With the UMP-45 in his hands, he knew that if he'd been spotted, he'd be automatically targeted as an intruder. The covert back entrance to the Green River facility had delivered him and Hermann Schwarz into the utility tunnels between the underground power plant and the rest of the base. Blancanales paused as the base went to emergency lighting, and he looked back at Schwarz.

"What the hell's going on?" he asked the electronics genius.

Schwarz pulled his combat PDA and tried to cue into his tap on the mainframe that he'd set up in the power plant. Instead of a connection, he ended up with a "no signal found" response on the screen.

"What?" Blancanales asked.

"Someone beat me to my punch," he answered. "The whole system has been hacked and shut down."

"You think the lady hacker used this as her contingency?" Blancanales asked.

"Has to be," Schwarz responded. He gave the PDA a slap, but nothing helped him reconnect. He shrugged and slid the portable unit into his vest. "Looks like Cortez wined and dined the wrong lady."

"According to the information that Barb passed on to us, the woman said that there were contingency programs for launching the so-called Fire Raptors in the event of a base shutdown," Blancanales replied.

Both men, as well as Lyons, were fully aware of the lady hacker's intricately mapped layout of the Green River underground facility. From where they were, it would take them several minutes to reach the launch hangars, but according to her information, the contingency launch plans would give them a full half hour to stop the Fire Raptors from taking flight to deliver their 20-kiloton warheads around North, Central and South America.

Schwarz keyed his LASH unit. "Ironman?"

"I read you," Carl Lyons replied from the concealed cave entrance that Schwarz and Blancanales had taken. "I just got back from town."

"Seems our vengeful hacker shut down the facility," Schwarz explained. "We're on a full countdown now."

"We'd have been on killing time the minute your own hack had been put into place," Lyons responded. "Head to the hangars and shut them down whatever way you can improvise."

"So much for bringing up the recoilless rifle," Blancanales added.

"That's okay," Lyons responded. "We'll just have to kill everyone with bullets and grenades instead of warheads. Any trip wires I have to worry about?"

"Nope. Double-time it and try to follow us," Schwarz responded.

Blancanales scanned the sparsely lit darkness, looking for enemy soldiers on patrol. A group appeared, heading toward the power plant and he leveled his silenced machine pistol at them.

With a pull of the trigger and a soft popping at the end of the suppressor, Blancanales began the final conflict against the Engineers of the New Tomorrow, .45-caliber slugs crashing through the unsuspecting guards in a whipsaw of carnage. Schwarz shouldered his own weapon, adding silenced thunder to his friend's, targeting the rear of the ENT guard patrol to keep them from retreating. The sights and the superb accuracy of the machine pistol made head shots, even in the dim light, very easy, copper-jacketed hollowpoints biting deep into skulls instead of deflecting off heavy curved bone, so that even if the 230-grain manstoppers didn't penetrate the thick natural armor around the brain, the jarring impact fractured the brain case, causing enormous trauma. It wasn't putting a .45-inch-wide steam shovel through soft, spongy gray matter, but it was still enough to put down the assembled guards before they could even react to Able Team's stealth assault. Corpses littered the floor, and Blancanales moved forward, Schwarz covering him from his position.

It took a few moments to make certain the gunners were dead. None of them had gotten the opportunity to radio back to the main security dispatch, but he noted that the gunmen were armed with suppressed machine pistols, as well. It wasn't for stealth purposes—gunfire in the confined corridors would result in permanent hearing damage and even brain trauma. Unfortunately the weapons were in 9 mm, not .45 ACP like the weapons Able Team had brought with them. While the two men were both laden with spare ammunition, they'd have liked the opportunity to stock up using their dead enemies' spoils. Blancanales signaled it was clear, and Schwarz joined up with his partner.

The two Stony Man warriors continued into the cybernetically crippled ENT facility, heading toward the UAV launch hangar.

CHAPTER TWENTY

Hal Brognola entered the Stony Man Farm War Room under full steam, chomping on an unlit cigar. With the Executioner, Able Team and Phoenix Force making their moves to ward off global extinction, the head Fed wanted to be on hand for live feed from the teams. It was a symbolic gesture, since Price could have relayed that information to almost any corner of the globe, but Brognola was concerned for his friends.

"We've got word from Gadgets," Price stated. "Power systems in the Green River location have been crippled by the hacker who leaked the layout to us."

Brognola's jaw set grimly. "The Engineers would have backup so that they wouldn't be left in the dark and unable to engage their plan, though."

"That's correct," Price said. "And Yao, that's the hacker, wasn't able to take care of all the emergency contingencies. I'm also certain that the rest of the Engineers' staff will be hard at work on bringing the base on line."

"Are the other teams reporting a similar situation?" Brognola asked.

"No new reports," Price said. "However, Yao only worked in the Green River facility. To accomplish that level of sabotage, she'd have had to been in the Chinese and Meggido bases and working directly in their power plant programming. You know how securely isolated each facility was from the other."

"Something to do with firewalls that could prevent the discovery of one leading to the disclosure of the whole network," Brognola stated.

"Only Cortez's information gave us the dirt on the three main facilities involved in the final launch, and if even one remained in operation, we're talking millions dead," Price told him.

"Can the Utah base still launch?" Brognola asked.

"Manual operation of the hangar doors is possible, and there is a secured system that takes a half hour of emergency self-diagnostics to start up," Price answered. "Since the power shut down four minutes ago, we've got twenty-six minutes for Able Team to reach the launch bay and shut it down."

Brognola nodded. He walked to the wall monitor, split into three orbital views of the disparate ENT subterranean headquarters. "Able and Phoenix have been able to set up relay communications from their entry points, but Striker's on his own with Jack in China."

"We won't know Mack's progress until he contacts us, or the Fire Raptors begin their launch from the base," Price explained.

"So we just count on Mack and Jack to take care of business," Kurtzman interjected. "We'll just be cut off from them. Whatever happens…"

"We'll know soon enough," Price said. "I've got activity. Able Team is in a firefight, but they're split up."

"Split?" Brognola asked.

"Carl had to get Susana Arquillo to medical attention," Price answered. "I've got a contact en route to take care of hospital paperwork and smooth things over with the local authorities."

Brognola nodded. "I'm sure Carl made a scene at the ER."

"The local 9-1-1 was called, but too late for the Green River Sheriff Department to do anything about him," Price replied. "And he's at the main facility, just a little bit behind the others."

Brognola nodded. "I should have known there was a good reason why he'd let his partners go into harm's way without him."

Price raised an eyebrow.

"Helping out a fellow soldier," Brognola returned. "He only acts shallow."

"I knew that. I was wondering if you did," Price said.

Brognola wrinkled his nose. "How are they communicating with us if they're under blastproof shelves of earth?"

"Simple design," Kurtzman said. He tossed a small object that resembled half an egg in size and shape. "Line-of-sight relay beacon. It's why Phoenix and Able can keep in touch with us, but Striker couldn't, even if he had the equipment."

Brognola turned the small half-egg over in his hand. The bottom had a powerful adhesive pad. The object was small, gray in color, easier to blend into a shadow. "Clever design."

"That's Gadgets for you," Kurtzman stated. "We'll see if we can saddle Striker with a couple of these the next time he wants to go underground."

"He doesn't need us to hold his hand, Bear," Brognola explained. "As much as I'd like to keep an apron string tied to his wrist, we tried that, and it failed miserably. Striker has to run free."

"One crisis at a time," Price said. "Chances are, if anyone blows it, Stony Man's going to take a backwash of fallout when Washington, D.C., becomes a glass bowl."

She paused and looked at Brognola. "Speaking of which, where's the Man?"

"Marine helicopter evacuated him from the White House," Brognola replied. "He's going to be in the air. Air Force One is especially designed to ride out short-duration nuclear exchanges."

Price nodded, watching the screen. "So he's going to fly over the country, and the pilots will just steer away from the mushrooms a poppin'."

Brognola regarded Price. "There's no way we can evacuate the cities targeted by the Engineers. Except for national capitals, we can't even fathom which populations are the intended destination for the Fire Raptors. And evacuating key cities might set off the Engineers' plans anyhow. You're not going to hide mass evacuations."

Price nodded. "We've protected the President enough times. It's part of our job."

"He doesn't like running with his tail between his legs, Barb," Brognola replied. "And the goal of "

"I've got Air Force One on screen five," Kurtzman interrupted. "It's ready for takeoff."

Price watched the screen, then grimaced. "If we can see the President, then so can the Engineers."

"The team's already on it," Kurtzman replied. "We're triangulating the observation software back to its origins."

"But the Green River site has been shut down," Brognola said.

"They could have a forward base here," Price replied. "Or anywhere on the coast."

"A remote station, remotely controlling Predator drones," Brognola snarled. "So we end up using the President as bait?"

"Not exactly," Price stated.

Tokaido spoke up. "We've got Raptor drones inbound toward Dulles. Projected path will put them over AF One in about two minutes. Emergency launch already engaged."

"Emergency launch?" Brognola asked.

"Cowboy has an update on a precision-guided bunker missile," Price stated. "Project XM-952."

"Right. He used that one when Able Team took on the Aryan Right Coalition in Georgia," Brognola stated. "When they were using a silenced assassination pistol ripped off from his design."

"Kissinger has been working on the design. We figured why not pit remote-control weapons against remote-control weapons," Price explained.

"I'm running the back track of their course," Carmen Delahunt noted.

Brognola turned to the screen and saw the countryside swooping beneath a camera lens. He looked at Tokaido, who was working a video-game-style controller, watching his monitor. Tokaido's reflexes and hyperactive energy made him a natural for manning the remote-control weapons.

"Interceptor will meet up with the Raptors over Chevy Chase," Tokaido announced. "I'm milking the engines hard."

"Projected flight speed is in excess of 230 miles an hour," Delahunt stated. "These aren't explosive-bearing drones. They more resemble the profile of the improvised gunships used in various attacks."

"I see them," Tokaido announced. "Ten seconds to weapons range."

The XM-952's velocity was 250 miles an hour. Inspired by drone usage in the two Gulf Wars, Kissinger had redesigned the television-guided missile to serve as an observation platform. It also was armed with two low-profile gun pods in its sleek shape. Instead of being an afterthought, mounted on wings like the improved Predators, the XM-952's guns were sleek, stripped-down M-60 machine guns, housed in streamlined blisters on either side of the television camera in the nose. Loaded with 250 rounds of 7.62 mm bullets per gun, the 952 was able to provide forward intelligence and fire support for any of the teams. The only weakness in the system was the requirement for one of the cyberteam to be on site, and the XM-952 was well over 1000 pounds of equipment to transport to foreign countries and expensive to operate as it was in the prototype stage.

However, in this instance, the Farm felt the expense was worth it for their stratagem.

Tokaido brought the Stony Man drone in behind the slightly slower ENT Fire Raptors. There were four of them, bristling with rocket and machine-gun pods. The obvious intent was to annihilate Air Force One while it was still on the ground. The firepower present was more than enough for any one of the enemy Predators to take out the grounded 747.

Tokaido switched from thrash metal to a sweeping science-fiction theme on his player. "Red Five going in!"

On the screen, the television camera shuddered as streams of machine-gun slugs licked out in fire-laced fingers toward the closest of the Fire Raptors. The machine-gun burst ripped across the UAV and ripped it in two. The fuel tank blazed and the engine belched smoke as it lurched and tumbled out of the sky. The other drones suddenly swerved off their preset course, racing in three different directions.

One was too slow as Tokaido juked his remote missile and caught the second Raptor drone with a withering blast of 7.62 mm armor-piercing rounds. Tungsten-cored rounds smashed into the missile pod, detonating warheads in an explosion that blasted the hapless aerial vehicle into a cloud of splinters.

"Two down, but the others are getting away," Brognola growled.

Another darting missile crossed the television screen showing Tokaido's camera view. Sleek, dark and stub-winged, as opposed to the swanlike Predators, it came up under a third of the enemy craft, guns flashing and chewing the drone apart.

Aaron Kurtzman grinned as Brognola caught sight of him. "Kissinger made a couple drones for us."

The head Fed nodded and looked back at the screen. The fourth Raptor was shredded by the combined firepower of the Stony Man remote missiles, four M-60s proving too much for the unmanned vehicle.

"Transmitting coordinates to FBI SWAT," Delahunt stated. "We've got their forward position locked."

"How hardened is it?" Brognola asked.

"It's an above-ground installation, but well outside of the Washington, D.C., environs," Delahunt stated. "We've had the SWAT team on alert for this eventuality."

"Too bad the other teams are occupied," Brognola mentioned. "I'd hate to put the FBI in over their heads."

"I've got a softening shot for the facility," Wethers commented. The tall former professor grinned as he guided a modified XM-952 missile. Loaded with a conventional 40-kiloton explosive, originally designed for taking out bunkers and tanks, the missile streaked from Stony Man Farm on a column of thrust, propelling it along at more than 450 mph.

It was less than two minutes between the launch and when the missile reached the forward ENT base, fifteen miles away. Striking Delahunt's GPS coordinates, the heavy warhead erupted with earth-shattering force, crating a twenty-foot-deep crater in the earth around the underground facility's entrance and smashing apart the heavy concrete shell of the base's concealing doors.

Kurtzman and Tokaido swung their drones over the blast site after having finished off the Predators. The camera noses showed a wrecked corridor leading down into the hillside. Stunned and staggered technicians lurched dazedly toward the blast hole, but Tokaido swept the entrance with a suppressing burst of machine-gun fire.

That gave the Engineers' conspirators inside the clue that leaving the underground facility was not in their best interests.

"Now the President can fly out of Dulles and get away from a nuclear blast," Price said. "We came up with the strategy when Able was buzzed in Colombia. We figured that the ENT wouldn't want the President escaping to his own Continuity of Government safehouse, so we pressed Kissinger's experimental missiles into service as hunters and seekers, as well as that bunker-buster."

"It was a risky play," Brognola stated.

"Not so much," Kurtzman admitted. "Hunt set up a false image of AF One preparing for takeoff to flush them. The President and his jet are still in the hangar, preparing for takeoff. It was just a recorded digital image we used to fool the entire Federal Aviation Administration network, and by extension, the Engineers."

Brognola took a deep breath. "Good work, team."

"You know, I could get used to this remote-control terrorist busting," Tokaido stated. "Maybe next time I go into the field with the teams, I won't end up being beat up, and can bring some thunder down on the bad guys instead."

"Don't count on it, Akira," Brognola said. "But good job protecting the President."

"He was never in any danger," Price replied. "But now that we've got the direct threat to the Man dealt with, we still have to put the rest of the Engineers out of commission."

Brognola took his chewed-to-death cigar out of his mouth and tossed it into a wastebasket. "It's going to feel like a long day."

BENEATH THE PLAINS of Meggido, the battle of Armageddon raged, as David McCarter cut loose with his M-16. Flesh-shredding 5.56 mm bullets ripped an Israeli rogue agent from crotch to throat, splitting his torso open. The Briton slammed his boot into the chest of the dying enemy gunman and kicked him off the crosswalk into the bottom of a crevice.

The underground facility had been installed in a series of subterranean caves, so excavation was less intensive. In some parts, the ceilings were twenty yards high, and prefabricated flooring had to be supported by scaffolding, cracks in the cave floor requiring bridges. Quonset huts were the main form of structure.

T.J. Hawkins had hung back at the power plant for the hidden facility, using a copy of Schwarz's combat PDA loaded with a specially programmed viral assault keyed toward the operating system and antiviral software. Utilizing code samples obtained from the Darien base, Schwarz and Kurtzman had designed logic bombs and viral worms that had been developed to target weaknesses in the base code of the Engineers' mainframe. Having five of the world's most skilled hackers on the same system-destroying program, they were able to develop a killer application that burrowed mercilessly into the chinks in the ENT's technological armor.

Right now, the Meggido base had been shut down, with the only illumination provided by muzzle-flashes, hand-held torches and emergency battery-powered lights. As the Engineers' defense force relied upon the emergency lighting, Gary Manning used his scope-equipped rifle to knock out every source of illumination that he could see from his vantage point in the cave system.

Phoenix Force had snapped red filters over their lights, the crimson coloration producing a weaker, shorter frequency of light that didn't show up as far or contrasted against the darkness. The dull red lenses of their illuminators would be difficult to target by enemy gunmen who had been operating with white lights without provision for filter mounting.

Thus, everyone who had a white light flare was a target for the Canadian's sniper skills.

McCarter crouched at the other end of the catwalk and saw a knot of ENT gunmen who had heard the brutal exchange on the crosswalk. He glanced back and flashed a signal to James and Encizo with his red-filtered pocket light. In the tight quarters of the crosswalk, the Stony Man commandos were able to see the crimson flash, and crossed the bridge while McCarter kept his eye on the Engineer se-

curity force. He'd turned his gun light off so as not to attract attention from the nearby enemy team.

James crouched beside McCarter, then unhooked a concussion grenade from his harness. The supply of grenades
had been a windfall when Phoenix Force had taken down
the enemy's armory. The cardboard-framed explosive shell
flew, landed amid the knot of sentries and detonated. Eight
ounces of high explosives released a shock wave that ruptured blood vessels and eardrums among the bunched-up
ENT gunmen. Two men flopped lifelessly to the floor in
the wake of the miniature bomb going off, while the others staggered, holding their shattered ears.

One of the ENT guards looked up, black streaks of his
blood pouring down his cheeks. The blood had turned
black in the glow of Encizo's gun light, and McCarter
knew that the hemorrhaging came from where the soft tissues around the victim's eyes had ruptured. He didn't suffer long, though, as the stocky Cuban triggered a burst
into his upper chest, slicing his heart in two.

McCarter and James joined in on the cleanup, raking
the wounded survivors with sweeping claws of 5.56 mm
copper-jacketed lead. Bodies jerked and collapsed into
boneless heaps under Phoenix Force's combined autofire.
In the darkness, without having to rely on position-betray-
ing white lights or heavy night-vision equipment, the five
warriors moved with smooth and fluid grace and stealth.
The darkened caverns that had housed and protected the
Engineers of the New Tomorrow from discovery by the authorities had turned into a pitch-black tomb with every
light source extinguished.

Not expecting a complete power shutdown, the defenders of the Meggido base were left as easy targets for the

quintet of hardened Phoenix Force warriors, who had trained both with and without the best in night-vision equipment. McCarter and his men used only brief flares of their gun lights to give them a memorized flash of their surroundings, then moved through the shadows in silence, while the ENT guardians bobbed around with glowing spotlights blazing beneath their weapons, allowing Phoenix Force to target and eliminate them.

Encizo heard footsteps around the side of a Quonset hut, and he flashed his handlight to James and McCarter to hold them up. The Briton and the medic halted. Encizo let his rifle hang on its strap and pulled his Cold Steel Tanto knife. An ENT soldier stepped into the open, his weapon light blazing harshly in the blackness. The Cuban reached out and grabbed a fist full of the man's hair and the shell of his ear, yanking hard. The guard stumbled against Encizo and was speared on the seven-inch chisel-pointed knife. With a wicked twist and a hard slash, Encizo disemboweled the hapless sentry, then threw the corpse to the floor.

Submachine guns ripped out ragged bursts at the corner of the Quonset hut, but Encizo had ducked behind cover. The Cuban took a moment to grab a concussion grenade off his harness, rip the pin out and pitch the bomb behind the hut. Encizo tucked himself down tightly and roared, holding his ears. After a second, the HE grenade went off, blazing off flashes of light and sound, signifying blindness and deafness among the enemy.

James and McCarter advanced and fired at the group of defenders that Encizo had stunned with his flash-bang bomb.

It was a ruthless advantage that Phoenix Force had gained over their opponents, but considering that the Engineers had two hundred city-destroying weapons perched to devastate Europe and the Middle East, fair play had flown out the window long ago. And since the ENT troops had shown no sign of surrender, the Stony Man warriors were left with no obligation to take prisoners or show mercy. Slaughter was the order of battle, and the defending guard had been given the overwhelming totality of the losses. The only thing slowing the team, other than how fast they could move, was an unwillingness to blindly stumble into an enemy trap.

Though the five professionals had an unfair edge, they also respected their enemies, and at any moment, the defending forces would adapt their tactics to render McCarter's initial battle plan useless.

"Defending forces have killed their illumination and shut down their emergency lighting," Manning announced from his vantage point. "It's pitch-black in there."

"So much for the upper hand," McCarter replied. "T.J., are you done wanking around back at the power plant?"

"I'm on my way. There was a backup team that had cut around through an alternate route. I had to deal with them," Hawkins answered over the LASH hands-free radio set he wore.

"Hope you left them a nice surprise in case they try to get the generators up and running," Manning told him.

"Grenade trip wires at the doors," Hawkins said. "And I used one of your spare mercury switches and a glob of C-4 with some pens stuck in it for backup."

McCarter chuckled. "Sounds like he's trying to steal your thunder, Gary."

"Trying? He stole the stuff I had him mule pack for me," Manning mockingly complained. "Heads down."

In the distance, a hollow tube gave off a pop as a projectile launched through it. A brightly burning ember bounced toward the Quonset hut where McCarter and the others had held their position. The bouncing flare burned brightly, producing a dome of illumination that burned brightly. Even though they were outside the main flare of light, Encizo, James and McCarter were visible as shadows to the side of the burning flare.

Another flare launched as rifles ripped in the distance.

McCarter and his partners tucked in tight to the floor as gunfire popped past over their heads, supersonic slugs cracking the air in miniature sonic booms.

"Too exposed here," Encizo said. He grabbed a piece of floor grating and wrenched it up and aside. With a hatch opened through the floor, he led the way, slithering into the space between the cave floor and the prefabricated walkways. James and McCarter came after, the Briton pausing long enough to drag the grating back behind them.

Encizo splayed his flashlight's cone ahead, looking through the support struts for signs of enemy soldiers taking the same route. He saw only shadows and uneven floor, and killed his light.

"Careful," Encizo whispered. He transitioned from his rifle, which he strapped across his back, to the light-mounted Glock 34 combat pistol. In the close quarters under the floor, he'd need the shorter, more maneuverable weapon in case he ran into an ENT guardian who decided to flank Phoenix Force by going under their feet. James and McCarter did likewise, trading their rifles for their Glock and Browning respectively.

"We went down below," McCarter informed Manning and Hawkins over his LASH. "Anyone above ground is fair game until I signal otherwise."

"Got it," Manning returned.

The crack of a rifle bullet slicing the air informed Mc-Carter that the enemy sentries were making their way forward to deal with Phoenix Force, perhaps expecting that they'd been pinned down in the Quonset hut they'd been hiding by.

Slipping between pipes and support beams, the Stony Man trio crawled in the darkness until they heard the clatter of boots on the metal grating over their heads.

McCarter looked up at the metallic cross weave and mentally measured it. He wouldn't be able to stick the muzzle of his Browning through the gaps, and without that bit of certainty, he wouldn't press the pistol against the metal, even though a 9 mm slug would slip through the holes. There was too much of a possibility of a backfire if his hand wavered and crossed a metal strip instead of empty space.

Instead, the trio moved on, slowly and surely.

"Gary can't see, but a larger part of the guard force is moving behind the flares. His night vision is being weakened by the brightness of the flare," Hawkins said. "But since the guards are between me and the light, it's easier to spot them."

"Take 'em," McCarter whispered softly, his words amplified by the vibrations in his throat.

Automatic fire rattled through a suppressor, and suddenly bodies collapsed on the metal grating above Encizo, James and McCarter. The Phoenix Force leader motioned to the Cuban, and Encizo rose, pushing up on the panel of flooring with his broad shoulders. A gunman atop the square of grating lost his balance and tumbled.

"Coming up!" McCarter whispered. "Check fire!"

The Phoenix Force commander and Calvin James rose through the hole that Encizo had made, their 9 mm pistols barking out suppressed slugs into the remaining survivors of Hawkins's ambush.

"I'm coming forward," Hawkins called over his radio. He scurried to the trio's side and knelt with them. The flares burned in the distance and the Southerner turned on the combat PDA, consulting his underground map. "We're only halfway through the complex. The hangar is another three hundred yards down that way, and up a staircase."

"It'll be heavily defended," Encizo stated. "We won't be able to do too much since fighting uphill is tough enough when it's the actual side of a hill. Going up stairs, you're confined and vulnerable."

"We'll figure that out when we get there," McCarter said. "Let's go."

CHAPTER TWENTY-ONE

Carl Lyons lifted his brawny arm and caught the running man across the jaw in a clothesline. Lyons was still catching up to his partners who had penetrated the underground base before he could. He leveled the UMP-45 at the stunned Chinese he'd laid out. A Glock pistol, dislodged when the runner had been clotheslined, clattered to the tile floor.

"Speak English?" Lyons growled, looking down at the stunned men.

"Don't shoot," Ling Jon croaked hoarsely, rubbing his sore throat. "I dropped my gun…"

Lyons poked Ling in the nose with the muzzle of the UMP machine pistol. "Do I really look like someone who cares? Stay still."

Lyons stepped over the man's chest, then kicked the Glock down the hall. Ling curled his arms to his breast and winced at the man's cold glare. "You didn't shoot me because I only had a pistol."

"I didn't see the gun," Lyons growled. "I should have just pulled the trigger."

"Wait…I wasn't going to protect this place!" Ling pleaded.

"Then where were you in a hurry to?" Lyons asked.

"To get out of here," Ling answered. "A dear friend told me to get the hell out of this place."

"Why's that?" Lyons pressed.

Ling met the cold, merciless blue eyes of the brawny blond commando standing over him. "I guess because she told me you were coming. You are here to kill the Engineers, right?"

"Still doesn't give you a free ride out of here," Lyons answered. "You're a conspirator…"

"Yes, yes, but I don't want to die," Ling muttered. "Please hear me out."

"You've got one sentence to convince me," Lyons told him.

"Backup launch system since Sunny Yao died," Ling sputtered. He winced, expecting a bullet in the face.

"Backup launch, like the mobile command center in Israel?" Lyons asked, lowering the muzzle of the UMP.

"I knew Sunny sent you to kill Cortez," Ling whispered. He caught a flash of impatient rage in Lyons's eyes and swallowed hard. "Yes. Yes, just like the Israel setup. A field command unit was set up in the hangar the day after Sunny died."

Lyons keyed his microphone. "Gadgets, it looks like the bad guys might have a different system than we thought to launch their Predators."

"Like the Israeli setup?" Schwarz inquired.

"According to the rat deserting the sinking ship," Lyons grumbled.

"Who is he?" Schwarz asked. Lyons relayed the question.

"Ling Jon, the director of information techno—" Lyons held up his hand, cutting off the man, letting Schwarz know.

"According to Sunny, he's someone we should take alive," Schwarz told the Able Team leader.

"Your girlfriend?" Lyons asked, prodding Ling.

"I wish," Ling said.

"Whatever. I'm no good at blowing the head off an unarmed prisoner who just gave me good intel," Lyons told him. "Get up."

Ling nodded and struggled to his feet. "But, if I tried to escape, you wouldn't have any trouble shooting me."

"That's the point of being a good prisoner, isn't it?" Lyons asked, menace dripping from his words.

Ling's shoulders fell. He wasn't a soldier, just a man skilled with a keyboard. The blond brute with the weapons hanging off his broad, powerful frame, probably knew hundreds of ways to kill him without breaking a sweat. "Yes, it is."

"You follow me. Step out of line and stop a bullet, it's your own damn fault," Lyons told him. "When we pass your Glock, pick it up."

Ling nodded nervously. For a moment he thought that the blond commando was oblivious to the fact that the Chinese hacker could shoot him to death. He reconsidered, noting the man's size. Ling didn't think that a single 9 mm bullet would hurt such a man-brute, and that would be all the shots Ling would get off before the commando tore off his head, jammed a grenade in his dead mouth and threw the decapitated skull at a knot of ENT defenders.

"Lead the way…um.."

"Ironman," Lyons said as he picked up Ling's Glock and handed it to him. "Let's go."

Ling accepted the pistol and followed the Stony Man commando through the ENT base.

GARY MANNING TOLD THE OTHER MEMBERS of Phoenix Force to hold on, at least until he got back from the Meggido base armory. McCarter trusted his long-time friend implicitly, and knew that Manning had a way to protect the members of the team from being chopped to ribbons on the stairway up to the launch hangar.

Manning finally caught up with the team, bringing along two crates that he'd loaded into a wheelbarrow. The big Canadian handed out gas masks.

"We're going to smoke out the hangar?" James asked.

"Among other things," Manning replied. He took out two MM-1 multishot grenade launchers from one crate and handed one to James. "You're our usual grenadier. You get one."

"I'll take the other," Encizo offered. "I'm usually the one who gets a backup launcher."

Manning nodded. "Here you go."

James opened his MM-1 and looked through the crates. "Mix it up?"

"Oh hell, yeah," Encizo said. "What've we got?"

"I brought a little of everything," Manning explained. He held up a small box of M-651 CS gas grenades. "Tear gas, some cluster flares, smoke and of course air burst and antipersonnel."

James and Encizo looked at each other. "We'll start with the M-397s," James said. "A volley of four should clear out any defensive positions."

"And then lay down the CS to discourage reinforcement," Encizo added.

"You guys move when we're firing the CS," James told McCarter and the others. "We'll empty these out, and then follow up."

Encizo rooted around in the ammunition crate and found a few more shells. "I'll reload with these on the way up."

James nodded his approval, looking at the brutal M-576 round. Each grenade was actually an oversize shotgun cartridge, holding two thousand pellets that, at their widest dispersal, could spray death across a ninety-eight-foot-wide arc. James smirked. "Any spares beyond your 12-load?"

"Here," Encizo said.

The black medic plucked two of his air-burst shells out and replaced them with the buckshot rounds. "Let me pop these. Then duck."

"You know it," Encizo said.

"Let's do this," James announced. He swiveled the cylinder on the massive launcher, then shouldered it and aimed at the top of the stairwell. With two rapid pulls of the trigger, he started the battle for the hangar, ducking back as the first of the M-537 shells' sheets of thousands of buckshot pellets struck the roof. At more than 800 feet per second, the metal balls hit stone and bounced wildly. The spreading cone hosed into the corner of the chasm leading up to the hangar level, but James was lucky to have stepped back when he did. A rain of steel slammed into the concrete floor where he'd been standing only a few moments ago. A few bounced, zipping through the doorway to the stairwell, but the team had stepped away from the entrance, allowing the lethal flesh-rippers to hurtle down the corridor harmlessly.

The rattle of dropping buckshot ended quickly, and both James and Encizo stepped into the open. Encizo's M-397 air-burst rounds struck the roof of the cavern, filling the area with thunder, shock waves crushing what was left of any surviving defenders at the top. James waited until the shells had done their job, then started to pump CS rounds at the top of the stairwell. As Encizo joined in on the barrage, McCarter charged up the stairs, Hawkins and Manning hot on his heels.

The MM-1s had a listed rate of fire of 30 rounds per minute, but that took into account reloading time. While not as fast as a revolver-style handgun, the two Phoenix Force pros were able to snap off the remainder of their weapon payloads in little under five seconds. Encizo lowered his weapon, snapped open the receiver and dumped out the empty 40 mm casings. James was halfway up the stairs by the time the Cuban had fully loaded his buckshot rounds into the 12-shooter. Encizo, however, wasn't burdened by the mass of the MM-1's fifteen fully loaded pounds. Forearms rippling, veins standing out as he gripped the brutal death-dealer, he caught up with James just as he joined the others at the top of the staircase.

Tangled corpses and choking capsicum gas filled the landing as Manning, McCarter and Hawkins cut loose on the far end of the corridor where gunmen tried to hold the entrance to the hangar. Utilizing pockmarked and heavily chewed crates for cover, the Phoenix Force trio was glad to have their allies back with them. The corridor, fifty feet long, was a no-man's land strewed with dead ENT guards, and would leave the Stony Man commandos exposed if they tried to get down the hallway.

James opened the breach on his M-203 under slung to the rifle he'd gotten. While the Palestinian drug dealers hadn't captured any 40 mm ammunition for the under-barrel launcher, it used the same ammunition as the MM-1, and James pulled an M-406 high-explosive grenade that he had pocketed. He fed it into the launcher's breech, since the buckshot rounds Encizo had would be relatively ineffective in clearing a doorway.

"Fire in the hole," James called. He aimed at the floor just behind the doorway and triggered the charge. The HE round hit only a few feet behind the door. Luck was with James, as the shell had traveled far enough to arm, and when it struck, it released a concussion wave that was completely lethal in a sixteen-foot radius. The defenders at the doorway were smashed to bloody pulps, bones ground to splinters and organs crushed like grapes by the horrendous shock. James had ducked down to avoid debris blown loose through the doorway. The M-406 was totally lethal for a relatively small radius, but could injure people over four hundred feet away. The whiz and whir of objects snapping over his head and the rattle of debris smacking against the crate he'd ducked behind reminded him of how much power he'd had in his weapon.

There was no time to relax, and Phoenix Force charged the doorway in a leapfrog pattern, half the team covering the others as they advanced forward. No response greeted the five warriors until they reached the jamb. The high-explosive shell and wafting tear gas had kept the enemy back. Concentrated fire hammered the doorway.

The CS was thinning, and McCarter was the first to pull off his gas mask. His eyes and nostrils stung with the burning power of the pepper extract, but he could live with minor discomfort in exchange for peripheral vision and better communication.

The others followed suit, except for Encizo, who was busy poking the muzzle of the MM-1 around the corner to tap off four buckshot rounds. Lethal cones of lead composed of eight thousand buckshot pellets ripped across the hangar. The stocky Cuban was rewarded with howls of pain and the temporary cessation of suppressive fire against the doorway. The other members of the team took the brief pause to enter the hangar proper, Encizo bringing up the rear, ripping off his mask.

An ENT defender popped up from cover near Encizo and took a shot at the swarthy warrior, hitting him dead in the chest. Protective armor blunted the blow, and McCarter and Hawkins swung as one, emptying two bursts of M-16 fire into the gunner. Manning hauled the stunned Encizo behind cover and opened his bullet-resistant vest.

"I'm fine," Encizo snarled. "The trauma plates stopped everything."

"Serious bruising there," James noted. "You might have a rib fracture."

"Listen, if a 9 mm slug couldn't punch through my un-protected forehead, how a damned glorified .22 going to break my ribs through a trauma plate?" Encizo asked.

"Well, you were struck dumb for a moment," James commented.

"Rafe, can you bloody well shoot?" McCarter asked.

"Yes!" Encizo growled.

"Then bloody well shut your gobs and do your jobs!" McCarter bellowed, firing a burst at the ENT defenders.

Encizo cut loose with another two rounds from the MM-1 before transitioning to his Glock 34 to save his big punch for later and because his rifle was still strapped across his back. Since the quarters were close, and the Cuban had trained to get head shots with the sleek tactical pistol at ranges of fifty yards, he didn't feel outgunned for now.

At the other end of the tunnel, light began to spill through.

The warriors of Phoenix Force realized that the Engineers' defenders had the launch bay open. It would only take a matter of minutes before the nuclear-tipped Fire Raptors would launch.

"No time to play, mates. Make a hole!" McCarter pulled a pin on his concussion grenade and hurled it toward the ENT guards.

The roar of the concussion bomb flattened the defenders and Phoenix Force threw themselves into the breach.

CARL LYONS FINALLY CAUGHT UP with his partners as they were held up at a juncture. Ling Jon paused as he closed with the intersection of corridors. The corpses of ENT soldiers were thrown about, like discarded, broken dolls. Ling had seen Lyons's brutal devastation when they'd encountered a patrol of defenders in the darkened tunnels leading here, but the hacker had been able to keep his distance from the shattered bodies. In this hall, Ling had no choice but to step over bodies ruptured like overripe fruit, faces locked in death masks of horror as they had been mercilessly hammered by heavy-caliber bullets or grenades. The smell of the recently dead, thick, heavy, coppery blood and opened bowels, was enough to make Ling want to vomit. He was lucky that the shadows had made it difficult to make out details of the bloody battle to clear a path to the launch bay, but the scent of carnage painted images more horrifying in his brain than the glinting highlights on blood-splattered flesh and exposed bone.

Schwarz looked at Lyons. "Got a concussion grenade?"

Lyons pulled one from his harness and whipped it toward the position that Schwarz had indicated. Ling knew from example and cleared his ears with a roar as the throw was made. Thunder crashed through the corridor, vibrations bouncing off the walls and rattling the untrained hacker with jolting spears of concussive force. He dropped and curled into a ball and came face-to-face with one of the Engineers' mercenary thugs, half of his face ripped away by a pair of .45-caliber slugs. The cavern carved by the twin bullets created a trap-door hatch that had been flung wide to expose gray, spongy brain while the white globe of an eyeball gleaming in reflection of emergency lighting.

Ling froze in horror at the glimpse of nightmarish mutilation and clamped his hand over his mouth to stem a sudden surge tide of bile rushing up his throat.

"Your new sidekick looks a little queasy," Blancanales noted, getting up to join Schwarz in mopping up the defense force crippled by Lyons's grenade.

"Might as well hork it up," Lyons told the hacker. "It'll help clear your head."

Ling turned away and let loose, spitting to get the bitter and sour vomit taste out of his mouth. His legs felt like rubber when Lyons's hand dropped heavily onto his shoulder.

"Let's go. We've got more work to do," Lyons told the Chinese.

Ling nodded spasmodically, shuffling after the Able Team commander. Movement out of the corner of his eye jerked the hacker's head upright, but before the impulse for words sprang to his lips to cry out a warning, Lyons whirled, left hand slapping him in the chest to push him against the wall. The machine pistol in Lyons's right fist ripped out an extended suppressed burst, brass flying from the breech.

Ling, with the Glock locked in his left hand, lifted it and opened fire wildly at the ENT gunmen. He screamed in blind panic, tugging the trigger and burning off the whole magazine. He wasn't sure if he'd hit anything, but in the cramped quarters of the corridor, it wouldn't have been too hard to miss the gunmen he had formerly embraced as comrades. His finger tugged on the lever of the trigger when Lyons put a hand over Ling's.

"You're empty," the Ironman told him. "Reload."

Ling patted his pockets. "I don't have spare clips."

Lyons shrugged. "Get them off some of these bodies. Maybe get something heavier, too."

Ling gulped audibly. He didn't want to look at the blood-spattered forms on the floor. "I don't even know how to use a pistol. I'm going to carry a complicated thing like a rifle?"

Lyons could read the reluctance in Ling's face, then bent down. With two swipes of his knife, he held up a magazine pouch for the hacker. "Take this. Press the button behind the trigger."

Ling did so, and the magazine fell halfway out of the bottom. It looked stuck, but he grabbed the stick and pried it the rest of the way free. Lyons handed him a fresh magazine, and Ling shoved it in until he felt the Glock click.

"Grab the slide by the rear and tug it back. It'll be loaded then," Lyons told him.

Ling pulled on the slide, and the gun snapped shut with a loud clack that shocked him so that he nearly dropped the pistol. Lyons stuffed the double pouch into Ling's free hand.

"Put that in your pocket," Lyons ordered.

"You going to babysit him all day?" Schwarz asked.

"I'm not going to let this guy be deadweight," Lyons explained. "Besides, he spotted an ambush."

"I didn't say a word," Ling muttered.

"No, but I saw you react," Lyons told him. "And I reacted."

Ling looked pleased.

"This doesn't mean we'll take long walks on the beach, holding hands, Ling," Lyons told him. "You've got a long road to walk before I let you off the hook for programming the Raptors to murder people."

Ling looked down the hall at the devastated ENT guards, and realized that whatever ice he stood on was so thin that the slightest shift would plunge him into icy death. He'd already proved to Cortez that he was untrustworthy, and the big blond commando made no bones about the fact that Ling was morally repugnant to him.

"Yes, sir," Ling muttered.

"Stay close and don't die," Lyons ordered. He took the lead, and Ling followed him, Schwarz and Blancanales bringing up the rear as they gathered fresh weapons and ammunition from the dead.

The underground war had depleted their initial combat loads, and only by scrounging from dead enemies were they able to stay at peak efficiency. It meant abandoning the UMPs, but the suppressed MP 5s used by the Engineers' forces were more than up to the task, and the guards carried plenty of ammunition, making each skirmish a chance for resupply. Concussion grenades were also found on various gunmen, restoring Able Team's ability to clear out corridors.

It was one small favor, on top of others they'd come across.

But small favors weren't going to finish the job. That would require ruthless efficiency and brutal combat, one dead ENT defender at a time.

YUAN HAN PACED the control room, his face cast in a mask of concern as communication with the other Alpha facilities was cut off by an invisible sheet of white noise. The links to the other sites were compromised, but that was the only hindrance that the ENT China base had encountered. Information still filed in from taps on the SAD and the People's Republic of China Ministry of Defense, and both agencies were in the dark about the Engineers' presence in their nation.

So far, so good, and the countdown to their projected launch against Taiwan and the coalition fleet made of American, British and Australian warships was still on schedule. An initial strike of a half dozen Fire Raptors bearing 20-kiloton warheads would get the ball rolling for a full-scale exchange of nuclear fire.

Yuan had fought long and hard to convince Cortez of this course of action. The small preliminary launch would set the stage. Once two major nuclear powers were engaged in conflict, it would prove easier to provoke other nations to war. Israel and the American base wouldn't have the range or nearby enemies who could start such a powerful conflict, while it could easily be imagined that Beijing decided to throw caution to the wind and tear apart the SEATO fleet in motion around Taiwan, a brutal response to saber rattling on both sides of the Bamboo Curtain.

Cortez allowed Yuan to implement the launch, and in fifteen minutes, he'd let loose the dogs of war.

Then the blackout hit.

Yuan's hands tingled with a mix of excitement and fear.

It was possible that the other bases had come under assault and were placed under an enforced blackout. However, considering that his people were still in contact over various branches of the Internet, it seemed as if he was locked down. He'd heard something about the Engineers coming under cybernetic assault from an opposing team, so it could have been that. The enemy hackers had invaded the network.

Yuan was glad that he had developed an alternate link, utilizing different software and connections to the outside world. Any assault would have to be more direct in regard to taking down the China facility, but the blackout still worried him.

He fought to control his discomfort.

Even if two of the three facilities were left impotent, he still had enough Fire Raptors to lay waste to dozens of major cities, and more importantly, unleash a shooting war between the United States and China.

There was nothing that could stop him now.

Alarm sirens blared and Yuan's pacing came to a halt.

"What's going on?" he snarled.

"The launch bay!" one of his lieutenants said. "We had an explosion in the fuel pumps. We've got fire-control teams responding, but the blaze is too intense!"

Yuan's forehead furrowed. "What?"

"The Fire Raptors are burning," another reported. "Look… No, we lost the closed-circuit cameras to the hangar."

Yuan grimaced. "How did that happen?"

"An emergency underground exit you didn't know about had a back-door passage up to your launch bay," a strange voice interjected.

Yuan Han whirled to the newcomer, but he only caught a brief glimpse of a tall man in black before a 230-grain hollowpoint smashed into the bridge of his nose and tore the dome of his skull away from his head.

The Chinese ENT commander collapsed into a lifeless

heap on the floor as suppressed gunfire ripped through his control center. The inferno in the launch bay wouldn't set off nuclear warheads, but rendered the hundreds of reconfigured drones useless charred remains. With the command staff eliminated, the potential for nuclear war between the U.S. and China was smothered.

But the Executioner realized that it was up to Phoenix Force and Able Team to stop the other several hundred warhead-equipped Predator drones, otherwise millions of lives were still at stake.

CHAPTER TWENTTY-TWO

The fight to defend the Meggido launch facility was going poorly. Ali Sindora ground his teeth as he heard the chatter of automatic weapons in the distance, thunderous booms punctuating the gunfire as an unholy weapon disgorged clouds of flying death that tore into his proudest and best warriors.

Sindora shouted in rage. "Kill them! Destroy them!"

He looked back at the command trailer. Its generator was sputtering, damaged by a rifle round. Technicians struggled to get the power source back on line while other drone operators made do with the battery packs in their laptops and a hand-cranked transmitter. The preflight programming for the swarm of lethal nuclear-tipped Predators was going slowly. The power outage that had crippled the Meggido base had caught Sindora off guard, but he managed to gather his troops.

It helped that the Engineers had developed a backup plan in case there was a cybernetic assault on the Meggido base mainframe. A secondary computer center, installed in mobile eighteen-wheelers, complete with portable generators, gave their fleet a supplementary control system in the event of a hacker's infiltration. Unfortunately for most of Sindora's soldiers, the cream of the crop from disparate forces as Basque separatists and Taliban veterans, the learning curve in night fighting had come much more slowly in response to the commando force that had hit.

So far, though, despite getting past the stairwell choke points he'd had his forces take over, the enemy had been held off.

Sindora fumed. He'd been in charge of four hundred men, and yet, through trickery, stealth and confiscated firepower, the small enemy force had depleted his command. There were still more than a hundred left after brutal, bloody fighting, but most of them were occupied with getting the squadron of several hundred Predator drones up and running.

Screams of pain revealing the weakness of his defense grew as the commandos fought for every inch of the launch bay level.

If only he'd been able to acquire a few RPG-7s before falling back to the hangar, but all he'd gotten were hand grenades and small arms.

The hand grenades might have evened the odds, were it not for the fact that the first of his defenders who tried had his hand nearly severed by a rifle shot as he threw it. The fragmentation bomb dropped amid his squad of defenders and shredded them in its kill radius. Others tried, but they were either cut down or were unable to penetrate the invaders' cover. Fragmentation and blast zones were good in open ground or confined rooms, but the tunnel leading from the freight elevator to the main hangar was too wide for concussion to do more than disorient, and there had been enough material to form protective barriers for a small, mobile squad of dedicated combatants.

Sindora was forced into retreat, and the prospect of defeat galled at his spirit.

The generator was protected, now, by a forklift parked in front of it. Bullets sparked against the small vehicle, but nothing could penetrate the bulk of its frame and reach the small electric motor behind it. His repairmen worked feverishly to get it running to provide power to the backup command network. Soon, Sindora hoped, the Fire Raptors would take flight, and the infidel governments of Europe, and their weak lapdog lackey governments in the Arab world would vanish in the blazing light of a nuclear sun. A cleansing flame would wash the world as hundreds of major cities would be destroyed.

Sindora knew that it wouldn't be a universal Muslim revolution, that different factions among the Islamic faithful would struggle for their true vision, but whoever won out would be free from Western imperialism's influence. In a world without oil barons and European or American corruptors, the will of God would once more ring loudly across the chosen lands.

"Come on, get the computers working!" Sindora shouted.

A rifle shot clanged against the forklift again. Sindora sneered in defiant glee. Let them try to punch a .22-caliber bullet through hundreds of pounds of steel. There was no way the generator would be vulnerable.

Another shot struck the forklift's fuel tank and gasoline gushed, pumping from the wound in its metal skin. Sindora's face paled as he saw the flammable liquid squirting from the ruptured tank.

"Take cover!" he shouted, diving toward the command module's sheltering mass.

A third shot clanged on metal, sparks flying from the impact, and the gasoline went up in a thump of superheated air. Fumes and liquid fuel turned into a fireball that sprayed the repairmen, roasting the flesh from their skeletons as they looked in confusion at Sindora's reaction. More defenders screamed as the flames spread across a fifty-foot-wide area.

Sindora looked out from behind his shelter and saw his warriors slapping at tongues of flame on their clothing or charred wounds on their exposed skin. He saw movement from down the tunnel and held up his AK-47 like a pistol, burning off half a magazine with a single pull of the trigger. Unfortunately, Sindora was afflicted with the same delusion that his manliness and faith in God had given him all the marksmanship he ever needed. Without shouldering the weapon or using the sights, however, all he did was waste ammunition and call attention to himself.

"Together, my champions!" Sindora bellowed. "We can repel—"

Encizo triggered the last buckshot round from his MM-1 40 mm grenade launcher and, in a flash, two thousand buckshot pellets struck Sindora and his rallying defenders at over 800 feet per second. The storm of projectiles hit Sindora like a brick wall, and while he stood, resisting the leaden wind, his flesh flayed from his skeleton as he took the brunt of the cloud. Gunmen who had gathered close to him were bowled over, blindsided by Encizo's devastating blast.

Face and chest peeled of skin and muscle down to the bone, Sindora stood for a moment, a grisly skeletal statue mutely testifying to the futility of his cause, and then the mutilated body folded into a crumpled heap of bloody remains.

"Good," the Cuban muttered. "I thought he'd never shut up."

A rifle shot smacked against the crate he'd taken cover behind, reminding him that the fight was far from over and mayhem still reigned in the cavernous mountainside hangar. Encizo discarded the grenade launcher and brought his rifle around and took out another defender with a short burst.

"Absolutely brilliant work with lighting up the fork-lift," McCarter said, complimenting Manning.

"It was relatively easy to lull them into a false sense of security with a few potshots. I just had to wait until they were committed to repairing the generator, pow," Manning said. "I'd have gotten to it sooner, however, if the guards hadn't had so many grenades."

The Canadian sniper ducked as a grenadier out of his arc of fire rolled a miniblaster that landed ten feet behind the steel pipes he was crouched beside. Shrapnel wire rang against the metal barrier, protecting his hide.

"Sooner or later they're going to get a signal through with the battery packs on the laptops, and once they do," Hawkins said, "those drones will get their takeoff orders."

The Southerner ripped off a short burst that sliced into the sternum of a Pakistani man who had used a crate as his shield. When the gunman leaned into the open, however, he hadn't seen Hawkins out on the far flank.

James and McCarter threw concussion grenades in unison, tossing them far and hard. The two blasters landed and detonated within moments of each other, giving the whole of Phoenix Force a space of a few seconds to gain another few yards, seeking out cover and continuing their blazing onslaught against the ENT soldiers.

It was a slow, miserable struggle, and they were lucky

to have taken down Sindora as he worked to rally the troops.

"I've got a line on the transmitter," James called. He fired off a short burst and was rewarded by a spray of sparks and shattered electronics. Gunmen rushed to the defense of the destroyed transmitter, but Hawkins scurried to James's side and backed him up with a fusillade of suppressive fire to take out the enemy gunmen.

"Well, that might have taken out their ability to launch the drones," McCarter said, "but we're still between them and the sane way out of this base."

"Unless they want to sprout wings and fly out of here," Encizo replied.

"Or they decide that if they're going to die, they might as well detonate a warhead or two and go out in style," Manning concluded.

Hawkins grimaced at the thought. "That'll ruin our day."

"Especially since Israel would take the detonation of a nuclear warhead in their territory as an attack by a foreign force, like perhaps Syria," James added.

"Or worse, Iran," Encizo noted.

"So now we protect the drones," Hawkins drawled. He'd long ago depleted the ammunition for his M-16 and had switched to a captured AK-47. The heavy-caliber rifle required fewer rounds to anchor an opponent, but the sights and barrel weren't in the best condition. His first shot would go wide, and he'd have to adjust for distance. He was tempted to toss the weapon away and grab another rifle, but a renewed slash of enemy fire pinned him down.

Rather than take a shot with the AK, he lobbed a grenade at his opponents, and tucked himself in against the shock wave. Concussive force rippled over the crates he was behind, and his teeth rattled, but having shouted to equalize the pressure in his head, Hawkins's eardrums were spared permanent damage.

Encizo cut loose with a captured Uzi, mopping up Hawkins's opponents in a wicked slash of damnation. Manning took another shot and cored a grenade-wielding terrorist through the sternum. The dying enemy trooper folded over and tucked the grenade to his bloody belly, a reflexive action to his pain, not a heroic act, but he took the brunt of the blast, shielding some of his partners.

It didn't matter for the dwindling defenders as McCarter and James added their fire to clean out the knot of ENT guards.

A gas can was hurled in front of Phoenix Force, an ugly black egg duct-taped to its side. The firebomb had fallen short, thanks to the withering fire put out by the commandos, but as soon as they'd seen the red aluminum container, they spun and raced back down the tunnel. The grenade exploded, igniting a couple gallons of gasoline in a brilliant blossom of flame. Hawkins hissed as a blazing tendril stabbed at the skin on his neck, but James hauled the Southerner behind cover and slapped out the flaming liquid.

"Damn, they got creative," Hawkins snarled.

"Shut up and let me fix that burn," James replied. He applied a wad of damp cloth to the burn as the skin turned red, the center browned to a crisp by the splash of gasoline. "You're just lucky it's a second-degree burn, and a small one at that."

"Yeah. I feel real lucky," Hawkins griped. "Next time I get this lucky, I should play the lotto."

Encizo, McCarter and Manning covered the medic as

he attended to Hawkins's fresh injury, but none of the ENT soldiers had dared to move past ground zero. In fact, the conspirators held back.

"Driving us off?" Manning asked. "Perhaps to buy some time?"

"I don't see why they wouldn't expect us to be an army, or the advance party of a larger force controlling a perimeter," McCarter said.

"So we're back to the possibility that they'll try to detonate one of the nukes manually, and hope for a chain reaction," Encizo stated.

"It's an outside chance, but considering that they're probably using 155 mm atomic artillery shells, we're looking at a minimum of half a kiloton, and up to twenty," Manning surmised. "Add in that they intended to knock out cities with each converted Predator, we can assume twenty kilotons."

"So enough to vaporize the top of this mountain," Encizo stated. "And since the vaporized stone would be made radioactive, as well as rupture the other shells, we're looking at the valley turning into a mass of lethal contagion, even if a shooting war doesn't start between Israel and anyone else."

Hawkins patted down the duct tape holding saline-soaked gauze to his burn and winced. "So we head back in and stop them from popping off a nuke."

"Easier said than done," McCarter replied. "But I think I see a solution."

Manning followed McCarter's eyes toward a forklift near the cargo elevator leading down to the lower levels of the Meggido base. "Yeah, but they'll know about shooting the gas tank. And we're going to have trouble from gas can grenades. There's no way—"

"I know. You think we'll come up with some kind of improvised tank and roll right into the hangar," McCarter said, cutting off his partner. "Nope. How much boom you got left?"

"I grabbed about five kilos of C-4 and detonators from the armory. I haven't needed to use any yet," Manning replied. His eyes narrowed. "Lock the steering in place, load it up with the C-4 and grenades…"

"Grab a crate and whip it up. Cal, with me. We'll hotwire the forklift and rig a steering block," McCarter said. "Rafe, T.J., grab all the grenades and ammunition you can find off the dead soldiers and dump it in the crate. Hell, any metal garbage, to boot. I want lots of nasty shrapnel."

Manning wadded his blocks of explosive into a cohesive glob, a radio detonator jammed in the core. Encizo and Hawkins, laden with armloads of magazines and grenades, packed them into the box. Loose ammunition, pocketknives, even nuts and bolts were poured into the wooden crate. When it was packed full, it weighed around forty-five pounds. With the gunpowder in the ammunition and the TNT in the grenades, there was at least fifteen pounds of explosives in the crate, the rest assorted metals.

Using tie-downs, James and McCarter had the forklift in neutral and aimed straight at the heart of the hangar. The whole process took around thirty seconds for all five Phoenix Force warriors to get it together. Manning hefted the improvised bomb while James had his hand on the stick shift of the forklift. It took a few more elastic cords to secure the explosive-packed crate in place to Manning's satisfaction. If the bomb fell out when the forklift peeled out, the team would have to fight their way into the hangar the hard way, giving the enemy enough time to figure out how to detonate one of the converted artillery shells.

"It's secure. Go!" Manning told James.

The Chicago native threw the forklift into third gear. A pipe jammed against the gas pedal put it down to the metal and the unmanned vehicle lurched forward, picking up speed as its gearbox whined and revved wildly.

Some ENT defenders rushed out to greet the forklift with their rifles chattering. Unfortunately for the conspirators' forces, the driverless drone sped on, ignoring the slaps of bullets against its metal skin. McCarter slid the cargo door shut on the elevator. The metal grating wouldn't provide much protection, but the stone sides of the shaft would shield them. If any shrapnel flew at the elevator door, it would be at an oblique angle, though ricochets off the walls might spear deadly fragments at them. Hopefully the grating and their own armor would be enough against such stray fragments.

Manning counted down the seconds on the forklift's advance and velocity. Reckoning the time right, he thumbed the stud on the radio detonator.

Even after the grenade blasts and gunfire, the explosion of the forklift bomb was tremendous. Despite being behind the thick granite corner of the cargo elevator shaft, concussion knocked all five commandos to the platform's floor. For a moment, Manning's heart sank as he wondered if he'd accidentally set off one of the nuclear shells. However, his logical mind took over. There was no heat wave that would have incinerated the Canadian and his allies, and the pressure front off the blast didn't burst their internal organs.

It was just a large explosion, amplified by the confined quarters of the corridor.

"Is everyone okay?" McCarter asked.

"Just knocked on my ass," Hawkins grumbled. "Anyone bleeding?"

It took a few moments for the Stony Man commandos to take inventory of aches and pains, but they'd lucked out. None of the shrapnel they'd packed into the explosive crate had come back at them.

McCarter and Manning both threw their strength against the cargo elevator door when the explosion had bent it out of shape, jamming it in place. Finally, out of frustration over wrestling with the door, the five Phoenix Force pros climbed over the top.

It was a slow approach, but they finally entered the hangar. Nothing stood, other than the blackened metal frame of the forklift, the bars of its roll cage splayed out like the legs of a gigantic spider. Several ENT defenders groaned in the distant corners of the hangar, badly wounded by shrapnel.

Predator drones were strewed about, wings snapped from being flipped over by the blast, but their warhead housings were untouched. Hawkins pulled a small mini-Geiger counter he'd found in the armory and tested the launch bay.

"No containment ruptures," the Southerner announced. "We're clear."

McCarter nodded. "Mop up the rest. Anyone still in a mood to fight, they get a bullet. Anyone willing to surrender, give them some basic first aid. They can turn themselves over to the Israelis. I want this hangar secured in five minutes, and then we're out of here."

Manning looked at the drones. "David, wait."

"What?" McCarter asked.

"Do we really want Israel to come into a couple hundred nuclear artillery shells?" the Canadian asked. "U.S.-manufactured atomic weaponry?"

McCarter grimaced. "That could lead to some sticky situations."

Manning nodded. "I could detonate a warhead in the lower levels."

"I thought that would produce too much fallout," Hawkins stated.

"Up here, sure. But down deeper into the mountainside, it would shake up the mountain and collapse the launch bay and other tunnels here. Especially if I dial down the explosive yield to a kiloton or less," Manning explained. "The Israelis could still retrieve the warheads, but the whole world would know because they'd need tons of digging equipment to get it out and haul it away."

"Collapse the roof on this place," James said. "But what about the wounded?"

"Triage, Cal," McCarter said. "Those who can survive long enough for medical assistance to arrive, we load them on one of those rolling carts and get them outside the mountain."

James looked at the bodies laying around the hangar. "Hippocrates would cry. I'm glad I'm not a doctor, just a medic."

"Rafe, help Gary carry a warhead down to the lower levels. T.J., with me. We'll police the survivors and the wounded. The dead and dying are left where they lay. Those that Cal says have a chance, we rescue."

The Stony Man warriors went about their tasks. It took a few moments for Encizo and Manning to crack open the nose housing of a Fire Raptor, finding an eight-inch shell inside. The weapon had dual fuses, the main safety and an impact primer. The safety had to be disengaged before loading and firing, otherwise the atomic shell would have been a menace with the slightest jostle.

Encizo rushed back to the armory and obtained more C-4 and a detonator to provide the impact force to set off the fuse. In the meantime, Manning ran a quick Geiger counter check on the confiscated warhead. Escaping the Meggido base would be a moot point if he and the others were exposed to radiation poisoning. Fortunately, the levels in the hangar were within the safe range for humans, and no leaks occurred around the eight-inch shell's containment casing.

If anything, James was faced with a more daunting task. The improvised Claymore mine had proved to be a horrendous weapon. There were sparks of life in some of the Engineers' survivors, but what was left of their bodies could hardly be described as human. While some were obviously dismembered by the sheering concussion forces of the explosion and its lethal shrapnel, others were flayed of all flesh on the side facing the explosion. One scoured skull rose at James's approach, jaw flexing in an effort to communicate. Eyeless sockets gaped in grisly, silent pleading. James drew his Glock and put a bullet into the man's forehead, putting him out of his misery.

"Mercy shots for anyone still kicking," James whispered, shaken.

"Absolutely," Hawkins agreed.

By the time Encizo and Manning finished with their bomb, James had tied tourniquets on a half dozen injured survivors, directing Hawkins and McCarter to load them into the bed of a pickup. It wouldn't be smooth transition, but there was a small access road off the entrance of the launch bay where extra supplies had been brought in by vehicle. Loading several wounded into the backs of the five trucks, they managed to get the thirty-two survivors to the base of the mountain in one trip. They took the more ambulatory wounded out of one truck, then destroyed the engines on the remaining four trucks to keep them in place.

Manning activated his radio detonator and the earth shook and a section of mountainside buckled. Hawkins tested the air with the Geiger counter.

"No radiation released from the mountain. Nothing ruptured, and no fallout cloud," Hawkins pronounced. "The valley seems safe from contamination."

"Then let's call the Farm to arrange to have these guys picked up," McCarter said wearily, looking at the truckloads of wounded. "And hope that the others stopped the other bases."

This phase of Armageddon was put to bed at last.

CHAPTER TWENTY-THREE

Cortez's true name was Javier Candida, and in his career, he had fought hard and long against those he had felt corrupt and imperfect. It was simply unfortunate that Candida's views of corruption and imperfection involved mere genetics. In nationality, he was truly an Argentinian by birth, but only because his grandfather had escaped prosecution after the Spanish civil war to the South American nation.

Tall, proud and blue-eyed, his blood was clean and pure. He knew, however, that he could not change the world alone. Cortez had required the help of who he considered to be mud people, the brown-mixed breeds of the Middle Eastern barbarians like Asid and Kovak. They had people in position in areas where he was sure to spark conflict. Kovak had potential, however. He was of European descent, and it was not obvious that he had Semitic blood in his veins. Kovak's courage in recent hours had shown that he was willing to let the past go.

But the survivors wouldn't matter because that Chinese harlot, Sunny Yao, had decided to take revenge upon him from beyond the grave. He cursed himself for a fool, not anticipating that the beautiful young hacker would have a contingency plan that would take effect after she was murdered. He also realized that the young woman would know how to exploit the defenses of the ENT information technology processes.

With a few lines of code, Yao had left the Green River launch facility a blind, helpless pit of darkness where emergency alarms blared.

Sure, he had the ability to get his Fire Raptors into the air, but there was no guarantee that the enemy force would give his forces the chance to complete the launch sequence. He also wondered if these assaults weren't coordinated around the globe. His doubts disappeared as fast as he realized that Ling Jon had complained about the kind of hacking activity that the enemy's cybernetic allies had thrown at them. The chattering thunder of automatic weapons ripped in the distance and Cortez, the would-be conqueror of the New Tomorrow, grimaced in disgust. The .45 in his fist might enable him to bring down one or two of the trio of commandos in a shoot-out, but years of rumors about the team, as well as firsthand experience, put that theory to the lie.

With skill, precision and explosive audacity, the trio had mowed their way through his forces as if they were children's toys tossed in their path.

Cortez shook his head and left the ENT soldiers, a conglomerate of right- and left-wing death squads he'd enlisted from across South America, to deal with the invaders blitzing through the underground base.

He had nuclear annihilation to unleash.

CARL LYONS LET HIS UMP-45 clatter to the floor, the last of its magazines drained by the last skirmish. "Going for weapons and ammo."

"We've got you covered," Blancanales told him. On the commando's ears were a set of collapsible, folding hearing protection muffs. The devices were a miniaturized, reliable version of range-specific ears that had the ability to filter gunshots to be no louder than a prop weapon sound effect on a TV screen, while the electronic microphones enabled clear hearing. Once their supply of suppressed weapon ammunition had been depleted, they had gotten out the hearing protectors, since many of the weapons being utilized by the Engineers' defense force were without calls.

"Oh, Christmas came early!" Lyons called. He picked up a black, polymer-framed weapon that looked very familiar in profile to the other two.

"Is that an Atchisson?" Schwarz asked.

"The AA-12, the update. Instead of being made out of tubular steel, they made the outer frame out of fiberglass-reinforced polymer," Lyons stated. "No wonder this guy's ears were bleeding before I put a burst into his head."

"Old home week," Blancanales said.

Ling, their reluctant companion, looked in shock at the weapon, which resembled the unholy union of an M-16 and a Thompson submachine gun. "What…what exactly is that?"

"A drum-fed, 12-gauge shotgun," Lyons explained. He ejected the drum and counted the remaining shells via the witness holes in the circular magazine. "He left nine in the drum. All he has for spares are seven rounder boxes, though."

"Like that ever inconvenienced you?" Blancanales asked.

Lyons grinned. "Hell no. Ling, make sure your muffs are on tight. This thing is as loud as hell."

"It looks it," Ling whimpered. Lyons could tell that the hacker was contemplating the kind of devastation such a blaster would wreak on his vulnerable, mortal body.

"Just don't misbehave, Ling," the big ex-cop told him. Finding loose 12-gauge ammunition on another dead gunman, he replenished the drum magazine to full 20-round capacity. "You'll be fine."

The hacker nodded.

"We're nearly to the main launch silo complex," Schwarz said, consulting his GPS-equipped map. "And according to Yao, the Fire Raptors are loaded to stand on their tails and launch in the more conventional ICBM-style launch ports."

"We decided to make use of the existing missile test facilities when we moved in here," Ling explained. "Plus, it seemed to fit Cortez's sense of irony to fire off the end of the world from a nuclear missile silo."

"It also beat the hell out of having to construct an underground hangar complex. According to the records Yao released as part of Cortez's teaser, the Meggido base had its mountainside artillery battery gutted and replaced with a launch bay," Lyons stated. "The same thing was done in Panama. This was the easiest to convert base he had."

"It took a little bit of work to modify storage racks for the Predator drones into standing launch scaffolds," Ling added.

"How long will it take the backup power systems to cut in to begin the launch sequence?" Blancanales asked.

Ling consulted his watch and frowned. "We're down to a little over seven minutes. We don't have far to go, but Cortez isn't going to make it easy for us."

"The feeling is mutual," Lyons replied.

He took point for the team, with Blancanales close behind him and Schwarz staying back to keep an eye on Ling, acting more as a babysitter and bodyguard than an actual captor. The Chinese hacker's spirit had been crushed by Yao's murder at Cortez's hand, and it had only taken a token display of manhandling on Lyons's part to convince Ling that he'd fallen into the hands of the baddest bastards on the planet.

Ling said that he was still useful, that he knew the setup of the launch computers, and could hack into their control systems. The Fire Raptors were fitted with CPUs that were already programmed with GPS coordinates that would steer them from Canada to Argentina, aimed at three hundred of the largest population centers and capitals across the Americas. While the devastation wouldn't be as complete with only one base firing as it would have been with the other two bases and their additional eight hundred warheads, millions would still die, inciting governmental collapse in at least one-third of the planet.

Schwarz decided to let Ling feel useful. While his combat PDA was equipped with a wireless connection with which he intended to fire off a lethal viral application into the Engineers' control center, there was always the possibility that the secondary systems would be as vulnerable as the original mainframe and be controlled by a less vulnerable operating system. Ling's description made the Able Team electronics genius doubt the efficacy of his program, and having someone with current password and administrator access would be a great shortcut should it come down to stopping the launch program.

Ling was the suspenders to Schwarz's belt. The thought

of three hundred out-of-control drones delivering atomic death across two continents forced Schwarz to look for every possible contingency.

Lyons's AA-12 roared out a thunderous burst, followed by Blancanales's M-16 ripping out a mop-up blast, informing Schwarz that the team had encountered another enemy defense formation.

"Don't worry," Lyons said. He paused long enough to feed a 7-round box into the Atchisson, slipping the partially depleted drum into his combat vest. "We got the drop, and they're down."

Schwarz looked at the knot of defenders, shredded by shotgun and rifle fire. He shot a querying glance to Blancanales, who winked to the electronics genius. Lyons's careless speech was bait for a trap that would be sprung when the site's defenders attempted to ambush Able Team. The two warriors had taken out only a few gunmen, but the area the ENT men defended extended into a larger room. A small army could have hidden in the shadows of the emergency-lit underground base, and Blancanales and Lyons's instincts decided to err on the side of caution.

Ling stood, confused as the trio of warriors pulled grenades off their harnesses, popped the pins, then hurled the bombs in unison. The trio of high-explosive eggs hurled into the darkened hall and Schwarz grabbed Ling, tugging him to the floor.

The grenades erupted, shrapnel and concussion waves slashing out toward the suspected ambushers, and even as the blasts faded, screams of pain filled the air. Gunmen bearing only minor wounds lurched into the open and Lyons cut loose first, his shotgun punching brutal holes in three guards' chests, buckshot ripping apart internal organs.

Schwarz and Blancanales cut loose with their M-16s, engaging further targets.

Stunned or wounded by the grenade barrage, the remainder of the ENT force proved to be no match for Able Team's guns as they cut bloody swathes through the survivors. It was a scorched-earth policy, and except for Ling, they were taking no prisoners. Despite Lyons's statement of mutual loathing, none of the Stony Man commandos relished the brutal extermination of wounded and incapacitated opponents, but the truth was that they didn't have time to restrain the enemy, and despite the destruction Able Team had wrought, they were still outnumbered. As well, history had shown how supposedly dead or unconscious foes had recovered long enough to fire a final lethal shot to bring down the men who'd killed them. Not needing a bullet in the back to hinder their odds of stopping the Fire Raptor launch, they pumped mercy shots into the downed opposition, then continued on.

The hallway, on examination by flashlight, was a utility tunnel. Schwarz recognized the section from the schematics downloaded to his PDA.

"The next door will put us in the launch facility," he announced. "And we're five minutes ahead of schedule for the emergency launch protocols."

Lyons stopped. "Bring up the facility schematics."

Schwarz did so, and Blancanales joined in on studying the map on the minuscule screen. The trio quickly pointed out several positions where the ENT could set up impassable cross fires that would cut apart any intrusion force. The construction of the silos also provided the Engineer gunmen a variety of areas where they could conceal themselves.

Ling was shown the map.

"We use this part of the complex to set up our backup computers," the man said. "We didn't use tractor-trailer set-ups like we intended overseas. The launch bay here was too confined, and we couldn't make a larger access way without destroying the silos we intended to use."

"No secondary access points so we can circumvent an ambush?" Lyons asked.

"The exhaust tunnels," Ling pointed out. "There was a maintenance access point back twenty yards where we could enter the exhaust tubes."

"They're large enough for us to walk through, because of the sheer volume of rocket exhaust," Schwarz stated. He and the others were already on the way back to the maintenance hatch.

"And using the tunnels, which connect all the silos, we'll be able to sabotage the launch mechanisms," Lyons added as he opened up the floor access to the exhaust vents. "Gadgets, you have enough C-4 for this?"

"If not, I can improvise something," Schwarz replied.

Blancanales dropped into the tunnel first. The pipe was more than six feet tall and smooth, wide enough for the team and Ling to walk abreast if they wanted. He shone his light down the tunnel in both directions, but no ENT forces greeted them. Schwarz was the last one down, and he secured the access plate behind him.

Able Team moved quickly, some of their lead eaten up by their planning to avoid the ENT's defensive ambush. Ling struggled to keep up with the trio of commandos as they reached the funnel area under the first silo.

A storage rack containing fifty modified Predator drones stood above them. Sunlight crept through a crack in the top of the silo as the bay doors struggled to open.

The hydraulics systems had been compromised, and it was a struggle to move the panels out of the path of the soon-to-be launched nukes. Unfortunately the rack was twenty feet above their heads, on the other side of heavy grating.

Lyons looked at Schwarz for guidance, but the electronics genius hit the transmit signal on his combat PDA.

"No way we can blow them all up in three minutes, not with what I have," Schwarz admitted. "Ling, the system is resisting."

The ENT defector looked at the portable computer unit, then tapped in access commands with a borrowed stylus. The miniature keypad required a nylon plastic pick to work the buttons, but Ling wasn't wasting time. He frowned

"Carter locked me out," the hacker said. "Must be because of Yao's betrayal. Maybe he suspected she would be looking out for me."

"He changed the access codes," Blancanales said. "That was fast."

"He had administrative authority, but I designed this system," Ling replied. "Give me a minute."

"If we have that long," Lyons noted.

Shouts resounded above. The Engineers had to have detected the presence of a cybernetic assault on their system, but Ling worked the stylus over the PDA, cracking through back-door protections. Hundreds of feet above them, the hydraulic motors of the doors clanked loudly as they pulled to a halt, then reversed, pushing back together to enclose the silo.

Ling's brow was furrowed in concentration as he worked feverishly on the keypad when one of the silo doors popped open.

Lyons jerked the AA-12 up and triggered buckshot

through the grated floor, but not before an ENT gunman triggered his weapon. Ling cried out in pain, dropping the PDA as he clutched his cored arm.

"Pol!"

"I got him," Blancanales answered, pulling the defector out of the line of fire. Lyons and Schwarz swept the silo with their weapons to give their partner some respite from the attack. Ling winced, but he'd grabbed the combat PDA while being dragged to safety.

"They'll be coming down through other access hatches," Schwarz noted.

"I've got the system wide open for you, Gadgets," Ling said hoarsely. "Hit the system with your virus."

Schwarz took the combat PDA and fired up the virus. Almost immediately, the lights powered by the emergency generators cut out, cries of confusion filling the air.

"You did good," Lyons said as Blancanales finished packing Ling's injury with a compress.

"Kill Cortez," Ling growled. "He killed the only person I ever really cared about."

"He was already dead meat walking. But I'll give him a little extra for you and Sunny," Lyons promised.

ENT soldiers, betraying their position in the tunnels with their flashlights, were cut down by thunderous automatic fire from Able Team's guns. It was akin to shooting fish in a barrel for the first minute of the conflict as the gunmen jumped down, lights glowing, into the exhaust tunnels.

Lyons led the way into one of the branches where a ladder had been dropped for sentries to climb down. He flicked the AA-12 to 3-shot burst and triggered a blast of thunder at the enemy. Three rounds of buckshot resulted in twenty-seven .36-caliber pellets, nearly the equivalent of an entire magazine from a submachine gun, into the clot of half a dozen defenders. The cone of projectiles shredded the enemy force, bowling them back. Six fell, but one struggled to get up, only suffering minor injuries from Lyons's assault. Before he could bring his weapon to bear, however, Schwarz ripped his head from his shoulders with a burst from his M-16.

Another side tunnel was filled with gunmen, but Blancanales burned off half a magazine into the group. A volley of 5.56 mm rounds punched through the trio at the front of the group, perforating the guards before screaming on into the soldiers behind them. The armor-piercing ammunition in the M-16 zipped through flesh and bone, slowing only slightly at the extreme close range. Additional bursts were needed to anchor the last of the group in the tunnel, emptying the weapon, but the skirmish was over as quickly as it started. He reloaded the rifle and joined Lyons and Schwarz as they advanced toward the hatch with the ladder.

Blancanales unclipped a concussion grenade and lobbed it to the top of the ladder to clear the hatchway. Shock waves ripped through Cortez's men, fading as they reached the base of the ladder, but Blancanales stepped back out of the way as a precaution. He let his rifle hang on its sling, pulled his high-cap 1911, and scrambled to the top of the ladder. He had to shove a corpse from the hatch hole, but once he was through, he saw the carnage wrought by the concussion bomb. Two gunmen struggled to recover their senses, while others either huddled in agony or were dead.

Blancanales cut loose with his .45, punching half-inch holes in the recovering guards. One triggered his M-16 in his death throes, bullets scoring the concrete just off to the Puerto Rican's side.

"Cleared," Blancanales shouted, holstering his pistol and transitioning to his rifle again.

Lyons and Schwarz climbed up and scanned for more opponents. The trio spread out, exploring the rafters and crosswalks above.

There was no movement except for a maintenance office.

"You're not going to get much protection in there," Lyons bellowed. He kept an eye on the hatch he and the others had come up through. There was a possibility that some of the gunmen had gone down into the exhaust tunnels as they'd come up. "Why not just give it up?"

A rifle cracked and Lyons ducked out of the way, concrete vaporizing as a bullet struck the outer structure of the silo. He shouldered the Atchisson and fired off five shots from the autoshotgun, smashing glass and chewing up sections of the prefab wall. Blancanales tossed a concussion grenade so it landed outside the office, giving the gunmen inside a chance to survive.

"On our six!" Schwarz warned, whirling and ripping off bursts from his M-16. A second after his shout, the grenade detonated. Had it not been for his warning, the others would have been distracted by the blast and left vulnerable to ambush.

Jason Kovak lead the flanking force from their hiding spot in one of the silos, an Uzi pressed to his hip, ripping off long bursts that forced Schwarz to dive for cover. Schwarz's M-16 fire sliced close to the Israeli ENT commander, two bullets plucking at his sleeve. Asid, who was behind Kovak, proved less fortunate. With half a dozen bullets burning in his upper torso, the Palestinian collapsed in a lifeless heap.

Kovak jerked and threw himself to the ground, reloading as he slid behind cover. Scanning the area, he saw René Dujon clutch his torn belly, trying to keep his bowels from spilling out onto the floor, messily excavated from his torso by a 12-gauge blast. Abbas Ghidorran cut loose with his pistol, his left arm hanging uselessly where an M-16 bullet had shattered it.

There wasn't going to be much left of the Engineers of the New Tomorrow after this battle if he didn't act quickly. Kovak pulled a grenade from his harness and whipped it toward Schwarz's position. The Able Team electronics genius raced from his hiding spot, sliding behind alternate cover as Lyons and Blancanales provided supporting fire. The grenade exploded, missing Schwarz by a mere second.

Lev Takarov's headless body, decapitated by a full-auto burst of 12-gauge fury, slid slowly down a silo wall, painting it crimson. Gidorran cried out in pain, paralyzed as Blancanales's marksmanship cored the African's heart.

Dujon continued to blubber about his horrific wounds as he sat in the corner, but at least his volume decreased with the growth of the bloody puddle he sat in. After another moment, the Frenchman's chin dropped to his chest, and he expired quietly. Kovak sneered, looking for Cortez.

The Argentinian had left him high and dry, and by all accounts, he was the last of the ENT leadership in the silo complex. A few gunmen remained, but after the ambush, the office had been riddled with rifle fire.

Kovak realized he couldn't count on anyone else. He didn't have many options, either. The Mossad would certainly turn the world upside down to find him if he cut and ran, and if he was taken prisoner, he'd be milked for covert information for as long as he was useful, and then suffer an "unfortunate accident" one day. The Israeli didn't want to go to hell alone, not with the rest of his murderous breed as his only company. He saw a flash of blond hair and aimed his reloaded Uzi. Bullets sparked against concrete in a waste of ammunition when a shadow fell across him.

Kovak whirled, but even as he did, he knew it was too late.

The .45 in Rosario Blancanales's fist blazed, 230-grain slugs punching through the Israeli's face.

And then the silo fell deathly silent.

Cortez was nowhere to be found.

HE'D LEFT HIS IDENTITY as Cortez behind, stripping out of his suit and stealing laundry from a basket. The clothes were battered and old, and hung loosely on him. He regretted ditching the .45, and any other weapon, as well as all of his identification, but if he was to survive, he had to disappear.

Candida's feet were aching by the time he walked into the diner. All he had were a few ten-dollar bills folded in his pocket, and he was hungry and thirsty. Maybe if he could find a job in the Green River diner, he'd submerge even further. No one would expect a middle-aged dishwasher of having tried to destroy the world.

Unfortunately no Help Wanted sign was in the window.

He paused at the door, but hunger and thirst drove him on. A slender Hispanic man with salt-and-pepper hair wiped down the counter. The diner was empty, but it was still an hour before dinner time, and too late for a lunch crowd to linger around.

"What'll it be?" the counter man asked. He pulled a notebook out of his apron pocket, and Candida relaxed.

"I'll have a beer and a hamburger," the Argentinian said.

He threw a ten onto the counter. "Know where a drifter could find work around here?"

The Hispanic folded his arms and thought for a moment. One hand dropped to his side and Candida lunged across the counter. The diner worker yelled in fear as the former ENT commander clutched a fistful of clothing at his chest, scooping a knife off a place setting. It was only a butter knife, but even the blunt serrated edge could kill if he speared it into the man's vulnerable throat.

"Don't kill me!" the counter man yelled. "I have a family!"

"You have a weapon in your pocket!" Candida growled, shoving the blunt tip of the knife against his victim's throat.

"No! No! My pockets are empty!"

Candida let his captive go. The man's surprise at the assault was genuine.

"Good. I was going to ask you to let the civilian go," a voice growled from the diner entrance. Candida whirled.

Carl Lyons stood in the doorway, stinking of cordite and the blood of other men. He was stripped to the waist except for a tank top drawn tightly across his powerful chest, tucked into fatigue pants. Lyons's muscular arms and shoulders glowed bronze in the setting sun, like the visage of some ancient Nordic god. He had no weapons with him, presumably to avoid inciting panic among the civilian populace. Gunfire would have drawn too much attention from the authorities, but one couldn't help to notice the tightly muscled figure, smelling of battle.

"Where are your partners?" Candida asked, still holding the butter knife.

"Cleaning up the mess you ran from," Lyons snarled. "You left a lot of firecrackers behind at the campsite."

Candida looked back to the diner worker, whose brown eyes were wide with horror.

"Are you going to come quietly?" Lyons asked. "Please say no, because I've been dying for a shot at you."

Candida smirked. "No."

The Argentinian lunged with springlike reflexes, lashing out with the butter knife's blade. Dull, serrated steel slammed hard into the side of Lyons's head, tearing into his scalp and ripping it down to the bone along the side. The Able Team leader had charged at the same time, so Candida's intended slash, which would have ripped out his cold blue eyes, went high. A thick, bronzed forearm smashed against Candida's wrist hard enough to jar the weapon from his fingers while a pile driver of a fist pistoned into the ENT founder's stomach.

Robbed of breath, Candida lashed out blindly, knuckles crashing against Lyons's cheek. The Able Team leader countered with a fist like a golden hammer, spearing into the Argentinian's side, over his kidney. In boxing, the move would have resulted in a disqualification, but in a real world fight to the death, it was simply softening up a cold-blooded murderer. Flaming agony splashed like napalm through Candida's torso, his leg muscles loosing their strength like overstretched elastic. Staggering back, the lead conspirator was left open for a knee to the groin. Instead of merely having his testicles mashed against his crotch, Candida felt his pelvis break with the kind of power only a trained *karateka* could unleash. Finally the Argentinian flopped to the ground, hips unable to support the weight of his body.

In blind panic and pain, Candida lashed out wildly, fists bouncing off rock-hard muscle and Lyons's face as the ex-cop straddled the crippled mass murderer. Lyons ignored the bruise-raising welts on his face and jammed his thumbs into Candida's eyes, fingertips clawing and tearing at the scalp over both ears.

"No!" Candida howled in terror as he felt the pressure on his eyeballs. Suddenly it felt as if his eyes had exploded in their sockets and his skin tore loose from his skull. It had. Lyons had burst the injured killer's eyeballs, driving his thumbs as deep as they would go into the orbital sockets. With his fingers jammed into the soft flesh behind Candida's ears, Lyons had enough leverage to twist the man's head until grinding vertebrae sliced through his spinal cord, severing the ENT founder's brain from the rest of his body in a sickening crunch.

Finally, Lyons released the dead man's head and staggered to his feet.

"Who…who was that?" the diner worker asked, terrified at the brutal execution on the tile floor.

"That used to be Cortez the Conqueror," Lyons told him. He wiped his bloody hands on Candida's stolen clothing. "Now he's just a mess your busboy has to mop up."

Lyons turned and walked out of the diner, disappearing in the bloodred flare of the sunset blazing through the glass door.

EPILOGUE

Ambassador Chong Sun Jung stepped out of the Chinese state department building, looking at the sun rising in the east. He'd been busy all night, and his eyes ached, burning from lack of sleep. Most of the planet wouldn't know just how close to annihilation they'd come, but the Korean statesman did.

Captain Zing Ho was by his side, carrying his briefcase. He'd been popping down caffeine pills and drinking coffee all night, and he was wired from the effort. In case the Engineers of the New Tomorrow had decided to interrupt the peace talks where North Korea, of all nations, was being the voice of reason, having the ear of Beijing in this international crisis, he wanted to be alert and ready for any attack. Fortunately, he hadn't had to resort to the concealed 9 mm handgun under his tunic.

"I bet you were worried that we'd never see another morning," Chong stated.

"Right now, I just want to come down off this coffee buzz and wrap my arms around a pillow," Ho admitted. "Remind me never to OD on coffee again."

"I'll make a point of it," Chong said with a chuckle.

His own government would never learn of the back-channel communications he'd made with the top-secret U.S. agency, with Ho's assistance. And that was for the best. Though Chong didn't always agree with the West, he wasn't interested in testing his nation's might against the U.S., or to anger China, either. In fact, Chong hoped, some-day, that his country would not be on hostile terms with the rest of the world. Starving citizens needed international commerce to sustain themselves.

It would take a lot of work, though, to bring North Korea to sanity. Maybe Chong's efforts today would be in-significant to that cause in the long run, but what mattered was that he did contribute to keeping two of the most pow-erful nations in the world from flying off the handle and annihilating each other.

One more day of peace meant one more day where the world could finally get its act straight.

It was a pretty dream that the future held hope and im-provement, but Chong was willing to fight for that dream. It warmed his heart to know that there were people who fought in the shadows to solve the world's problems, not add to them. There were too many conspiracies, but as long as the folks who had been in contact with him were around, the chances that he would see another sunrise, unobscured by clouds of nuclear fallout, were golden.

"Come on, Captain," Chong said. "Let's get some breakfast. My treat."

The attaché nodded numbly. "Sounds good."

SUSANA ARQUILLO OPENED her eyes as the door to her hos-pital room opened. Carl Lyons, eyes red from lack of sleep, shoulders slumped in exhaustion, stood there. He was dressed in jeans and a T-shirt. A baseball cap partially obscured bandages around his forehead, and his face was covered in healing bruises.

"I guess you saved the world," Arquillo whispered. "Which hospital am I in?"

Lyons smiled, a little energy pouring back into him. "We had you transferred to Bethesda."

Arquillo looked at her left hand, wrapped completely in bandages. It didn't look like she had room for fingers under them, and she remembered after the explosion in the jeep.

"You'll get the best rehabilitation here," Lyons said, coming closer to her. He took her good hand in his and gave it a squeeze.

"My field career's over, though," Arquillo said glumly. "And it looks like I'll have to throw out half my shoes."

"You'll be hooked up with a new leg. And maybe a new job," Lyons said, taking a seat by her bed. He stroked her dark hair. "I have connections."

"Thank you," Arquillo whispered. She wrapped her right arm around his shoulders, and Lyons held her tight for a long time. Sooner or later, duty would call him away from his vigil at her bedside, but for now, Lyons was taking some quiet time, healing time.

Look for

PROVENANCE
by AleX Archer

Finding the relic is a divine quest.
Even if it means committing murder.

When a mysterious man orchestrates an attack on
archaeologist Annja Creed and then offers her an
assignment, Annja is baffled.
She must find an object
that possesses a sacred
and powerful secret,
offering atonement to
anyone who uncovers
it... or wreaking havoc
on the world.

**Available March
wherever you
buy books.**

James Axler

OUTLANDERS®

GHOSTWALK

Area 51 remains a mysterious enclave of eerie synergy and unleashed power—a nightmare poised to take the world to hell. A madman has marshaled an army of incorporeal, alien evil, a virus with intelligence now scything through human hosts like locusts. Cerberus warriors must stop the unstoppable, before humanity becomes discarded vessels of feeding energy for ravenous disembodied monsters.

Available May wherever you buy books.

ROOM 59

A research facility in China has built
the ultimate biological weapon. Alex's job:
infiltrate and destroy. His wife works at the
biotech company's stateside lab, and Alex
fears danger is poised to hit home. But when
Alex is captured, his personal and professional
worlds collide in a last, desperate gamble to
stop ruthless masterminds from unleashing
virulent, unstoppable death.

Look for

out of time
by
cliff RYDER

*Available April
wherever you buy books.*

GRM592